MW01244450

SATAN
LIKE SPAM

The Disillusioning Art of Shell Formation
Volume II

"For where your treasure is, there your heart will be also."
– Matthew 6:21

A NOVEL BY

NICOLE GARBER

Dust Jacket Press
PO Box 721243
Oklahoma City, OK 73172

www.DustJacket.com
Info@DustJacket.com

Cover art: Abby Stiglets aby3.com
Cover & Interior Design: ZAQ Designs

To Brooks and Madison.
You are my sunshine.

ACKNOWLEDGEMENTS

First and foremost, I want to thank God for absolutely everything. Thank you for purpose and guidance and for placing special people in my life to help me through the process of writing another novel.

Jimmy, I never could have done any of this without you. Thanks for being there for me. I love you.

Dad, for editing my manuscript and encouraging me when I'm going through rough patches. Thanks for your love and support. You have one of the kindest hearts I know.

Mom. You always seem to have the perfect book to inspire me, motivate me, and encourage me, and the words inside always come at the perfect time. Thank you for your love and understanding.

Karen. You're amazing. Thank you for your support, encouragement, editing skills, and marketing genius. You always steer me in the right direction and offer the best advice.

Thank you Marty for helping me with the business side of things. If it were up to me I would stay in my office and write all day. But you have given me drive to get out there and market my book. Thank you for introducing me to so many wonderful people. Thank you for caring about my story and my cause.

Brian, thank you for always making me laugh. I needed a lot of laughs this year.

Thank you to Brooks and Madison for being patient when I get a little scatterbrained. I couldn't ask for better kiddos. I am so proud of you. You truly are my sunshine.

Thank you to my Switch girls… I thought I was supposed to be teaching you, but you teach me new things every week. Your love for Jesus and your desire for purpose inspire me more than you know.

Thank you to all my friends who offered suggestions, editing help, and encouragement.

Abby, thank you for painting another beautiful cover. You are a master with the brush and a wonderful friend.

Kara and Jeremy. You have been so supportive and your friendship means the world to me. I can't thank you enough. You also rocked the book trailer. You are both amazing talents, and I am so proud of you and your accomplishments.

Amanda, thank you for your input, enthusiasm and understanding. I look forward to our upcoming adventure. You have been my friend through it all and I love you.

Susie, a fellow author and friend. Thank you for always having an ear to listen.
Becca, your encouragement was much needed and your advice was so helpful. I'll miss you while you're in Italy.

To Louis Skipper. Thank you for your superb editing skills. Because of you, I no longer have a headache. You are the book doctor.

Thank you, Stacy. Commas are my weakness, and I love that you know exactly where to put them. Thanks for your feedback. It means a lot.

Adam. Thanks for believing in my book and supporting my cause. I feel blessed to be with Dustjacket and the past year and a half has been such an amazing journey. You are the best publisher out there.

PROLOGUE

I was gasping for air, standing in at least twelve inches of snow, in front of a lake and beside a tree that was marshmallow white; its green leaves had disappeared long ago, and now its bare branches looked like crooked, white fingers twisted high above my head. My racing heart was beginning to slow and despite the cold, my forehead was damp with sweat. I had been running from something, although I could not remember what, and the fresh powder that covered my tracks made it impossible to determine the direction from which I had come.

The snow that had been falling steadily for quite some time was both beautiful and deceiving, giving the illusion of an earth that was soft and white, but doing nothing more than masking the hard, frozen ground beneath it and concealing the lake that had long since turned to ice. Hunched over, with one hand on my knee and the other planted firmly on the sturdy tree beside me, I continued to take in shallow breaths of air until the pain in my chest began to subside. It wasn't until I stood up that I began to survey my surroundings. My periphery was dead… frozen… white, with no signs of life.

But the smell of wood burning somewhere in the distance suggested that someone was near, triggering an emotion that was an equal measure of hope and fear. It was so quiet, I could hear the sound of snowflakes making contact with the ground, creating a delicate sound that was more lonely than rain. I had no idea how long I had been standing idle by a tree… long enough for my vitals to return to normal… long enough to watch the sky turn from a solid, wintery white into a thick, chalky gray. I leaned against the trunk of the tree, letting it support the weight of my body and started to slide slowly down the powdery, white bark until I was sitting rather than standing. I stuck my tongue out and let a fat, white flake land on the tip and wiggled my fingers inside my gloves to warm them. The snow had been falling hard for hours but was now beginning to slow, and as my visibility increased, I could see the outline of trees to my left, a forest in the distance that had been hidden moments ago.

A sound startled me, interrupting my silent surroundings. It was the sound of footsteps crunching across the ground and cracking through the thin layer of ice just below the fresh powder. But it was what I saw that captured my attention: there stood a figure shrouded in a veil of snow. I grew tense as the figure walked out of the forest and toward the tree where I was sitting. The silence had been broken and my suspicions were confirmed. Life did indeed exist. And I was not alone. As the figure drew nearer, I saw that it was a girl, a girl dressed too scantily for the snow. I relaxed a bit when I realized she had not seen me. If she had, she was indifferent to my presence. She was wearing a short-sleeved tee shirt and her ungloved hands were tucked into the pockets of her jeans. She walked with her head down, staring intently at the solid, white earth. She appeared to be searching for something. Occasionally, she would stop, bend over, and brush the snow away from the ground with the fingers of her bare hand.

"What are you looking for?" I whispered.

With my body still tense, I watched as she changed direction, walking away from me and onto the hard, frozen lake that expanded wide before us.

The smell of smoke was still wafting through the air. When I looked over my shoulder to follow the scent, I noticed the silhouette of a house about 100 feet behind me. The smoke that bellowed out of the chimney and into the air filled my nostrils with something sweet and musky, and it suddenly reminded me of my freezing fingers and toes. My socks were damp and cold, my feet were painfully numb, and I was certain my toes were a frosty shade of blue. I wiggled them around inside my boots. I curled them up tight and let them relax, pumping the blood to keep them warm. How nice it would be to curl up beside that fire. The house was beckoning me, and the smoke from the chimney was drawing me in.

Suddenly, a deep cracking noise caused me to turn my attention from the house and to the lake. It sounded like a tree being uprooted, the branches splintering into sharp and tiny pieces. When I turned to face the lake, two things happened almost at once: the mysterious girl fell through the ice, dropping into the hole she created without making so much as a splash, and I leapt from the ground and ran onto the frozen lake, away from the house, away from the tree, toward the spot where, less than a second ago, I had seen the girl disappear. I did not consider the fragile ice or how the pounding of my feet on the surface of the lake might render me as helpless as the girl I was trying to rescue. It didn't even cross my mind that I might not be able to bring her back. But when I reached the round and jagged circle and looked down into the still, dark green water below, I was shocked to see nothing.

I inched closer to the ominous pool of liquid, peering inside the hole until I could see my reflection. I plunged my arm into the water, intent to rescue the girl by using all my strength to pull her to safety, but when I felt something grab hold of my fingers, I instinctively recoiled. Angry and desperate, I tried again… but she was gone. When finally I pulled my arm from the lake, the cold air felt like a thousand needles stabbing my skin. On hands and knees, I began to push the snow away from the ice, searching for the girl who was trapped somewhere beneath. I cupped both of my hands and used my fingers as claws to dig. When the tips of my fingers hit something hard, I knew I had found what I was looking for: the ice below the snow. With more speed, I began to clear a large circle of snow away from the ice.

And then I stopped. I was both bewildered and surprised. I was staring at myself beneath the icy blanket. My eyes were bright blue, cold, and forced wide open, unblinking. My hair was spread out like a fan and was floating weightless in the water. My lips were blue with death. I pressed my hand to the ice and watched my body sink deeper and deeper until it had completely disappeared.

CHAPTER ONE

*C*old crept its wispy, ghostlike fingers out of my dream and wove them into my reality. I was startled awake. My bare feet were hanging from the end of the queen-sized bed, and the chilly morning air was nipping at my toes. I glanced at the clock beside the bed: 7:45. Still exhausted, I exhaled in frustration, my breath visible. I exhaled again, this time because I was fascinated by how my breath became a dense, white cloud that suspended itself in midair before becoming one with nature. I shivered. This was only my second morning in Alexandria, but so far May in Minnesota felt like January back home. The air was cold and residual ice lingered on the lake where it was shaded beneath the trees. I tucked my knees to my chest and pulled the blankets up around my chin. Cocoa, my two year-old, black Goldendoodle, was curled up with her head resting on the pillow beside me. I lay in bed, still, beneath the vintage quilts and thinning sheets, wishing that I were wrapped in Alex's sleeping arms. Forty-five hours and counting. Forty-five hours since I walked away from my parents' home in the middle of the night and hopped into the car with Alex. Minnesota bound.

For the past forty-five hours, I had willed myself to forget the reasons for which I had left my past behind. But now, as I lay in bed with the cool air blowing across my body, everything I had pushed out of my mind came rushing back. As the euphoria faded, I began to reflect on the events that forced me to run away from my home. I didn't feel guilty for leaving. To feel guilt would mean that I had left on my own accord and for very selfish reasons... like for love... like for Alex, perhaps. I wished it were that simple. But the kind of love that made me leave my home was not a romantic kind of love. It was the kind of love that left me with no other choice. I hurt my parents in order to protect them. I broke their hearts to keep them safe. This kind of love was foreign to me. It was a kind of love I didn't know I was capable of giving. When I left my home of nearly a year, when I left my parents sleeping in their bed, leaving them nothing more than a letter of farewell, it was out of necessity. For the past eighteen years, they had managed to protect me from pain or death or both. They had done their best, and now it was my turn to protect them. It was my turn to fight, and I hoped that my absence would be enough to keep them safe. There were people who wanted me dead, and these people were willing to hurt anyone who got in their way. Minnesota was magical, but there just wasn't enough magic to make my problems disappear. The last forty-five hours had been perfect, but I could no longer ignore reality. I was 750 miles away from home and away from my parents. I had four states separating Alex and me from Chloe Pierce and Benard Bodin, and I wondered how long it would be before they found us.

The waves crashed onto the shallow shoreline with a rhythm that could have easily lulled me back to sleep. Instead, I slid out of bed, stretched, and opened one of my three pieces of luggage, searching for my running gear. Goosebumps formed on my arms, so I slipped a heavy sweatshirt on over my tee, pulled on my running tights, and tied up my shoes. There was a light drizzle in the air when I stepped out of the cottage, but the rainwater that sat in puddles on the side of the road told me that something more severe had taken place the night before. The flowers that I watched Alex plant on our first day in Minnesota looked a bit rumpled from the rain, but the assortment of bright colors still made a bold statement against the stark, white cottages. Keeping Cocoa on a short leash, I tiptoed past the cottage where Alex was staying, being careful not to wake him, and let my feet crunch the rest of the way down the gravel drive. I took a left onto the county road without the slightest idea of where it would take me. I plugged my earbuds into my ears, hit play on my iPOD, and let the reality of my life come rushing back. I thought about Mom and Dad because I missed them. I thought about all the things that made me both angry and sad. I thought about the lies my parents had told to save my life; I was still furious about that. I thought about my friends, or the lack thereof. I thought about how I had been lonely for most of my life. I thought about all the untold secrets, and although I was nowhere close to uncovering the truth, I wondered what I would do when I did. I thought about my archenemy Chloe Pierce and her accomplice Benard Bodin, or was it the other way around? Who knew? They both wanted me dead. But why? Revenge did seem to be a likely motive, but this motive did not satisfy me. Finally, I thought about September 13th and how it was fast approaching. It was a day that was synonymous with both death and lies. On September 13th, 1990, three cars collided on a small Minnesota highway just outside of Alexandria. It was on that night, almost nineteen years ago, that I was born and others died. Ten people were involved in that crash, but only three survived: my mother, my father, and me. Alex and his parents weren't so lucky, neither were the Bodins. Nor my sister. I never got to meet her and have lived with the question: Why did I survive? For the past year, Alex's presence had been enough to ease the anger and alleviate most of the pain, but the notion that I would never meet my sister still made me sad. The notion that perhaps it was my life that caused her death still flooded me with guilt.

When I was eight, I was old enough to put together some of the pieces. When I discovered that my birthday was also symbolic of death, I was filled with pain, and I was convinced that it was deserved. Making matters worse, my mother and father were so consumed with their careers that they had forgotten about my happiness. They had moved up and down the coast of Europe to help the less fortunate, but they had completely neglected to see the unfortunate things that were taking place in their very own home. I had no friends to confide in, and I blamed myself for my sister's death. I was sad and all alone. That would be enough to cause anyone to self-destruct. I suppose I could have rebelled as I grew older. I could have done a slew of things to make myself feel better, but I did not; instead, I built a shell around my heart, which made me cold. But what if my parents had told me the truth? Would that have made a difference? Did they know the secrets they kept in order to save me only hurt me more? I was numb inside my shell, and that was fine with me… until Alex came along. He cracked the shell around my heart and his presence eased my pain. He freed me, and when he did, I began to discover secrets that had been right in front of me all along - the secrets of my past, the secrets that I was finally strong enough to face. I learned that my parents were not obsessed with their careers; they were obsessed with my life.

There was nothing about life with Alex that was normal. First of all, he was the dead that had come back to life, or resurrected if you will. All of this happened so that he could protect me from Chloe and Ben, but mostly he just saved me from myself. Strange as it may seem, I had accepted the fact that my boyfriend, my eternal soul mate, was dead. This news wasn't shocking. When I first met Alex, I knew that there was something different about him. He was absolutely perfect and that seemed a little off, because in my world, perfect didn't exist.

In a matter of three short months, I had gained a lifetime of knowledge, but I knew that there was something more I was missing. There were questions that needed to be answered. For instance, what were my parents doing in Alexandria, Minnesota, on the night of September 13th? My parents worked for A-Omega. But who was A-Omega, and why had A-Omega sent them here? And of course, I had to consider Chloe and Ben. Maybe revenge was the reason they wanted me dead, but was that the only reason? Was there something more? Luckily, the most important question was one that I could answer without hesitation. If I could go back, would I? Would I trade this complicated and dangerous mess to have a normal life again? Not a chance. In a normal life, Alex wouldn't exist. In a normal life, I would still be inside my shell - pain free perhaps, but missing absolutely everything life had to offer. Although the world outside my shell looked dangerous, it was different and beautiful and full of possibilities.

Five miles later, my feet crunched back up the gravel drive. I could see Alex's silhouette in the kitchen window. The outline of his body brought a smile to my face, and my body became a melting pot for emotions. I felt more confident than ever before, but there was a bit of self-doubt that lingered. I felt strength like I had never known. Yet there was something inside of me that was still very, very weak. My heart was finally open and free. If only I could figure out how to use it.

CHAPTER TWO

I opened the door to the cabin and sat down on the bench at the kitchen table. Alex was sitting across from me. He had a bowl raised to his lips and was draining the cereal milk into his mouth.

I smiled as I watched him. This supernatural being, my supernatural being, was in the middle of such an ordinary task like eating. I ignored the milk dribbling down his chin and focused on his angelic features: his unique pinwheel eyes and the long lashes that extended from each lid; his thick, messy chocolate brown hair; the square shape of his jaw. I focused on his soft, full lips. And then there was the scar at the corner of his eye. It was the only portion of his appearance that was of this world. Even though Alex had told me on more than one occasion that he was not an angel, I would often stare at his uncommon beauty, convinced that he was wrong. But then my eyes would fall upon his scar, and I was reminded that Alex had once walked this earth as a living, breathing human boy. It was this single defining feature that told the truth. So small, yet so significant, it told a story.

I watched as he refilled his bowl. Round two. He wasn't the only one that was hungry. Cocoa had already made a habit of greeting Alex first thing in the morning. She would nuzzle him with her nose until he scratched her head. But the run had made her ravenous, and she was in the corner of the kitchen inhaling her doggie food and lapping up water from her bowl.

"How did you sleep?"

"Okay," I lied. I didn't want to tell him about the dreams or that it was the second night in a row I dreamt that I had drowned. Alex would know that my dream was more than a dream; it was an omen.

"How about you?" I returned the pleasantry. "Did you sleep well?"

"I've slept better." This was an understatement and the dark circles under Alex's eyes spoke so much louder than words.

"I didn't wake you, did I? I was trying to be quiet. Cocoa was chasing this chip—"

"It wasn't you that woke me," Alex interrupted before I could finish.

"Good."

I moved my eyes away from his and toward the bay window, looking at the hummingbird feeders we had just filled with sugary, red syrup, and the intricate and colorful birds that were already flocking to them. I noticed the flowers in the box beneath the window were already springing back to life after just a little bit of sun. The grass outside was bright green. Drops of rain were lingering on the tall, skinny blades. Wind whipped through the living room and into the kitchen. I shuddered. Nervously, I twirled my promise ring around my finger.

"Does the oven work? I mean, assuming that we have electricity or gas or whatever."

"Already taken care of," he slurped, and milk spilled off of his chin onto the blue, vinyl tablecloth. I tried to remind myself that, despite his sloppy cereal habits, he was perfect. Not just in my eyes, but absolutely perfect.

"How did you go about that?"

"Just like everyone else does. I gave the electric company my name, and then I gave them a deposit. *Voilà.*"

"I sincerely hope that you didn't give them your real name."

"You underestimate my intelligence, Sunshine," he teased.

"Just making sure," I scowled. "We can't leave a trace. My parents' lives depend on it."

Another gust of wind blew into the kitchen and I shivered. Despite the chill in the air, we had the windows open because the cottage smelled a bit stale when we arrived. Of course it would. Besides Alex's brief stay at the cottage last winter, no one had been here in almost twenty years. I was surprised that everything was in working order when we arrived. The kitchen was functional and, despite the fact that it was more than a bit outdated, it was totally my style: kitschy. Pushed to the far edge of the table near the window was a chipped turquoise Fiesta sugar dish, an old transistor radio, a crystal toothpick holder, and a wooden napkin holder in the shape of a fish. Hanging on the towel rack just below the sink was an embroidered dishtowel; yellow stitching spelled out *Monday* near the bottom. As Alex continued to slurp down his second bowl of cereal, I studied the outdated, mismatched kitchen. Brown, blue, and white linoleum squares covered the kitchen floor. The colors did not come close to coordinating with the yellow laminate countertops. Seventies... no.... sixties, I thought. Between the oven and the wall stood a large, rusty hot water tank. I was almost positive it heated up water that came straight out of the lake.

Alex set his bowl down on the table and eyed the box of cereal as he considered pouring himself another. He shook the box to find it empty, save a few sugar coated squares resting at the bottom. Trying not to show his disappointment, he diverted his eyes from the empty box of Mini-Wheats and rested his piercing green eyes on me. I exhaled and looked out the window.

"So what name *did* you give them?"

"Ian Limbeaux."

At least thirty seconds passed before I found humor in the name. "Real funny, Alex. They didn't ask for I.D.?"

"Of course not," Alex said as he got up from the table and placed his dishes in the sink. "Come on. I have a little something planned, and I think you'll enjoy it."

"Where are we going?" I demanded.

"To the lake. Grab your phone and follow me."

His request was strange but intriguing, so I obliged. I had no choice but to accept his invitation.

Alex was halfway to the lake and his voice was barely audible over the wind. "Yo... di.. et... brefst."

I quickened my pace to catch him. Even from a distance the lake was a sight to behold-an emerald pool of water bordered by sandy shores and grassy lawns. It was beautiful, no doubt. But after the dreams, I had been keeping my distance. I scampered up beside Alex and slipped my arm around his waist.

"What did you say?"

"I said," Alex spoke louder this time. "I noticed that you didn't eat breakfast... again."

"Not hungry."

Alex ruffled my hair with his hand and pulled me closer. "If you say so."

As we neared the dock, Alex pulled his cell phone from the pocket of his fleece. "Did you grab yours?"

"I did," I returned, holding out my phone for him to see.

"Are you ready?'

"For what?"

Alex fixed his eyes on the lake and threw his phone across the surface like he was skipping a stone. "To being untraceable," Alex said.

I watched the phone make several splashes before slipping under the surface.

"You think of everything, Alex Loving," I said, a smile tugging at the corners of my mouth.

"I believe it's your turn, Sunshine."

"To being untraceable," I repeated without hesitation, and then I flung my phone into the lake. I was amazed that such a simple action could be so freeing.

When my phone disappeared into the waves, Alex sat down on the end of the dock and massaged his whiskery chin. He hadn't shaved since arriving at the cottage and the stubble made him look a little rough around the edges. I didn't mind. He had a melancholy expression on his face, which led me to believe he didn't find the ceremony quite as liberating as I did.

"You're aware that we can't stay cooped up inside of this cabin forever," he began. "I have no intention of hiding. We're going to have to venture out. Not eating the two pieces of bread in the brisker will only *delay* the inevitable, not *prevent* it. We need to eat to stay alive, and we need to go to the store for food."

"I'm not ready."

"I'm worried about you. You're turning into an agoraphobe."

"So?" I was familiar with the term because my parents were both shrinks and psychobabble had become my second language.

"And that doesn't bother you?"

"Well, I'm not afraid of you. I just don't have the desire to see anyone else."

We were both aware of the complicated circumstances that brought us to Minnesota, but I was beginning to realize that our reasons for coming here were very different. My mom and dad… that's why I ran away with Alex… to keep them safe. And now that I was gone, they finally were. Alex, on the other hand, was here to find answers. He was determined to put a stop to Chloe and Ben. He was on a mission, while I was content to enjoy the little time that we had left together. He was all strategy and preparation, while I was content to sit and patiently wait. For the past two days, I had succeeded in distracting Alex from his assignment and was successful in delaying point number one on his agenda: to fervently dig around in my family's history.

"I bought you something." Alex said, trying to change the subject. He reached back into the pocket of his fleece and pulled out a small plastic bag. "Take your pick," he said, handing it to me.

I reached my hand blindly inside the bag and pulled out a small cell phone.

"I don't understand? I thought the point was to be untraceable?"

"We still are. It's a prepaid. I didn't have to sign a contract. It's perfect."

"Once again, you think of everything." I kissed his cheek and his whiskers scratched my lips. "You look tired," I told him.

"I am."

"You need to relax."

"Relax? And this is coming from the girl who doesn't want to leave the cottage?" he began.

I didn't respond; instead, I turned my head and looked out across the water.

"I'm sorry. Look, I'm not trying to be mean, and I'm not trying to discredit what you've gone through, either. God knows it's been a lot. But just because we are here in this very beautiful place doesn't mean that anything has changed. Ben and Chloe want you dead, Rae."

"Thanks for the reminder."

"You act like you no longer care."

"I'm not sure that I do."

"Do you want to know why I'm so tired? Do you want to know what keeps me up at night?" Alex paused, but not long enough for me to respond. "You, and the thought of not having you by my side. The fear that I might fail. That my protection might not be enough. And do you want to know what wakes me in the morning?" Alex's pause was even shorter this time. It seemed as though he was merely trying to catch his breath rather than give me a chance to answer. "It isn't you scurrying around outside of my cottage. I can tell you that for sure. You slipped through my fingers once before, and I swear to you that if it happens again it will be over my dead body."

I didn't respond. I was too busy thinking about how he was, as far as I knew, already dead, and I was beginning to worry about what his promise held for my future. The first time I slipped through Alex's fingers was on the night of September 13th. That was the night he died, the night I was born, and the night our souls touched, if only for a moment. I thought it might be rather brash to tell him that it was through his dead fingers that I first slipped. I wanted to remind him of how much one could learn by reviewing history and that doing things over one's dead body was not the method I preferred, nor was it a method that produced the most desirable results.

"You know, maybe you should follow your own advice."

While I was lost in reverie, Alex had been talking to himself. But his last statement was so potent that it snapped me back at once.

"And what advice would that be?"

"This isn't something you can just brush under the carpet and hope it will go away. We've had two perfect days. Vacation is over. Now it's time to get to work."

CHAPTER THREE

*M*y dog, Cocoa, is a Goldendoodle. Her defining feature is her fur. I call it fur, but really it's more like human hair. When it's long, it's shaggy… curly. It keeps her warm. It makes her look ten pounds heavier. It makes her appear tough. She wears it like a warrior. And while the heavy coat of fur is very functional, there are certain seasons that it makes her absolutely miserable. During those seasons, we cut her hair so that it's short, sleek, smooth, and easy to care for. It gives her skin a chance to breath.

I will never forget when we moved to Oklahoma. It was the summer before my senior year, and the heat came as a shock to my family, Cocoa included. Her fur was at its longest, and it was a sweltering 104 degrees outside. She was so miserable that she barely moved. When Dad got out the shears, her ears perked up at once. When the fur came off she was like a different dog: spunky, full of energy, rambunctious, and ready to play. There was no question that we had made the right decision, but we failed to consider one thing. Not only had the thick fur kept her warm and comfortable in Europe's temperate climate, it had cushioned her paws as well.

Later that night, after the temperature dropped into the nineties and the sun was beginning to set, Cocoa and I went for a long run down the country road by our house. The next morning I found her curled up on the kitchen floor licking her paws. She couldn't walk. I was terrified. Dad looked at the pads of her feet and noticed they were bleeding. The thick cushion of fur had served as protection, armor if you will. When we removed her heavy coat, we did so with the best intentions, but we had no idea how vulnerable it would leave her. We did all that we could do to comfort her. Mom flushed out the wounds and bandaged her paws. All we could do was wait for them to heal.

While I really hate to liken my heart to the paws of Cocoa, I can think of no better comparison. Much like the fur that guarded Cocoa's feet, the shell around my heart served as a cushion. It made me feel safe, sheltered… comfortable, and it had done so for a decade. But then Alex came along; he brought me into a new *season* of life, and the shell around my heart became a burden. After it was gone, I felt liberated. I felt like Cocoa did right after a haircut: light, happy, vivacious, and ready to conquer the world. But in the middle of the excitement, I looked down and saw that my heart was bleeding. For years, I hid myself beneath a heavy coat of steel. My shell had covered my pain, but didn't make it go away. I had not forgotten how it felt to crumple on my parents' closet floor. And the memory of the pain on my mother's face when she found me holding Laney's funeral program had intensified over time, not faded.

I rummaged through my luggage until I found what I was looking for: my scrapbook and the brown leather journal. The journal had been in my possession for almost two months. I had yet to tell Alex about it. I hadn't even looked at it myself. It held secrets that I desperately wanted to uncover; I couldn't deny the temptation. I found it in Chloe's basement, and I just knew the contents would tell me everything I needed to know about the Pierce's past. I was also aware that this book might have everything to do with my future. The link between Chloe and Ben and Alex and me was inside the journal… I could feel it. But I was afraid to open it. Why? My fear seemed irrational. I held the brown leather book in my hands and began to drum my fingers on the cover.

The information in this book might just save my life. I pulled the corner back and peeked inside. The paper was yellowing, and I could see the flourishes of handwriting. I smoothed the cover flat and held it to my chest. To open this book would be like opening a can of worms. Once it was open, it could never be shut. I knew this. Would the words inside haunt me forever? Why couldn't I tell Alex about the journal? It wasn't because I was being vengeful or spiteful, it was because I was being selfish. Alex told me that he was meant to save my body, and that I was meant to save his soul. If the journal was able to provide the clues Alex needed, then he would be able to get rid of Chloe and Ben for good. With them gone, Alex's job would be finished, and he would leave. He would return to where he belonged. That was the plan... his plan, but I never agreed to it. And saving his soul... that was impossible; it was a weight too heavy for me to bear. I certainly never agreed to that. I didn't want to be the one responsible for Alex's eternity and, selfish as it may be, I would rather have his body here with me than his spirit up in heaven. The journal was sure to give me answers, but finding answers might cost me the man I loved.

First way to lose Alex Loving: let him get sucked back up to heaven... not if I could help it!

I slid the journal into the drawer of my nightstand and picked up my scrapbook. I turned to the back of the book and had just pulled out an old letter that was stuck between the pages, when I heard Alex call out.

"You ready?" he shouted from the kitchen. "If you hurry I'll buy you a Caribou Coffee."

Alex knew how to bribe me. Between the two of us, we had very little money. Back home, I was used to a frequent latte; now I was enjoying cheap, drip coffee with cream and Splenda at the cottage. I placed the scrapbook back inside my luggage and reluctantly gathered my dirty clothes, pulling them out of my luggage and stuffing them into a white mesh bag.

"Do we really have to go to the Laundromat?" I asked when I entered the kitchen.

"Yes," he said, grabbing the bag from under my arm and slinging it over his shoulder.

"Did you know that we've been in Alexandria for exactly a week? Our one week anniversary and we're celebrating by doing laundry."

"I've always known how to charm you." A mischievous smile spread across his face. "I'm just excited to be getting out of the house... finally."

"I guess it's not so bad... doing laundry. There's nothing else I'd rather be doing...as long I'm with you. Besides, it makes me feel like we're an actual couple."

Alex looked taken aback. "An *actual* couple?" His smile vanished in an instant.

"Doing laundry makes you more human... more like me," I said, trying to smooth things over. "It makes me think that maybe you will stay," I continued, only making matters worse.

I knew that what I said did not please Alex. The look on his face was so revealing. Alex didn't like to discuss his inevitable departure, and he would be content if I never brought it up again. I was just about to apologize when an unexpected knock came from the back door, catching both Alex and me off guard. My heart practically jumped into my throat, and I noticed that, once again, Alex had a small furrow in his brow. Peeking into the living room, I could see a petite woman in her early forties waiting patiently on the deck, just outside the paned glass door.

"I'll get it," I told Alex, who didn't object. I only had the door halfway open before she began to speak.

"Hello there. I'm Mrs. Harvey from down the street." She had a higher-toned voice, yet it was unmistakably rich and bold. Her shoulder length hair was platinum blonde, and her skin was fair.

"I wanted to welcome you to the North Shore," she said with a smile.

"Oh, thank you," was all I could say. I couldn't ignore the fact that she smelled like a bakery, just like my nana did after she had been cooking all day.

"Please excuse the way that I look," she laughed. "I've been in the kitchen since six this morning. We're having a get-together tonight. The seniors are graduating, and we're having a small celebration. It is my daughter Corrine's graduation," she said with pride.

"Congratulations."

"We would love for your family to join us. Bass season has only just begun, but already we have enough to feed the masses," she laughed. "My husband, Jerry, is a pro fisherman. He knows all of the tricks for catching bass early in the season."

I was fumbling with my words when I heard Alex coming up from behind. I watched Mrs. Harvey's look of pleasure turn into one of surprise. She tilted her head and studied Alex; a puzzled expression rearranging her delicate features.

"And this must be your... brother?" The softness I heard in her voice a moment ago had vanished.

I looked over my shoulder and saw Alex shaking his head.

"I'm sorry," she said, refocusing her eyes on me. "You look too young to be on your own. I assumed that you were here with your family." Mrs. Harvey paused and twisted her mouth. It appeared that she was at a loss for words. "Well… we would still love to have you over, if you'll come."

"You can count us in, Mrs. Harvey," Alex replied in a way that turned my stomach. "Can we bring anything?"

"Not a thing. And you can call me Candice, if you like." Mrs. Harvey gave us a quizzical look, and then turned to leave.

I waited until she was halfway across the deck before I shut the door and locked it. But I was still watching her through the glass. She was craning her neck, trying to catch another glimpse inside the cottage, almost tripping over herself as she made her way down the stairs of our small wooden deck. I waved to her through the glass panels and watched her scurry away.

Neither Alex nor I said a word to each other until he pulled into Nokomis Square, the strip mall that housed both Caribou Coffee and Coin Laundry. I had kept my mouth shut for nearly ten minutes. Alex had made plans to spend the evening with a group of strangers. He knew how I felt about that. He knew that I was feeling vulnerable and that the last thing I wanted was to be around a bunch of people I didn't know.

"Why did you tell her 'yes'?" I spat, breaking the silence.

"I thought it sounded fun."

"I think you did it because you were mad."

Alex put the car into park and returned his hand to the steering wheel. "You know, I'm trying my best not to leave you. I wish you would quit making me feel so bad about something that is completely out of my control," he said as he opened his car door and slammed it shut behind him.

"I'm sorry."

"It's fine. No damage done. You are a bit grouchy without coffee in your system. You better go fill up," he teased. "I'll wait outside."

I took a sip of my latte and let the door to Caribou Coffee shut behind me.

"Better?" Alex asked as I approached him.

"Umhum," I nodded, taking another sip.

"I thought the coffee might help."

"Are you still mad at me?" I asked.

"No, I'm not mad at you. How could I stay mad at you? And I didn't agree to go to the party because you made me mad. I think it's a good idea for you and me to get out of the house. It's not healthy to be cooped up in the cottage like we have been."

"We've only been here a week. Besides, I feel just fine," I told him as he opened the door to Coin Laundry. I looked around the large open room. An older woman with shoulder length grey hair was busy mopping the floors, which were already perfectly clean. It smelled like Tide mixed with bleach. I inhaled deeply, taking in the scent that brought back memories, all of which were good. What Alex didn't know was that I felt as though I was the queen, or the princess, of Laundromats. I was a Laundromat connoisseur.

My family had never owned a washer and dryer until we moved to Oklahoma and had a place of our very own. When we lived overseas, Mom would take me to the Laundromat on the weekends and we would play games. We would play *I Spy* and card games like *Go Fish*. She would always let me win. Sometimes, she would experiment with my hair while we waited for our clothes to dry. The Laundromat was where I got my first French braid.

Often I associate people with places. For instance, when I see a small pond, I can't help but associate the body of water with my papa. When I was small, he used to take me fishing every summer. With Alex, it's the park by the bridge where he took me on our first date. It was and will always be our spot. And not to disparage my mother in anyway, but when I see a Laundromat I think of her. It was the one place where I had her undivided attention... her soft voice rising above the tossing and turning of the clothes in the dryer... the warm, clean clothes that she would press to my cheeks just before she kissed me.

Here we were, celebrating our one-week anniversary away from Mom and Dad at the Laundromat, the place that I associated with my mother. Now I felt a sadness my latte couldn't fix.

Alex could sense my discomfort. "We could play *I Spy*," he offered, throwing a load of laundry into the washer. Normally, I resented the fact that he had the ability to see me from the halfway. He had seen my entire life play out like a movie. For eighteen years, he has seen me in both good times and bad. He knew more about me than I did about him. But at times like these, I found it comforting. He knew exactly how to cheer me up, no guesswork involved.

"I can start," I said. "I spy with my little eye something green."

"That lady's shirt," he said.

"No."

"The green stripe on the box of detergent," he said, pointing his finger in the direction of the vending machine that housed an assortment of detergents and softeners.

"No."

Alex put his hand to his head, holding it there while massaging his temple with his forefinger and thumb, deep in thought, then he began to scan the room. After a moment, he turned to me with a gleam in his eye.

"I know. The pair of green underwear in the basket to my left," he told me.

"You got it," I said through hiccups of laughter. "Your turn."

"Let me think about this." Alex's hand returned to his temple. It was strange. I had never seen him do this before. Alex was superhuman. He wasn't supposed to have to think things through. He just always knew the right answer.

"Okay. I spy something blue."

"You have to say, 'I spy with my little eye,'" I informed him.

"Fine. I spy *with my little eye* something blue, and you're never going to get it."

"Your shirt?"

"Sorry."

"The little square of blue on my cup of coffee."

"AIHRR," Alex did his best imitation of a buzzer, and I shook my head with a bit of impatience.

"Um, the blue pen that is wedged in between the two dryers," I said hopefully.

"Wrong again."

I wasn't certain, but by the tone of his voice and the look of satisfaction on his face, I was under the impression that Alex was gloating.

"My eyes," I spat.

"Finally. I was staring right at them the whole time."

"I'm up. I spy with my little eye something silver."

"The washing machine," he said.

"No."

"The vending machine?"

"Nope."

"The cell phone lying on the counter behind you?"

"Sorry."

"I give up," he said.

"Ahhh. To hear you say that is music to my ears. The silver sign over the register is the correct answer. So, did I win?"

"No. But if you guess the next one, then you're the winner. If you don't, I take home the prize."

"What's the prize?"

"Loser has to fold the laundry."

"Agreed."

"I spy with my itty bitty eye....something...black," he said.

"The hand on the clock," I shouted with positivity, because just seconds ago I saw him staring at it.

"Nope," he said smugly.

"The stripe on your shoe."

"Again... NO."

"The lid on the red water bottle that the lady over there is holding in her hand."

"Wrong again."

"Now I was searching frantically around the room. Not because I didn't want to fold laundry, but because I wanted so desperately this victory over him. I was a sore loser. That I could admit.

"By the way, this is your last guess, so you better make it good."

"My last guess?"

"You can't keep guessing all day."

"Oh! I've got it!" I pointed to the fashion magazine I had left open on the counter. "The fingernail polish in the advertisement."

Alex picked up the magazine and studied the page. "The polish is purple."

"It's black... ish."

"It's purple, and you're not right."

"What is it, then?"

"The black sedan outside the window."

"That's not fair. The rules are that the object has to be inside of this room," I said, craning my neck to see the car in question. After a moment's hesitation, I turned my whole body around for a better look. The sedan was an older model, and it was a little banged up. My eyes followed the curve of the car, beginning at the dulled Cadillac emblem and moving up the hood toward the windshield, which was covered in dirt and bugs. I squinted my eyes, struggling to see past the bug splattered glass, focusing until I found myself no longer staring at the window, but through it. The driver's features were indistinct from where I was standing, but it seemed that he was staring directly at me. When our eyes met, the driver put his car in reverse and began to back away.

I'm not sure how long I had been staring out the window with my back toward Alex, but what felt like an eternity was probably only several seconds.

"Are you pouting, Rae, because you didn't win." Alex approached me from behind and began to massage my shoulders, freeing me from the daze I was in.

Stop it, Rae. I scolded myself. *Stop it. Stop it. Stop it. Not everyone is out to get you.*

"Looks like you get to fold."

"It was a tie. And no, I'm not pouting. I think I'm just going to read a bit, if you don't mind. I only have a couple of chapters left in my book."

"Sure," Alex said, just as the spin cycle came to an end on all three loads of our laundry.

Alex had his back toward me as he pulled our wet clothes from the washer and put them into one massive, industrial-sized dryer. I observed him for a moment. Tall, but not too tall. Sturdy. Powerful. Invincible. I reached for the bag of quarters on the counter. Without thinking, I threw it directly at Alex, testing the acuity of his reflexes. I wasn't sure why I did it. Perhaps to reassure myself that he was still agile enough to protect me. In one fluid movement, he reached up and caught the bag of change. When he turned around to face me, he had a bewildered look in his eyes.

"Are you trying to *kill* me?" he asked.

"Just trying to keep you quick on your feet."

Alex rolled his eyes and finished putting the laundry into the dryer. I reached into my bag and pulled out my book.

CHAPTER FOUR

*A*s I was getting ready for the fish fry, I could feel my anxiety beginning to resurface. I still couldn't believe that Alex had accepted Mrs. Harvey's invitation. Mrs. Harvey was nice and I did appreciate that she had thought to invite us, but it was easier to pretend that my life was okay when it was just Alex and me. Painting other people into the picture only made things messy. I was also a bit irritated that Alex seemed so eager to attend. I grabbed a couple of shirts that were folded neatly on top of my dresser. I held them up against my body and studied myself in the mirror. Disagreeing with both of them because they were too dressy, I tossed them onto the floor and picked out something more casual: a pair of jeans and a pink tee shirt. I loved the well-worn, thinning tee shirt with the image of two very different trees printed onto the front. One tree was barren; the other was full of life and foliage. But the beautiful, green tree had a tear in its eye and a sad face because of the caption over the top of the barren tree.

"That's so last season," the barren tree said to the one that was full of life.

I was sure the barren tree was jealous. I slipped on a long-sleeved grey cardigan over my tee shirt and met Alex, who was patiently waiting for me on the deck.

"You shaved," I said, running my fingers across the smooth skin of his cheek. "And you're kind of dressed up… compared to me. Should I change?" I asked.

Alex was wearing jeans, as usual, but he had traded his tee shirt for a freshly ironed navy blue and green checked button up. The sleeves of his shirt were rolled up, which gave him a more casual look. "You look like a J-Crew model; I look like I just rolled out of bed. I *should* change."

"You look perfect. I like your shirt," he smiled.

"I liked your beard. Why'd you shave?"

"It added a couple of years to my age. It made me look a bit too old for you. I'd hate for people to start talking."

"Are you kidding me? I'm sure they already are. Didn't you see the look on Mrs. Harvey's face when she found out you weren't my brother?"

"I'm sure they have better things to talk about than us," Alex said as we walked down the lane toward the Harvey's house.

Mrs. Harvey saw us when we arrived and, with a smile on her face, waved to catch our attention. She was standing under an enormous ash tree next to a long table and, despite the chill, was wearing a sundress. I pulled my thin sweater tight around my torso and followed Alex. Festive lights hung from the trees near the lake, but the sun was still too bright to see them glow. The smell of citronella wafted through the air. I supposed that someone was burning a precautionary candle because, although it was the first of June, the bugs weren't too bad yet. I hadn't received a single bite. Mrs. Harvey, "Candice" as she reminded us, had been stirring something inside a casserole dish, but as we approached, she set it on the table which was filled with food and wiped her hand on the tiny apron she had tied around her waist.

"You're just in time," she said in a jovial voice. "Jerry is frying up the fish right now. Follow me. I'll introduce you. He is so glad to hear that someone is finally living in that old house. It's been vacant for nearly twenty years. Such a sad story."

Alex's shoulder stiffened; I brushed my hand across the back of his neck and felt his muscles relax to my touch. Candice wove in and out of the guests who were dotting her lawn. As the crowd thickened, the level of my anxiety began to increase accordingly. The unfamiliar faces brought back unpleasant memories of being the new kid at school. I thought that after graduating I would never have to feel that way again, like a stranger. I looked over at Alex. A huge smile plastered his face. It appeared that touching the back of his neck had done more than loosen his muscles. He was now as cool as a cucumber, saying hello to every person that he passed, and I was a bit annoyed by the effect he seemed to be having on the females at the party. I had never seen so many eyes glued to the same thing at once. I didn't disagree. He always looked handsome, but tonight there was something exceptional about the way he looked. Very possessively, I slipped my arm through his and followed Candice around the side of the house to meet Jerry.

Jerry wasn't what I expected. He was tall, at least six foot five, and standing next to the petite Mrs. Harvey only accentuated his size.

"Jerry, I want you to meet…I'm sorry, but I never got your names."

"I'm Rae," I answered just above a whisper.

"I'm Alex," Alex said with a broad smile.

"They've just moved into that old cottage down the way. For the life of me I can't remember the name of the family that used to live there."

My heart was in my throat.

"Is that so," Jerry said over the sound of popping oil. "What brings you here?"

"School," Alex said without hesitation.

"Where will you be attending?" Mrs. Harvey interjected, looking Alex in the eye.

"We're here for Rae. She'll be going to the University of Minnesota in the fall. She's an artist, and a very talented one at that."

"That's quite a drive. Two and a half hours, at least."

"We're bound and determined to make it work."

"Why did you choose Alexandria? I hope you don't mind that I ask."

"Lake L'Homme Dieu just feels like home, I guess. I love it here. We love it here."

"You betcha. It's a wonderful lake, that's for sure." It seemed that Mrs. Harvey could have gone on and on about the splendors of L'Homme Dieu but something had caught her attention. My eyes involuntarily followed Mrs. Harvey's. A tall and curvy girl with white blonde hair was walking toward us. It wasn't hard to tell that she belonged to Candice and Jerry. She had her mother's delicate facial features and white blonde waves, but as far as height was concerned, she took after her father.

"This is our daughter, Corrine." Candice said with a smile. "She will be in the Twin Cities for school this fall as well, but she'll be staying in the dormitories. Wontcha, Corrine?"

I couldn't help noticing Corrine's outfit. She had paired black cowboy boots with a very feminine dress that was filled and fitted at the bodice and full and flowing from the waist all the way down to where the layers of sheer material ended just above her knees. The dress was beautiful, white with a plumage print down one side and across the bottom. Her long hair cascaded down her back. She looked angelic, almost as angelic as someone else I knew. I dipped my head to acknowledge Corrine, but she didn't seem to notice. Her pale brown eyes were fixed on Alex.

"I don't mean to be nosy." Candice lowered her voice. "But you two look awfully young to be married." Mrs. Harvey stole a glance at my ring, but Corrine, who was still studying my boyfriend with intent, didn't appear to notice the sparkly object on my finger. I began to twirl it around in an attempt to show it off.

"We're not married," Alex interjected much too quickly, I thought. I stopped twirling at once.

"Do forgive me," she replied. "I guess I just assumed that since you were living in the same cottage…"

"There are actually three cottages on the property. I gave Rae the one by the lake. The middle one's all mine." Alex's voice rose over the snapping oil and the friendly chatter of old friends.

"Well, that's different."

"You can be so old fashioned at times, Mom," Corrine interjected, catching only the pieces of conversation she wished to hear.

"And there is nothing wrong with that." Mrs. Harvey gave us a disapproving look. Corrine, on the other hand, seemed to be intrigued by our arrangement. I thought she might be more intrigued with Alex than with the thought of us together.

Jerry could sense the tension in the air and, at just the right moment, he pulled Alex aside and began to discuss, what I assumed to be, his favorite topic: fishing in Minnesota.

"Bass season doesn't open until the last weekend of May. Generally Memorial Day weekend and runs through the end of the year," he told Alex while adjusting the settings on the Fry Daddy.

"Your wife said that you might have a few tricks up your sleeve… as far as fishing is concerned." Alex returned.

I was surprised by Alex's newfound interest in fishing and wondered if it were merely an attempt to butter Jerry up. I thought that this was most likely the case considering that, in the living room of the main cottage, there was an entire rack of fishing poles that had yet to catch his attention. Still, he seemed to have a genuine interest in what Jerry was saying.

"Oh. You flatter me boy. I wouldn't call them tricks, but I do know some of the best spots on the lake."

I was getting bored with the conversation and so, without another alternative, I did the only thing that I was good at. In a wallflower fashion, I leaned against the side of the Harvey's house and tuned in to what Corrine was saying. One of Corrine's friends had joined her. She was petite with mousy brown hair. She had a bulbous nose and a tiny mouth. Her skin was pale beneath the freckles that spread across her cheeks. I quickly learned that her name was Gretchen. I continued to listen to Corrine's voice bob up and down with enthusiasm.

"Party. That's what I'm talking about." Corrine looked over her shoulder to make sure that her mother was out of range. The devious look in her eyes told me that my first impression of Corrine was very wrong: she was no angel. "Seriously, Gretchen," she said to the girl with the mousy brown hair. "The dorms are a complete joke. I heard that there is only one RA per floor, and you can like bribe them with food."

Corrine liked to talk with her hands. She moved them enthusiastically around her body, showing off her neatly manicured, neon colored nails. But it was the wide assortment of expressions that formed so naturally on her face that brought everything she said to life. Her fair porcelain skin was glowing with thoughts of deception, and her light brown eyes sparkled when she spoke. At first glance, Corrine looked womanly, no doubt. But in the middle of the excitement, her maturity gave way to a childlike quality that I envied, and I couldn't figure out why.

"Whatever. Don't rub it in," Gretchen remarked bitterly.

Alex was still trapped between the house and the industrial sized Fry Daddy. I was pretty sure that he hadn't gotten a word in edgewise, but he didn't seem to mind.

"The rushes don't come up until early June and die off when the ice comes in. Usually November or December," Jerry continued. "Bass will generally go to shallow water in the summer and then return to deeper water when the weather gets cold."

After Jerry had covered the ins and outs of Minnesota fishing in the summer, he moved on to another season. The talk of cold weather brought up the subject of ice-covered lakes and the conversation quickly shifted from fishing boats to drills, ice shacks, and parkas. Before I could object, Jerry handed over his Fry Daddy duty to a friend and began walking toward the dock where he had his brand new, metallic-green fishing boat tethered to the side. Alex followed close behind, leaving me with nothing to do but eavesdrop. Corrine noticed Alex's departure as well, and her conversation shifted quickly from college to the statuesque build of my boyfriend.

"I am standing right here, Corrine," I said in a voice so low that only I could hear. I groaned and was seriously considering the option of returning to the cottage, when I noticed that Mrs. Harvey's conversation had changed direction as well. I stood stock-still and listened with intent. It was her tone that first attracted my attention: she had quickly lowered her voice to a level more suitable for gossip. There was a hush-hush quality about it that told me they were no longer discussing who had the most luscious lawn on the lake.

"It happened twenty years ago," she said, completely failing in her attempt to whisper. "Gosh, I was only twenty-five at the time. I was pregnant with Corrine. Jerry and I were up here at the house for the weekend visiting Mom and Dad. It was normally just the parents and the little boy. Uggghh. I wish I could remember their last name. It's on the tip of my tongue. I think it might have been Lovelace. Love something or other. They weren't here often, so we never had the chance to meet. Very private people. That's why I was surprised to see they had company... another couple... with the cutest little girl you've ever seen. She was darling and about the same age as the boy."

Better able to control the level of her voice, the lady standing next to Candice successfully whispered something so quietly that I couldn't hear. I inched closer, but kept ample distance between the ladies and myself so as not to be caught listening in.

"Oh Candy, dontcha remember the *other* lady?"

"I had completely forgotten about her," Candice returned. "She was definitely odd, if you ask me...."

A chubby lady on the other side of the circle chimed in, and she was so successful in lowering her voice that I was left picking up only bits and pieces of the conversation.

"Pregnant... sick... I heard... delusional... screaming... I know.... so sad...."

"And they were only at the cottage for a day before... well you know," Mrs. Harvey interrupted.

I was drawn to the story, while at the same time it hurt to listen. After reading the letters in my scrapbook and discovering that my parents had met Alex's, I often wondered if my family had stayed at his cottage. There were many holes in Mrs. Harvey's story, but based on timing alone, I assumed that the Loving's guests were my mom and dad. And Laney. The "darling" little girl had to have been my sister. As I replayed the fragmented conversation between Candice and the chubby woman standing in the circle, a chill developed inside me and swept outward, leaving goose bumps on my arms and legs.

"Pregnant... sick... I heard... delusional... screaming... I know....
so sad."

Pregnant. Mom had been pregnant with me at the time. I could
easily fit that piece into place. But delusional? Screaming? There was also
mention of another lady, "an odd lady." Who was this other woman, and
why had she been invited to the Loving's cottage? What was the relation?
This was new information. Information that had not been included in the
letters. The letters. I looked in the direction of the lake and was relieved
to find that Alex was still on the dock with Jerry. I was glad he had not
heard this gossip.

By moving into the Loving cottage, we had unearthed a story that had
been buried for nearly twenty years. This topic was far from extinguished;
it was only heating up. Not only was I keeping secrets from Alex, now I
was going to have to keep Alex away from the neighbors. Still, I couldn't
deny the gossip session had whetted my appetite, and I couldn't deny
that my curiosity for uncovering the truth was growing stronger. But
how could I forget what was holding me back in the first place? Digging
deeper might just cost Alex his life on earth and uncovering the truth
about September 13th might leave me all alone.

The wind picked up midway through the celebration. The locals
suggested that the storm the weathermen had predicted was finally moving
in. Some of the neighbors helped wrap up the food and unstring the tiny
lights from the trees. But when Mrs. Harvey and her husband moved
the party inside, I was pleasantly surprised that Alex suggested we call it
a night.

Alex retired to his cottage much earlier than usual, but I wasn't tired.
I lay in bed, tossing and turning. I listened to the wind blowing the water
onto the shore. The trees were moving outside my window, creating a
deep and chilling sound. I was on edge and had every reason to be. I
thought about the black sedan I saw outside the Laundromat. I wondered

if I were making it into something more than it actually was. When I thought about the man inside the car I felt frightened. I couldn't shake the feeling. Our eyes met just before he pulled away. And then I thought about other eyes, Corrine's eyes to be exact. Her eyes had been glued to Alex the entire night. In fact, she hadn't taken her eyes off Alex long enough to recognize that I was even there. It was like I was invisible. Feeling invisible was nothing new to me, but it was just that, until now, I had never really minded. Corrine was so vivacious. So full. Full of the curves I lacked. Full of beauty. Full of life. I now understood how the barren tree on the front of my shirt felt. Yes, the barren tree was definitely jealous. I thought about Mom and Dad. I wondered what they were doing. Were they searching for me? Did they miss me? Of course they did. I missed them, too. Sorrow ate away at me until I drifted off to sleep.

CHAPTER FIVE

*T*he morning air was chilly and the breeze that blew onto the north shore pushed through the cottage windows we had propped open with blocks of wood. There was a crow outside my window caw-cawing, and I was wishing that it would go away. I slipped on my robe and pulled the soft hood up over my ears. When I opened my bedroom door, the stillness of the cottage told me something was very wrong. The clock on the mantel read 8:45. The morning was well on its way. The clinking sound of a spoon against a cereal bowl. The careless slurping of milk. That was what I expected to hear; instead, I was greeted with silence. I stepped into the kitchen and found it empty. Alex wasn't where I expected him to be and this concerned me. I froze to the kitchen floor in fear as I considered the implications of his absence. I peered out the window; his car was parked beneath the tree. This wasn't necessarily a comforting sign. Alex running an errand was the least of my concerns.

The notion that Alex could leave this earth at any given moment was still rather fresh in my mind, as it was something that I thought about each night before I fell asleep. I dreaded going to bed at night; I feared when I woke he might be gone. When another gust of wind swept through the cottage, I regained my senses. I took a deep breath. All at once, I could smell something that I couldn't smell when I was frozen inside my little block of ice. Coffee. Alex was here, on earth, and he had made me coffee. I walked over to the white, bead board cupboard and pulled out a yellow speckled mug. I grabbed a spoon from the drawer, walked over to the coffee pot, and filled my cup. I tied my robe tightly around my waist and slipped on my UGGS, which were thrown down in front of the door.

I stepped off the deck into the yard, with Cocoa following close behind. She began sniffing at the limbs and leaves that littered the lawn from the storm the night before. She treaded cautiously through the wet grass; however, when she realized we were headed toward the lake, she raced to the water's edge and jumped in. Last night's wind had been enough to pull the weeds from their sandy beds and they now lined the lake's shore. This morning the water was clear, green, and inviting. Except for the occasional ripple, the water was calm and smooth as glass. I walked to the end of the narrow dock and lay on my stomach. Hesitating, I dipped my fingers into the water and immediately recoiled. You could not pay me to jump in, I thought as I warmed my cold, numb fingers. I pulled myself up, took off my boots, and sat on the end of the dock. I let my legs dangle over the edge so that my toes were just inches from the icy water. The only occupants on the lake this morning were the two loons fighting to the left of me and, Cocoa, who was paddling with her head above water toward an unidentifiable object near the middle of the lake.

I took a sip from my mug and watched the fish swimming below my feet. They were so close, I could catch them with my hands if I tried. And then I saw the strangest thing. While a small perch was feasting on a mayfly, an enormous bass came up and swallowed the perch whole. It was a mixture of shock and remorse for the perch that caused me to spring to my feet, spilling hot coffee down the front of my robe. It would be okay with me if I never again saw the food chain in action. It was a different world under the water, but the occupants of the aquatic world were much the same as humans. The strong devoured the weak. It was survival of the fittest.

I heard Cocoa splashing and looked up to see that the unidentifiable object in the middle of the lake was now swimming by Cocoa's side.

"Alex!" I waved my hands in the air, letting him know I was out of bed and ready to play.

They were still about seventy-five yards out, but they were drawing closer by the second. It was Cocoa who reached the shore first, sopping wet. She was shaking and twisting her body to rid her fur of water. Alex swam over to the dock where I waited.

"I had my bets on you. I have to admit, I am a bit disappointed," I said.

"You know I let her win." He smiled a crooked smile and pointed to Cocoa, who was now lying in the sand licking her belly dry. I jumped off the dock, sat down next to Cocoa, and began to scratch her head.

"Get in the water with me."

"No thanks," I laughed.

"You're up early."

"All thanks to the crow that made its home outside my bedroom window."

Alex shrugged, and dog-paddled toward the shore.

I remember the first time that I saw Alex without his shirt. It was only a flash of his skin that I remember, but one I will never forget. I felt ashamed or embarrassed or something, but I couldn't keep myself from staring. But now, as I lay on the beach beside Cocoa, watching Alex move out of the water, I was neither embarrassed nor ashamed. Already Alex's pale skin had turned a light golden brown. The wet shirt clung to his body, and I could see the outline of every muscle of his chest. His shirt... Why couldn't he just take it off?

His hair was wet and when he reached the shore, he shook his head in much the same way Cocoa had done just moments ago.

"Sure you don't want to get in?"

"I'm sure. Besides, I'm still in my pajamas and robe."

"Go change."

"I'll pass."

"Why are you so scared of the water?"

"I can't swim," I mumbled, but he heard me clearly and responded with haste.

"I know you *can* swim. I've seen you. But you don't want to. Why?"

"I'm more of a land kind of girl, I guess. I run. You don't understand that. You swim, and I don't want to."

"But I've run for you before."

"And if you hadn't I would have died."

Alex shrugged his shoulders without saying a word. Lack of ability was not the reason I avoided the water. In fact, water had never bothered me much until the dreams began. But I didn't think that I was ready to tell Alex about the dreams just yet. How could I tell him that after only a week in Alexandria, I felt that I was in mortal danger? If I was going to tell anyone at all, it would be Alex, because if anyone could save me, it would be him.

Several months ago, my bad dreams had become reality. I couldn't explain it. Alex told me he thought I might have a sixth sense. It was the first time in my life anything like that had ever happened. It was surreal. That's the only way to explain it. I don't know why, but now that several months had passed the events that had taken place on the path in Oklahoma no longer seemed real. The dreams had returned and, even though the nightmares were not the same, they had many similar qualities. For instance, I still faced a cruel and painful death.

"I just figured with you living on a lake that you might want to get in."

"It's cold."

"Just jump in. It's not so bad if you do it that way. You don't have time to change your mind."

I inched toward the lake, getting just close enough to feel the cool water on my toes. I let my feet adjust, and then I took a step further. My heart began to accelerate. The water was now up to my knees.

"Baby steps. Whatever works," he said as he walked toward the end of the dock. He dove into the water and then resurfaced. "Now that's how it's done."

"You shouldn't dive there. It's shallow."

He began to swim toward me with a menacing look upon his face.

"Don't even think about it," I warned him. When he did not heed my warning, I retreated from the water onto the sandy beach.

"What? I wasn't going to do anything." Alex emerged from the water once again, but this time, he joined me on the sand and wrapped his cold, wet arms tightly around me.

"Do you really think that I would let you drown? I thought you had more trust in me than that, Sunshine."

We sat in silence for a moment before he spoke again.

"I think I might just have the perfect idea. It's foolproof. Totally safe. There's no way you'll drown."

CHAPTER SIX

*T*hirty minutes later, I emerged from the cottage. I was no longer in my pajamas and robe, and I was holding a bag of necessities in one hand and a blanket in the other. I tossed a bottle of sunscreen into the bag along with a few Diet Cokes, some chips, fruit, and two sandwiches: peanut butter and honey for myself, and turkey and Swiss for Alex. I let the screen door slam behind me. I had just descended from the deck when I saw Alex's 'bright' idea in tangible form. What was supposed to be shiny and silver was dirty and tarnished with age. It weighed at least a thousand pounds and it was a very, very bad idea.

"I've never been in a boat," I told him as he pushed the giant hunk of aluminum into the water.

"I know."

"Not *ever*," I told him again.

"I know, and you've been missing out."

"Really? That thing looks like a death trap. Do you even know how to drive it?"

"It's a fishing boat. It's pretty straight forward."

Alex handed me a life jacket and, with a little persuasion, was able to coax me aboard. I felt dizzy when I climbed into the boat. Although the lake was still, the boat rocked on the water as I moved toward the seat in the back. Once situated, Alex started the engine. With a sputter, the boat began to move away from the beach. It cut through the water and disrupted the calm. Alex did not stay close to the shore like he promised me he would; instead, he kept the boat at least a hundred feet from solid ground.

flooding (fluhd-ing) *n*.: in psychotherapy, a popular and successful exposure technique where the client is immersed in their greatest fear until that fear is gone.

I was terrified of water, yet Alex had successfully coerced me into a tiny aluminum boat and taken me to the middle of the lake. Only now did I find this ironic. I closed my eyes and prayed to God that the term "flooding" would not take on a more literal meaning.

I had just finished up my prayer when I heard the sputtering engine grow silent. My heart began to race. Had Alex stopped the boat in the middle of the lake to "flood" me even more? Had the boat's engine fizzled? Maybe the battery was dead. The boat was old, so it wasn't out of the question. When I opened my eyes, I realized I was wrong. While I was busy begging God to spare my life, Alex had put the boat in idle and was maneuvering the small aluminum craft through a narrow tunnel beneath a bridge. I looked over the side of the boat and noticed that we were moving through water that was barely waist high. At once, I began to relax. Awe replaced fear as I beheld the beauty before me. Reeds of varying lengths poked out of the water, providing refuge to a pair of ducks that paddled near the shore. My eyes roved from the beach to the bridge. I recognized the structure. It was the bridge I jogged over every morning. It was the bridge that led into town, and as we drew closer, I realized it served another purpose as well: It blocked the wind. While *L'Homme Dieu* was perfectly smooth, *Carlos*, the lake on the other side of the bridge, the lake we were approaching, was a miniature ocean, filled with waves. Alex eased our boat through the tunnel, but when we emerged on the other side, fear gripped me once again. This time, Alex stayed close to the shore in an attempt to avoid the larger waves. I tightened up my life jacket and focused on Alex. I was cold and my body was beginning to tremble.

"Where... where are we going?" my voice shook.

"Darling."

"What?" I groaned.

"Darling," he said again, louder this time.

"And I said 'what'," I yelled over the boat's sputtering engine.

"I said we're going to *Lake Darling*."

"Oh... okay... are we almost there?"

"Just about ten more minutes, I think."

Last year, Alex would have told me to be patient, but ever since we made the promise to tell each other everything, Alex had become a wealth of information. He was completely different from the boy I knew last year. I tried to smile, but my teeth were still chattering.

"Why are you looking at me like that?"

"You n...n...never tell me w...ww...here we're going." I spoke through chattering teeth. "You always w...ww..ant everything to be a s...s...surprise, even though you know how much I hate s....s..s..surprises. But just now you told me." I wrapped my arms around my torso to warm my body.

"We made a deal. Remember? No more secrets. Not even little ones."

I nodded and looked down at my finger and the diamond-encrusted ring that encircled it. "How could I forget?"

How *could* I forget? The ring symbolized an eternity together, an eternity with no secrets. But on the night he gave me the ring, I was keeping a huge secret from him. I had snuck into Chloe Pierce's basement without his knowledge, and I couldn't bring myself to tell him. I also couldn't forget how angry he was when, weeks later, I finally confessed. He made me promise that I would never do anything like that again.

His reminder made me feel guilty. It reminded me of the journal that I had taken from Chloe Pierce's basement. He didn't know about it. I had been hiding the letters from him, too. They were still tucked away in a scrapbook that he had yet to see. And then there was the conversation I overheard while standing on the Harvey's lawn. I hadn't bothered to tell him about that either. Secrets… secrets… secrets.

I could see a resort in the distance. It looked deserted. Not a single attendant stood on the dock.

"Perfect," Alex said, steering the boat into shallow water. When he turned the key in the ignition the boat grew silent. Alex rolled up his jeans, hopped into the lake, and pulled the boat onto the sandy shore with an effortless tug.

I pointed at a sign that read "Private Property."

"Are we supposed to be here?"

"I don't know. It doesn't look like there's anyone to stop us."

"Breaking the rules, are we?" I said, pointing to the sign. "Just look at what the world is doing to my little angel."

"You're a fine one to talk. Besides, I've told you all along that I'm no angel."

"I'm beginning to worry about your future, Alex Loving. You may no longer be fit for eternity."

Alex rolled his eyes. "You see that spot over there?" He pointed to a spot about fifty yards down the beach. "That's where we're headed. Follow me."

With a steady hand, Alex helped me out of the boat. Dizzy and a bit dazed from the adventure, I said a short prayer of thanks when my feet touched solid ground. I waded through the cold water until I reached the shore. I followed Alex up an embankment and across a short measure of grass to a small private beach. Everything looked much the same as it did from the boat: deserted. A fire pit had been fashioned in the sand. Large stones formed a perfect circular border, but there were no logs inside and the ash had blown away.

Alex spread out our blanket beneath a drooping tree. Its limbs hung so low they dipped into the water.

"This reminds me of our spot by the bridge."

Alex simply nodded his head in agreement. I lay on the blanket and looked up at the sky. The clouds were still heavy despite the rain we received the night before. Regardless, this spot was beautiful. I was beginning to think that the boat ride was worth it. A reluctant smile began to turn the corners of my mouth. I glanced at Alex and was surprised to find we did not share the same expression. His face was consumed by a look of concern. I nervously twisted the ring around my finger.

"I love you."

"I love you, too."

"You look worried, Alex."

"Now what on *earth* do I have to be worried about?" He gazed at me and smiled. "I have you, and that's all that matters."

"You know what would make this moment absolutely perfect?"

"I thought it already was."

"I can think of one thing that might make it better."

Alex regarded me with suspicion.

"Will you tell me about us? Tell me about our life in heaven.'"

"No," Alex said very matter-of-factly, and I began to pout. "Will you settle for something that I wrote while I was in the halfway?"

My eyes lit up at once and my lower lip, which I had intentionally made very full, was now spread thin with a smile. "I guess that will have to do."

Alex cleared his throat, lowered his voice, and began to whisper a song he had written years ago.

> *Running round the castle wall*
> *Yellow Dress and nearly five feet tall*
> *With your dad you look so sweet*
> *Long black waves and innocence*
> *You swept me off my feet.*
> *Yeah, you swept me off my feet*
>
> *So naïve and unexposed*
> *You choose a daisy and then a rose*
> *Pick the petals one by one*
> *You pick the petals one by one*

He loves me, he loves me not, you say
So, do you think about him everyday?
Just like he thinks about you
Just like I think about you

All grown up and different
Insecure and indifferent
I whisper that it will be okay
The world is hard
But I am harder you say
I'm harder you say

Listening to his voice was like looking into his soul, the deep down part of a person that one rarely gets to see. I couldn't help myself. I couldn't help that his soul was so inviting and that when he showed me just a little piece of it, it did strange things to my body. On any given day it was hard to resist Alex Loving, but when he recited poetry the task became impossible. Without waiting for him to object, I pressed my lips against his and held them there. With his hand on the small of my back, he pulled me so close to his body I could feel his heart beating in his chest. His fingers wound through my hair and tugged. I felt desperation in his fingertips just before he came up for air.

"I didn't know my poetry had such a profound effect on you," he laughed.

"I remember that yellow dress," I whispered back. I could still feel his breath, ragged, on my cheek. "It was my favorite. I remember that day, too. It was just after we moved to Paris. We were at Luxemburg Gardens. I wasn't supposed to be picking the flowers, but I did it anyway. Dad told me it would be okay as long as no one was looking. I can't believe you saw that. I can't believe you remember. If it wasn't so sweet, I would feel completely violated."

I expected him to laugh, but he didn't. His lightheartedness had vanished once again. It seemed as though something was weighing heavily on his soul. His eyes looked sad and watery. His mouth was slightly agape and his lips were trembling. He relaxed onto the ground and stared blankly up at the sky.

"I brought you here for a reason, you know."

"To romance me with your poetry," I cooed and hovered over his body casting shadows upon his face.

"No. What I have to show you is definitely not romantic, but none-the-less, I think you need to see it for yourself."

I fell onto my side and placed my head upon his chest. In an instant, my mood had changed as well. When he spoke, I felt like a child whose dreams had just been shattered. With more soothing strength than desperation, Alex ran his fingers through my hair while I lay crumpled at his side.

"Come on. Let's walk," he said without moving. Normally, I was so full of questions that Alex didn't know which one to answer first. I suppose that he was waiting for me to say something, waiting for me to ask where we were going, but I didn't. I couldn't, because deep down, I already knew. With a look of understanding, Alex took my hand in his, pulled me up from our sandy spot on the beach, and led me across the rocky shore to a trail that wound uphill through the woods. It was so quiet, we could have heard a pin drop. Broken tree limbs littered the path, and the green leaves beneath our feet were soft from rain.

As we ascended, my heart rate did as well, and I tried my best to focus on my surroundings instead of what lay ahead. I closed my eyes and let Alex lead the way. I took in the smell of trees still fresh with rain. I listened to the now distant sound of water crashing over the rocks and a woodpecker in a tree somewhere far away. But even with all my senses working together, I could not push the image of death from my mind. I often thought about this place and had considered, on more than one occasion, what it might look like. I envisioned monstrous, black waves surrounding a narrow, winding road. I saw matchbox cars that were smashed and crumpled, but I never saw anything real. I liked it better that way; swirly drawings of death that belonged on the page of a book. It was a night so filled with sadness that not even the stars would shine. But this place was real. And to face it would be to acknowledge that this place did indeed exist. It would be to acknowledge that we were not living inside a storybook and *happily ever after* might not be written at the end. This was real. Could I face it? Alex was real. Chloe and Ben were real. But perhaps our love *was* like a book: there *would* be a final chapter. When Alex stopped, I opened my eyes and was pleasantly surprised.

"I thought it would be best if we didn't come by car. Besides, you can see it better from the hill."

My first glance proved me wrong, and I quietly sighed in relief. A ray of sun peeked out from behind a cloud, confirming that the storm was over and better weather was headed our way. Still holding onto Alex's hand, I moved slowly to the edge of the hill and looked down at the newly paved highway that stretched out like a smooth, silky ribbon some thirty feet below us. The road was flat and straight with gentle bodies of emerald water residing on either side. I sat down on the damp grass and let my feet dangle over the edge of the bluff.

"Careful," Alex said, not loosening his grip on my hand until he was seated comfortably beside me.

"What is this place?" I asked, now confident that I could handle any answer that he gave.

"This is the place where my body first met yours."

"This isn't what I imagined. It doesn't even come close."

"It's beautiful, huh?"

"Surprisingly so." My voice cracked. I was on the brink of tears. "I'm ready to go." I stood up and grabbed my bag. "And I don't ever want to come back."

What is it about trying to forget that makes you remember all the more? The one thing that you try to push from your mind seems to be the only thing that occupies it. It's much like trying to forget someone special, only to remember his touch with more strength. I had been trying my hardest to forget about the accident, but being at *the bluff* with Alex brought to the surface a plethora of emotions. Now more than ever, I needed my mom and dad. Now more than ever, I felt a longing to uncover the truth. I thought about the journal. A part of me wished that I had never taken the book. The words inside were at my fingertips, and I could think of nothing else. Discovering the secrets inside the book might cost me the man I love. So why was it such a temptation? I pushed the journal out of my mind and grabbed my scrapbook instead. I flipped to the back of the book and pulled out the letter that was pressed between the pages.

Dear Mr. and Mrs. Colbert,

On the 23rd day of June, A-Omega received intelligence that a certain package thought to be safe is now in jeopardy. For the past couple of months, we have been attempting to eliminate any problems that might hinder the delivery of said package into your hands. Under optimal circumstances, this package would have been delivered for your safe keeping at a later date, just as we had previously discussed. We can no longer wait. The risks are much too high as we have already learned. We feel that the package would be safer in a more remote location, and have confidence that you will do everything in your power to protect it. We at A-Omega cannot emphasize how important it is that we get this package to safety. As physicians, you are well aware that there will be some care involved. The package will be in grave condition when it arrives, but not beyond repair. However, we must inform you that the requirements for this mission may exceed your level of expertise.

The arrangements for delivery will be simple. Your family will be arriving into the Minneapolis/St. Paul International airport at 6:15 PM on the evening of September 12th. As we at A-Omega have already informed you, this should be a very simple operation, but in the case that complications should arise, we will arrange for a contact to meet you at the airport. Your contacts will be Paul and Sarah Loving. They will be equipped in areas that you are not. Transportation will be prearranged and a vehicle will be ready for pick up at the transit center in terminal 1-Lindbergh between Concourse C and G. You are to follow your contact to the designated place of safety and wait for further instruction. Your family's patronage has not gone unnoticed.

Arm yourself well,
A-Omega
Ephesians 6: 10-18

I knew there must be clues on this aged and rumpled note, but I hadn't been able to find any. I couldn't connect the dots. Would Alex be able to? As I closed the book and returned it to the bag at the foot of my bed, I thought about Alex's two years of life as a human, and I realized it was the first time I had ever considered his life on earth. Many times I wondered what his life might have been like in the halfway. We had talked a bit about the time he spent there. We had also talked a lot about my life as seen through his eyes. And although he had yet to tell me of our life in heaven, I knew that he could remember it with ease. But I had never considered that Alex might recall his life on Earth as well.

There was one day last year when I was sitting at the dinner table with my parents listening to my dad discuss a case he was working on. For a month, he had been counseling a ten year old who could vividly recall abuse inflicted upon him at the tender age of three. My dad was amazed. He told me that most children have no memory before the age of four or five. After reviewing several studies, he found that, if an experience is particularly traumatic, a child may develop memories as early as the age of two. Alex was two when he died, and I would consider the events of September 13th nothing short of traumatic. I wondered if Alex could remember anything about his life on earth, about his life as a human boy. Perhaps he already knew about the package. Perhaps he already knew that my parents were acquainted with his parents. Maybe I wasn't the only one keeping secrets and perhaps, I wasn't the only one still telling lies.

CHAPTER SEVEN

Gone with the Wind. I picked the biggest book on the shelf, and I did it for one very specific reason. I pulled it from the shelf where it was nestled between a copy of *The Catcher in the Rye*, which I had already read for school and *On the Road* by Jack Kerouac. Besides the missing dust jacket, it was pristine. A cream and maroon hardback with the title embossed in gold upon the spine. It weighed at least ten pounds and had just over a thousand pages. And because the brown journal in my nightstand was strictly off limits, I intentionally chose a book that would keep me busy for a while. *Gone with the Wind* was one of the most famous love stories of all times. Everyone has heard of Rhett Butler and Scarlett O'Hara and because I had long been a fan of romantic novels, this classic would surely exceed my every expectation. But visions for how I thought the book would go were soon shattered when I learned that, instead of being a gentle lady as most women of her day were, Scarlett O'Hara was a dramatic, conniving girl willing to do anything to get the things in life that she desired. The object of her desire was Ashley Wilkes and, once again, I was baffled. I thought Scarlett was supposed to be in love with Rhett. So who was this Ashley character that Scarlett was pining after? She could have had any man, but she wanted the man who didn't belong to her: Ashley Wilkes, the man who was engaged to marry his cousin, Melanie. And yet, Scarlett still wanted him.

"Look what I found." Alex appeared out of nowhere. He had an old camera around his neck and was holding a rectangular object in the crook of his left arm and a small wicker basket in the crook of his right. I had just finished the first chapter when Alex fell into the chair opposite the sofa where I was sitting.

"Where'd you get the camera?" I asked, closing my book and wedging it between my hip and the cushion.

"In the back cottage."

"Does it have film?"

"There was a roll already in it."

"And what's that?"

"It's a cassette player."

"For music?"

"Yes."

"How do you listen to music on it?" I asked, pointing at the silver rectangular object.

Alex set a basket down on the coffee table and pushed a button on top of the machine. A door popped open, revealing the small plastic object that was inside.

"With these things, I suppose," he said, pulling it out and reading the writing on the piece of plastic. "The B-52's."

"Let's hear it. Do you think the, um... cassette player even works?"

"I'll plug it in and we'll find out." Alex seemed fascinated by the sheer simplicity of the machine, which surprised me. His affinity for technology far surpassed mine. To see him so mesmerized with this artifact left me feeling perplexed.

Alex nodded and, without saying a word, pushed a button on top of the machine. A song called "Love Shack" blasted from the speakers.

Alex laughed and leaned back into the chair to listen. I climbed onto Alex's lap and he kissed me on the cheek.

"I think I like this song," I giggled.

"What am I going to do with you, Rae?" Alex kissed my cheek again, then pushed a button to turn off the machine.

"Was that in the back cottage, too?"

"No. This was in my cottage."

I studied the silver box and the cassette that sat inside. I examined the dimensions and the condition of the machine, wondering if perhaps it was 'the package' referred to in the letter I had found in the scrapbook.

Within the walls of my Oklahoma bedroom, I had read the letter in the back of my nana's scrapbook at least a dozen times. There, I was surrounded by mocha colored carpet and whimsical wallpaper. There, I focused on only certain aspects of the letter that I deemed important at the time. For instance, my parents had not been strangers to Alex's parents; they knew each other. But now that I was in a new state, a new town, and a new home, the vintage feel of the cottage and the worn condition of every item inside spurred me to consider the beat up nature of the package. I wondered why I had never considered the package before. After much deliberation, I decided that the package was the key to it all.

At first, I imagined it to be small and wrapped in brightly colored paper, but then I quickly changed my mind. The letter was foreshadowing something sinister, so I reconsidered the package. I envisioned a medium-sized box wrapped in brown parcel paper. No ribbons, no bows, no card of any sort. Then I was struck with another idea. The package might simply be an object with something hidden inside. With that I began to search high and low, examining any object that was close to coming apart. The desk in the corner was old and banged up. Plus, there were many things inside. But just as soon as I considered this possibility, I disregarded the idea based on size alone. I was convinced that the package had to be small and easy to move in a hurry. I had also considered the clock on the mantle. One night, after Alex had gone to bed, I pried off the back of the clock and, much to my dismay, found only a mainspring and a mess of gears. Over the past couple weeks nothing was exempt. And even though I could come up with no reasonable explanation for why A-Omega might want to give my parents an electrical box in which they could toast their bread, I had definitely considered the toaster this morning while making my breakfast. I had been on the hunt for weeks and my searching had yet to pay off. I was leaning toward an option that was hardly satisfying: perhaps the package wasn't here at all. But when Alex walked in with a banged up silver box that played music, my interest was sparked once again. The cassette player might not be the package, but the package was here… I could feel it… I could feel it in my bones.

Breaking my train of thought, Alex interjected, "I think there is a thrift store on Broadway. We should see if they have any more tapes. It'll give us a chance to go into town. Our trip to the Laundromat hardly qualified. We've been living like hermits. The only people we see are our neighbors. Plus, I'd like to swing by a one-hour photo and get this film developed. I can't wait to see what's on it. No one has used this camera in nineteen years. We might find a clue in one of the pictures."

"I doubt it." I tried to sound convincing, but my heart was caught in my throat and I was finding it rather hard to speak. There was a very good chance that Alex would find something on the role of film to aid him in his quest.

"It's worth a try. I just hope the pictures turn out. The film's old."

"I don't want the film developed," I said rather bluntly.

"What? Why?"

"I like things how they are. I don't want anything to change. And… I'm scared."

"There's nothing to worry about. Just let me take care of you. You have to let me do what it is that I was put here to do. Don't worry about Chloe and Ben. I'll take care of them… I promise. You have to trust me."

"I'm not worried about Chloe and Ben. I'm worried about losing you."

"I told you I would try my best to stay. Isn't that enough?"

"No," I said. "Of course it's not enough."

Alex let out an exaggerated sigh. "There's just one other thing that you have to promise."

"What?"

"No more secrets and no more lies. Do you think that you can handle that?"

I looked out the window, pondering his question for a moment before I could respond.

"Yes," I lied. "I think I can handle that."

When we turned onto Broadway, I saw a sign for Cherry Street Books. I stopped in to have a look around while Alex walked down a block to the thrift store. After pulling a few titles from the shelf, I settled into a comfortable chair and began to read the synopses, choosing only the books that sounded romantic or mysterious or both. I adored romance. In fact, romance was my favorite genre. But I wasn't a fan of the trashy sort. I liked tragedy. And in the past couple of months, I had been reading books that could make me feel, which was odd considering that, for ten years, I had worked so hard to feel nothing at all. Alex had changed me more than I realized. I was now drawn to books about lovers being torn apart by circumstance. I wanted a book that would make me sob for hours. I picked up a copy of *The English Patient*. The cover alone was enough to make me want to buy it: a picture of two people in the middle of a passionate kiss. I flipped open the cover of the book and when I discovered that the story took place in both Italy and Africa in the middle of World War II, I added it quickly to my stack. By the time I was finished, I had an armful of books that included mystery as well as romance.

An hour later, I walked down the street to the thrift store and found Alex sorting through piles of tapes.

"Whatcha got?" I asked, sifting through his pile. "*The Queen is Dead* by the Smiths. Good one." I nodded with approval, holding up the cassette and studying the picture of Alain Delon from the 1964 film *L'Insoumis*. His stack also included Beastie Boys, *License to Ill*; The Cure, *Disintegration*; Annie Lenox, Violent Femmes, and Talking Heads.

"You're trying to keep it 80's, right?"

Alex looked at me, confused, as though my rhetorical question was causing him to second guess his selection process.

"This album was released in the late seventies." I held up the case so he could see the cover. "Thus the title, *Talking Heads: 77.*"

Alex snorted and returned to his sorting. "Don't you want to look at the clothes or something?"

"Just saying. It's not 80's, but get it anyway. It's good."

Still rummaging through a stack of tapes with one hand, he began to shoo me away with his other. If I hadn't been so eager to see what was hanging on the rack, I would have been inclined to say something smart in return. I loved both vintage and vintage inspired clothes, namely circa 1960's and 1970's. Europe had the best thrift stores, hands down, but they were expensive. Plus, I didn't have much room in my luggage. When we lived overseas I would wander through the thrift stores, mostly just looking, but on occasion, I would find something I couldn't live without and would make a purchase. Trying to find something valuable buried beneath a pile of junk was very similar to a treasure hunt. One time I was at the Parisian flea market, and I found a black crystal choker. After purchasing the necklace, Dad took me to a jewelry store, and the jeweler told me that it was from the 1940's. The necklace had been made in Germany during World War II, and I wondered who might have worn it. It had survived when so many people had not.

There were plenty of vintage rock tees hanging on the rack. I pushed them aside and sorted through the tops and dresses. I finally found a white and black polka-dotted sleeveless top from the 50's and my absolute favorite: a lacy white Victorian-style blouse that I just knew would fit me to perfection.

Alex and I left the store with three full bags. He had a bundle of cassettes, but I had more. Four books, two vintage tops, and a phone that wasn't brand new, but newer than the one in the cottage. And for an added bonus, it had caller ID. Alex rolled his eyes when he saw it, because he knew exactly why I had picked it up.

"I don't think Chloe and Ben are going to be calling."

"But now I'll know if they do. Besides, what if Mom and Dad try to call? I promise, this thing will come in handy."

"If you say so."

We were halfway down Broadway, halfway to the car, when a building in an alleyway just off of the main road caught my attention. My eyes drifted from the building to the black sedan that was parked in the lot. It looked like the same black car from Coin Laundry. It had to be. In a town as small as Alexandria, how many cars like that could there be?

"I'm going to run across the street and see if the film's ready."

"Huh?" I turned my attention away from the car and focused on Alex. "You coming?"

"Yes," I said, trying to hide my shock.

"Are you going to finish *Gone with the Wind* before you start on *The English Patient*?" Alex asked as we walked across the street toward Kyle's Cameras.

"Of course. But I just started it this morning, so I'll have to get busy."

"I'm not sure you're aware of the implications, but with you reading all of these romance novels, you're setting the bar a little high. I mean, how am I supposed to live up to Rhett Butler and Ashley Wilkes?"

"You've read *Gone with the Wind*?"

"I read it last year when I was staying at the cabin by myself."

I gave Alex a taunting look.

"What?! I was bored and it was cold outside," he shrugged. "Besides, it's not just a book about love; it's a book about war."

"If you say so," I teased. "I wondered what you were doing up here by yourself. How does it end?"

"You're crazy. I'm not going to tell you. You have a thousand pages to go and then we can talk," Alex said as he opened the door to the camera store.

We approached the counter, and Alex rang the silver bell beside the register for service. I had never seen him so eager... so excited. I wish I could say I felt the same.

"I have a roll of film to pick up for 'Loving'," Alex said when the man behind the counter finally appeared.

"Just the one?"

"Yes, just one," Alex told the clerk and began to rub the palms of his hands together in anticipation. "I think this roll of film is the key to it all, Rae." Alex lowered his voice. "I just know it. It's all we have. If the film doesn't tell us something, then I'm afraid I don't know where else to look. I guess we could look through your scrapbook."

"No."

"Why? Because there are pictures of your parents inside?"

"Yes, that's certainly one reason." The other reason I didn't want Alex poring over my nana's scrapbook was because of the letters that were tucked between the pages.

"You feel guilty for leaving? Is that it?"

"Yes. In a way."

"Don't. You did the right thing. You did the only thing you could do. You came here to keep your parents safe."

The clerk returned with a single package in his hand, and Alex cleared his throat.

"There were a few pictures that didn't turn out, but the rest are not too bad, considering the age of the film. I suggest you take a look before I ring you up," the clerk apologized.

Alex hesitated a moment before accepting the envelope of photos. We now shared the same expression. His anticipation was replaced with worry. Slowly, he pulled the pictures from the package. The first picture was blurry.

"Just set the blurry ones aside. You won't have to pay for those," the clerk chimed in.

Alex set the photo on the counter and fixed his eyes on the second picture in the stack. It was a picture of a woman with long blond hair holding a little boy in her arms. Alex and his mom. I looked at Alex out of the corner of my eye. He ran his finger across the glossy finish but didn't say a word. As Alex continued to sift through pictures of his parents, I began to realize that this role of film was exactly what he needed. It was a connection to *his* past, not mine.

"Rae!" Alex nearly shouted. "Look at this one."

I studied the picture he was holding. The image was sharp, the colors were vibrant, and the setting was one I had seen before. It was a picture of a woman standing in the Loving's backyard. She had her back toward the photographer and was gazing out onto the lake. Her long black hair was blowing in the wind.

"Who is this woman?"

"I don't know," I said, taking the picture from Alex and inspecting it closely.

There was a quality about the picture that felt familiar. There was something about the photo that made me feel sad. The woman standing on the Loving's grassy lawn seemed misplaced. The conversation I overheard at the Harvey's fish fry came back to me.

"Oh Candy, do you remember the *other* lady?"

"Pregnant... sick... I heard... delusional... screaming... I know.... so sad...."

A chill crept up my spine. Could this be the *other* woman that Candice and her friends were talking about? Maybe our trip to the camera store had done more than reconnect Alex with his past. I was pretty sure we had just found our first clue.

CHAPTER EIGHT

*M*ay turned into June, and June turned into July. We spent most of our time outside when the weather was nice. Besides the intermittent downpours and the occasional chilly day, it was gorgeous. I loved to lie on the beach and watch Alex swim. Because Cocoa and Alex shared an affinity for the water, Alex seemed to be her new best friend. On occasion, I would dip my toe into the cool liquid of the lake, but then would return to my warm spot on the sandy beach. Some days, I would spread my towel out on the sand and read. On other days, when I was irritated with Scarlett O'Hara, I would look at *People* or *Cosmo*. I never thought I would say it, but magazines can be just as interesting as books. For instance, I learned that high-heeled clogs were 'in' because Sarah Jessica Parker had been spotted in a pair of peep-toe Hasbeens. I also learned that many readers had a strong aversion to the trend. I was with Sarah Jessica. High heel clogs were cool.

The best tidbit of information that I found inside one of my magazines was from an article called "Odd Foods and the Libido." According to *Cosmo*, baked goods worked just like love potions. I had never heard of such a thing. I had heard that the way to a man's heart is through his stomach, but I never knew that certain foods could produce such a desirable reaction. There were still other days when I felt like reading nothing at all.

I would lie mindlessly on my back and soak up the sun. The temperature never rose above ninety degrees, but my skin was changing from a light olive to a deep golden brown. Even Alex's skin, which was far fairer than mine, was nearing a Coppertone bronze.

Our days were leisure filled and, for the most part, completely free of stress. The only drawback was watching Corrine and her friends frolic around in their bikinis, trying to steal Alex's attention in a very childish and obvious way. This reinforced what I already knew. Corrine looked much older than she acted. I tried my hardest but couldn't shrug it off. I told Alex that Corrine was crushing on him. He told me I was delusional.

Alex had grown quite fond of snapping pictures and photography was quickly becoming his favorite pastime. As for me, I was getting very close to the halfway point in *Gone with the Wind* and was having trouble putting it down. I would read until the wee hours of the morning, and I was getting into the habit of sleeping until noon.

On the night of July 15th, I stayed up late, my nose buried in my book, until I fell asleep at two in the morning. But three hours later, I was awake, drenched in sweat. Once again, I had dreamed that I was drowning. The cottage was quiet. Darkness poured through the open windows and the absence of any sound whatsoever was chilling. I was used to lying in bed listening to the breeze softly blow the cotton curtains to and fro. I was used to the wind moving the lake water onto the shore, creating a metronomic sound that, no matter how bad the dream had been, could put me back to sleep.

It was the stillness that pulled me out of bed. I walked the short distance to the living room and sluggishly collapsed onto the sofa. I didn't want to fall back asleep. I tried to think of something other than death, something happy, but I could think of nothing. No matter how exhausted I was, I didn't want to return to my nightmare. I turned on the television, not really watching the late night infomercial, but listening because the background noise brought me comfort. Still holding the remote, I closed my eyes and listened to the voice of the lady on TV. She was trying to sell a kitchen device that would not only cut up potatoes, but fry them as well. I wondered what my life would be like if I were that efficient. If my body was a machine that did everything I needed it to do. How easy life would be if, like the machine, I could do everything myself. The lady was selling the product well. Some chimes sounded on the TV: In just five short minutes, over 1,000 potato machines had been sold. In a syrupy voice, she told the viewers that if they called in the next ten minutes, they would receive a free ketchup dispenser that could be attached to the side. This machine really *did* do it all. Her voice started to fade away, and I felt my fingers gradually loosen around the remote, relaxing until I could no longer feel it in my hand. My mind began to drift into a dream.

Mom was standing in the kitchen making a pot of tea. The kettle on the stove was screaming that the water was hot enough. With a delicate hand, she reached up into the cabinet and pulled down a box of tea bags.

"I want a little cup of tea, too. With honey in it, please."

"Just a small cup and then it's time for bed, okay."

"Will you make me some banana goodies?" I asked, hugging her leg.

"I know a little girl who is trying her hardest to get out of going to bed."

"But *I'm* hungry!" I demanded.

"You just ate dinner. You're hungry again so soon?" she asked, picking me up in her arms, then setting me down on a stool behind the counter.

"Please, Mommy," I begged.

"Well, I think we might just have everything we need to make them. Let's see." Mom had the cabinet door open and within seconds, pulled out a jar of peanut butter and grabbed a banana off the counter.

"You forgot about the chocolate chips."

"Oh, you don't need the chocolate chips. It's almost bedtime."

"They won't be banana goodies without the chocolate chips." I sat at the barstool and kicked my legs back and forth inside my blue, silk nightgown. "I'll be your best friend, Mommy."

"You already are my best friend, Sunshine."

"Please!" I pleaded.

"Oh, all right." She gave in and began to place miniature sized chocolate chips on top of the bananas, making a smiley face on top of each slice. She poured a small amount of tea into a cup and then sat down beside me. "Now you have to pay the toll," she teased, kissing my nose and tickling me before taking a few slices of bananas from my little plate. And then something strange happened, something very out of place. As soon as my mother's fingers touched the plate, it began to slide across the counter. I continued to watch as gravity pulled it to the floor, in slow motion, my mother scrambling to catch the plate in midair. Something was wrong. The plate wasn't supposed to fall, but every time her hands made contact, the dish would slip and continue its descent. I never saw it reach its final destination, but I heard it crash into a thousand tiny pieces just as the screen door in the kitchen banged shut and woke me from my dream.

I rubbed my tired eyes. I had been exhausted at five, but after my little nap, I was in worse shape than I was before.

"Why are you asleep on the sofa?"

Still in a semiconscious state, my head jerked and lifted off the pillow. I was expecting to see my mom, but it was Alex.

"Is there room for me?" he asked, sitting down beside me without waiting for an answer. "Were you dreaming?"

"No," I lied, wiping a bit of drool from my mouth.

"You must have been sleeping hard. You needed it. You shouldn't stay up so late reading books," he smiled. I rolled onto my side to make room for Alex to snuggle up beside me.

"You have a tear in your eye," he said, wiping the corner of my eye with the back of his hand. He moved in close and pulled a thin woven blanket over our bodies. "You've been crying."

"No, I have not! My eyes water when I sleep."

"Is that what you're going with?"

"I swear I wasn't crying."

"Just so you know, if you were crying, I would do anything to make you feel better."

Without saying another word, Alex wound his fingers through my hair and very gently began to rub the back of my head, soothing me back to sleep.

I woke up a couple of hours later still curled in Alex's arms. I tried to shift my body a bit and slide off the sofa without waking him, but I nudged him with my elbow. He stirred a bit, but didn't wake up. I grabbed another blanket from the back of the chair and stepped outside to let Cocoa take care of business. Wrapped in a blanket, I relaxed in one of the grass green Adirondack chairs on the small wooden deck. I kicked my feet up on a makeshift ottoman. Still adjusting my eyes to the sunlight, I used my free hand to rub them until the lake came into focus and when it finally did, I began to count the boats. I wasn't sure of the exact time, but the lake was already busy. The wind was nonexistent, and the water was like glass. I noticed several skiers out this morning; they were being pulled along while observers on the shore cheered. I shivered. You couldn't pay me to do that, I thought, for more reasons than just one. Water just wasn't my thing and after my dream last night, the fear of water was still fresh in my mind. I thought about my morning run, the one that I was missing. For the first time since being in Minnesota, I was too tired to go. My body wasn't working right, and it felt a bit stiff after sleeping on the sofa. I stretched my legs out, popped my shoulders, and rolled my neck. My eyes were closed, and I was just drifting back into a dream when Cocoa let out an obnoxious howl that caused me to jump halfway out of the wooden chair.

When I opened my eyes, she had her head buried in a Hosta plant. She was rustling the leaves with her nose and wagging her tail. She must have found a varmint hiding beneath the foliage. For weeks, the chipmunks had been driving Cocoa crazy, and during her morning exercise, she liked to chase them. She pounced on clumps of grass and bunches of flowers if she so much as heard a tiny noise. It drove her crazy when the chipmunks darted across the road and hid in something green and bushy. They were teasing Cocoa. She was on a leash and the chipmunks knew it. I think they knew that, no matter how badly they teased her, she could never catch them. Well, this morning was different; Cocoa wasn't on her leash, and I felt something close to pride as I watched her go after her prey.

"Go girl!" I cheered her on, watching but not caring as she dug up a beautiful, twenty-year-old leafy plant. "Get that chipmunk," I chanted. All at once, she stopped and set her eyes on the yard next door. With mud flinging everywhere, she ran through the row of hedges that separated our house from the neighbor's in pursuit of the tiny rodent. Still wrapped in my blanket, I chased after her. She stopped at a large tree and began to circle it, sniffing at the bottom to make certain she had correctly followed the tracks. Patiently, Cocoa sat down and stared up at the branches of the enormous tree, and I stood next to her, also looking up. An old man in the yard next to us, peered through a gap in the hedge trying to discern where all of the commotion was coming from. He had stern eyes that hid behind a pair of glasses, and I could immediately tell by the way he combed his pointy goatee that he was the only grouchy person on Lake L'Homme Dieu. Bored with her failed conquest, Cocoa considered the elf-looking figure standing less than twenty feet away, and then she ran, mud flying, into his backyard.

I had heard once before that animals have emotions, that they are capable of sensing both fear and anger in others; apparently my source of information was incorrect, because I was shaking in my UGGS while all 70 pounds of Cocoa leapt into the air and knocked the man to the ground. She was licking his face and slobbering all over him. This was out of character for Cocoa, because she didn't like strangers. Besides Alex, I couldn't think of a single person outside my immediate family that Cocoa was fond of. If animals were indeed capable of emotions, and perhaps rational thought, then releasing this poor man was something that Cocoa had not considered. She had pinned him to the ground with her front paws digging into his collarbone. I was horrified by the muddy paw prints across the front of his shirt. When I called to Cocoa and she would not remove herself, I grabbed her collar and pulled her away. I thought I was prepared for the look on my neighbor's face, I knew it would not be pleasant, but when he finally scampered to his feet, his expression was one like I had never seen before. Rage would be too modest a word to describe what I was seeing. His entire head was scarlet, the color of a tomato… no, much redder than a tomato. I knew my best bet would be to turn in the opposite direction and run back toward my cabin, but it didn't seem right to leave without apologizing. Besides, in awkward times like these, I found it hard to keep my mouth shut.

"I am *so* sorry. Now is probably not the best time to introduce myself." As I held out my hand to shake his, I noticed it was covered in mud and Cocoa's drool. The elf-looking creature regarded my hand with disgust.

"I'm Rae Colbert. I just live…"

"Get… get… ga… get out of my yard," he stuttered. That was all he said and, all stuttering aside, I could tell by the tone of his voice that he meant it. I stood there stupidly for a moment, before I turned my back and walked away.

"It's all right, Cocoa," I cooed and I rubbed her muddy head. When I reached the cottage, I found a hand towel on the deck. I carried it over to the spigot that was in the middle of the yard by the old oak tree. I turned on the water and soaked the rag. Cocoa followed close behind.

"Sit," I told her and then began to rub her fur clean. "If you continue to get this muddy, I'm not going to let you go outside… and if I do let you go outside… I'm not going to let you come back in. One or the other… you decide."

I stood back and looked at Cocoa. She was still a muddy mess, but she looked very pleased. I regarded her sternly.

"Go jump in the lake," I demanded.

Cocoa didn't budge. She looked up at me and wagged her tail. "Go on," I encouraged her, now using my finger to point toward the water.

Cocoa followed my finger. It took a moment for understanding to set in, but when it finally did, she took off toward the lake, running down the long, narrow dock, and jumping in. It wasn't until I settled into the hammock that I allowed myself to succumb to the stillness around me. There was only one skier left on the lake, and the sound of the boat's engine was soft and distant. Only then, when absolutely everything else was quiet, did I hear the voices coming from within my cottage.

I toweled Cocoa off at the back door before opening it. Because it was dark inside the cottage, I couldn't see who was paying us this unexpected visit. I listened while I continued to dry her fur. It was definitely a girl's voice, but it didn't sound like Chloe's, and I was relieved until I opened the back door and saw Corrine sitting in the chair opposite my angelic boyfriend. I scowled. I almost wished it were Chloe Pierce. Alex must have heard me scowl, because he turned his head and rolled his eyes. He was still in his pajamas - a pair of loose fitting sweat pants and a tee shirt. Cocoa bounded into the house behind me. She was a bit wound up after bathing in the lake and did not appear to mind Corrine's presence, which surprised me. I was beginning to think my dog was a traitor.

"To think that I just stood up for you when you were so, so bad," I muttered under my breath as I watched Cocoa curl up beside the fireplace and look into Alex's eyes. I was familiar with that look. She was begging him to start a fire that would fully dry her fur.

My walking through the door didn't seem to affect Corrine. She hadn't shut up. She was talking about fishing while rubbing her fingers delicately across her neatly polished nails and making rapid gestures with her hands. I already knew that her dad, Jerry, was a professional fisherman. But Corrine was talking about fishing like she had firsthand knowledge. I couldn't imagine Corrine with a fishing pole in her hand. I thought she would be too worried about breaking a nail or touching a worm. I sat down beside Alex, placed my hand upon his knee, and listened. I was too angry to speak.

No longer able to look Corrine in the eyes, I shifted my focus to Cocoa, who was already asleep. "Lazy dog," I muttered, and Alex pinched my knee.

Corrine was now talking about college. She was still undecided and a bit anxious about going potluck. Alex told her that, because she was so easy going, she and her roommate would surely get along. He then went on to tell her that she should consider going to culinary school if she was still undecided after the first semester, because her cookies were great. That's when I noticed the cookies that were on a plate in the middle of the coffee table, right next to Alex's new copy of *Car and Driver* magazine. Alex was eating one of Corrine's cookies, and I wanted to rip it out of his fingers. I pushed the plate aside, picked up the magazine, and began to leaf through the pages. Some of the pages were dog-eared; I looked at those first. A BMW M5. A Porsche 356 vintage speedster. A Mercedes Maybach. I only needed to look at three pages before I came to realize that Alex was developing a liking for fast... shiny... pretty... things.

I looked back up at Corrine and noticed the subtle stripes of pink and purple running through her platinum hair, coordinating perfectly with the neon polish on her nails. Despite her womanly figure, there was still a childlike quality about Corrine, and I couldn't figure out why it bothered me. She just rubbed me the wrong way. Maybe it was because she was perfect. Maybe it was because she was womanly. Or maybe it was because she was so very confident. Regardless, I couldn't stand Corrine. But mostly, I couldn't stand Corrine because of how she looked at my Alex. She wanted him for herself, and I was sure that everyone but Alex could see it. He was oblivious to her advances, which made me angrier because, as a result, he did nothing to stop them. I liked to blame it on the fact that he had little to no real-world experience. He had no idea how ruthless girls could be. I looked at my hand on Alex's knee and noticed it was caked with mud. I reached up with my other hand and discretely felt my face. With the tips of my fingers, I followed the strip of mud that ran from my left ear all the way down to my chin. I looked at my white shirt. It was damp and the bottom half was now a dingy brown. Why would Alex want me? I was a mess. Why would he want me when he could so easily have someone like Corrine? All he had to do was say the word, and she would be on him like white on rice. I had envisioned losing Alex, but the only scenario that I considered was the version where he got sucked back up to heaven. Until now, I hadn't taken into account that I could lose Alex in another way. All at once it occurred to me that I was all that Alex had ever seen, all that he had ever known. What if I was no longer enough?

Second Way To Lose Alex Loving: Lose him to another girl

I ran a bath, poured in some shampoo because I didn't have any bubble bath, and began to slosh the water around with my hand, watching as tiny bubbles formed on the surface. I let the hot mixture soak all the dirt from my skin while simultaneously soaking all the sorrows from my soul.

CHAPTER NINE

I'm not sure what it was about the look on Mr. Finnegan's face, but when I passed his house this morning while out for a run, his expression triggered something inside me. Mr. Finnegan was standing in his yard, which wasn't entirely out of the ordinary. There were many vacationers and locals along the North Shore that spent every morning in their front yard pulling weeds and planting flowers. The part that I found strange was that Mr. Finnegan was doing nothing of the sort. It was obvious he was staring at me, and I didn't really want to stare back; however, I did look at him out of the corner of my eye and when I did, there wasn't a single gardening tool in sight. It seemed to me that Mr. Finnegan had sensed I was drawing near and was standing in his yard, close to the road, as a form of intimidation. And, although there was hardly anything about the barely five foot Mr. Finnegan that was intimidating, the look in his eyes was enough to send me running for the hills. His eyes held a distinct look of disdain, and it reminded me that, in my entire life, very few people had ever really liked me. There was crazy Carly, of course. She had been my friend through thick and thin. But for some reason, I began to focus on the negative and right now, the worst thing in my life was Chloe Pierce and Benard Bodin. Things had been going so perfectly that I had almost forgotten they exist.

As I ran past Mr. Finnegan's, I thought about my adversaries. We had been here for almost two months and they had yet to find us. I wondered why. I wondered why they hated me so. I wondered why they wanted me dead. I thought about Benard and reconsidered all the reasons he might want me out of the picture. The crash had taken everything from him, and now he wanted revenge. He blamed my mom and dad for the death of his family (perhaps because they were the sole survivors of the crash), and now he wanted to take from them what he had lost: family... and himself. He wanted them to feel the pain he had been feeling for years. Taking my life would be his revenge upon my parents. I guess I could understand why. In a mind as sick as Ben's, the loss of my life might be appealing. But there were several pieces of the puzzle that were not fitting. In the past couple of months, I had learned that in my life, there were no coincidences, and I couldn't help but wonder why Ben and his family were in the tiny town of Alexandria, Minnesota, on the night of September 13th. It was no coincidence that my parents and the Lovings were on the exact same road at the exact same time. I had documentation that proved this. I was almost certain that the presence of the Bodin's car on Highway 26 was no coincidence either, but I had no proof... at least not yet.

The second discrepancy was Chloe Pierce. A year ago, when I first met Chloe, I could immediately sense she didn't like me, but I hadn't spent much time thinking about it until she tried to run me off the road on that snowy day in March. Alex reminded me that he had spent time with Ben in the halfway, and then he explained it to me like this: "Chloe is to Ben like you are to me. Chloe is his other half; his evil other half, but they're soul mates none-the-less." So for the next mile, I tried my hardest to put myself in Chloe's shoes. From what I understood, Chloe had a passion for Ben much like the passion I had for Alex. I wondered if passion could ever be strong enough inside me that I would want to take another's life. I decided the answer was "NO." Even though Chloe and I were like night and day, I decided passion wasn't enough for her either. There had to be some other reason why she hated me with such ferocity. There was something more to the story, and I desperately wanted to find out what it was. And once again, I found myself at a dead end. I was faced with the same dilemma. I feared that the deeper I dug into the past and the closer I got to the truth, the closer I would be to losing Alex. I was absolutely torn between my desire to learn the truth and the need to keep him by my side. I wanted both, and I was becoming more and more determined to find a way to make that happen.

As I turned onto the gravel drive, I watched Alex's silhouette shift in the kitchen window. I quickened my steps. My heart was beating like a drum, and the anticipation of his touch was warming me from the inside out. Despite my warm and fuzzy feelings, I walked into the kitchen with a scowl on my face.

"What's wrong with you?"

"I think that Mr. Finnegan might be a spy... or at the very least, retired CIA. I bet he has a booby trap set up in his yard. He turns it on at night to catch anyone who dares to walk through his yard. I bet he's hiding something. What do you think he's hiding? I bet he's hiding a body." I didn't give Alex a chance to speak. "I bet he's hiding a body, and I bet it's buried somewhere in his yard. That's why he doesn't like Cocoa. He's afraid that she's going to dig it up."

"Are these the things you think about when I'm not around?"

I bunched up my lips and began to pout, because it was obvious Alex didn't agree with my conspiracy theory.

"There is another more reasonable answer, you know. Maybe he doesn't like Cocoa because she pounced on him with all fours."

"I think it's a body."

"Whatever makes you feel better," Alex responded coolly while simultaneously stuffing a large hunk of something into his mouth.

"What are you eating?" I asked, noticing that, instead of his usual bowl of Mini-Wheats, Alex had a loaf of some kind of bread in front of him, probably banana nut. It was unwrapped and already halfway gone.

"Banana nut bread." Alex confirmed my suspicions while stuffing another hunk of bread into his mouth. "We don't have to worry about dinner either because the girl that lives on the other side of Mr. Finnegan, I think her name is Gretchen, brought us enough food for a week. It looks like enchiladas, and I think the other dish is meatloaf."

I wrinkled my nose at the mention of the word 'loaf' and pointed to the food on the table. "At least our neighbors are hospitable. Most of them, anyway." I rolled my eyes, but Alex didn't see. He was still stuffing banana bread into his mouth.

"What is that supposed to mean?"

"Nothing. I just haven't had the best morning. That's all."

"Oh, and Gretchen brought garlic bread too."

"Great. Your good looks might just be our meal ticket... literally."

The bitterness in my voice grabbed his full attention, and the smile on Alex's face was quickly fading. "You're jealous," he said with finality, and his smile returned just as quickly as it disappeared.

"Am not." I grabbed a chunk of banana bread off the table and shoved it into my mouth, because if my mouth were full of food, I would not be expected to respond.

"Are too." Alex nudged me gently. When I didn't respond, he wrapped his arm around my waist and pulled me in so that I could feel his breath on my face. His lips were so close I would have kissed them if I hadn't been so annoyed. "We're cosmic, Rae. No one can break us apart."

I could feel a smile forming against my will.

"Cosmic... I like the way that sounds," I kissed his lips. They tasted like banana bread.

"So, why is your day starting off so bad?"

"I was just thinking about Chloe and Ben and Mr. Finnegan. I was wondering why everyone in the world seems to want me dead."

"I wouldn't go so far to say that Mr. Finnegan wants you dead."

"You didn't see the look on his face when I ran by his house."

"So, you're having a pity party while you were out for your morning run?"

"You want to join?"

"No, I'm fine."

"Did Gretchen bring by the banana bread too? It's good."

"What's the ladies name that lives several houses down?"

"Mrs. Harvey." I no longer sounded bitter. I sounded suspicious.

"Mrs. Harvey's daughter."

"Corrine?" I scoffed.

"Yeah, Cory," Alex said. Had they become so close while I was out for my run that he now called her by her nickname? "In fact, you just missed her. She and her friends have been so considerate since we've moved in. Look," Alex said, pointing to the bread. "There's even little chocolate chips in here."

"That Corrine, she thinks of everything."

"I think the chocolate chips add the perfect touch. It almost tastes like dessert."

I rolled my eyes again. "You know what they say, 'The way to a man's heart is through his stomach.'"

"Who's 'they'?"

"You know…'they'. Meaning, *everyone* knows that you get a man to like you by making him food, Alex, including Corrine. Why can't you see that? Stop eating her banana bread," I demanded.

"You shouldn't jump to conclusions."

"Stop blaming this on me. This has nothing to do with me. This has everything to do with you and, what do you call her now? Cory."

"This does have to do with you. It has to do with you being so insecure."

"I can't help it. She drives me to it. If you had ever been jealous, you would know how it feels."

"I have been jealous, plenty of times, more than you will ever know."

"Then you should know that it's not insecurity that drives me to say the things that I do; it's the fear of losing the only thing in life that I have ever loved."

"Every time you feel scared of losing me, just look down at the ring I gave you and try to remember what it means."

"Well, it's not an engagement ring," I said without thinking. I immediately sensed my blunder.

"No, it's not." The sweetness was gone from his voice. "It's so much more than that," Alex spat and stormed out of the kitchen without saying another word.

I took his place on the bench seat, and I could feel the wood, still warm, from where he had been sitting. I fixed my eyes on the ruby throated hummingbird eating her breakfast outside the kitchen window. The tiny bird was hovering in midair while feeding on nectar. How many times must she beat her wings to stay in flight? Several thousand times per minute, or maybe more? I could relate. Sometimes I beat my wings so hard they hurt. I eyed the banana bread, and then I took a reluctant bite. Among other things, Corrine was a very good cook.

Third Way To Lose Alex Loving: Run him away with my words

It had been several hours since Alex left me standing in the kitchen all alone. I had tried to bide the time by reading, but I hardly wanted to read about romance when my own romantic affairs were not in order. I walked into my room and pulled open the little drawer of my nightstand. I gently removed the brown journal and held it in my hands. It was screaming for me to open it, but a voice inside me was saying to keep it shut. I reminded myself of all the things that might happen if I caved in. I returned it to the drawer and fell back onto the bed. I was bored. For the first time since being in Minnesota, I had absolutely nothing to do. I thought that I might like to paint, but I had no supplies. But even with a storeroom full of supplies, a concept that would have excited me on any other day, I wouldn't know where to begin. I knew I would paint something for Alex, something that would show him that I was sorry. But what? What could I paint that would take back all of the words that I had said? I wished I could shove them back into my mouth. And then I thought about the banana bread he had been shoving into his mouth all morning. This in turn made me think of Corrine. If she could bake him bread, then so could I. Two could play at this game.

Reminded of the article in Cosmo about food and the libido, I opened the magazine to refresh my memory. Pumpkin pie, sure to drive a man wild: a possibility, although I didn't have a can of pumpkin, and I wasn't about to go to the store. Buttered popcorn, too easy. Licorice, yuck. Cinnamon rolls, totally doable. I found a recipe book in the kitchen (a thirty year-old copy of Betty Crocker), and opened it to the section on breads. The recipe for cinnamon rolls seemed easy, but when complete, the result was an edible masterpiece, a peace offering, something to give Alex the impression that I had spent hours in the kitchen, even though I had not. I heated up the milk in the microwave and when it was almost scalding, I added a cold stick of butter to cool it down. In a separate bowl, I mixed yeast with a bit of warm water and let it sit for a short time while I mixed together the dry ingredients. Two hours later, after the dough finished rising, I punched it down, rolled it out thin, spread butter and sugar and cinnamon over the top, and rolled it up. I cut it into rather large slices, lined a circular pan with the sugary dough, and placed it in the oven to bake. I thought the smell of baking bread would be enough to lure Alex from his cottage, but I was wrong. Only Cocoa noticed the smell, and it seemed to be driving her mad.

It was two in the morning and still no luck. Alex hadn't emerged, not even for a single bite of food. I knew he must be furious, and I was worried because I had never seen him this angry before… at least not with me. I couldn't stand it, this feeling. Alex keeping his distance from me was hard enough, but knowing I had hurt him was almost too much to bear. The love I felt for Alex filled my heart completely. There wasn't room for anything else, but I could no longer ignore the tiny hole in my heart that was beginning to drain. Alex had the ability to replenish any portion of my heart that was depleted. In an instant, he could fill my emptiness with something beautiful and satisfying. I looked at the Celestial clock on the mantle. The writing near the bottom said it was time to plant your flowers. The hands of the clock said it was way past time for bed. I had been without Alex's company for just over fifteen hours. As soon as he walked out of the kitchen, my heart began to leak and after nearly fifteen hours, I felt completely empty. What would I do when he left me? How could he fill my heart if he were gone?

CHAPTER TEN

*B*y the age of ten, I was well acquainted with the great minds of psychology. My parents were both shrinks, and they talked about Sigmund Freud and Carl Jung around the dinner table in a way I envisioned normal families to talk of sports or their plans for the weekend. Dad was of the opinion that Freud was, for the most part, correct. Dad and Freud both believe that dreams are driven by sex. My mother sides with Carl Jung, who said that our dreams revolve around the fear of death. Jung also said that dreams are a tool used by the brain to help us grow; this was the only thing my parents agreed on when it came to dream analysis. I'm not sure with whom I agree. I guess it depends on which morning I'm asked. Normally, I would say that I am with Jung 100%, not only because all of my dreams are rather violent in nature, but because they have a peculiar way of coming true. But after my dream last night, I am willing to bet my life that Freud is right.

I was desperate to fall back into my dream, but my mind was going in too many directions. I exhaled slowly, then pushed my sheets back and stood on the edge of the bed. I studied my reflection in the mirror above my dresser. It's true that I still lacked most of the curves I desired, but my legs were long and lean and muscular. I lifted up my tank top and studied my stomach. Flat. I climbed down from the bed and came face to face with the person who looked out at me from the mirror. I touched my finger to her cheek and studied her eyes, searching for the childlike innocence that I knew was trapped somewhere deep inside. Instead, I found worry mixed with wisdom.

The past year of my life had been a whirlwind; certain events had occurred that, no matter how hard I tried, could not be erased from my memory. When I looked into the mirror, when I looked into her eyes, I saw a *woman* trapped inside the body of a *child*. Her eyes had seen more than most see in a lifetime. Her eyes told a story. Her eyes didn't fit with the soft cheeks and smooth skin of a girl who had yet to turn nineteen. Much like the maturing of skin with age, my soul had weathered. Like wrinkling of the skin, my memories folded over one another distorting my perception of time and the truth.

My heart had gone through a transformation as well. Alex had to know this because he was the one who chipped the shell away. He was the one who set me free, and yet he still looked at me as though I were a little girl. But after our fight yesterday, after being separated for nearly twenty-four hours, I realized that my heart was far from free. There was a piece that belonged to Alex. When he left, he took that piece with him and in its place there was a gaping hole through which my soul was slowly leaking. Now more than ever before, I realized that it was his job to make my heart full. Full of love, full of passion… full of whatever it is that makes a person happy. I slid the ring around my finger, the promise ring he had given me on the night I graduated. The ring was his promise to love me for an eternity. That was the night he shared with me his thoughts on marriage. He told me that marriage was worldly and mundane. He told me that what we had before was something greater and more beautiful than that. But he didn't realize that I was worldly. I was mundane. I was simple where he was not. He thought that marriage would tarnish our love.

I continued to twist the diamond-encrusted ring around my finger and fell back onto the bed. It was hard for me to think about our fight when all that I wanted to remember was the dream. The fight had been my fault, and I knew it. I was ready to accept the blame. Still feeling a bit sorry for myself, I curled up into a ball and hugged my knees. With the old quilt wrapped around my body, I stared at the window shade I had pulled down to keep out the sunlight. I thought about the world on the other side of the roller shade. It seemed like everyone else's life was easy, and I wondered why life inside my body had to be so agonizing and so confusing. I wished someone would just tell me how to do it. I wished someone would just tell me how it would end. I wanted to know when Alex would leave me again. I needed to know how much time I had left.

This sky was clear this morning, but I could hear the wind outside my window, and I knew it would be chilly. I traded my pajamas for a pair of running tights and a sweatshirt and walked the distance between my cottage and his. I shivered as I tiptoed across the sidewalk connecting our cabins, and I ran my hands up and down my arms to warm them. I felt goose bumps forming on my legs, but on the inside I was warm. His cottage was wide open when I reached it, save the flimsy screen door that kept out the bugs. Quietly, I pushed the door open and slid inside. He was still asleep. I knelt beside his bed, and I watched the thin sheet that covered his body, his very alive body, move up and down as he breathed. His chocolate hair fell perfectly just where his eyes began. His eyelashes were long and dark. I studied the scar next to his eye. It took all my restraint not to reach out and trace it with my finger. I loved the delicate curve of his lip. Even when he was asleep, he seemed to be smiling. I wondered if he would still be mad when he awoke. Could he forgive me for all of the things I had said the day before? Everything I wanted was just inches away. With a deep breath and a gentle hand, I touched the bare skin of his forearm. He jumped.

"What in the world are you doing?" Alex sat up with a confused look on his face. "What's wrong? Is something wrong?"

I let out the breath I had taken in moments ago, the breath that I didn't realize I had been holding. "Nothing's wrong." I sighed, stood up, and was starting to walk back out the way I had come, when he grabbed my hand.

"Then what are you doing in here?"

"I was in the area… I thought I'd stop by," I said sarcastically, sitting on the edge of his bed.

"You look tired," he said, brushing a piece of hair away from my face and tucking it behind my ear. "What's on your mind?"

Alex wasn't bringing up the fight from the day before, so I thought it might be best not to bring it up either. I was sorry, though. I wanted to tell him all the reasons why I had said those horrible things. I knew that I couldn't erase the words, but if he only knew why I had said them, then maybe he would understand.

"Nothing," I lied.

"I don't believe that for a minute," he said, stretching his arms over his head, allowing the sheets to drop down to his chest. "What's going on?"

Alex scooted to the opposite side of the bed, and I lay down next to him.

"I've changed. I'm not the little girl I was when you found me. I'm not the nine year old girl you saw picking flowers with her daddy." I ran my hand across his shoulder and closed my eyes, letting the tips of my fingers move up the back of his neck until they were ruffling his chocolate brown hair.

"I know."

"I'm a woman now." I moved my lips so that they brushed against his ear.

"I know."

"Does that scare you?" I whispered.

"A little." His voice was shaking, his breathing heavy.

"Why?"

"Because you know what you want and that makes it so much harder… harder for me."

"Why does it have to be so hard? Shouldn't this be easy?"

"I recall telling you that nothing about us being together would be easy."

"It's not easy," I agreed. "I feel like something's missing. It's been missing all along, but I didn't realize what it was until last night. When you're around, my heart is full, so full it's about to burst. But there's still this tiny hole in the center that is a drain. And when you're gone, all of the happiness leaks out."

"I can't be the one who fills that empty space. It's not fair of you to expect that from me. I'll only disappoint you in the end. Because in the end, I am only human... well, sort of."

"Yesterday, you told me you had been jealous before. When were you jealous?"

"When you had the crush on Micah Peatree in the third grade."

"Micah Peatree? I did not have a crush on Micah."

"Well, he seemed to be fond of you."

"Regardless, I never liked him. He wet his pants everyday right after lunch. I felt sorry for him. I was nice to him when no one else was. I knew how it felt to be shunned, but that is very different than having a crush."

"Little Micah Peatree," Alex taunted.

"You know, I hardly think it's fair that you bring up things like that. You weren't even here. You think you know everything about me just because you could see my every move. But you never knew what I was thinking."

"Don't be so hard on me, Rae. You so easily forget that those are the only memories I have... of you... on earth, anyway."

"I'm being hard on you because you're not playing fair. - Corrine and Micah Peatree are not the same."

"Why?"

"Because I was in third grade. And it's different with Corrine."

"I don't like Corrine, so why are you so concerned?"

"Because she's pretty. She looks like a woman, and you still look at me like I'm a child."

"No, I don't."

"Yes, you do."

"*No*, I don't. Believe me, I don't."

"RrRR." I flipped over onto my back and stared at the large crack running through the white plaster ceiling. I could feel a fire kindling inside of me. The flames were growing larger by the second. I was burning inside; he had witnessed my entire life from above, like a movie he had watched from the comfort of a soft cloud. He told me that he could feel my pain from the halfway, and that it was torture that he couldn't save me every time. But he couldn't possibly know what it was like. I was the one who was on this earth, in the middle of the fire, engulfed in flames. I was burning inside because I envied him. He knew all about us. He could remember the type of love we had before we were placed on earth. He knew our perfect love, the sort of love where envy and jealousy, the kind that I was experiencing at this very moment, was non-existent. Finally, I was burning inside because he knew me better than I knew myself. I discretely shifted my gaze to the left and peeked at him from the corner of my eye. He was staring back at me. His face was just inches from mine, apparently waiting for me to make just that sort of move. He interpreted my simple gesture as permission to open his mouth again.

"Don't be mad, Sunshine." An impish grin spread across his face, forcing his eyes into a half squint.

"Well, I kind of am!" I huffed.

"Look at it this way; I've only been on earth for about a year, this time around. I have never forced you to talk about your past, but I never complain when you do. In fact, I encourage it. If I never talked about mine then, I presume, I would be a little boring."

"The only part of your past that you talk about seems to involve me and my most embarrassing moments. Anyway, I don't talk about my past. It's painful. Nothing good has ever happened in my life... until you. That's the part of my life I like to talk about. You and me. That's it."

I turned from my back onto my side, looking directly into his eyes. I was toying with a few ideas. I was wondering how I could convince him into telling me about 'us'. The 'us' I didn't know about. The heavenly 'us', I nibbled on my lower lip because he liked it when I did that, and then I began to twirl a piece of my hair around my finger and watch him squirm. He inched toward me. I eased back, making the gap between us a bit larger, and then I spoke.

"If you want so badly to talk about the past, then why don't you tell me about 'us'. Tell me about our life in heaven," I cooed.

"No."

He said it with no emotion whatsoever. If he had shown even an inkling of anger or annoyance, I could have used that emotion to get my way. But determination was the only thing I could detect when he said "no." I settled onto my back again and stared up at the crack in the ceiling.

"Please." I was halfway begging and halfway pouting, something I had told myself I wouldn't do.

"You know I can't. Now you're the one who's not playing fair."

"Why can't you?"

"Can't you just enjoy what we have right now? Is it really so bad being next to me in this cold and drafty room on this hard and lumpy bed?" He grinned and pulled me close. "Look, I'll make you a deal. I won't tell you about heaven, but I will tell you two stories: one good and one bad. In return, you tell me two stories about your life: one good and one bad."

"You already know everything about me. What could I possibly tell you?"

"Maybe, but I want your perspective. I want you to tell me what it felt like to experience those things as a human. You forget that I was only human for two short years. I'm new to all of this. So... do we have a deal?"

"I guess, but I don't know if I can think of anything good."

"I'm sure you can think of something."

"Well, you're going first," I said.

Alex nodded like he had figured this much. He slowly ran his fingers across the top of my arm, making the tiny hairs stand on end. I glanced at him from the corner of my eye and noticed that he had arranged his other arm over the top of his head so that his forearm covered his eyes. He was silent, which made me unsure of what to say, unsure if I should say anything at all. Finally, he spoke. His voice was soft and full of emotion.

"I'm going to start with the bad. The day I died. There's not a lot I remember about being human, but I do remember the little things. I remember the smell of my mother's hair. It smelled like mint. I remember how she seemed to float when she walked. I remember my dad telling me the same story every night before bed. It was a story about a horse named Brown Sugar. I wish I could remember the rest."

His arm was no longer covering his face, and his eyes were now focused on the small window that sat lonely and peeling in front of us. It framed perfectly the green shrubs that lay outside the thin, single pane of glass. His voice was without expression, and his mind was somewhere far away.

"I remember the night I died. It was raining outside, and I was playing with my toy cars in the middle of the kitchen. My parents were fighting over something. My mom didn't want to get in the car, but my dad had all of our bags packed. He had already begun loading the luggage into the car despite my mother's protests. He kept coming back into the house to grab another and another, each time leaving puddles of rainwater on the kitchen floor.

"I have a bad feeling about this," she told my father.

"Orders are orders."

"What about intuition? Where does that fit in?" she pleaded.

"In this case, your intuition makes no difference. They left five minutes ago. We have to hurry. We have to catch up."

"What does any of this have to do with us?"

"Nothing that we have done in the past five years has been about us. That was a decision we made a long time ago."

"I realize that, Paul. But I don't think we're going to make it out of this alive."

"Don't be silly, Sarah." And with that, my dad picked me up off the ground, and I watched as tears rolled down my mother's cheeks. Taking everything into consideration, it seems strange that I felt a sense of peace as my father placed me in the car, but I did. When my dad buckled me in I felt safe, and when my mother slid into the car and my father began to drive, I knew that everything was going as planned.

It was extremely dark that night. The dim light from the dashboard illuminated the rain on the windshield. Each drop sparkled and glistened...and then...the drops turned crimson red.

"After that, everything went black. Imagine how it might feel if your body and mind were numb. You see nothing, you hear nothing, and you feel nothing… except heavy. It's hard to explain. I guess it's kind of like when you've been sitting in an uncomfortable position for too long, and when you finally get up, your leg is completely numb. It feels like you're dragging this heavy thing around, this thing that doesn't belong to you. It feels like your leg is no longer attached. That's how my soul felt, no longer attached to my body. I don't know how long I stayed this way, but it couldn't have been very long because, the next thing I remember I was standing, hovering, on the side of County Road 26, and the carnage was very visible around me.

I was pretty sure I was dead. It felt like electricity was running through my body; it warmed and illuminated me. Although it was still dark, I could see. Although my body was visible and still appeared human in form, I could run my fingers through it with ease. It wasn't natural. Without much effort, I lifted myself higher so that I could get a bird's eye view. I'm certain there were three cars below me, and each car was so strategically placed that it made me think of the little toy cars I was playing with before we left the cottage. It was as if a hand had reached down from the heavens with purpose and made them collide.

After the crash, it grew quiet. The pounding rain had turned to drizzle. I could distinguish my parents' car amid the wreckage. Once, it had been a small white convertible. Now it was a mess of twisted steel. There was a perfect hole in the rear of the convertible's soft top, directly above where I had been sitting. It looked as if a skilled hand had extracted something from the backseat. I lowered myself so that my feet were touching the asphalt and walked over to the wreckage and looked inside. My body was in the back, right where my father had placed me, and the belt was still fastened tightly around my tiny frame. My dad was in the front seat. It looked like he was doing nothing more than taking a nap.

The passenger door was open, and it looked like something had been trying to gnaw my mother's seatbelt in half; only a few nylon threads remained, barely holding her body inside the car. The fingertips of her right hand delicately touched the ground. I couldn't see her left arm.

I wasn't sure if it was even there. I didn't feel sadness like you might think, but still, I turned my back because I couldn't bear to look. For the longest time, I hovered over the wreckage, observing my body still fastened snuggly inside my seat. And then something happened. There was movement. A set of hands reached through the rip in the convertible top, unbuckled my lifeless body, and pulled it from the car. I watched this stranger as she held my body close to hers, positioning me with care in the crook of her left arm while she positioned the body of a smaller child in the crook of her right. She rocked our bodies back and forth, slowly. It was so dark, I couldn't see her face, but I knew that she must have been an angel.

I rolled over onto my side and stared at Alex, who seemed far away. I wondered why he hadn't told me this before. He began chewing the inside of his cheek, and then he pulled his pillow gently over his face. All of his beautiful features disappeared behind a soft white cloud of pima cotton and feathers, with the exception of his lips. Their soft pinkness stood out against the white, and I watched as the little freckle on his lower lip moved up and down when he spoke. Hypnotized, I could barely breathe.

"And that's what I remember about the night I died."

I pulled the soft cloud of feathers away from his face and kissed him. "And what about your best memory?"

"That's easy." He pulled me into the place where I felt safest. "That was when I first saw you."

He had whetted my appetite, and I wanted to hear more. Who was the woman holding my boyfriends lifeless body on that cold and rainy night. I had to believe it *was* an angel, just as Alex suggested. There could be no other reasonable explanation. I wanted to ask him if he had seen my parents. I wanted to know if he had seen my sister, Laney. Was her spirit, too, lingering above the wreckage? The angel was holding Alex in the crook of her left arm, was she holding Laney in the crook of her right? But I would save these questions for another day, perhaps one day very, very soon.

CHAPTER ELEVEN

When I was a little girl, Dad would read me a book called *Goose Goofs Off*. It was about a very lazy goose that lived in a house all by herself and in order to make her life easy, never did a stitch of housekeeping. One day, the stork came to her door to deliver her mail, and he found a house that had been turned upside down. Ice cream was dripping off the cabinets, dishes were stacked in the sink, and the lazy goose was taking a nap.

I was reminded of the story when Alex peeked into my room yesterday afternoon. Messy. Haphazard. Unorganized. Unkempt. Calamitous. Bedraggled. Any of these words could be used to describe the state of my bedroom. My clothes were strewn across the floor with about five dozen other items. Books. Sunscreen. Fashion magazines and tabloids. Dirty towels. And to make matters worse, two weeks worth of dishes were stacked on any structure that was flat and sturdy. To top it off, my room was dark and dreary.

When we first arrived, I treasured the cool breeze that blew off the lake and through my half opened bedroom windows. I used to love the sound of waves crashing on the shoreline. If I woke up in the middle of the night the sound could lull me back to sleep. I used to love the light that woke me up at dawn, beckoning me to tie up my shoes and go outside for my morning run. But then…*Gone with the Wind* happened.

I couldn't seem to put the book down. At night, after Alex went to bed, I got lost in Scarlett's world. I was quickly learning that even though Scarlett lived a hundred years before I was born, we had a few things in common. History is a funny thing; surroundings might change, but people never do. I had adapted so easily to my new schedule. I read until the wee hours of the morning and slept until almost noon. My routine would have been absolutely perfect if the pesky crow hadn't been caw-cawing right outside my window. I quickly fixed the problem. I shut my bedroom windows, thus eliminating the noise, and I pulled down the shades and drew the curtains to create a more suitable atmosphere for sleep. I shut out the crow and the morning sun, and subsequently, another little piece of the world.

This morning, after several very discrete hints, Alex told me that my room looked like an extremely messy bat cave. He told me he was scared to step inside.

"Point taken," I told him, then I immediately began by sorting through my clothes. I made two piles: one for dirty clothes and one for clean. I stuffed my dirty clothes into my white mesh laundry bag and slid the bag beside the dresser. Done! Next, I took inventory of all the dirty dishes that had collected over the past couple of weeks. There were cereal bowls with curdled milk at the bottom and chocolate flakes stuck to the side, a mug half filled with a mixture of coffee and separated hazelnut creamer, and a single glass of orange juice that was showing tell-tale signs of mold. I made five trips back and forth between my bedroom and the kitchen. When I was finished, the sink was overflowing with dirty dishes but my room was beginning to look clean. Cocoa was still lying on the bed when I returned. The back of her head was resting on my pillow, and all four of her legs were in the air.

"You're just going to lie there?" I scolded, bending down to pick up a piece of trash from the floor. I was still mad at Cocoa. She had devoured the entire pan of cinnamon rolls I had made for Alex. Apparently, both men and dogs are fond of the smell of baking bread. She had her tail between her legs when we entered the cabin yesterday morning and the crumbs were still on her chin. I was mad, not just because I had worked so hard, but because the cinnamon rolls had been my single-handed attempt to entice Alex and now they were gone. I felt like even my own dog was trying to sabotage me. Alex, on the other hand, thought it was funny. He called her the black bearded bread bandit, but I was just about to call her something much, much worse. Instead, I scowled and returned several bottles of sunscreen to the bathroom and an armful of books to the small shelf in the living room where they belonged. My room was nearly as clean as it was when I arrived at the end of May, but it wasn't until I pulled on the roller shade and let in the afternoon sun that something changed, not only inside my room, but also inside me.

My room no longer felt like just a room, it felt like a home. I lifted the windows and propped them open with blocks of wood. I let out the smell of something stale and musty. I let in the smell of flowers and freshly cut grass. I let in the smell of life. My room felt more like home than ever, but there was one more thing to do. My little yellow bird. My prized possession. It was a simple wooden bird; yellow with green and red details. It was a silly souvenir, but when I saw it dangling from a decorated branch in the window of a store overseas, I knew it was meant for me.

The bird was hanging by a single string from the ceiling fan. She was in a state of never-ending flight, with no hope of rest. I, too, had spent my entire life flying, moving from place to place without control, suspended from an invisible string, going nowhere in the end. Not until I graduated from high school did I realize I was finally free. The strings had been cut. I could fly away if I wanted to; the difference was that I was finally free to choose. With a pair of scissors, I cut the small loop of thread that was attached to the bird's head and placed her on the sill of my window. If I was free, then she should be as well.

I was just about to shoo Cocoa off of my bed so I could make it, but something startled her and shooing wasn't needed. She began to bark and howl, then ran from my room to the back door. She usually did this when someone was walking through our yard and because our yard was unfenced, this had become a regular occurrence. I tugged on the sheets, pulling them tight and smoothing them flat. I picked the quilt up from the floor and placed it neatly on top of the bed. I was slipping fresh pillowcases onto the pillows when Cocoa's barking turned into a growl.

I told Cocoa to hush. She responded with a single whimper, and I scratched her head. A rapping on the frame of the screen door startled me, and I glanced at the clock. It was 1:00, and I was still in my pajamas. I waited to see if Alex would get the door, but he didn't. I scowled and threw on my robe, hesitating before peeking into the living room, wondering if perhaps Chloe and Ben were standing on the back deck waiting patiently to knock me off. Finally, I stuck my nose around the corner and sighed. What was standing on the back deck of the cottage, face pressed against one of the windows, was far worse than Chloe and Ben... much, much worse: It was cranky Mr. Finnegan. Apparently, he was convinced someone was home. With much aggravation, he pulled his gaunt face away from the glass, leaving a steamy triangular shaped smudge on the window and began tapping his foot with agitation. The sight of Mr. Finnegan outside my door was terrifying. In a way, I wished it were Chloe or Ben. I think I would rather be killed than yelled at.

"I want you to know that I have had it with your dog and her droppings," he began as soon as I opened the door.

"Excuse me but..."

"No, let me finish. I have had it up to here," he said, moving his hand so that it was level with his pointy little beard. "with your dog running through the lanes as she pleases. And the barking. *Annnnnd theeeee baaaaarking*," he repeated. "She is from hell, I tell you, from *h...h....h.... hell*," the elf like creature stuttered.

"But Mr. Finnegan..."

"You let me finish. I have already called the authorities concerning this ma.... ma.... ma.... mess. You are on probation. One more dropping, one more howl," his voice squeaked. He cleared his throat and continued. "One more complaint from me, and that dog is going to the pound...do you hear me? I don't want to see her f...f....f....f...."

Mr. Finnegan was stammering again, his "f's" firing like a semi automatic that was using spit instead of bullets as ammo. Mr. Finnegan took a deep breath and continued.

"Her furry butt again. I don't want to see her furry butt again. Is that clear?" His voice had been a steady crescendo, culminating in a climactic burst that left me wiping saliva from my cheek.

I knew good and well that the North Shore of L'Homme Dieu was filled with dogs, and I knew that Cocoa was not the only dog that barked, nor was she the only dog that, on occasion, got loose and ran down the lane. I was also certain that the only time Cocoa took care of business was when we went out for our morning run, and I always disposed of it properly. Her routine was like clockwork, but there was no use in arguing. I slunk my shoulders in fear, fear that I would be soaked in saliva if I didn't agree with everything he said. I told him I would be right over to pick up the droppings in his backyard, and that I would make sure he never saw the likes of my dog again. Mr. Finnegan lifted his nose into the air, turned briskly, and began talking to himself as he scuttled away. I wasn't really sure what it was that I was promising. Was my promise sentencing Cocoa to a life of confinement? That wasn't really fair, especially when she was completely innocent. When I finally saw his shiny head disappear behind the last row of hedges, I waited a moment longer. After hearing his screen door slam shut, I made my way to his cottage, armed with a plastic baggie for poop.

When I returned, Alex was in the kitchen eating lunch. I wondered how he had so conveniently escaped the wrath of cranky Mr. Finnegan. My feet slid haughtily across the old linoleum floor toward the coffee pot, and I found it filled to the brim with the dark colored liquid that I loved.

"Mr. Finnegan stopped by this morning," I informed him, my tone of voice as artificially sweet as the yellow packet of sugar I was dumping into my coffee.

"I know. I heard him."

"And you didn't even come to my rescue?" I asked. The sweetness in my voice was gone. "You don't mind fighting for my life, but I'm on my own when it comes to a grouchy neighbor."

"The guy likes me. I wouldn't want to do anything that might ruin our friendship."

I snarled as I stirred the creamer into my cup of coffee.

"What did he want, anyway?"

"He's mad at Cocoa… and me, too, I suppose."

"I guess it could be worse."

"I guess. I thought we were living in heaven until I found out that Satan lived two doors down."

"He's not that bad."

"What do you mean? He's a terrible man."

"I think that people are inherently good."

"Was I dreaming? Because I thought you were the one who told me this world was a terrible place to be."

I had always been under the impression that this world was less than perfect. Alex and I saw the world in a very different light. So, it was with great surprise when I listened to him explain to me his views of the earth and how he saw it from the halfway, the place where he experienced the first seventeen years of my life. He said that the earth was an enormous sea below him, swallowing whole every living thing that was born unto it. He said, "The earth truly is a tragic place to be." And I said, "Finally, something we agree on." It was the only time I ever remember us agreeing on anything other than our love for one another. It was a bonding moment, at least for me.

"I said the world is a truly tragic place to be, I didn't say the people were truly tragic. I don't think people act terribly without good reason. I'm not saying that I condone it, I'm just saying that everyone has their own way of covering up the pain."

I knew Alex was right, because I was a prime example. It hadn't even been a year since he had found the key to unlock the chains that bound my heart, and already I had forgotten how it felt to merely survive. I had forgotten how life was when I was locked inside my hardened shell. How it felt: dark and lonely. How I felt: cold and numb. Mr. Finnegan was no different than me. The cause of his pain was most certainly different, but his coping mechanism was much the same. I shut people out. He chewed people out. I was no better than him.

I looked over at Cocoa who had plopped down on the kitchen floor.

"Maybe I just need to run her more."

"If you run anymore your legs are going to fall off."

"I like to run."

"You like to paint, too."

"I know," I said without looking him in the eye, because I knew where this was going.

Alex had made me promise that I would go to college and pursue my love of painting. I remember telling him that my parents wanted me to follow in their footsteps and become a doctor. Alex had said, "I'd say you're more of a Picasso than a Florence Nightingale."

And I said, "Actually, Florence Nightingale was a nurse, not a doctor."

"Freud, then," he said. "I see you as more of a Picasso than a Sigmund Freud."

"We'll see," I told him.

To appease Alex, I had applied to eleven schools and received eleven letters of acceptance, finally choosing the University of Minnesota in the Twin Cities. But summer was coming to an end and driving two-and-a-half hours three days a week just to get to school did not sound appealing nor was it realistic. I would spend a minimum of fifteen hours a week driving. Not to mention the thirteen credit hours that I was enrolled in and the at home study time that I would need. I had done the math. I could easily spend a good forty hours a week on college, and that kind of time was more than I was willing to give. I had promised Alex I would go to college. But I had made a promise to myself as well. I promised to spend as much time as possible with Alex before he left. There had to be a happy medium.

"You haven't picked up a brush all summer. When you get a brush back in your hand, you're not going to be able to put it down."

"I don't have a brush. I wasn't able to bring any of my art supplies with me. No room. No time."

"There's an art store in town we can go to tomorrow. I should have already bought them for you as a back to school present."

I didn't respond.

"I hope you haven't changed your mind. You're going to art school. I am not going to stand by and let you waste your life away on me."

"No, I haven't changed my mind." All at once I was struck with an idea. "What if I was able to take most of my classes online?"

"We need internet access." He twisted his mouth in thought as he considered how to make my idea work, and then, just as quickly, he frowned. "But you can't take art online. And that's the whole point, right?"

"I could at least check into it."

"When do classes start?"

"First week in September."

"That's just a little over a month away."

"I know," I said, not believing it myself.

"I'll check into getting the Internet hooked up. It was on my list of things to do anyway."

"You have a list of things to do?" I said, unable to hide the surprise in my voice. I don't know why it seemed strange to hear him say it. Making a to-do list seemed like such a human thing to do, and Alex was anything but human. I thought about his strengths and all the abilities he had, all of the abilities I had yet to see, and I thought that, if he wanted to, he could make one sweeping movement with his angelic hand and his entire to do list for the month would be complete. But no, Alex was making a to-do list, and I didn't know what to think.

It was late in the afternoon when the Century Link guy left, and we were officially connected to the rest of the world. I couldn't deny that, in a way, it made me feel sad. For a couple of months, it seemed that Alex and I were in another universe, away from the world that brought us so many problems, the world that told us it would never work out for the two of us to be together. Alexandria was paradise, and the cottage on Lake L'Homme Dieu was our heaven. Now, Cal from Century Link brought a piece of the world into our little home and when he left, he took a tiny chunk of our paradise with him. It's not that I disliked Cal. He was a slightly overweight blue-collar worker who thought he was doing us a favor. He didn't know any better. He didn't know that, by bringing the world to us, he was actually taking *our* world away. Despite my aversion toward the computer and all of its capabilities, I sat down immediately, clicked on Firefox, and surfed the web for a while before I thought to check my Gmail account.

Only now did it occur to me that my parents might have tried to contact me via email. In fact, I was almost certain that they would have, considering they had absolutely no idea how to reach me any other way. Email would be their only hope of contacting me. Gmail popped up, and it was with much hesitation and a sick feeling in my stomach that I entered my user name and password. If there was mail from Mom and Dad in my inbox, would it be angry mail? Would they be furious that I had left them in the middle of the night, giving them no indication of why I was leaving or where I was planning to go? And then another pang of guilt rippled through my body. I knew they wouldn't be angry. If they were angry with me, then my actions would be easier to live with. My parents would be sad and concerned, possibly even confused, but never angry. They loved me, and I left them. If only I could tell them that it was for their own good I had run away. When my email account appeared on the screen, I realized it might take a little sifting to sort out the legitimate emails from the junk. I had 2,567 emails in my inbox, the result of neglecting to check my account since the end of May. Most of them seemed to be spam: mail from a TracyTada who wanted to sell me pills that would make my boobs bigger. Another one from Diceman47 with the subject heading: grow rich gaming. And another from RiccoPBL: attract the RIGHT girl with wonder pills. There were others that promised to help me lose weight and rid myself of wrinkles instantly. It took me nearly thirty minutes to check the little box beside all of the spam and hit block sender and delete, but afterwards, I was left with an inbox that was more manageable.

"For someone with mixed feelings about technology, you've sure been in there a long time," Alex shouted from the kitchen.

"Deleting spam," I answered.

"Right, right."

"What are you doing?"

"Cooking dinner."

"What is it? It smells good."

"Enchiladas. I'm just warming them up."

"Yum," I said, rolling my eyes. Even though it was the banana bread, not the enchiladas, that caused the fight the other day, I wasn't about to go down that road again. Besides, Gretchen made the enchiladas and, in my opinion, Gretchen wasn't anyone I needed to worry about. Gretchen's enchiladas were filled with cheese and chicken... not ulterior motives.

Although my account was more manageable, I was still left with an inbox that was rather full. Impatiently, I scrolled down the list, searching for mail from Mom and Dad. Finally, I took a shortcut and entered their email address into the box at the top of the page and hit search. Sure enough, in less than a second, a single email appeared on the screen. I hesitated before I clicked on the search result and began to read.

Rae,

It doesn't come as a surprise that you left, and I think I know the reasons why you did. Unfortunately, you must think that everything bad that has happened in your life and in our lives is your fault. It is not. We are no safer now that you have left than we were before you came into our lives. Your dad and I chose to make a difference in this world, and when we did, we were fully aware of the storms that would be coming our way. You cannot expect to change the world without a fight. Even after choosing to live within the light, the darkness is always close behind. In fact, after making the choice, darkness will come at you faster than ever before. I do not know what it is that you have learned about me, your father, your sister, or your grandparents for that matter, but what I do know is this: you do not know it all. There are things about your father and I, things about your life, that we have neglected to tell you for your own safety. There are things that I should tell you now, but these things I can't tell you in an email. I need to see you, Rae. I need to tell you that I'm so very sorry, and I need to do this in person. It's the only way you'll understand. If

*you are not ready to see me I will try to be patient, but please, I beg
you, send me something back so that I know you are okay.*

I love you,
Sue

The first thing I noticed was the date at the top of the email. It
was dated June 15. It occurred to me that my mother and father didn't
attempt to email me until seventeen days after I departed. Maybe they
didn't know what to say. Maybe it took seventeen days for them to gather
the courage to tell me what was in the body of this email. She wasn't
telling anything I didn't already know. I knew that my parents were
hiding something. I knew there was more to our lives than met the eye.
The only difference was that, until now, my mother had never admitted
it. What else did she need to tell me? Was she going to tell me the reason
behind Chloe and Ben's unquenchable hatred toward me? Would she tell
me about A-Omega and what it was like to work for them? Or maybe she
would tell me I wasn't the reason my sister died. But what I really wanted
and needed to know was how they knew Alex's parents and why they were
assigned to work as a group. I needed to know how the Lovings fit into
this mess, and I needed to know what they were doing on the night of
September 13th that ended in sudden tragedy. I wanted to know about the
package: what it was and where I could find it? Did its contents still exist?

I had just begun to re-read the email when I heard Alex leaving the
kitchen and entering the living room. If the cottage had been larger, I
would have had more time to reflect on the word at the bottom of the
email that left me baffled.

'Sue'

That's how my mother signed her name. It was odd, to say the least,
and it bothered me; it made the letter seem very impersonal. Was she
trying to tell me something? Was I no longer allowed to call her *Mom*

because I had run away? With a flick of my wrist, I moved the mouse over the back arrow. By the time Alex was standing beside me, I had managed to produce the Alexandria Chamber of Commerce home page, the page I was looking at before Gmail, on the screen in front of me.

"Alexandria Chamber of Commerce... that's some serious surfing you're doing there."

"I was just seeing what this town has to offer," I retorted.

"Really? The girl who never wants to leave the house is all of a sudden interested in the local..."

"If there *was* something worth seeing, then I wouldn't be opposed," I interrupted. "That's progress, right?"

I scrolled halfway down the page and then stopped. "Look," I said, pointing to the screen. "Art in the Park is this weekend. We could go to that," I offered.

The art festival *was* the last thing on my mind. I was still thinking about the email, but I couldn't tell Alex about it. I couldn't deny that a part of me wanted to, and although that part was small, I couldn't ignore my need to say aloud the words that were stirring around in my head. Alex adored my family. I thought it was probably because he never really had a family of his own, and he craved all of the things that a family could offer, all of the things that he had never been allowed to experience. I also thought that his fondness for my parents might stem from the unusual vantage point he had been given. When he died and spent seventeen years in the halfway, he observed the interactions between my parents and me. Mom and Dad were good parents, and he grew to love them as his own. He thought that, far too often, I took my own family for granted. I told him he was wrong, but deep down, I knew he was right. If I told Alex about the email, he would use it as ammo and because I was already feeling vulnerable after reading the note from Mom, I didn't trust myself. The slightest persuasion would cause me to raise the white flag and as part of the treaty, Alex would have my parents at my side. Nope. I couldn't tell him that my mother had attempted contact and, even more importantly, that she had news.

CHAPTER TWELVE

*T*he next day I got up early and ran Cocoa extra hard. The morning was cold, and the air bit my cheeks and stung my eyes. I licked my lips, a habit I had just recently developed, and the chapped skin around my mouth began to burn. When I returned to the cottage, the warm shower thawed my body and loosened my joints. I dried my hair quickly, threw on a chunky sweater with a pair of tapered jeans, and coated my lips with a thick salve that Alex brought home from the store last week. He said it was made from beeswax, the only thing that would actually heal my lips. I wasn't sure I agreed with him, but then I tried it. Instantaneous relief. I loved, and hated, how he was always right.

Since being in Alexandria, I had only made a few trips into town. One trip to the thrift store and several trips to Coin Laundry. Hiding away with Alex was fun but unrealistic and as our car crossed over the bridge into town, I felt extremely anxious, like an animal being let out of its cage and into the wild. I studied the world on the other side of the window because I was certain it had changed since my last visit to Coin Laundry. I listened to the way people talked on the radio. For the first time since arriving in Alexandria, I noticed the houses and how they looked different from the homes in Oklahoma. They were built mostly out of wood instead of brick and stone. I observed the people at the park and regarded their attire, noticing how, even in August, a lightweight jacket wasn't out of the question. I remember the blazing August heat in Oklahoma and how I had no need for outerwear until the end of October. And then, I noticed an older model black Cadillac following too closely behind us.

I did a double take. It couldn't be, I told myself. The black sedan resembled the one I saw parked outside of the Laundromat just a week after we arrived. Was it a coincidence that the driver had backed away just seconds after we made eye contact? It also appeared to be the same car I had seen parked in the alley near the thrift store. My eyes were glued to the side mirror. The black sedan kept ample distance, but my chest felt tight and I could barely breathe. But when Alex took a left onto Hawthorne Street in route to the art store, the black sedan continued on. I sighed in relief, but my body was trembling.

Something occurred to me as we pulled into the parking lot of Artist's Edge. For most of my life, I had kept my heart under lock and key. The hard shell around my heart let nothing in or out. And though my heart had finally found freedom, had I? I was still trying my best to keep myself inside a shell. The cottage had become my new and perfect shell, my safe haven, and it was the only place where life was perfect. Inside the walls of the cottage, nothing could go wrong. It was the one place where Alex was always close by, where Chloe and Ben did not exist, and where my previous life seemed to be just a very, very bad dream. My new shell wasn't built from steel and rivets, locks and chains; it was built from wood and concrete and shingles. Same game, different rules.

I recall having a conversation with Alex on this topic. I told him that it was easier to have a shell around my heart. I said that if I couldn't feel, then I couldn't be hurt. Alex didn't agree. He told me that the shell in itself was disillusioning. He told me it did a good job of keeping the bad out, but it kept the good out as well. It wasn't until after the shell around my heart had crumbled that I realized Alex had been right. I had been living in darkness and missing out on so many beautiful things. Since arriving in Minnesota, Alex had been encouraging me to leave the cottage, to live life, to mingle with others, to have fun. Once again, he was trying his hardest to dissolve my shell, to pull me from my isolation, to save me from myself. And once again, I was having trouble letting go.

With the exception of a brand new, charcoal colored BMW, the parking lot of Artist's Edge was completely empty. Alex pulled up next to the BMW and shut off the engine.

"Look at that, Rae."

"Look at what?"

"That M5 has enough horsepower to annihilate *any* car on the road. 8200-rpm. V-10."

"Are you trying to tell me you like fast things?"

Alex ignored my remark and began to follow the curves of the car with his eyes.

"What I wouldn't do to take that car out for a spin. You go in and start looking around. I'm going to peek in the window."

"When did you start caring so much about cars?"

Still ignoring me, Alex slid out of the old Wagoneer, walked over to the dark grey BMW, and pressed his nose against the tinted window. He was caressing the car, moving his hand gently down the hood toward the headlights. I rolled my eyes and walked inside.

The Artist's Edge was inside of an old wooden warehouse. The building was a perfect square and freshly painted in a bright leaf green. In the middle of the glass door was a decal of a crow holding a paintbrush in its mouth. I pulled the door open and when I did, tiny bells jingled over my head. On the drive into town, I had been focusing on all the things that seemed different, but when I stepped inside, I realized that nothing at all had changed. The smell of paint was the same as I remembered and the feel of a brush in my hand was just as comforting, just as inspiring. I had begun filling my basket with paints when I heard the bells jingle again. Alex had stopped drooling over the car in the parking lot and was now looking at art books. Behind the front counter, the twenty-something clerk was looking at a magazine. He was tall, six foot at least, and well-built. He had sun kissed skin and blond hair that was cut like a rock star's, longer in the front than in the back with a little bit of spike on top. Several times, I noticed he was staring at me, but every time I looked his way, he would look back at his magazine. I could read his name tag from where I was standing: Flynt. With my basket in hand, I walked to the back of the store where the easels were displayed. I had just about settled on a lightweight, wooden easel that I could move from room to room, when 'Flynt' snuck up behind me.

"You look like you could use some help."

I turned around and smiled. "I think I've got it," I told him, nearly dropping my basket as I tried to pull the prepackaged wooden easel down from the shelf.

"Are you planning to do a lot of painting outdoors?"

I set my basket on the floor. My puny biceps immediately thanked me. "I don't know. I suppose. We live on Lake L'Homme Dieu," I replied, looking past Flynt at my boyfriend, who didn't seem to notice that I could use his help.

"Really? I have a few friends who live out that way. Do you live on the North Shore?"

"I do," I replied, the sense of commonality making me feel more comfortable.

"Well, it's beautiful there. You should paint outside whenever you get the chance… while it's still warm."

"I guess you're right."

"What size canvases do you plan on working with?"

"All sizes. I'm starting school in Minneapolis next month. Eighteen and still getting school supplies," I laughed.

"Right, but these are the fun kind."

"I suppose. I don't really know what I'm going to need for school, so I need an easel that's adjustable."

"The one you have is great. It's light. But it won't hold a canvas much larger than 30x24. This one over here is a bit pricier, but it will hold a fairly large canvas. It's made of aluminum, so it's extremely sturdy but still lightweight. It has a built in palette holder, too. Plus, you can adjust the height and even tilt it if you want."

"What's the price difference?"

Flynt glanced at the label above the display. "This one…" He appeared to be calculating the difference in his head. "…is about $50 more."

I bit my lip and did a little calculating of my own. I looked into my basket and tallied up the damage I had already done with brushes and paints alone. I was well over budget, and I had yet to pick a canvas.

Flynt must have noticed my dilemma, because he said, "I guess I could give it to you for the same price."

"Oh… you don't have to do that."

"I know I don't have to… I want to. Consider it a welcome gift… since you're new in town."

I wondered if it was my black hair and olive complexion that gave me away. In a single sentence, Flynt confirmed that, once again, I didn't seem to fit in. It must have been the look of bewilderment that consumed my every feature that caused Flynt to respond with haste.

"I was born here. I know everyone. In the summer, it's hard to tell the newcomers from the vacationers, but I thought I had a fifty-fifty chance. And besides, you have a bit of a twang."

My look of bewilderment changed into one of shock. "A twang," I retorted. I had lived in a variety of places, but I had never been in one place long enough to pick up any sort of accent. A twang? I was horrified. I wasn't sure how to take Flynt's remark. I was pretty sure that it wasn't a complement, so I decided to make his previous offer retribution for the insult.

"You're positive about the easel?"

"You betcha."

After listening to a brief overview about the different surfaces on which I could paint, I settled on two rather large canvases, an 11x14 piece of hardboard, which I had never painted on before, and a pad of canvas paper. They had supplies that I had never experimented with and things that I would be tempted to buy if I only I had the money. I followed Flynt to the register and cringed as he began to tally up my order.

"Do you paint?" I asked.

Flynt looked up from the counter. He had just begun writing down the cost of each item on a pad of paper that was embellished with a crow.

"I do… some. But mostly I sculpt."

"With clay?"

"Not usually. I make sculptures out of recycled metal."

"What do you do with them when you're finished?"

"I sell them. Mostly I do commission work for large companies in the Twin Cities. They buy them as landscape pieces. On occasion, I get individuals that want me to make something smaller scale. I do alright."

"Sounds like it. That must be amazing to make money doing what you love to do."

"It pays the bills. Plus, it allowed me to open up this shop." Flynt tossed back his head and laughed. "This store was one of my childhood dreams. While the other kids my age dreamed of owning a toy store, I was dreaming of having a store filled with paints."

"Well, that's okay. At least you knew what you wanted. Not many people can say that."

Flynt began to punch the numbers on the calculator, and then he paused.

"You wouldn't want to grab a bite to eat later, would you? Or even just get a cup of coffee? I'm thinking about closing up early today. I can be out of here in a couple of hours…"

Flynt was blushing. He was nervous and he was rambling. I was going to have to stop him in the middle of his sentence before he embarrassed us both.

"I'm with someone," I told him, wondering how he could have missed Alex walking into the store behind me. I glanced over my shoulder and pointed to where he was standing, engrossed in a book on Miro.

Flynt looked at Alex, and then he looked at the ring on my finger. "You're married? You look a little young to be married. I hope you don't mind me saying so."

"It's a promise ring," Alex interjected without so much as glancing in our direction. "As in, we're promised to one another for the *rest* of our lives."

For the last forty-five minutes, Alex had been so totally immersed in Miro that he wouldn't even give me advice on which canvas size to choose. And yet, he was so quick to tell Flynt that he and I were promised to one another that I gave him a menacing look. It seemed that the promise ring took on a different meaning depending on who he was talking to.

Without saying another word, Flynt returned to his calculating, and I began a quick tally of my own. Each 120ml tube of paint was $35.80, and I had eight of them. I reached into my bag, pulled out my wallet, and very discretely I began to count my money. I had exactly $253. I checked for change. Two quarters. I was already over budget with paint alone. My very small savings was dwindling quickly, and I didn't know what we were going to do. I was about to tell Flynt that I would need to exchange the large tubes of paint for the smaller size when he presented me with the handwritten receipt.

"It's going to be $253.50."

I felt my jaw drop. I looked down at the green bills in my left hand and then at the two quarters in my other.

"That can't be right." I wasn't sure if I was more surprised with the discounted cost or the fact that the cost of my supplies was the exact amount that I held in my hands. Not a penny more and not a penny less.

"It's right." Flynt pointed to the receipt. $143.20 for the paints, $24 for the large canvas, and $10 for the small. Another $10 for miscellaneous items like the pastels and charcoal pencils, and $52 for the easel. I told you that I would give it to you for the price of the wooden one."

"But the paints alone should be more than that."

"It's buy one get one on the paints today." He pointed to the sign on the wall.

"You've got to be kidding me."

"Nope. You saved almost one-hundred and fifty dollars on paints."

"One-hundred and fifty dollars that I didn't have," I mumbled under my breath and then handed him all of my money.

"Now all you have to do is paint something. I'll bet you already have something in mind. I'll bet you're an impressionist."

"To tell you the truth, I don't know what I am at the moment. I've been lacking in inspiration since arriving in Minnesota."

"I know what you mean. When I'm stuck, I like to look at the work of other artists. You know Art in the Park is this weekend. You should come. It might give you the inspiration that you need."

"I think we're planning to be there."

"You should try to make it out on Saturday. Sunday they're calling for rain."

"Isn't that always the case? I think the best fix for a drought is an outdoor festival."

"Never thought of it before, but I think you're right." Flynt handed me my bag of paints, and I took it. "Do you want to be on our mailing list?"

"No, thank you."

"Can I at least help you to your car? You've got your hands full there."

"No. I can manage." I turned around and was surprised to find that Alex was still fascinated with the book he was reading.

"Alex," I nearly shouted. "Can you give me a hand?" Alex set the book on the shelf and reluctantly made his way to the counter. Without a hint of intimidation, he stood with his arms folded across his chest. Alex was fuming, and I realized that, while I thought he was busy reading, he was actually eavesdropping. He had heard our entire conversation. He was fully aware that I had just been asked out on a date. I twisted my mouth into a mischievous smile. Now *he* knows what it feels like to be jealous, I thought.

"Well, if you change your mind… about anything… you know where to find me."

I blushed because I knew that Flynt was no longer talking about the mailing list. Without responding, Alex and I turned to leave the store, both of our arms loaded up with supplies.

"Where are you from, anyway?"

"I guess that depends on which day you ask me."

Flynt gave me an awkward smile. "Well, if you don't like coffee, and you don't want to be on the mailing list, then at least take a flyer. It has the address and phone number of the store at the top. That way you won't forget about me."

I nodded, took the flyer, and turned to leave.

"By the way," I said with a smile. "I never said I didn't like coffee."

CHAPTER THIRTEEN

*A*lex made snide remarks about Flynt the entire way home, but after a while I tuned him out and began to listen to the voices on the radio instead; the familiar Minnesota accent was quickly becoming synonymous with our safety. Alex's rendition of the conversation that took place between Flynt and me in the Artist's Edge was almost more than I could handle. And because he had the dialogue memorized word for word, I was positive he hadn't been looking at Miro at all.

"You wouldn't want to grab a bite to eat later, would you? Or even just get a cup of coffee," Alex said, mimicking Flynt's accent in a way that would have neared perfection if he hadn't intentionally overdramatized the nasal quality of his voice. Sometimes he would ad-lib, saying things like, "What I would really like to give you is more than a cup of coffee." He would always finish each sentence by plastering a super cheesy smile onto his face. I didn't respond, which seemed to provoke him even more.

On Saturday, I tried to convince him to get out of the house and go to Art in the Park. He responded by punching the power button on the TV and giving me the cold shoulder.

When I woke up Sunday morning, I decided that if I heard one more word about Flynt, I was going to have to say something harsh. But Alex was in the kitchen; dressed and having already eaten breakfast, he was revved up to go to the art festival… on Sunday of all days… when there was a 90 percent chance of rain. I was sure it was out of pure stubbornness and as we made the drive into town, I had to listen to him talk about what a beautiful day it turned out to be and how, not only the weather men were mistaken, but so was Flynt. I bit my tongue, because I didn't want to start the day off badly.

When we reached the bridge that separated L'Homme Dieu from Carlos, I looked into my side mirror and noticed the old black Cadillac creeping slowly behind. Our cottage was a good five miles outside of town. Could this be another coincidence? Had they followed us to the cottage? I recalled how nothing in my life had ever been a coincidence and so this probably wasn't, either.

Bound and determined not to have to park at the fairgrounds and take the shuttle in, Alex circled the park looking for a spot to magically appear. Whether it was persistence or luck, I do not know, but after driving around for nearly twenty minutes, he found one. Once out of the car, Alex's mood seemed to improve. I'm not sure if it was the smell of popcorn or the sound of panpipes heavy in the air, but my mood seemed to lighten as well. Hand in hand, we walked toward the gate. A lady was standing at the entrance handing out programs. I grabbed one and then stepped off the gravel onto the bright green grass.

"In two hours, belly dancers will be performing in the pavilion," I said, taking off my flip-flops and letting my bare feet brush across the cool green blades.

"Well, we can't miss that," he replied, motioning for the program so that he could have a closer look. I handed it to him, and I lifted up my long skirt a bit so I wouldn't trip as I walked down the small incline toward the festival. I looked at Alex and smiled. It wasn't until I saw him smile back that I realized the tension in our little cottage had been so thick we could hardly breathe. This day was exactly what we needed. Maybe Alex was right. Maybe we did need to get out more often. Before descending the small hill that led into the park, I took a moment to capture the scene that was unfolding below us. A park dotted with tiny canvas tents. Art. Beautiful pieces that people had made with their hands. Things that people had created with love. And of course, there was Lake Agnes, the lake that bordered the park. Its water wrapped itself around all of this perfection.

"This would be it, Alex. This would be my heaven moment."

I looked over at Alex. He was clutching a blanket in the crook of his arm and his newest toy, the old camera he had found in the back cottage, was hanging around his neck. He simply nodded in agreement. The determined expression had disappeared from his face and at once he appeared more relaxed.

"Didn't I tell you it was beautiful here?" Alex said as we lay on the blanket near the water's edge.

"Yes, but you didn't describe it very well. If you had, I would have come sooner."

The panpipes were telling a melancholy story, and I stared at people as they walked by, trying to discern what they might be like based on the outfit they were wearing. A big burly man in motorcycle regalia walked past us, and I thought that, despite what he wanted people to think, he had a soft heart behind his rough exterior. An older woman walked by with her grandchildren: one boy and one girl. The little girl had on a princess crown, and the little boy was shooting a rubber band gun at his sister's behind. The grandmother reprimanded the boy while the little girl howled. Now more than ever I wished for a sibling. I wished for Laney. I began to wonder what she might look like had she been allowed to grow up. She would have been twenty-one. She would have been beautiful. She had our mother's porcelain skin. She would have looked just like Mom, except with blond hair.

"I smell hamburgers," Alex said, getting up on one knee so he could take a close up of my face.

"Put the camera down, Alex. Quit taking pictures of me."

"You're no fun."

"Yes I am. And you're wrong. All I smell is popcorn."

"It's kettle corn. It's sweeter," he said, setting the camera down and kissing my neck, this time with more intention, "than popcorn." He ruffled my hair with his hand. "Let's go get something to eat. I'm hungry."

"Okay. And we might want to look around before it starts to rain."

"It's not going to rain," Alex said, looking up at the sky, studying the clouds that were masking the sun.

The twenty-minute line was worth the wait. Alex was right. Kettle corn was far sweeter than popcorn. I held the clear plastic bag, and we nibbled as we walked from booth to booth, stopping to talk with each artist. We learned tidbits of information, like where they were from and what their lives were like traveling from show to show. The bag of popcorn was nearly empty, and we had almost made our way around the entire park.

"I could do this for the rest of my life. I could be just like these artists. I don't need to go to art school. I just need to paint and take my work to shows. Maybe I could make enough to pay the bills."

Alex didn't respond, and I was certain it was because he disapproved of what I had just said. However, when I looked over at him and saw that he was eyeing a trailer several booths down that was selling hamburgers, I realized he hadn't even been listening.

"I can't believe you're still hungry. We ate that whole bag of popcorn."

"A man's got to eat."

"You go get a burger. I'll finish looking around."

I had just finished picking out a pair of earrings at the booth cattycorner from the hamburger stand, when I heard a voice that made me jump. It was sweet and deep, a voice that I had recently stored into my memory but couldn't place, a voice that, at the moment, I couldn't put with a face.

"Hey there!" The voice came again. My stomach lurched when I saw Flynt at the next booth. I was pleasantly surprised, but I was also completely shocked. Flynt's arm was in a cast from the fingers of his right hand all the way up to his shoulder. His eye was swollen, and he had a gash at the corner of his mouth. Despite the scabs and swelling, his smile was welcoming. Flynt was standing behind a table underneath a blue and white striped canopy. There was a sign on the table that said Artist's Edge. In the center of the table was a neat line of brochures. In front of the table was a homemade Wheel of Fortune style spinner divided into twenty different colored pie shaped sections. Each slice was labeled with something different: 20% off your total purchase, $15 off any easel, Free tube of Schmincke Mussini Oil Paints with any purchase, BOGO on artist brushes, and finally, the grand prize, the bright red slice of pie, 50% off for one full year.

"I heard your voice around the corner," he confessed. "Did you find a pair of earrings?"

I glanced at Alex. He was still standing in line waiting for a hamburger.

"Yes, I did." I moved closer and pulled them out of the bag, holding them up to my ears so that he could see my purchase.

"I saw this exact pair yesterday. They're great earrings. The artist is from Duluth. She and her husband make them. They're here every year," he told me. His fingers brushed against my cheek as he reached out to touch the earrings. "If I had a girlfriend, I would choose this pair for her."

I noticed that Flynt was no longer looking at the earrings. He was looking at me in a way that sent redness to my cheeks. Not the kind of blushing that Alex was capable of bringing; it was the sort of flushing that was brought on by an uncomfortable situation, a situation that left me not knowing what to say in return. I glanced down at the spinner, and then I snuck a quick peek at Alex. He was still standing in line but, instead of looking hungrily at the hamburgers, he was staring at us. The expression on his face told me he wanted to break Flynt's other arm and, if Alex didn't have such a kind heart, I didn't doubt that he would do it.

"By the way, what happened to your arm?" I asked, changing the subject, my voice a mixture of innocence and concern.

"I was getting ready for a competition."

"Must have been a rather large sculpture."

"No, not art. Hockey."

I must have had a puzzled look on my face, because Flynt laughed and explained: "The lack of ice doesn't stop us from training in the summer. Rollerblades instead of skates, ya know. We have a few indoor competitions during the warmer months to keep us competitive."

With his uninjured arm, Flynt pointed to the path on the other side of the lake. "I was a couple of miles out on the path when a doe jumped out in front of me. I had two choices: slam into the deer and hurt the both of us, or smack into the tree beside me."

"I'm guessing that you chose the tree?"

"I did. But I think I scared the doe to death, anyway," he laughed.

"I'm sure."

Flynt was staring at me with intent, which made me feel uncomfortable, and then he began to chew on his lip.

"You should have come out yesterday. I'll give it another fifteen minutes before it starts to rain."

"Well, you know. Yesterday was a wash. Didn't get a lot done."

Flynt looked at me with a suspicious smile that I didn't understand.

"So, are you selling anything?" I asked, stepping back to study the homemade wooden spinner once again.

"Selling… nothing. Just letting people know I'm here. Good advertising. The store's a bit off the beaten path, and it's rather new. I don't have a lot of traffic just yet."

"Do you have sales on paint often? Buy one get one really helps when you're a starving artist."

"Just had the grand opening sale. I'll probably have another one soon. Why don't you give it a try?" Flynt said, pointing to the spinner. I looked at Alex. He was nearing the front of the hamburger line.

"Quit worrying about Boy Miro and give it a spin."

I forced a laugh and spun the wheel as hard as I could, hoping that it would land on the grand prize: 50% off for a year. Although I had yet to use a dab of paint, I could see how the savings might come in handy. I watched hopefully as the wheel spun, and I couldn't hide the look of disappointment that flashed across my face when the arrow landed on a triangle that was completely blank.

"Oh well. I've never been lucky."

"I can make an exception just for you. I can give you a permanent discount. I was going to tell you that yesterday when I saw you at the coffee shop but… I have to admit, I was a bit confused."

He raised his eyebrows, as if he were waiting for me to explain something.

"I wasn't at the coffee shop."

"It had to be you. I know everyone in this town and there is no one here that has hair like yours. It's like black silk." Flynt looked flustered. "Your hair… *you*… are beautiful. I hope you don't mind me saying so."

My heart was caught in my throat, my pulse began to quicken. My chest felt tight. My body was reacting to what he was saying, but my mind was still catching up. I didn't leave the cottage yesterday. Not even for my morning run. The girl Flynt saw at the coffee shop couldn't have been me. Why was I reacting this way? I wanted to tell him that it couldn't have been me, but I was unable to form the words. I considered what he was telling me. He said that he had seen me, but what he saw was a girl with long black hair. That in and of itself was not alarming. Before making the move to Alexandria, I had stereotypically imagined that every resident of Minnesota would be a towhead, and I envisioned myself sticking out like a sore thumb with my raven hair and olive complexion. I was pleasantly surprised when I arrived. Even though white blond hair seemed to be a predominant feature, my appearance definitely did not single me out. Flynt saw a girl with wavy black hair standing at the counter in the coffee shop. Calm down, I told myself. Coincidence… that's all it was. Calm down. Calm down. As my heart rate began to drop back into the realm of normal, Flynt's voice drifted back in. But when he said, "Boy Miro," he grabbed my full attention.

"What? What did you just say?"

"I said, 'That definitely wasn't Boy Miro'," Flynt smirked. "Should I be offended by the fact that you turned me down for coffee just the day before? I mean… the only reason my heart wasn't completely shattered on the spot was because you were already in a relationship. And then I see you with this tall, dark haired stranger. Now I'm beginning to take it personally. It's the dark hair, isn't it? Or maybe it's the tattoo that you like. I've always thought about getting one. Not to knock lions, but that wouldn't be my first choice if I were going to get something permanently inked on my skin.

His voice was drifting in and out. I could hear the pan flutes in the background, but the peaceful melody did nothing to calm me. Coincidence? I think not. How could this be happening? Had they found us? Were we safe? Was I going to have to tell Alex everything? Was I ready to tell Alex about the journal? I could feel the color draining from my face. My head felt light and I felt dizzy.

Flynt must have seen my face had gone from a rich olive color to "titanium white" in a matter of seconds, because he reached out and took my hand.

"Are you okay?"

I didn't respond; instead, I looked over my shoulder and saw Alex at the booth across the way. The lady in the trailer was handing him a plate with two hamburgers on it.

"I'm sorry. Did I say something wrong? If it makes you feel any better, I promise I won't tell Boy Miro that you were sneaking around behind his back."

"I have to go!" I snapped. Still shaking on the inside, I caught my breath and tried to regain my composure. "I'll swing by. Next week," I promised, moving away from the booth and toward Alex.

In a daze, I walked past Alex toward the pavilion and wiped a tear from my eye. The belly dancers were on stage, dancing to an Arabic tune that was drawing the crowd in for a closer look. Like me, they too were shaking. But while I was shaking with fear, they were shaking their hips to the rhythm of the Tabla drums. They were hypnotizing the audience with their guiles, with their charm. If they had a worry in the world, it didn't show. An old man on the corner of the stage began to play the lute, and a single woman came forward for a solo performance. She was dressed in a brightly colored fitted top adorned with fringe and golden beads. She had on a long flowing skirt with a slit up the side. The music drew me closer. Heavily lined cat eyes. A face covered with a veil of golden chains and coins. Moving with grace and confidence. All of her emotion was hidden behind a mask of gold. Mysterious. Alluring. I wanted a mask. I needed a mask. I needed something to hide behind. But if I had a mask, what kind of mask would it be? The rain the weatherman had predicted began to fall. The crowd began to thin, and I found myself standing in the pouring rain, watching the belly dancers and the musicians clear the stage, still thinking about masks.

CHAPTER FOURTEEN

I decided to set up my studio in the back cottage; a single room cottage, completely vacant, with an open space for my blank canvas. I had to keep my hands busy to prevent my mind from wandering and, contrary to my nature, began to organize my brushes and paints, arranging my oils from lightest to darkest hue, and my brushes from the shortest to the longest handle. It took me the rest of the afternoon and most of Sunday evening to do so. For many reasons, this cottage was a perfect fit, but it felt lonely and so, after only half an hour, I decided to return all my supplies to the main cottage, thus having to start the organization process from scratch. I finally settled on the perfect spot, a spot that provided both inspiration and closeness to Alex during the daylight hours.

I pushed a small chair out of the way and made room for my easel in front of the large glass window that overlooked the lake. Now I could gaze upon the water as I worked. I sat down in the chair and placed a fresh canvas on the easel. I paused for a moment to take in the picture perfect view and stole a glance at Alex, who was still brooding over the fact that I had spent a significant portion of my Sunday conversing with Flynt... last name still unknown. But despite his momentary preoccupation with Flynt's intentions and his undeniable irritation over my response to Flynt's advances, I knew he would still be there to save me should I need it.

And after the alarming news that Flynt shared with me, I would need his strength to save me very soon.

Sunday night, just before I went to bed, I unscrewed the lid from a tube of paint and inhaled deeply. The fumes must have been lingering around my room while I was asleep, because that night I received inspiration for my first painting.

I'm sure the dream was more detailed than I remember, but the vision that stuck in my head, the vision I couldn't forget, was of me back in high school with Chloe and Claire standing beside my locker. Claire's voice was more robotic than ever. Her bangs were shorter than I remembered, but her hair was still that same shade of artificial black. Claire fixed her eyes on me and spoke. Her words shook me to the core.

"You could pass for Chloe's twin, you know," Claire said in a dreamy but robotic voice.

All at once, I was walking toward my locker, walking toward Chloe. I inched closer and closer to Chloe until we were standing face to face. I was examining her expressionless features, her cold blue eyes, her long black hair, and the locket that lay just below the hollow of her neck. I reached out to grab it, to reclaim it as my own. She didn't object as I had expected; however, when my fingers brushed across the locket, I felt a jolt of electricity and my body slipped inside hers. We were now one person, one body with two separate souls. We were wrestling and twisting. We were trying to escape each other's presence. And then, as if we had reached a truce, we turned our body to face my open locker, two separate souls looking through the same set of eyes, looking into the mirror that hung askew just below the three little vents in the door. What I saw when I looked into the mirror was not what I expected. It was not me, but a stranger. One half Chloe Pierce, one half Rae Colbert. The eyes were different, too. Both eyes were large, blue, and almond shaped, but the left eye was icy and cold while the right eye was warm, inviting, and pure. A sneer formed on the stranger's lips, and then she opened her mouth to speak.

"Blood is behind it all," she hissed, and then I woke up. My sheets were drenched in sweat.

"What are you thinking about?" Alex asked as we sat at the breakfast table Monday morning. He was shoveling cereal into his mouth, and I was swirling mine with my spoon. "It seems like there's something wrong this morning."

"Nothing's wrong. I'm just tired, that's all."

"You didn't even go for a run. Something has to be wrong."

"I'm just tired."

"You didn't sleep well?"

"No." Not appearing alarmed over the sharpness in my voice, Alex stared at me without expression, waiting for me to continue, but I didn't. Normally, when Alex asked me if I had slept well, I would always tell him I would have slept better if he were staying in my cottage. But this morning, I said nothing of the sort. I was a battlefield of emotions and the war was hardly over. I was going to have to tell Alex the news. I was going to have to tell him that our enemies had found us, but I didn't know where I should start. I poured a bit of cream into my coffee and began to stir, watching the two totally different colors blend together to create something new… and then it struck me.

"That's it!" I shouted, jumping up from the kitchen table.

"What's it?" Alex asked, following me into the living room.

I ignored him. I picked up the pencil that was lying on the table behind my easel, and for the first time in months, began to sketch. The sofa creaked as Alex sat down and again, louder this time, when Cocoa jumped up from her spot in front of the fire to join him.

"You're inspired. Maybe the art festival *was* exactly what you needed. What's it going to be? You seem determined."

"You'll have to wait and see."

"Do you have a title for your piece?"

"It's going to be called 'My Evil Alter-Ego.'"

"Your parents would be proud. It sounds so…. so… Freudian."

"I suppose."

"Should I leave you to it?"

"Fine," I said without really considering him for a moment. When I painted, when I received inspiration, it was as though nothing else in the world existed. Alone with my canvas, I worked until I could see all my inspiration in visual form.

"I'll just be snapping pictures. I'll probably go into the woods across the street."

Silence.

"Might take Cocoa along. I'm sure she would like to go for a walk."

Silence.

"If you need me, I'll be in heaven. I received word from God this morning that today would be the day. Yep... I'm leaving."

Silence.

"Getting sucked up to heaven in a few. See you on the flip side," he said, trying desperately to grab my attention. "I'm leaving now."

Silence.

I heard Alex pick up a magazine off the coffee table, I assumed *Car and Driver*, and then he stormed out of the room with Cocoa close behind.

I wasn't completely sure I would be able to make the vision in my dream come alive without a picture. I thumped my pencil on the side of the table and exhaled. My frustration was beginning to mount when I realized I had just the thing that would help. With haste, I ran into my room and began to dig through my luggage. I unzipped the first piece and then zipped it back up. I tried the second piece of luggage. Except for a small manila envelope, it was empty. I froze when I saw it. I had forgotten all about it. Inside the envelope was the letter I had written to my father just before I ran away. I felt for the two little lumps in the envelope. The potassium pills. They were still there. I thought about the night my mother was rushed to the ER, the night she was poisoned. Doctor Connelly told us she had suffered from a heart attack. But when I got home, I discovered that someone had replaced her daily vitamins with potassium pills. Someone had tried to kill my mom, and it was my fault. They wanted me, not her. That was the night I decided to leave.

A chill swept over my body. Mom's heart attack was not an accident, and I should have told them, but I didn't. The words were in the letter I had yet to mail. I zipped up the bag and placed the envelope on my dresser. Back on task, I unzipped the third piece of luggage. There it was. My senior yearbook. I had no idea why, out of all of the things that I could have brought, I had chosen it, but right now, I was glad I did. For most of my life, I had a love-hate relationship with school. I loved the academics, but I hated the social aspect. And flipping through page after page of cheesy smiles and groups of friends only reminded me that I had never fit in. For most of my academic career, I had been ridiculed and bullied because I was the new kid, because I didn't have the right clothes, because I was not like the others. I flipped past the pictures of students posing on rows of bleachers for group organizations like the choir, the student council, cheerleading, debate and finally, my eyes fell upon the group picture for cross country.

Because I was taller than most of the other runners, the photographer had placed me on the back row. I stared at the picture, relieved that I was no longer stuck inside that book. It seemed like another life. In the picture, I looked like a different person, a person I no longer knew. I sneered and turned to the page where the senior pictures began. I flipped to the P's and began to scan the page for Chloe Pierce. There she was. I was shocked to see an expression on her face that halfway resembled a smile. That was not how I remembered Chloe Pierce. With the book in my hand, I walked over to the desk in the living room and began to search for a pair of scissors.

Finally, my search produced an ancient metal pair that I hoped were sharp enough to do the trick. With great care, I cut around the small square that framed Chloe's face and then, with even greater care, I cut her face right down the middle. I repeated the process with my own senior picture. When I was finished, I took a piece of tape and fastened the two halves together, making them one. One part Chloe Pierce, one part me. It was a bit of a botched job, but it would do.

Two hours later Alex returned to the sofa. He picked up another magazine and began to read while I continued to paint.

"What are you reading over there?"

"An old copy of *National Geographic*."

"Anything interesting?"

"Yes, actually. I'm reading about how a lion kills its prey. It's *very* interesting. They kill by suffocation. They clamp their jaws around the prey's throat, pressing its trachea closed so it can't draw a breath. Afterwards...."

"That's enough. I don't want to hear any more."

Alex snorted and looked up from the magazine. "You've made some progress. But I can't tell what it is."

"Well, progress is right, but it's still in the works." I sighed and looked at the canvas as if there was nothing more I could do at the moment. "I think that I'm done for the day." I stood up and discretely grabbed the manipulated photo from the tray on the easel and slid it into my pocket before Alex could see.

"That's the best news I've heard all day. I'm bored."

"Don't you have superhero things you should be doing? Shouldn't you be out saving the world from Chloe and Ben?" I laughed out loud.

Alex didn't seem to think it was very funny.

"I don't get you. You're so all or nothing. Most of the time you pretend like Chloe and Ben don't even exist, like our problems don't exist. Now you're joking about it."

"Brushing things under the carpet is a trick I learned from you." When Alex didn't respond, I continued. "It's like this Alex. I was hopeful that they wouldn't find us, but it seems as though they have."

"What are you talking about?" Alex's eyes flashed with excitement, and his cheeks glowed at the mere mention of conflict. I couldn't relate. I wanted to crawl into a hole and hide. Alex wanted to fight. It wasn't hard to see that, between the two of us, Alex was the stronger creation.

"For the life of me, I can't understand why you look so excited."

"I just can't wait to get this over with."

"What you really mean to say is that you can't wait to go home. You can't wait to fulfill your purpose so that you can leave this awful world behind, leave me... behind."

"Don't start with this Rae. I'm not in the mood." Alex exhaled deeply. "So, are you going to keep me guessing?"

The timing could not have been worse. From the moment we arrived in Minnesota, Alex had been ready to start fighting, ready to solve the puzzle that was my past. I was the one who had stalled, delayed the inevitable, and I had done so for selfish reasons. Now, after Flynt's warning, I was suddenly concerned. Alex was still sore over the whole 'Flynt' thing and to tell him that I was heeding Flynt's warning rather than his own would be like kicking him while he was down.

"Do you remember what we did Saturday?"

"Yes. Nothing."

"Right. I never left the cottage."

"Get to the point, Rae."

"Flynt said he saw me at the coffee shop."

"That means nothing. Could have been someone who resembled you. Your doppelganger, perhaps."

"That's what I thought. But then he told me that he was just about to say hello when a tall, dark haired boy walked up beside me."

"So."

"A boy with a lion tattoo on his forearm. Does that ring a bell?"

I felt like I was sinking. I was expecting Alex to be angry, but he smiled instead.

"You know, maybe Flynt is useful after all. Don't get me wrong. I'm not saying that I like the guy, and I still think that he is a complete idiot, but he might have just given us the heads up we need. We might not be able to find Chloe and Ben before they find us, but at least we know they're on their way."

"Well, we do have one clue. They like coffee," I chuckled. "Are we going to wait outside Caribou Coffee day and night?" I asked, scooting closer to him and placing my hand upon his leg.

"I don't know. We might," Alex said, lifting my hand with his, examining it. "You know, you never told me a story. You were supposed to tell me one good story and one bad."

"I know," I groaned. *I* hadn't forgotten, but since the subject hadn't been brought back up, I was kind of hoping that *he* had.

"So you're up," he said, still studying my hand.

"Which do you want to hear first? The good or the bad?"

"How about the bad."

"Are you sure?"

"Positive."

I was silent for a moment, allowing myself some time to gather my thoughts before I told him a story that was both the good and bad all wrapped up in one. It was a complex story, one with many facets and, even though my understanding of the incident was better now at the age of eighteen than it was at the age of seven, my comprehension was still incomplete.

"Just tell me. Just start with something. It's easier once you get started," he urged me. He was now examining my fingers, studying each one individually, attempting to scratch the caked on paint from my skin with his nails.

I looked away from Alex and trained my eyes on the fireplace. I wasn't sure where to begin.

"I was seven years old when I had my first nightmare or at least the first nightmare I can remember. It was horrible. I dreamed I was living in the apartment over my nana and papa's garage. It was a tiny space. The walls of the apartment were made of white plaster and were cracked with age. There was a TV in the corner of the living room; it was turned on to the news channel, but the volume was down. The drapes were drawn and the apartment was dark, but the light that peeked in through the gaps in the curtains told me it was well into the daylight hour. Mom was asleep on the sofa with a box fan blowing on her. The room was smoldering, but she had blankets piled on top of her body and pulled up over her head. The coffee table was stacked with dirty dishes.

I looked into the kitchenette, hoping to find Dad, but he wasn't there. I crept quietly down the stairs into my grandparents' two-car garage hoping to find him, but it was completely empty. My papa's baby blue El Camino was gone and so was his bag of fishing gear. I stepped outside. The pavement was hot on my feet, and I darted across the driveway to my grandparents' house. I was standing on their back porch, and I could see Nana through the window. She was in the kitchen cooking. The clock on the wall over the kitchen table read 5:30. The small air conditioning unit in the window was turned to high, but when I opened the back door and stepped inside, the house was hot. Nana didn't hear me come in. I sat down at the table and colored while I watched her cook. I felt invisible. I felt like a ghost. I was coloring a rainbow and had just finished up with the purple stripe when she reached for the dial on the old stove and shut the burner off. She turned around and looked me in the eye, finally acknowledging my presence.

"I'm going to clean up before dinner, Sunshine," she told me, using her apron to wipe away the beads of perspiration from her forehead. "You know the rules. You aren't to go outside without an adult."

I chose to ignore her. I focused on my coloring book, choosing the picture of a blackbird to color next. "Bye-Bye Blackbird," read the title over the blackbird's head.

"Do you hear me, Rae?"

"Yes ma'am, I do. I'm not to go outside without you or Papa."

"Don't go bothering your mama either. She's not feeling...well today. She needs her quiet."

"Fine."

"Rae."

"What?"

"I love you, Sunshine." Nana's face lit up when she smiled. Her whole body was glowing. She stood watching me for a moment before turning to leave, and then I heard her bare feet pad up the wooden stairs toward her bedroom. "Bye-bye black bird," I said, picking out a crayon that was bright enough to transform the old crow into something beautiful. Sitting at the kitchen table, I could see other children outside playing, and

I remember thinking how it looked like they were having fun. I moved the red crayon between my fingers, and then I snapped it in half. I set the broken pieces down on the table and picked up the black one. Some things will never change, I told myself.

I was peeling the paper away from the crayon when I heard a knock at the front door. A single knock that was barely audible over the steady hum of the window unit. I knew better than to answer the door. I had been warned on more than one occasion. "You never know who might be standing on the other side." That's what my parents always said. I crept into my grandparents' dining room, moved the curtain away from the window, and peeked outside. There was a girl standing on the veranda. She looked to be about my age. She was holding a small brown dog. More than anything, I wanted to meet her. I didn't really see how opening my grandparents' door to a seven-year-old girl could be dangerous. My mom had told me that there was nothing wrong with having friends.

I studied the girl outside the window. She had on a pair of jean shorts and a white tank top. Her strawberry blond hair was pulled up into a ponytail. I walked around the corner, resting my hand on the doorknob for a moment before finally opening it up. The girl smiled. She seemed nervous. I could relate. She told me her name was Katie and while holding the small dog in one hand, she used her other hand to point at a van parked on the corner. It was a white van with a blue stripe down the side. Katie told me she got her dog from the lady in the van. She had more just like the one she was holding. I told her I couldn't have a dog, and she told me they were free. It was the first time in my life that anyone other than my family had shown interest in me, and so when she asked me if I wanted to go and look at the puppies with her, I was reluctant but finally agreed.

I shut the front door softly and followed her to the van. Her dog began to yip. As Katie and I approached the van the back door swung open, and I felt the sleeve of my shirt rip as I was pulled inside. The van screeched away, and I pressed my hand against the back window and looked outside, expecting to see Katie, but instead I saw my mom. She was dripping with blood. She was screaming.

"That's when I woke up from the dream." I shook myself out of the daze I was in and moved my eyes away from the fireplace and fixed them on Alex. He looked dumbfounded.

"So are you ready to hear the good?"

Alex nodded without saying a word.

"The good began when I woke up from the nightmare," I started. Although I hadn't let myself think about that night in years, the details were still fresh in my mind: how I let my legs dangle over the side of the bed before I had the courage to let them touch the floor, how I tugged at my pink nylon nightgown that was stuck to the back of my thighs, how my heart felt like it was beating a thousand times per minute. I spared him the details.

"It was our first night in London, and I christened our tiny apartment with a nightmare. Our flat was so small, I could hear my dad snoring through the partition that separated my bedroom from theirs. I stood stock-still, listening for movement, or even a breath. In my nightmare, my mother was covered in blood. But the dream, it felt so real. I needed to know that Mom was okay. More than anything, I needed to hear her breathing. I stepped quietly across the floor, pausing every time I heard the floors creak beneath my feet, hoping the sudden noise had not roused my father from his sleep. The flat was so small, I could make it from one side to the other in less than fifty steps, but on that night, when I needed my mom more than ever, when I needed to know she was okay, it felt like I was crossing an ocean.

When finally I reached their makeshift room, I stood at the foot of the bed and watched them sleep. The moon outside the window was full, and my mother was drowned in a perfect pool of yellowish, white light. I tiptoed toward the side of the bed where she was sleeping. I wanted to whisper her name. I wanted to tell her I was scared. I had hoped to see her porcelain face and perfect features, but the bruises that defiled the left side of her face were more prominent than her beauty. The gash on her forehead had been mended with stitches, but it was red and still very swollen. The bruises reminded me that my nightmare was not a dream. It really happened. My mother had nearly died saving my life, and now

I felt it was my turn to protect her. I studied my mother's body beneath the sheets and noticed how, with each breath she took, they moved up and down. I was comforted by the fact that she was okay.

That was when I felt the happiest. I felt relief. I felt really, really happy that she was still alive."

Alex was still studying my fingers, but instead of trying to pick the paint off, he squeezed my hand, then he lifted it into the air.

"Did you know your hands are like a work of art?"

"Thank you, I guess." I laughed. "How so?"

"They're like a Jackson Pollock."

I rolled my eyes. At first I thought he might actually be paying me a complement, but now it was obvious he was not.

"They're beautiful. I could look at your hands for hours on end. Only you could have hands like these, Rae." When he brushed his lips over my fingers I realized that he wasn't teasing me. I wasn't sure why he loved my paint splattered hands and speckled fingernails, but he so very obviously did. "Don't ever change. I love you exactly the way you are."

"Don't ever leave. I love you exactly where you are. Right here in this exact spot. Right here on this plaid sofa for the rest of our lives."

"I promise you, I will do my best. I'll do my best for you."

"I love you, Alex, and I don't think you'll ever know how much."

"I love you more."

"No, I love you more."

"Doubt it," he whispered into my ear, then kissed me softly on the cheek.

"I love you more than the universe and the stars above," he breathed.

"I love you for an eternity," I said. "And that is definitely more."

The next three weeks passed more quickly than I had hoped or anticipated. I enrolled for the fall semester online through the University of Minnesota digital campus so I could take my prerequisites via Internet.

I was surprised to find out that I wouldn't even have to be present for testing. All tests were to be taken online at a registered satellite campus; the closest one was a learning center on the south side of town. I couldn't have been more pleased. Unfortunately, science was a requirement and the only online class with available slots was botany. I wasn't pleased about that. I knew a lot about the subject, but I didn't find it all that interesting. On the first Monday in September, Alex and I drove to Minneapolis so I could take a tour of the art department and talk with the professors. The two and a half hour drive to the university took over three with traffic, so I was glad Alex had thought to set up an appointment with the dean at the college of art to discuss the possibility of my painting from home; There's no way I could have made that three-hour trip on a daily basis. They had asked to see my portfolio and because my life's work was still in Oklahoma, Alex convinced me to bring along the painting I had given him on our first night in the cottage: the giant painting of his head. I pleaded with him not to bring it along, but he didn't listen.

"It shows feeling." That's what the dean told me, and then he agreed to let me do most of my work from home on one condition: I had to take pictures of my progress and send him weekly updates.

Back at the cottage, Alex, Cocoa, and I were inseparable, and Cocoa seemed to be favoring Alex over me, but I wasn't jealous. The weather had warmed and reached its high by the middle of August and now, at the beginning of September, fall was approaching quickly and beginning to chill the air. We spent most of our days on the beach, picking up tiny shells. The shells were not as big as the ones you get from the ocean, but they were still pretty. When the sun went down, the air would chill and Alex would start a fire in the fireplace. I was beginning to dread what winter would bring, and the stories the neighbors told only made me dread it more. In the evenings, I would cook dinner while Cocoa slept several feet away from the flames drying her wooly fur that was wet and packed with sand. At night, we would lie on the sofa by the fire and talk. Sometimes, if I was lucky, Alex would read me a poem from the book he kept under lock and key. School would be starting on the sixth, only a few weeks away and, if truth be told, I was excited about it. What I wasn't excited about was the day that fell seven days after that. September 13th was right around the corner, and I couldn't think of a more horrifying place to spend it.

CHAPTER FIFTEEN

*T*he beginning of September was wet and dreary. The rain hadn't let up for a solid week, and the temperature made a drastic drop from the mid-eighties, which was balmy, beautiful, and perfect, to the mid-sixties, a wet cold that had settled in my bones and left my body aching. For months, my only wish was to be confined to the cottage with Alex. And then, just when I was beginning to venture out, just when I was beginning to move outside my zone of comfort, the rain came, and we were forced to stay inside. It seemed as though I had become the butt of Mother Nature's joke, and I felt inclined to blame her for the dark places my mind had wandered to over the past couple of days.

Already, I had lost several nights sleep attempting to link Chloe and Ben to the man in the beat up black sedan. I had yet to come up with a plausible connection, and the lack of a good night's sleep had caught up with me: I was cranky. Even so, I couldn't seem to let it go. How was this man involved? I had considered Carl Pierce, Chloe Pierce's father, as a suspect; however, the pieces just didn't seem to fit. I hadn't been able to get a close look at my stalker, but from what I could tell, he looked older than I imagined Chloe's father to be.

Secondly, there was the issue of the car. My stalker drove a beat up Cadillac that was at least twenty years old. I couldn't fathom why a man living in a multi-million dollar mansion in Tulsa, Oklahoma, a man who let his daughter drive a brand new Range Rover, would choose a beat up black sedan for himself. It didn't add up. I pushed that possibility from my mind and began to reevaluate the situation. I was now considering that this man might be a private investigator... or worse... a hit man.

And then there was Flynt's forewarning, which I had taken to heart, but only now had considered the timing. Chloe and Ben had decided to make their presence known a month before my birthday. It occurred to me that they were waiting for September 13th to roll around before striking. How symbolic of them. They wanted to end it on the exact day it all began.

Even though it was a month ago that I began to consider the actions I would take against my stalker, only now, when my hands were idle, did I develop a plan that would not only reveal the driver's identity, but lead me to Chloe and Ben as well.

When I turned onto Sixth Street, I could see that the "car in question" wasn't in the parking lot. I continued down the road, took a left on Irving, and pulled around the block. It was ten o'clock when I came to a stop in front of the building I had only seen from the side street. My eyes made a futile attempt to absorb the size of the building. It was a much larger building than I had envisioned, stretching across half a city block and rising up two stories in the front. My windshield wipers were on high, and my headlights beamed into the distance. I put the Wagoneer into park and strained my eyes to see out of the rain-streaked window.

"Surely not."

The sign in front of the building read Cherith Interdenom-inational. A church? It couldn't be. It had been several months since I had seen the black sedan parked in the lot behind this building, the day that I went to the thrift store with Alex. The details of that day were still fresh in my mind, but now I was beginning to second-guess myself. I quickly made a u-turn, took a sharp right onto Irving Street, and drove south two blocks.

I took another right at Seventh Street and continued on. When I reached Broadway, I came to a stop at the red light. Not a single car was on the road. The rain was still coming down in sheets, and the windows were beginning to fog up. I turned on the defroster while waiting for the light to change, but it didn't seem to be working and the car began to make a strange noise. I stretched over to the passenger seat and began to roll the window down. The condensation immediately began to clear, but raindrops were sneaking in through the crack, making a small puddle on the leather. Quickly, I pulled off my sweatshirt and sopped up the water. Now the seat was dry, but I was freezing. The light turned green.

I pulled onto Broadway and headed north. I read the store names as I passed them: Dawn's Quilt Shop, Coldwell Banker, Alexandria Thrift, Hedine's Jewelry, and the Vikingland Book Trader. I came to a stop at another light. I was at Sixth Street once again. I put on my blinker, turned right onto Sixth Street, and pulled into the parking lot where I had previously seen the black sedan. Broadway sloped down to Sixth Street, so the church's parking lot actually sat lower than the front of the building. From this view, it was three stories tall, but so plain that it looked far less impressive than the front. I squinted to get a better look at the rear entrance.

I could see black lettering on the glass door. Cherith Interdenominational. This was the right place. The black sedan had been parked behind a church and for the life of me, I could not come up with a reasonable explanation as to why a man who was in cahoots with Chloe and Ben would be hanging out in the house of God. If you asked me, it seemed like a conflict of interest. I continued through the empty lot and parked across the street, waiting for the off chance that the old black sedan might appear.

After thirty minutes, the church lot was still empty, and I was beginning to get bored with my mission. The rain hadn't let up. It was pounding heavily on the old Jeep, creating a sound akin to a war zone. The huge drops bouncing off the hood like bullets did little to ease my anxiety. I took a long sip of my Diet Coke and shivered, wishing I had chosen something warm to drink instead of something cold. My sweatshirt was soaking wet and no longer served its purpose. I twisted in my seat and began to dig around in the back of the Wagoneer. With a bit of luck, I found an old jacket stuffed beneath the bench seat and held it up in front of me. It didn't look like anything Alex would wear. It was maroon with a small boat embroidered on the front. I slipped it over my head and warmed my hands inside the fleece-lined pockets. Now comfortable, I was able to focus on my surveillance. The lot was still empty, and I was still bored. I scowled and reached into the compartment on the car door, pulling out Alex's Sudoku book of puzzles. I grabbed a pencil from my bag and began to fill in a few of the boxes. My hand was shaking, but I wasn't shivering, I was positive the trembling was a manifestation of my fear and had nothing to do with the weather.

"Settle down," I said out loud. "Plan C. I'm just going to copy down the license plate number. That's it. Then I'll go home." I recalled the other more dangerous options I had considered several days before.

Plan A: Take extraordinary measures to uncover the identity of my stalker. If he went into the building, I would follow. It was by far the most risky plan of the three.

Plan B: Not without risk, it involved getting out of my car and snooping around.

Plan C: Completely safe, and this was the plan I had chosen. If I stuck with it, all my detective work could be done from a distance, no confrontation whatsoever. It was simple: I would copy down the plate number from the safety of my car then, after I returned to the cottage, I would figure out what to do with the information. I hadn't researched it, but I was sure there had to be some way to find out who a vehicle was registered to based on the plate information. I put my pencil to the paper and began to fill in a few squares of the Sudoku puzzle. A five, a seven, and a three were given to me, but I needed to fill in six empty boxes on the first row. I toyed with the numbers, jotting them down lightly in pencil and then erasing them when I realized the order in which I had placed them was not congruent with the second row. Starting from scratch, I reversed the order but got the same results. I gave it another shot, this time taking a vertical instead of horizontal approach. Nothing was adding up.

Frustrated, I tossed my pencil across the car. I was just about to reach over and pick it up when a light caught my eye. I looked up from what I was doing. My heart rate began to quicken. I tapped my fingers against the steering wheel in anticipation. A set of headlights beamed through the rain, the first set of headlights I had seen all morning, and they were drawing closer by the second. I sat stock-still and strangely enough, after days of strategizing, planning, and preparing for this moment, I was kind of hoping it would drive past. Holding my breath, I watched the vehicle turn into the rear parking lot of Cherith. Without question, it was the Cadillac. Even in the pouring rain, I could easily make out the oblong shape of the older model car. So the question remained: What was a hit man doing at a church?

The car pulled into a parking slot near the back door of the building. I realized immediately there was a major flaw in my plan: first, due to several factors, I couldn't read the license plate from where I was parked; and second, Plan C might tell me who was following me, but it was not going to tell me why. Was I okay with that? September 13th was fast approaching and Chloe and Ben were nearby. Would that information be enough to save my life? I thought of Alex. He would be furious with me for thinking about doing any kind of detective work without his knowledge. We weren't supposed to be keeping secrets. Without taking my eyes off the Cadillac, I lifted my drink out of the cup holder, took a slow sip, and studied the car.

"What is he waiting on?" I wondered out loud. "I'll bet he's waiting on Chloe and -"

I stopped mid-sentence when I saw the door of the Cadillac open. The first thing to emerge from the sedan was a man's shoe; the first shoe was eventually followed by a second. Both feet rested on the ground for a moment before the remainder of his body began to materialize. Slowly, slowly, my stalker came into view. I squinted, straining to see through the rain splattered windshield.

"Turn around. Turn around," I chanted softly to myself.

It was as if he heard me chanting and decided to oblige. Awkwardly, the man turned in my direction… but the timing was wrong. His eyes were trained on the ground and, just as he began to lift his gaze, he opened a huge black umbrella, covering not only his face, but the top half of his body as well. I quickly shuffled through my list of options. I had promised myself that I wouldn't get out of the car. But the scene was not unfolding the way I had hoped. My plan needed a revision. I was going to have to go with plan B - I was going to have to get out of the car. I would wait. When he was inside the building, I would sneak across the street, copy down the license number, jump back in my car, and drive away. I let out the breath that I was holding and sighed in relief. My eyes followed the man as he shuffled across the parking lot. I mentally crossed 'hit man' off the list; he was too old and he moved too slowly.

I continued to watch the man move from his car to the door of the church. And then, I watched as he did the strangest thing. He reached into his pocket, pulled out a key, and inserted it into the door of the building. This man wasn't just visiting the church, he *worked* at the church. I tried to come up with a reasonable explanation for who this stalker might be. If he wasn't a hit man, could he be a private investigator? But why would he have a key to the church? I watched him slip through the door and out of sight, wanting desperately to follow. I had promised myself that I would not, but I was still asking 'why?' Why was this man following me? That was what I really needed to know. Last night, I was lying in bed trying to imagine how I would feel when I finally stood face to face with my stalker. I thought of all the things I would say to him. I thought of all the questions I would ask. I wondered if I'd be brave enough to say anything or would I chicken out?

My legs were shaking uncontrollably as I slid out of the car. But I wasn't scared. Maybe it was because I was close to a church. Maybe it was because my stalker was old and weak. Regardless of the reason, I felt safe. Anxious, but safe.

The rain was still coming down in buckets. I hadn't even made it into the parking lot of the church and already, I was sopping wet. I pulled up the hood on the jacket and bolted across the street. I was halfway between my car and the door of the church when I stopped short. At a most inconvenient time, my conscience decided to chime in. I had heard my conscience before, but it had never been so potent.

Are you sure that you want to do this?

"I don't see the harm in it," I silently convinced myself. "What danger could possibly be inside of a church?"

Perhaps the danger isn't in the action, but in the lie.

"I'm not lying."

Your lies are ones of omission!

And then, like the flicking of a switch, I extinguished the small voice and continued running through the rain until I reached the back of the church. I hesitated at the door, wondering if it might be locked, but when my hand met the curved handle of the door and I pulled it open, I realized that it was not. Quietly, I slipped inside. I stood in the lobby for a moment to gather my thoughts. I turned and gazed out the glass door, giving the old Wagoneer a longing look. I wondered if I should make a run for it. I could be back inside the Wagoneer in twenty seconds flat. No. I had come this far. There was no turning back. I surveyed my surroundings. The church was massive, and it appeared to be empty. It would take hours to search the entire building. I felt discouraged. I studied the white walls. Normally, I couldn't stand the lack of color; it reminded me of the apartments I lived in as a child. I longed for a warmer, richer hue. But the white walls made a perfect backdrop for the colorful paintings that were hanging along the corridor. I shifted my gaze to the flooring, a rough white tile. I looked at my feet. I was standing in a puddle of rain. Evidence of my presence. And then something occurred to me. My eyes roved the white tile, stopping only when they rested upon a puddle a couple of feet from where I was standing.

Humph, apparently I was not the only one leaving tracks. I followed the puddles of rainwater down the dimly lit corridor, observing the multitude of doors to my left and right. Colorful, child geared biblical paintings hung above the entrance to each room. This must be the nursery section of the building. I continued to tread lightly, so that my footsteps wouldn't echo. And then I came to a stop. The white tiles ended where carpet began. This was both good and bad. The carpet would absorb the sound of my footsteps, and no one would hear me coming. On the other hand, the carpet was absorbing more than just the sound; it was absorbing the rainwater and with it, my stalker's tracks. Ahead of me, I could see a set of stairs leading to the main floor of the church. Slowly, I took the stairs one by one, hugging the wall as I went. The top of the stairs was lit by natural light pushing through the windows; even on such a rainy day, it was radiant. Then, I found myself standing in the main lobby of the church. The doors to the sanctuary stood open before me, and I felt myself being drawn toward it.

Walking into the sanctuary, I noticed the architectural features first. Unlike the low ceilings in the hallway, the ceilings in the auditorium were vaulted. The floor of the sanctuary was made of stone. An aisle stretched up the center of the room and stopped at a set of steps leading to the pulpit. There were rows of pews on either side of the aisle. A weak light streamed through the stained glass windows and faintly covered the stone floors with dull jewels of light in every color of the rainbow. But it wasn't what I saw with my eyes that made this room so very different, it was what I felt when I stepped inside. An unexplainable peace washed over me, and my anxiety was gone. I walked down the stone aisle and took a seat in a wooden pew. I pulled a hymnal out of the seat back in front of me and randomly flipped it open - "Morning Has Broken."

I read the first stanza.

> *Morning has broken,*
> *Like the first morning,*
> *Blackbird has spoken*
> *Like the first bird;*
> *Praise for the singing,*
> *Praise for the morning,*
> *Praise for them springing*
> *Fresh from the Word.*

"Blackbird has spoken," I said out loud. "A blackbird, huh? A pesky old crow?" Reminded of the annoying bird outside of my bedroom window, I couldn't help but laugh. I returned the hymnal to the seat back and closed my eyes. I felt like I should pray, but I didn't know what to say. Was I supposed to get down on my knees? That just didn't feel right to me. I thought about how Mom prayed: often and quietly. Mostly she prayed alone, but sometimes she would pray with Dad. Sometimes she would pray with me. I fixed my eyes on the crucifix above the pulpit, and I began to talk to Jesus like a friend.

"I hope that You're listening. Not really sure if You know who I am. I'm Rae Colbert, and I have a whole host of problems. First of all, I'm a wanted girl. Everyone seems to want me dead, and I can't seem to figure out why. I'm not saying that I'm innocent… don't get me wrong. While I'm sitting here in Your holy house, I am guilty of, not only lying to my boyfriend, but causing my parents to worry. I'm a little mixed up. I am also angry. Is it okay to say that I'm angry with You? I know that it was You… or Your Father who sent Alex here to protect me. By the way, that was a really nice thing to do, and I'm eternally grateful. But I'm angry and hurt that You want to take him away. I understand that he belongs in heaven. But can't he just stay here? I need him here with me. I don't need his protection. I can protect myself. I've done it for years. He makes me happy. That's all. That's all I have to say."

Halfway through the prayer, I had unknowingly closed my eyes and bowed my head, but I didn't realize that my eyes were wet with tears until I opened them. I wiped my hand across my eyes, sniffled, and stood up. Just before I stepped out of the sanctuary, I glanced over my shoulder and, once again, fixed my eyes on the crucifix. Jesus with nails in his hands and feet. Jesus with a thorny crown upon his head.

I was still thinking about the sanctuary as I continued up the carpeted stairs to the top floor of the church, but when I saw the light at the end of the hallway, I was reminded of my mission at once. The door to the room was slightly ajar, and I came to a stop just outside. It was an office. I searched for a nameplate that might indicate to whom this office belonged, but there was nothing. I held my breath, listening for movement, trying to decide how to proceed. Where was my conscience now? I didn't here any sounds from the office, so I slowly pushed the door open. I stopped in my tracks; my heart jumped into my throat. I couldn't move. I couldn't speak. I couldn't breath. What I saw was not at all what I expected.

CHAPTER SIXTEEN

A wooden desk stood in the middle of the room with a man sitting behind it. I stared at him, my feet stuck to the floor. I was terrified. His eyes were closed, and he was slumped over in his chair. He was either asleep... or dead. The only thought going through my mind was that I was trespassing. I had entered this church and this man's office without invitation. I tried to ask my conscience for advice, but it was gone.

"Hello?" I heard myself say. I'm not sure who was more surprised to hear my voice, the man behind the desk or me. He jumped when I spoke and for a moment, looked a bit disoriented. But he quickly regained his composure and straightened up in his chair.

"I must have drifted off. Please sit down," he said. "I've been expecting you."

"Huh?" The single word escaped from my mouth before I had time to think.

"Your car was parked across the street, my dear."

I said nothing in return, but his response only confirmed my suspicions. He had been following me. There was no doubt.

Only slightly thawed from the fear that held me frozen to the floor, I moved rigidly over to the sofa that was in front of a window and to the left of his desk. I sunk into the soft cushion and watched as the old man shuffled over to the chair opposite me. I stared into his eyes and prepared myself for the worst. I was afraid of what he might say. Would he scold me for sneaking into his office? Would he tell me why he had been following me? I let my eyes wander to the cross hanging on the wall beside the bookshelf. I studied its intricate detail. Solid silver with a gothic flare. He cleared his throat, commanding my attention. My eyes fell back on him at once. It wasn't until that moment that I really began to study his every feature.

He was old, there was no getting around that, and it looked as if he had seen better days. His face was ashen, a pasty white covering otherwise ruddy colored skin. He looked like someone who had just seen a ghost, or perhaps something far more concerning. His blue grey eyes looked tired. His hair was salt and pepper. I gathered he was a humble man. He was dressed in a navy blue suit that looked a bit aged but cared for. The soles on his brown oxfords were worn down to nothing, but the leather was still shiny and without a scuff. I didn't know him from Adam. But what I did know was this: for the past couple of months, he had been tracking me. It had taken me a while, but I had gathered the courage to follow this man I didn't know and confront him. It was with mixed emotions that I sat in his office waiting for him to speak. I was terrified, but at the same time, I was at ease. I was no longer terrified that he would harm me. He was gentle, feeble, and harmless. I was terrified of what he was about to say. I tried to relax as I waited for him to speak. I felt connected to this stranger, and I felt that he held a secret even greater than mine. A secret that was responsible for the grayish white tint to his face.

"I'm Pastor Joe, and this is my church. I'm sure you are here today because you discovered I've been following you. Now you would like to know why." His voice cracked when he spoke. It was a voice marked with age but filled with wisdom. I looked into his blue-grey eyes. They were warm and understanding. I nodded for him to go on, and he continued.

"I saw Alex before I saw you. It was the old Wagoneer in the parking lot of Elden's Food Fair that caught my attention. I hadn't seen one like that in years, and I couldn't deny that seeing the old car reignited a sorrow I thought had been extinguished long ago. Curiosity got the better of me.

I drove into the parking lot, parked next to the Wagoneer, and waited patiently to see who might climb into the car." The old man paused to gather his thoughts. He lifted his eyebrows in concern. For a moment, I thought he was waiting for me to respond, and I was getting ready to open my mouth when he began right where he left off.

"When I saw him walking to the car, it was as if I had seen a ghost. Just before he climbed inside the car, he turned to look at me. The first thing I noticed were his eyes. This boy had the same hazel colored pinwheel eyes that my Alex had. Of course, he looked more mature, but there was no denying that it was Alex Loving. I thought about it all day, and I swore to myself that in my old age I was growing senile, seeing things that weren't really there. By nightfall, I had completely disregarded the idea. Several weeks later, I saw the Wagoneer at Coin Laundry. And a couple of months later, I saw it again, this time driving down Third Street. When Alex turned onto Hawthorn, I continued on. I didn't want you to think that I was stalking you, for heaven's sake. I parked in front of the church and stayed there for a while. I guess I was trying to gather strength to do what I needed to do. I'm an old man; I'm well aware of that. I'm approaching eighty and my body just doesn't work the way it used to. I know the mind is sometimes the first thing to go. I knew I could very well be chasing a figment of my imagination. The last thing I wanted to do was scare a couple of innocent teenagers. But on the other hand, I needed to put this silly notion of mine to rest. Finally, I got up the nerve to wait for you outside the art store and started to follow you home. I made it as far as the bridge, but I couldn't bring myself to follow you all the way. I hadn't made it that far in almost twenty years.

"That night I tossed and turned. I was upset with myself for giving up so easily. I decided that when I woke up, I would drive by the cottage. Seeing that it was still boarded up, just the way I saw it last, would make me feel much better. If I could see the vacant cottage with my own eyes then I would finally be able to rest. I could get on with my life. The next morning, I drove five miles outside of town to a place I used to know. I had fully expected to see the cottage deserted, just the way I remembered it, but instead, I saw a chimney bellowing smoke and the old Wagoneer parked beneath a tree." Pastor Joe paused and gave me a sharp look. "So tell me, how is it that my Alex has come back from the dead?"

I thought it was strange that the pastor referred to Alex in a possessive sort of way, but for some reason, I felt I could trust him completely, so without reservation, I told him who I was, and I told him about meeting Alex for the first time. I told him about the halfway, or at least all that I knew about the halfway. I brought him up to speed on the happenings of the past year, about Chloe and Ben, and I was shocked when he didn't appear surprised.

"I'm sorry, but I didn't realize who you were. I was under the impression that the Colbert's had only one child, the child that died in the wreck. The story you tell seems impossible and yet it explains so much; it's the only explanation that makes sense. It's nice to know I'm not losing my mind. But do you know what's even better than that?" Pastor Joe laughed and shook his head. "After eighteen years of waiting and testing, it's beginning to make sense."

He seemed far away. As he gazed out the window, color started to return to his face. His eyes looked restful and full of thought, still tired but less troubled.

"Alex's father worked for the government. Right before he died, he became increasingly involved in the fight against the exploitation of women in Eastern Europe. A modern day slave trade was going on right before our very eyes. About a month before the accident, Paul stumbled across a bit of new information, the missing link. He was about to single-handedly expose the truth. My faith was at an all time high; the world as I knew it was beginning to make sense. It's hard to live with faith in a world that is so evil, so far from God. You hope that one day you will be around to witness God make everything just, for the bad to get what they deserve, and for good to win over evil. So like I said, my faith couldn't have been stronger. Then the unthinkable happened. Not even the life of little Alex was spared. It didn't make sense. And I began to wonder about God."

Tears were rolling down my cheeks, and I realized I had never truly thought of Alex's death. Perhaps because I never had a reason to. It's hard to mourn the loss of someone when he's right beside you in the flesh. It's hard to comprehend the reality of what had happened to him when, for me, nothing had. My shoulders were shaking and tears flowed down in steady streams. I felt my mother's pain for the first time in my life. I felt sadness and loss and the despair that comes with losing someone special. I turned to face the window and silently looked out upon the empty playground across the street.

"Ofttimes, people find the good that comes through something tragic. It's taken me eighteen years, but today I have finally found the silver lining. Alex is here on earth. I'm sure you realize that his presence is nothing short of a miracle. I'm left to believe that all of this has happened for a reason."

"I always thought that if you were doing something good that God would protect you." I paused. "I feel kind of let down in a way. If God's not going to protect those who love him, then who will?"

"I don't mean to frighten you or make you sad. And I don't mean to paint a nasty picture of the world. But you have to remember that we are not the home team here, Rae. The earth is the devil's playground and because of this, sadness and loss will exist."

"So you're saying that God can't protect us while we're on earth."

"I'm not saying that at all."

"Then what are you saying?"

"What you're wanting to know is whether or not God will or can save us from death. Are you talking about death, Rae?"

"Yes, I'm talking about death."

"Death is inevitable. Every single one of us will die, there's no avoiding it, and you have to believe that when your life on this earth is over, it's for a reason."

"But if Paul was doing something to better humanity, why wasn't he allowed to finish?"

"Maybe Paul wasn't the person who was appointed to finish the task. Maybe that was left for someone else. It's called passing the torch."

"Then who is the right person?"

"After Paul passed, my faith was tested, which is a hard thing for a man of God to admit to himself, much less to anyone else. I had dedicated my life to serving God and studying His word. I had been out of seminary for many years, and I thought I had it all figured out. I was a seasoned pastor. I thought I knew everything I needed to know. I knew the Bible front to back, I quoted scripture, I lived in a way that I thought was pleasing to the Lord, and most of all, I thought that I knew Him. When I looked at Paul, I saw a man who fought courageously for humanity. I thought that if ever there was a man for God to protect, it would be Paul and his family. And then he died in a senseless car crash. Such a tragedy. Such a random, senseless tragedy. And because the God I loved had never been a random, senseless God, I started to question whether my God existed at all. Of course, I knew the verses that were supposed to help me through this tough time. 'Trust in the Lord with all your heart and lean not on your own understanding.' Or my absolute favorite is 1 Peter 1:6-7: 'For a little while you have had to suffer grief so that the proven genuineness of your faith may result in praise.' My faith came back around, but my understanding never did."

"So who's holding the torch? The one that Paul was forced to drop."

"Good question. Maybe it still needs to be picked up."

"Who's supposed to pick it up?"

"That's not for me to know, but I will say this: sometimes God chooses the least likely of us to do his work. That way when the task is done, we know it was His strength and not our own that allowed us to carry through."

"How will this person know? What if they don't figure it out? What if Paul and Sarah died in vain? And my sister? And Alex, too? What if they all died in vain?"

"The only advice I can give you is this: find the Truth, Rae. Dig deep and pull it out."

The finality of his statement assured me that our conversation was over. Besides, so many thoughts were flying around in my mind that I needed some alone time to sort through them. Unbelievable. I got up from the sofa and started toward the door.

"Rae, there's something I think you should know." He exhaled in a way that made me think he wasn't sure where to start.

"I knew Paul, Alex's father Paul. I have told you this. He was a good friend. And with all of that said, I first met Alex Loving on the day he was born. I'm his godfather."

When I had considered going into the church, I was only thinking about my safety. I was reminded of what my conscience had tried to tell me.

Perhaps the danger isn't in the action but the lie.

My conscience had been right. My actions hadn't resulted in bodily harm. But the lie... it had opened up another can of worms. From the very beginning, this had been about me. It no longer was. Alex had a godfather. He had a link to his life before. Alex craved his past. He craved all of the things that he was never allowed to have. He craved family, and Pastor Joe was the closest thing to family that Alex had on this earth. There was more to Pastor Joe than met the eye, and I was sure that he would be a wealth of information. He knew things about the night of September 13th. I just knew he had some of the answers we were looking for. But there was no way I could tell Alex about his godfather. It would be too risky. And yet I knew it would mean the world to him if I did. I was stuck between a rock and a hard place. I wanted to make Alex happy, but at what cost? Was it worth losing him? Absolutely not! With a little persistence, I convinced Pastor Joe to give me time to prepare Alex for their meeting, and I desperately needed this time to figure out what I was going to do.

CHAPTER SEVENTEEN

"*Of* all days, why would you bring me here? I told you I never wanted to come back. Are you trying to rub salt in my wounds?" I asked. "I vividly remember telling you I never wanted to see this place again."

I had planned to lie in bed all day and numb the pain by reading but instead, I found myself sitting on the bluff with my legs dangling over the edge, cursing Alex and looking down upon the place where, nineteen years ago, my sister had lost her life.

"Give me a little bit of credit, Rae. I made a promise to myself a long time ago that if I ever made it to earth, I would see to it that you never have another horrible birthday. I made last year fun, didn't I?"

I remembered my eighteenth birthday well. Alex took me to the Philbrook Museum of Art. He had taken my mind off Laney, and it was the first birthday in years that I had not dwelt on her death. This year he seemed to be taking the opposite approach.

"For your information, this is not fun. This is just about the worst thing that anyone has ever done to me."

"I have to disagree. I respect your parents and have grown to love them as my own, but they were wrong when they kept this a secret. They were wrong when they allowed you to think that any of this was your fault."

"You're my boyfriend. You should want to take my pain away. Have you forgotten that my sister died here?"

"No, I haven't. But you seem to have forgotten that I did, too."

"Why are you doing this to me?" I shrieked. I fell back onto the grass and let a breath escape me. I felt too weak to argue. My birthday had never been a pleasant experience but this year, I felt more anxious and guilt ridden than ever before. "You're mean; you know that, right?"

"No. I'm not," he told me without expression.

I scowled and closed my eyes.

"So what's wrong this morning? Is it the usual birthday blues? To me it seems like something more."

Alex was right. There was something more. For starters, I was almost positive that today was the day I would die. And after everything Alex had done to save me, how could I tell him I was ready? How could I tell him I would rather die than spend another day being hunted by Benard Bodin? It wasn't the fight that was wearing me thin; it was the waiting. Even during my happiest moments, thoughts of Chloe and Ben hovered over me like a heavy cloud. And then there was Pastor Joe. For a solid week, I had managed to keep Alex's godfather from him. I could hardly stand to look at myself in the mirror, much less look Alex in the eye. I was deceitful, and I deserved anything that came my way. On top of everything else, I was tired. Physically tired. Emotionally tired. Tired of fighting. Tired of searching for reason. Tired of looking for answers. Tired of being me. And while all of these concerns were valid, they were only a couple pieces of the pie. How could I tell Alex that the real reason for my horrible behavior stemmed from the realization that Scarlett O'Hara and I were exactly alike?

For the past several months, I had grown to hate Scarlett. She was cruel. She lied. She kept secrets. She wanted things that were not hers and was willing to use any means to get them. And then, at two o'clock this morning, I came across a passage that stopped my eyes in their tracks. It left me feeling restless… uneasy. Scarlett had just killed a Yankee soldier. And although it was in self-defense, a shell formed around her heart soon after and it began to thicken over time. I couldn't believe the luck I had reading this passage on my birthday of all days. Reading was the one thing that I could do to escape from reality, and now this book was bringing me back. So odd that Scarlett, like me, would have a shell around her heart to keep it from breaking into tiny pieces. I often wondered what it was that caused my heart to harden. I could blame it on a slew of misfortunes: the lack of friends, the lack of consistency, the lack of personal beauty, or any other thing that stood in the way of my happiness. But deep down, I knew the reason why. Like Scarlett, it was the loss of a life that caused the shell to form. It wasn't with misgivings that I had begun to construct the shell; I had taken pleasure in the process.

After a moment, I opened my eyes and motioned to my bag lying on the grass beside me. Just as I expected, Alex hesitated before he peeked inside. He reached in and pulled out my copy of *Gone with the Wind*. He looked puzzled, so when finally he met my gaze, I nodded for him to continue. It seemed that my simple gesture was the only affirmation he needed and, without further delay, he opened the book to where it was marked: page 455. I had successfully piqued his curiosity, and I was thankful that his attention was now on the book instead of me. He studied the page for a moment and then began to read. His lips moved in silence while his finger skimmed the words. Halfway down the page, he stopped. He had found something of interest. He silently re-read the sentence over and over until finally, a look of understanding spread across his face.

"Ah. I see. 'I've done murder and so I can surely do this.'" Alex rubbed his whiskery chin and began to recite the next sentence in a very sugary southern accent.

"'She had changed more than she knew and the shell of hardness which had begun to form about her heart when she lay in the slave garden at Twelve Oaks was slowly thickening.'"

The southern accent began to fade near the end of the sentence and in its place was a voice heavy with concern.

"You know you're nothing like her. You're nothing at all like Scarlett O'Hara."

"Oh, yes I am," I choked back a sob. My jaw began to quiver and tears were welling up in my eyes.

"Scarlett killed a man, Rae. She pulled the trigger."

"Does it matter how you do it if you get the same result?"

"Yes, I think it does. I think it's the heart that matters most."

"I'm much worse than Scarlett. She killed a man in self-defense. I killed my very own sister... my flesh and blood. My heart deserves to be hard, much, much harder than hers."

"How could you have caused your sister's death when you were still in your mother's womb?"

"I don't know exactly how or why, but it was my birth that caused her death, and I know that for certain."

"You're hard on yourself. You think your mother blames you, but she doesn't."

"You haven't seen the look on her face when I open my birthday presents."

"You forget that I have."

"Not with my eyes, you haven't." With my arm, I covered my face to hide the tears.

"I think there is only one problem, and it lies within the eye of the beholder."

"You can't know how I felt opening gifts on my birthday. It was almost cruel that they even made me do it."

"Some might say that it would be cruel if they did not."

"How could I have been delighted about a gift when I knew that they were thinking about her? How can I be happy in their sadness, especially when I was the cause? But on the other hand, to show no excitement over the gifts they gave would make me look ungrateful. I tell you, I couldn't win."

"You're just like your parents in many ways. But you're also very different. You only see the bad while your parents see the good. They celebrate the living, instead of dwelling on the dead."

"I didn't know you could also read minds from the halfway," I said with more sarcasm than I had intended. "I guess you left that part out."

Alex's voice was now more cool than condescending. "From where I was sitting, I didn't have to read minds. She doted on you and so did your father."

"Name one time," I challenged him, knowing full well that he could produce.

"Do you remember that day in Prague when you walked home from school by yourself?"

I nodded silently. I did remember. It was a fall day, and I was twelve years old. I was angry with my parents because they treated me like a baby. They kept me inside a bubble. They sheltered me. They never let me see the world. I told my parents that, because of them, I didn't fit in with others. That day I took matters into my own hands. I was going to walk home from school by myself whether they liked it or not. And so, after the dismissal bell rang, while my mother waited for me in front of the school's entrance, I hid myself in the shadow of Jan Jorgenson and slipped past my mother without her noticing. I remember getting lost. I remember how I wasn't reunited with my parents until ten o'clock that night. But I will never forget my punishment for disobeying.

"What you couldn't see was your mother's panic as she searched for you and her pain when she thought you were gone. What you couldn't see was your father crying over having to punish you when all he really wanted to do was give you a hug."

I swallowed hard. I didn't know what to think. I had never considered how my parents might have felt, and I wasn't really sure that I was ready to consider it now. I shrugged him off. "Name another."

"What's the real problem, Rae?" Alex sighed.

The real problem was that I loathed Scarlett O'Hara, only to realize that we were exactly alike. Did I hate myself? Was that it? Tears were rolling down my cheeks at a rate so steady, I was no longer attempting to wipe them away. How could I tell Alex how I felt? And even worse would be to tell him the reasons why. Like Scarlett, I was keeping secrets, and just like Scarlett, I was a master manipulator. I hated myself because I was a liar, and because I was too weak to say it aloud. I had been sneaking around behind his back, and my tracks were still fresh. Alex had a godfather that I so wanted to tell him about but couldn't. But what I hated more than anything else was that there were some nights when I was almost willing to lose the man I loved for a peek inside the little brown book. It was a temptation that I struggled daily to resist, and I was disgusted with myself for being tempted when I knew the stakes. How could I tell him that?

"You know, Scarlett's not all that bad. In fact, I kind of like Scarlett." Alex now sounded somewhat sympathetic.

"She's a terrible person."

"Are you still referring to how she killed a man?"

"No. I'm talking about the kind of person that she is, and I'm talking about Melanie Wilkes. There are saint-like people in this world, people like Melanie Wilkes, and no matter how hard I try, I will never be one of them. My mom is like Melanie. Everything she does is kind and right and good. I'm just like Scarlett. Everything I touch just falls apart."

"I can't say that I know what you mean."

"Everyone I love always ends up in pain. I used to think my family was cursed, but now I know it's me."

"It's just a book," Alex said with finality. He moved my arm away from my eyes and wiped the tears away. "It was easy for Melanie Wilkes to lie back in her sick bed and be gentle and kind," Alex said, pulling me from the ground so that I was now sitting comfortably beside him. "She was about to die and Scarlett was the only one left to take care of her. Of course, Scarlett was a bit hard. She had to be. She was the only one fighting to save the lives of the ones she loved. She took all of that upon herself. She took on the weight of the world and the weight of the war. She did exactly what she had to do." Alex laughed and then turned serious again. "Remind me to never let you read *The Bad Seed*."

"I already have, and that's not funny."

Alex put his arm around my waist and squeezed me tight. "I'll quit laughing if, for just today, you will put Scarlett O'Hara out of your mind."

"You know that Scarlett and I are the exact same age?"

"The book was written in 1949. Scarlett has waited this long to meet you. I think that she can wait another day."

"Did you really read the whole book?"

"Yes. And no, I'm not going to tell you how it ends."

"But it's my birthday. You could give me just one hint."

"Sorry. I'm already giving you something else," he whispered into my ear and then kissed me lightly on the cheek. "But not until later tonight."

"So now what?" I asked smartly.

"Well, I didn't bring you here to discuss the character traits of Scarlett O'Hara. I know it's painful, but I was really hoping that bringing you here on your birthday might start the healing process."

"And where did you get that horrible piece of advice?"

"I Googled it," he mumbled.

"Seriously," I scoffed. "My emotional wellbeing is now in the hands of Google? Is that what you're trying to tell me?"

"It's a start."

"I don't know a lot about healing, but I do know this: it is supposed to make you feel better… and this hurts."

"Just give it a try… if you won't do it for yourself then do it for me."

"Fine. Tell me what I'm supposed to be doing?"

"Try closing your eyes," Alex offered.

"Okay, they're closed."

"Now feel."

"Feel what? Pain?" My eyes snapped open immediately, and I gave Alex a sharp look. "I'll tell you what I feel. I feel like I'm sitting here with my parents, not my boyfriend. I don't understand why everyone wants to psychoanalyze me. First my parents and now you. It's understandable coming from my mom and dad… that's their profession. They can't help themselves."

"They don't like seeing you sad and miserable, and neither do I."

"I was miserable when you came into my life. I was broken when you found me. Did you ever think that I might want to stay that way? You don't have to fix everything, Alex."

"Just let me try. That's all I'm asking."

Defeated, I looked into Alex's eyes, trying my hardest to be compliant.

"Like I've said before, the way you see the world is a little skewed. Try closing your eyes and using your other senses."

"This is ridiculous."

"Just give it a try."

"You're being mean," I informed him.

Just before I shut my eyes, I took in my surroundings; my foul mood had prevented me from noticing the beautiful weather. The rain that had been pounding hard for a solid week and a half had finally let up, and now the sun was shining though scattered clouds. There was a slight chill in the air. I pulled my jacket around my body and did as Alex instructed: I closed my eyes and felt. I felt the breeze blow across my body, and I wondered if it was chilly on the day they died. It had been raining, so I imagined that it was. Then I remembered the picture of my parents and Laney standing in front of the lake. They were wearing short-sleeved shirts and the sun was sparkling on the water. Just like the weather, their lives had been bright and sunny just before the storm. I listened to the birds chirping. I could hear the lake softly crashing onto the shore. Someone nearby had started a fire.

With eyes closed, I couldn't see the smoke, but I could smell it. Blindly, my fingers reached for the cool blades of grass beside me. As I was feeling, it occurred to me that everything in my presence was full of life. The accident had not stopped the world from turning. It had not stopped the rest of the world from going about their day. I was the only one still frozen in the past. My fingers moved up and down the blades for a moment, and then I felt Alex take my hand in his. In the cool green blades, I found a bit of hope, but in Alex's hands I found something more.

When finally I opened my eyes, I realized that Alex hadn't had his shut at all. While I had been 'feeling', he had been rummaging through his backpack and now he sat with a bouquet of flowers resting in his lap. I knew that they were not for me.

The car ride home was quiet. I didn't want to talk because I was still 'feeling'. The windows were down and cool air was nipping at my cheeks and whipping through my hair. My senses were finally awake and what

I wanted most from life was to live it to the fullest. In a few short hours, I had regained a bit of strength. And even though I was still crippled with guilt, I was now strong enough to spend the rest of the day with Alex. I was strong enough to unwrap my birthday present and enjoy the spaghetti dinner he was getting ready to prepare. A tiny weight had been lifted from my shoulders, and I felt like I was flying... soaring. There was energy inside me that I had never felt before. Alex hit the nail on the head when he took me to *the bluff*. I needed healing, and now that I was feeling better, it was much easier to admit that he was right.

It was nearly four o'clock when we pulled into the driveway of the cottage and the sound of gravel crunching under the tires was comforting; it reminded me that I was home. One of the things I loved most about the cottage was that it never changed. It was the same today as it was yesterday and as it was twenty years before that. But this afternoon something was off, and yet, I couldn't put my finger on it. Alex pulled beneath the old oak tree that shaded our lawn, and I began to take in my surroundings. The flowers that Alex planted on our first day in Minnesota were still in bloom but beginning to wither. The hummingbird feeder was filled with sugary red syrup and tiny winged creatures were still flocking to it. Wood was stacked up against the side of the house, just as it always was. The shutters were still red, and the house was still white. Just when I was beginning to think that all this healing had not only changed the way I felt, but also the way I perceived the things around me, I noticed the small object on the front porch that was skewing my visual perception. The implications of this small brown package were huge. Alex, too, noticed the box; however, while I was staring out the window, bug-eyed, he was more discreet. With a quiet ease, he shifted the car into park, then placed his hand upon my knee.

"What does this mean?" I asked.

Just moments ago, I was feeling lighthearted. Now my chest felt cramped. The weight had returned to my shoulders, but it felt heavier now than before.

"I'll get the groceries," Alex offered. "Why don't you go take a look?"

I agreed with a simple nod and opened the car door. I took slow and careful steps toward the porch and came to a stop several yards away from the package. I could read the label with ease from where I was standing. I was still staring at the box when Alex approached me from behind; I could hear the rustling of a paper grocery sack coupled with his footsteps.

"It's addressed to you," he said. He stood beside me, massaging his stubble while studying the box.

"I can see that," I said with sarcasm. The label was unique. It was solid white and my name was spelled out with black marker in the middle.

"There's no address. No return address. No delivery address."

"I see that, too," I said through clinched teeth.

"It's from Big Bend Collectables."

"Thanks for clearing that up, Alex," I snapped.

"Are you going to open it?" he asked, still smoothing his facial hair with the tips of his fingers.

"I haven't decided."

Alex stopped smoothing and stared at me. He shook his head in disbelief and then, without another word, he picked up the box with his free hand and took it inside. I stood on the steps for a moment pondering the meaning of the package. There could be so many different things inside the box, but I was more concerned with the fact that it was on my front porch. It was official: someone knew where I was. The game was over and our fairytale had come to an end.

I sat at the kitchen table while Alex cooked. I drummed my fingers on the box and studied the label. Big Bend Collectables. I checked for postage. It was shipped priority. It gave a tracking number, but the label didn't indicate where the package was shipped from. I was still drumming my fingers on the package when Alex brought dinner to the table. He pushed the box aside and sat down.

"You know that I'm going to make you open that, right?"

"You can't *make* me do anything," I told him, twirling the noodles with my fork.

Alex gave me a sharp look.

"If you don't open it, then I'm not going to give you your birthday present."

"Trying to bargain, are we?"

"Come on, Rae," Alex groaned. "The suspense is practically killing me."

"What do you care? It's not even addressed to you."

"Are you trying to tell me that you're not the least bit interested to find out what's inside?"

"It's intriguing." I scooped some of the meat sauce onto my cheese bread and took a bite.

"So what are you waiting for? Open it."

"But what if it explodes when I open it?" I pressed my ear to the box and listened. "It's ticking," I teased.

"The only thing ticking is the clock. You've been staring at that box for forty-five minutes. Open it." Alex handed me a knife.

I scowled, took a huge bite of spaghetti and, with reluctance, grabbed the knife from his hands. After making a slit in the tape, I lifted the lid.

"What is it?"

"Popcorn."

"Popcorn?" Alex questioned, unable to hide his disappointment.

"Packing popcorn."

"Okay… well… dig around in there and pull the present out," he commanded. The only time I recall seeing Alex this excited was when he was discussing Benard Bodin.

"I'm scared. What if it's something bad?"

"Oh, it's nothing bad. Stand back and let me do it."

Alex pulled the box toward him, reached inside, and pulled out two brown leather books with gold embossing across the front and on the spine.

"Books?"

"Very old books," Alex corrected.

"Hand them over," I demanded, and Alex obliged.

"Be careful with them. They're close to coming apart."

Delicately, I took the books from Alex and turned them so I could read the spines.

"*Uncle Tom's Cabin.* Volumes I and II. I didn't know there was more than one volume."

Carefully, I opened up volume one to the copyright page. The paper was brittle and browning with age.

"1852," I said. "Do you think this is a first edition?"

"By the looks of it, it very well could be."

"Have you read this book before?"

"Yes."

"It's about slavery, right?"

"Yeah. Supposedly, the release of this book was the fuel the fire needed to begin the Civil War."

I turned to the next page and began to read out loud. "*Uncle Tom's Cabin or Life Among the Lowly,* by Harriet Beecher Stowe."

I ran my hand across the page and felt something hard beneath my fingers. With care, I held the spine of the book and delicately shook until a small white envelope fell out. Alex and I looked up from the envelope and into each other's eyes. I knew we were thinking the exact same thing. I pulled the card out of the envelope and began to read:

> Dear Rae,
> Happy Birthday. I hope that you are enjoying your time in Minnesota. We at A-Omega know how much you love to read, and we are excited for you to read this book. As you can see, these books are old and are of value, but the real value isn't in the physical nature of the book, but in the words and in their meaning. We are interested to know what you think, and we hope that it will be an enjoyable read. Have a happy birthday, Sunshine. We will be contacting you soon.
>
> Arm Yourself Well,
> A-Omega
> Ephesians 6: 10-18

"What do you know about this?" I asked.

"Nothing. I promise. I swear."

"Well, they know where we are. Do you think they'll tell my parents that we're here?"

"If they were going to do it, they would have already done it by now."

"You're right." I smiled at Alex and pushed the box to the far end of the table. "I'm ready to open my present. A deal's a deal."

"Don't you want to wait until after dinner?"

"I'm done," I said, taking the last bite of my spaghetti and wiping my mouth with a paper napkin.

Alex's hand moved behind the table and when it reappeared, he was holding an unwrapped piece of poster board.

"It's not much. But I worked hard on it."

Just looking at the piece of poster board was enough to bring tears to my eyes. The back was blank, but when I flipped it over, it was covered with pictures of us during the past year of my life.

"It's a birthday collage," I gasped.

"I thought you might like it."

Alex grabbed my empty plate and carried it over to the counter. He began to clean the dishes, and I began to reminisce. My mother was the one who came up with the idea of pasting a years worth of pictures onto a small piece of poster board. She kept it small, so I wouldn't have to leave it behind when we moved. Not only was it the birthday gift that I could count on, but it was also the one I loved best. She took pleasure in collecting mementos throughout the year, and she took pride in arranging them on a small piece of cardboard that she referred to as my birthday collage. It bothered me that I was not with my parents on my birthday. But this gift from Alex made them feel so close. I began to think about the gift from A-Omega. The sender was Big Bend Collectables, but there was no return address. The letter inside side was from A-Omega. My parents worked for A-Omega, or at least they had in the past. Even though they both had new jobs, they were always there for A-Omega. Or perhaps more importantly, A-Omega was always there for them. It seemed that they had given their lives over to this.... this.... I don't know what. Was organization the right word? No, it seemed bigger than that. Corporation? No, that didn't feel right either. My biggest problem right now was that A-Omega knew my location, and I was terrified they would tell my parents where I was.

"You can't know how much this means to me."

Alex was still standing with his back toward me, but he was no longer cleaning dishes.

"You forget that I do."

"Alex."

"What."

"The box was from Big Bend Collectables. But the letter inside was from A-Omega. Why?"

"I haven't the foggiest."

"Don't you think it's a little strange?"

"A little. I'm sure there's some sort of explanation."

"I'm sure you're right." I tilted my head and studied Alex. "You're being awfully sneaky over there. What are you doing?"

In response to my question, Alex turned around and flicked off the kitchen light. All at once I could see the candles glow.

"A birthday cake? For me?"

"It's not a proper birthday without a cake," he said holding the petite cake steady and making his way toward me.

"How did you manage to squeeze nineteen candles on top?"

"You so quickly forget that I have supernatural abilities."

Alex set the cake on the table, the candles bathing his face in a yellow pool of light. "Make a wish," he whispered, sliding the plate toward me.

I was in awe. I stared at him with my mouth slightly agape. Sitting aglow in the darkness, Alex looked like an angel, but it was what poured out of his heart that made him so good. There was no expression for how I was feeling right now, so I closed my eyes, made a wish, and blew my candles out.

What does it mean that beauty can exist in a place that was once so filled with tragedy? That the sun can shine in a place of darkness? That a flower can grow out of soil that is stained with death? Is it God's way of promising that everything is going to be okay?

"God, are you there?" I whispered softly. "*The bluff* was beautiful today. Is this your way of easing my pain and offering a bit of hope?"

The spot on the hill was pure beauty, and when I looked over the side, I didn't see a deep pit of darkness or an angry, raging sea. Instead I saw hope, the first inkling of hope that I had seen in quite some time. Maybe life would end happily ever after, after all.

CHAPTER EIGHTEEN

*M*y birthday had gone perfectly, and I had several things to be thankful for. First and foremost, I hadn't heard from Chloe and Ben. Second, I had a first edition of *Uncle Tom's Cabin* in hand, and I couldn't deny that I was intrigued by the method in which it arrived. There was also the birthday collage. Alex always thought of everything, and I was thankful that I had the best boyfriend in the universe. And last but not least, I think I was finally beginning to heal. The time we spent on *the bluff* might have been the perfect medicine. I knew I wasn't quite there, but I was on my way.

So, the next morning when I woke up on the sofa beside Alex, when I found myself lying in his arms, I closed my eyes and tried to relish the moment. My birthday wish had just come true, and I was expecting to feel satisfied... at ease... fulfilled; instead, all I felt was guilt. He was bending over backwards to make me happy. In return, I was keeping secrets, and it was my latest secret that bothered me the most. I had followed the black sedan and by doing so, had found Alex's godfather. After my conversation with him, how could I keep it a secret? Pastor Joe was a wealth of information, and I realized right away that I would have to keep him the biggest secret of all. I was having trouble justifying my actions. I was having a hard time shaking the guilt. So, in order to clear my conscience, I decided I was going to have to tell him something.

With Alex still asleep beside me, I weighed my options. I wasn't going to tell him about the journal. I hadn't even looked at it myself, and I wasn't ready to either. And even though the conversation that took place during the fish fry had sparked my interest, and even though I was anxious to know more about the strange woman that had stayed at the Loving cottage, I wasn't about to let him in on that. There was a chance that Alex might see Mrs. Harvey as an important source of information and the last thing I needed was for him to start hanging out at the Harvey's house with Corrine and Candy. The scrapbook was the only reasonable option. Of course, it wasn't going to be pleasant when he discovered the letters that were tucked inside the book. He would be angry with me for not showing him sooner. But I thought I probably deserved it. I could handle him being angry. What I couldn't handle was the idea of him leaving for good. I had looked at the scrapbook over and over again. I had yet to find anything significant, and I wasn't any closer to discovering the truth by looking at the pictures inside. I doubted that Alex would make anything of it either. It was the perfect offering. I could clear my conscience while making him happy and the risk was slim to none.

At nine o'clock, Alex was still asleep. I had been watching him for nearly an hour and, as much as I would like to lie perfectly still and watch him for another, I decided to wake him up and share the news.

I kissed him on the cheek.

"Good morning," I cooed.

"Why are you always watching me sleep?" Alex groaned. "It's creepy." Alex seemed a bit cranky. He ruffled his hair with his hand and rubbed his eyes.

"It's not creepy. I like the way you look when you sleep. You look more like an angel than ever."

"You should take a picture. It will last longer."

"That's kind of why I woke you." Alex raised his eyebrows in surprise. "I want to talk to you about pictures. More specifically, the pictures in my nana's scrapbook."

Alex rubbed his eyes one last time and then sat up with attention.

"My papa told me that a picture has the ability to tell you something that words cannot. I've been thinking that maybe he's right. I can't find anything inside the book to help us, but you might be able to…. that is… if you want to."

"You've got to be joking. I've been ready for months." Alex was now all smiles.

"Well, it's in my bag at the foot of the bed if you want to go get it."

Without another word, Alex jumped off the sofa and disappeared inside my bedroom. I patted the cushion and Cocoa jumped up beside me.

"You'll never leave me, will you girl?" I whispered in her ear and scratched her head. Cocoa licked her chops and rolled onto her back so I could scratch her belly.

"I found it," I heard Alex shout from the bedroom.

I took in a deep breath and held it. There was a chance that Alex might discover something that would change our lives forever.

"So, a picture's worth a thousand words," Alex stated when he walked back into the living room.

"Huh?"

"What your papa said. I think he's right. I think we're going to find something in here that will help us out. I know you've looked at the scrapbook… on more than one occasion, I'm sure. But I just keep thinking that I might find something you've overlooked."

I exhaled. "Maybe you're right," I sighed.

Alex flipped open the cover and we studied the first page. It was a picture of my nana and papa on their wedding day. It was the day her new life began.

"Your nana looks sad," Alex observed.

I hadn't noticed it before, but Alex was right. I flipped to the next page and saw a picture of my nana holding my newborn mother. My Aunt Eva was sitting on the hospital bed beside Nana touching the top of her brand new sister's head. Nana's expression was different in this picture. She looked full of life, and so happy. I wondered why there weren't any baby pictures of Eva. At least five years had passed between picture number one and picture number two. I wondered what had happened in between.

What had happened during those five undocumented years? I sighed because I would never know, and then I flipped to the middle of the book, to the page I loved most.

"Turn it back," Alex whined. "I want to see the whole thing."

"In a minute. I want to show you my favorite page."

At the top of the page was a picture of my mom, dad, and sister, Laney. Below the picture Nana had written, "Sue, Will, and Laney. September 13th, 1990. Alexandria, Minnesota. I chilled when I saw the date. I had viewed this page countless times and the effect it had on me never changed. There was something ominous about this picture, but I couldn't put my finger on it.

"Your mom and dad look so young."

"That's because they were. This picture was taken when my mom was pregnant with me, nineteen years ago."

A peculiar look formed on Alex's face as he studied the picture. He ran his finger across the glossy finish. After a moment, he shrugged.

"What's this?" He pointed to the envelope at the top of the page. I hadn't forgotten about the envelope, but now I was having second thoughts about letting him read the two, very short letters that were inside. Without waiting for me to answer, Alex pulled out both letters, unfolded the first one, and he began to read aloud.

September 10
Mom,

Sometimes I wonder how you and Daddy did it for so long. I love what I do and I owe that to you and Daddy, but I have never been one to patiently wait. One step at a time has never suited me and yet, I have a career that requires me to do just that. For the past five months, Will, Laney, and I have had the luxury of a much-needed sabbatical. As you know, we were in the process of preparing for our upcoming assignment in January. But that is what I have written to tell you. We have received correspondence from A-Omega that the date for the assignment has been moved up. We will be leaving tomorrow. I am scared. All of this is just coming so fast. I wish that I could have your faith right now because I cannot see how any of this will work out. I have never had such a bad feeling in my entire life. I am sorry to say that, even though you and Daddy are still actively involved in A-Omega, I cannot disclose the location of our assignment. You have every right to know and I am very sorry. You have been waiting for this moment just as long as I have. I do not know how long we will be gone and I'm afraid that our only correspondence will be by mail. I will write often and keep you as informed as I possibly can, but A-Omega has made it clear that the details of this assignment are confidential. The mission depends on it. I love you. Tell Daddy I love him, too.

Sue

Alex said nothing for a moment. He stared at the letter while running his hand through his tangled, chocolate locks.

"What do you think?"

"I think your mom sounds scared. I think she sounds strong but worried."

"She said she had a bad feeling. Do you think it could have been a sixth sense?"

"Of course," Alex returned at once.

"She was right, you know. She should have listened to her gut. If she had listened to her gut, nobody would have died."

"You don't know that." Alex refolded the letter and quickly unfolded the next.

Alex read the salutation: *"Dear Charlie and Irene Roth,"* he whispered, and I began to panic. This letter was all about the night he died. Ever since that day in the cemetery, the day when I stumbled upon his grave, he had spoken openly with me about his death. But this time it was different. He was no longer the storyteller, he was being told. For the first time, he was hearing details about the accident from someone else's point of view. The house grew quiet. I swallowed the lump that had formed in my throat. Because of the content, I was relieved when Alex began to read the letter silently to himself.

I had read the letters over and over so many times that I had memorized them word for word and by observing where Alex's eyes fell on the page, I was able to determine the portion of the letter he was reading; the expression on his face told me exactly what was going through his mind. His eyes moved smoothly from the salutation to the body of the letter. He was reading about the car crash and Laney's death. His expression was concerned but not surprised. A quarter of the way down the page; he was reading about the scar on my mother's arm. Several lines down from that: he was silently reading about the number of fatalities. There were ten people involved in the accident, but only three survived. Alex had died and so had his parents, but the letter didn't directly mention their names. I wondered how that made him feel. My mom and dad had survived the crash, and I was survivor number three, but my name had been omitted as well. His face relaxed a bit and then he began to read the next line, the line about the package and how, despite its tattered condition, my parents had been assigned to protect it. I observed Alex. No longer smooth in movement, his eyes jumped backward on the page, rereading the sentence several times over. His brow furrowed as he traced the words with his finger.

"What is it?" I asked. There was a momentary pause before Alex spoke.

"A package?"

I said nothing in return. Alex continued to study the letter. The pause was greater this time. It seemed as though several minutes passed before Alex spoke again and, when he did, he reread the last paragraph of the letter aloud.

The package entrusted to Sue and Will was beyond repair, but the contents of the package were saved and, despite the gravest of circumstances, the objective of the mission was carried out. Sue and Will are under strict orders to remain silent about the assignment

and their present location; however, we at A-Omega
will keep you well informed.
We thank you for your patronage and your faith. You
will be greatly rewarded.

Arm yourself well,
A-Omega
Ephesians 6: 10-18

"It's nothing that I didn't already know." I could tell that Alex was a
bit shaken, but also that he was trying his best to shrug it off. "Except the
package. I guess I didn't know about that."

"I was really hoping that you would." I hadn't realized I was holding
my breath and when I spoke, the pressure that had been building up inside
me was finally released. "That's the part I can't figure out."

Alex folded the piece of paper and returned both letters to the envelope
from which they originated. Still, he didn't say a word. He began to
massage the side of his head with the tips of his fingers.

"Are you still thinking about the letter?"

"No. I'm thinking about the picture."

I studied the picture in the center of the page. I loved the picture of
my mom, my dad, and Laney. It was the only picture I had of the three of
them together. When I first saw it, it made me feel warm and fuzzy, but
after I read the letters, those feelings were replaced with something more
foreboding.

"There's something about this picture that seems a little off," Alex said.

"Tell me what you see." Once again, I found myself holding my
breath, waiting for my world to change.

Alex looked at the picture again. He turned his head sideways and
studied it from a different angle.

"I don't know. Something doesn't seem quite right, but I can't put my
finger on it."

"I know what you mean." I paused. "So do you think the package
might be here?"

"What would give you that idea?"

I sighed and closed my eyes. For some reason, the thought of showing him the letter in the back of the book made my chest feel hollow... empty. "What?"

"I have another letter that you need to see." The words flew from my mouth before I had the chance to change my mind. I flipped to the back of the book and pulled out the letter that was pressed between the pages. After a bit of hesitation, I began to read.

Dear Mr. and Mrs. Colbert,

On the 23rd day of June, A-Omega received intelligence that a certain package thought to be safe is now in jeopardy. For the past couple of months, we have been attempting to eliminate any problems that might hinder the delivery of said package into your hands. Under optimal circumstances, this package would have been delivered for your safe keeping at a later date, just as we had previously discussed. We can no longer wait. The risks are much too high as we have already learned. We feel that the package would be safer in a more remote location and have confidence that you will do everything in your power to protect it. We at A-Omega cannot emphasize how important it is that we get this package to safety. As physicians, you are well aware that there will be some care involved. The package will be in grave condition when it arrives, but not beyond repair. However, we must inform you that the requirements for this mission may exceed your level of expertise.

The arrangements for delivery will be simple. Your family will be arriving into the Minneapolis/St. Paul International airport at 6:15 PM on the evening of September 12th. As we at A-Omega have already informed you, this should be a very simple operation, but in the case that complications should arise, we will have arranged for a contact to meet you at the airport.

> Your contacts will be Paul and Sarah Loving. They will
> be equipped in areas that you are not. Transportation
> will be prearranged and a vehicle will be ready for
> pick up at the transit center in terminal 1-Lindbergh
> between concourse C and G. You are to follow your
> contact to...

Midway through the letter, I felt Alex heating up beside me. So it was no surprise when he interrupted me before I had even finished.

"I can't believe that you didn't tell me about this." He sounded both hurt and angry.

"I assumed that you knew and that *you* were the one who was keeping the secret."

"What would make you think that?"

"You were here when it happened. Are you telling me that you don't remember meeting my mom and dad? Laney?"

"No, I don't remember. I was only two."

"You remember sitting on the kitchen floor playing with toy cars just ten minutes before you died, but you don't remember my parents? I find that hard to believe."

"I remember some things. But I don't remember this."

"Fine," I said, exasperated. "Why is this letter any different than the others? You weren't mad when you read the other letters."

"I wasn't surprised by the other letters. There was no information in them that I didn't already know. I knew about your parents' assignment. All of this I knew. I just didn't know that *my* parents were involved. I had no idea our parents knew each other. All of this time, I thought that some cosmic force put our parents on the same road that night. I guess it wasn't like that at all."

"Cosmic? What does cosmic have to do with any of this? Why does cosmic matter?"

"It matters. It changes everything."

"Why?"

"It's stupid, and I don't want to say it out loud."

"Just say it."

"Fine," he responded with haste. I was surprised that no further coaxing was needed. Normally, getting answers out of Alex was like pulling teeth. He was obviously taking the promise we made to each other very seriously.

"I realize that the accident was an absolute tragedy. But in general, I believe that all things work together for the greater good."

"Is that so?" I smirked.

"Let me finish before I change my mind. I have stayed up many nights wondering what little bit of good came from that crash. I have tried my hardest and still, I can only come up with one thing."

"I'm surprised that you were able to come up with anything at all."

"Are you going to let me finish or not?"

"Fine. Sorry."

"I just thought that, you know… being on the same road that night… meeting by chance on a lonely Minnesota highway… it all ended in tragedy… our souls passed each other by." He fell back onto the sofa and put a pillow over his face. "It reminded me of RommoanJulet," he mumbled.

"What? I can't hear you with that pillow on your face."

Alex groaned and tossed the pillow across the room. "Romeo and Juliet… all right! The whole thing reminds me of Romeo and Juliet."

I stifled a laugh. Very discretely, I covered my mouth with my fist and coughed.

"Star crossed lovers," he explained. "My body dying just as yours was waking."

"You are really turning lemons into lemonade."

"I told you it was stupid." Alex blushed.

"I'm sorry. It's not stupid. It's sweet… but there's only one flaw. I didn't stab myself with a dagger."

"You're right. You didn't even know that I had died. In fact, you didn't even know that I existed."

"It's still romantic, Alex. In a sick and twisted kind of way."

Alex shook his head but didn't say a word.

"Alex. Come on. It's not like our parents knew each other very well. They were assigned to work together. Look at it this way. Out of all the people in the entire world, your parents were assigned to work with mine. What are the chances of that?"

"You're right," he smiled. "Maybe we're cosmic after all. But it's still unsettling that I don't remember your parents being here, at my family cottage."

Alex began to study the picture. "I guess I now know why the picture struck me as odd. Your parents were standing in my yard. I'm not sure why I didn't realize that before." Alex got up, fetched something from the fireplace mantel, and returned to the sofa. He was holding a picture in his hand, the picture of the 'other' woman standing by the lake.

"I knew that this picture had to be a clue. I just didn't know what to do with it. Look at this picture."

"What about it?"

"Look at the chair in the background. There's a striped towel thrown over the back of the chair."

"So."

"Now look at the picture of your parents. The same towel is thrown over the back of that chair. These pictures were taken on the same day. Someone else was at the cottage with our parents. This is a big deal, Rae."

"So what about the package? Do you think it might still be in one of the three cottages? The letter did say that the contents of the package were safe."

"I suppose that it could be."

"What do you think it looks like?"

"I haven't the foggiest."

Alex thumbed through the book, then let it fall open to a page I had seen many times before. It was the picture of my mom and her sister Eva leaving for the prom. My mom was wearing a baby blue dress, and my Aunt Eva looked almost exotic in her tight fitting purple one.

Not belonging: a feeling that I frequently experienced.

I need only take one look at my mother and father to know we look nothing alike. There was hardly anything about our personalities that matched either. I often wondered if I really belonged to my mom and dad… if I belonged in the Colbert family at all. I remember the first time I saw this page, the first time I saw the picture of my Aunt Eva. It was on that day that everything made perfect sense. I looked like her. I did belong. My eyes were blue like my mother's eyes and like Eva's. But my eyes are almond shaped, and when I looked into Eva's eyes it was like looking into my own.

"She looks very familiar," he observed, his voice starting out strong but trailing.

"That's probably because we look exactly alike. Plus, I am just about the same age as she was in the picture."

"You have your aunt's eyes… and her hair," he said, studying the picture with care.

"I love this picture. If I'm having a bad day, I think about it, and it tends to make me feel a little better." I hesitated. "My mom hates it. I don't think she really liked her sister all that much."

"Why?"

"She never gave me any details. She just said something about my Aunt Eva being the black sheep of the family, and then my nana got mad and tried to make her take it back."

"Did she?"

"No. But then my nana said something about how my aunt had made some poor choices. She said that in the end she redeemed herself, or something like that."

"And that makes you feel better? To know there was something in your mother's past that you might not ever know."

"No, I guess it just makes me feel better that Eva screwed up. I feel like maybe I'm not all that bad. Living with two perfect parents hasn't been easy. Sometimes it was hard to measure up. At least I know there is hope for me. At least I know I can be redeemed."

CHAPTER NINETEEN

September 13th had passed without consequence, and now that fall was here, everything seemed to be going my way. The temperature had dropped into the low seventies and the leaves had just begun to change. The weather was perfect and things at the cottage had never been better. I had so many things to be thankful for. For starters, I was still alive and glad of it. I had yet to hear from Chloe and Ben, and I was beginning to think that all of the time I spent worrying about them had been in vain. My parents seemed to be on the mend as well. I had received a birthday email from my mother and the lack of any alarming news led me to believe that they were safe and, considering the circumstance in which I left them, that was about as much as I could hope for. I was also thankful that the black sedan was no longer a threat. It was a relief to scratch it off my list of worries. And even though it was probably wrong to keep Alex's godfather from him, I was right about one thing: showing him the scrapbook had lessened my guilt. But the icing on the cake came three weeks ago when I saw Mr. and Mrs. Harvey loading up the car. They were shipping Corrine off to college and for the first time in several months, I could finally breathe. Oh, how I love fall.

School had only just begun and as planned, I did all my work online. I had already perfected my daily routine: I rush through my homework, then paint. The best news came when I received an email from my art professor and, after reading over the instructions for my first project, I was pleased to discover that the painting I was currently working on would fit perfectly into the curriculum. Over the course of the semester, I was to finish a project that correlated with another subject I was taking. In addition to art history, I was taking botany and psychology. And because my piece was entitled My Evil Alter Ego, I felt it correlated perfectly with the latter of the three.

When I woke up this morning, the note on the kitchen table confirmed what I already knew: Alex had gone into town to run a few errands and wouldn't be back until later in the afternoon. He left a fire blazing in the hearth and a pot full of coffee in the kitchen. Not only was Alex the most attractive boyfriend in the universe, but he was the most thoughtful one, too. I grabbed a banana, laced up my shoes, and put Cocoa on her leash. I was ready to go. I zipped up my fleece and rubbed my hands together to warm them. Cocoa was eager to get out of the house, practically pulling me down the gravel drive until she reached the road. I passed Mr. Finnegan's house and found that, like always, he was standing in his front yard like a fixture. I wondered why he hated me so much, but on a day like today, I refused to dwell on grouchy neighbors. Instead, I tried to focus on something positive, like the fact that Corrine Harvey had just shipped off to college and was no longer available to ogle my boyfriend. Nearly all the weight had been lifted from my shoulders, and I felt like I was flying down the road.

But when Cocoa and I reached the bridge that separated L'Homme Dieu from Carlos, we just had to stop and stare. It was serene, even more so than it was during the summer; perhaps this was because there was not a single boat on the lake. There wasn't a single wave either. Not on either side of the bridge. I thought about the day Alex took me out in the boat trying to make me face my fear so I could overcome it. The drowning dreams had stopped, so I guess his effort wasn't futile. The water was rough that day, but today it was smooth and inviting. Still, I had no desire to submerge my body in it. With a sudden tug, Cocoa yanked me out of my reverie and began to pull me down the road. The weather was invigorating, and it pushed me even farther, made me run even harder, and I found myself halfway around the lake before I finally started for home. Forty-five minutes later, I was relieved to be nearing the cottage. The muscles in my legs were on fire, but my skin was covered in goose bumps. I wanted nothing more than to take a hot shower.

Still a quarter of a mile away, I could smell the smoke coming from our cottage. It was comforting. The smoke permeated the chilly fall air in a way that wasn't possible on a warm summer day. I pushed harder until I reached home. When my feet hit the gravel drive, I unhooked Cocoa from her leash and nearly collapsed. I hadn't realized how tired I was until I stopped. Cocoa was barking at the door. I hurried up the walkway to shush her. After Mr. Finnegan's warning, I was still a bit edgy. I knew his threats were not empty, and I knew that if I didn't make my dog obey, he *would* call the cops. In a bit of a rush to get Cocoa inside, I grabbed her collar and opened the cottage door. I was surprised when she pushed passed me and, instead of going straight to her water bowl, began to sniff around the house.

"What is it girl?"

Cocoa brushed up against my leg and whined.

I grabbed a bottle of water out of the fridge and started to shed my clothes in the kitchen, so I could more quickly hop into the shower. I took off my fleece and tossed it over a kitchen chair, then kicked my shoes into the corner. My socks and shorts went into the hamper, then I headed for the bathroom and jumped in the shower.

I stood under the hot water for several minutes and let it wash all the tension from my body. My hair was still a bit wet when I finally sat down in the chair behind my easel. Wearing only an oversized tee shirt and a pair of UGGS, I looked out the paned glass window onto the lake, taking in the peace and quiet, relishing my luck, and thinking about how my day had begun with such perfection. It was strange to look out the window and not see a single soul, not hear the sound of boats or children running through the lanes. Alexandria was a small town that was flooded with vacationers during the summer months but now that school had started, almost everyone was gone. The Harvey's were locals and lived on L'Homme Dieu year round. Mr. Finnegan was a local as well. And, of course Gretchen and her family too. But most of the other residents had already headed back to the city. The boats were off the lake and the cottages had been closed up for the winter. I looked at Cocoa. She had finally settled down and was curled up in a ball by the fireplace. I had never seen such a lazy dog.

I studied my canvas and the progress I had made so far. The face was almost complete: half Chloe, half me. Originally, I thought there would be plenty of contrast between the two halves, but other than the slight variance in eye color, it looked like I was painting a portrait of myself. I relaxed into the ladder-back chair I had pulled up in front of the easel and grabbed the manipulated photo so I could take a closer look. Besides the eyes, I tried to determine what it was that made us so very different. And then I tried to determine why it was that we looked so much alike. The eyes. They were the same. The cheekbones too, perhaps. My cheekbones were higher than Chloe's, but was it enough of a difference to make the painting pop? I thought a cup of coffee might help me see things in a different light. As I got up, I heard a faint noise. Trying to pinpoint the source of the sound, I slowly walked into the kitchen and saw where it was coming from: Alex's cassette player was sitting in the middle of the kitchen table and the red power button was on. An uneasy feeling began to grown in the pit of my stomach. Someone had come in the cottage while I was in the shower. I looked out the kitchen window. Alex's car was still gone and the feeling of unease began to build. I pushed stop on the cassette player, turning the music off, and the cottage grew quiet; everything looked in order.

I poured myself a cup of coffee to settle my nerves and reached in the refrigerator for the creamer. I added it and some sugar to my coffee and began to swirl the liquid around in my mug with a spoon. My mind was still on the cassette player, so it took a moment for me to realize what was sitting on the kitchen counter. Much like meeting someone on the first day of school and then seeing them at the grocery store later that night and not recognizing them, what I saw on the counter wasn't registering. I held my mug tightly, allowing the transfer of heat to warm my hands. I studied the object. It was green and black and small enough to fit in the palm of my hand… or on the loop of my belt. I gasped when I made the connection, and a moment later, my body went numb. I didn't feel the cup of coffee slip from my hands, but I saw it as it fell; the perfect mocha colored mixture inside my mug shot out in every direction when it crashed onto the floor. I was now standing in a warm puddle of coffee, but I was frozen as solid as ice. Slowly, I walked closer to the counter and saw that the object was holding down a single slip of paper. With a shaking hand, I pulled the piece of paper free and began to read.

I have returned something of yours. Now return what is rightfully mine. - C

With my hand still shaking like a leaf, I placed the note back on the counter and let my eyes fall on the walkie-talkie. My fingers brushed across the plastic and then, after careful consideration, I picked it up. I took myself back to the night when it had come unfastened from my belt loop when I fell down the stairs into Chloe's basement. Scrambling to escape, I hadn't tried to retrieve it. It never occurred to me that Chloe might find it lying on the floor. And furthermore, it had never occurred to me that if she had found it, she would realize it was mine and realize that I had been in her basement unannounced and uninvited, snooping through all of her belongings. Just moments ago, I had been so lighthearted, now I could barely breathe. I was scared to move. What if Chloe was still in the cottage?

I quickly weighed my options. I couldn't go into town because Alex had the car. I could take off on foot, but even though I was fast, I knew that I wouldn't get far. Besides, I was half naked and the last thing I wanted to do was draw attention to myself, or our situation. I could call 911. But then the police would be involved and that absolutely could not happen. Besides, what would I say? Would I tell them that I left the door unlocked while I was in the shower and someone had returned my walkie-talkie and turned on my tape player? That hardly seemed a criminal offense. There was one last option, and I didn't like it. I was going to have to be brave. I opened the kitchen drawer, searching for a suitable weapon, something I could use to defend myself. I rummaged through the drawer until I came across a small paring knife. Perfect. Chloe wanted something from me, and I needed to find out what it was. If she got it back, maybe she would leave us alone. Maybe I really could do all of this without Alex's help, and if I pulled it off, maybe he could stay.

The main cottage was only around 600 square feet, but I still spent almost an hour searching every nook and cranny for any sign of Chloe's presence. I checked behind the doors, inside the closet, and under the bed. Only when I realized the coast was clear did I begin to rack my brain for answers. I had been under the impression that Chloe Pierce wanted me dead. I tried to recall what I based this assumption on. My first impression of Chloe was that she hated me, so when her car tried to run me off the road, everything just seemed to fit. But I wasn't one hundred percent sure that Chloe was the one behind the wheel; the windows were so heavily tinted, I was unable to see inside her SUV.

Regardless, there was still the issue of the boxes in her basement. I couldn't forget about that. They were stacked up and labeled according to every school I had attended. Still, this only suggested that someone in the Pierce household was following me, tracking me perhaps, but not necessarily trying to kill me. The only one who had tried to do that was Ben. If Chloe wanted me dead, she could have hung out at the cabin and waited for me to return... but she didn't. She didn't take anything either. She just wrote a simple note, returned my walkie-talkie, and left. I began to wonder what it was that Chloe wanted. What could I possibly have of hers? I studied the cassette player on the coffee table. Why did she put it there?

I turned the power back on and let the tape rewind. I replayed the song I had heard earlier, but this time I listened to the words, wondering if she was trying to tell me something. Music came out of the speakers: a melancholy song about being the victim or the crime. I continued to listen to the lyrics. When the song was over, I was even more confused. I fell back onto the sofa and crossed my legs. The song made me think about the past: making mistakes and wanting to be forgiven. The past.

Maybe she wants something from the past. Or maybe there's something about her past that she doesn't want me to discover. But how would I find out about her past unless she told me? I had just begun to relax when something occurred to me: The *past* was in the little brown journal. Chloe's past was in my nightstand.

In an instant, I was off the sofa and in my room. I pulled out the drawer of my nightstand. The brown leather journal was right where I had left it. Chloe wanted her family history back. That had to be it. I smiled despite my shaking legs and trembling fingers. I had no intention of giving the journal back, and her wanting it made me want it even more. I didn't know if I could resist it any longer and the simple fact that Chloe did not want me to look inside made it more appealing. Curiosity was getting the better of me. I was no longer thinking about all the reasons why I should not open the book; instead, I was thinking about all the reasons I should. I twirled the twine between my fingers and then, very slowly, began to unwrap it. I closed my eyes and opened the cover. I lifted my lids and read the words in front of me.

The Dark and Unfortunate Life of Eva Pierce

I slammed the book shut and stuffed it into the drawer of my nightstand. I was gasping for air, sucking in tiny breaths. I was disappointed in myself for giving into temptation, and I was fearful of what my moment of weakness might cost me. I had been right. The words inside this book *would* haunt me. My mind was now clearer than ever. I no longer wanted to open the journal, and I promised myself that I would never look at it again.

CHAPTER TWENTY

A week had passed with no more notes from Chloe. I was hoping time had taken care of that problem but one morning, I woke to find another one in its place. Alex was at the kitchen table massaging his temples and studying a pile of bills stacked in front of him, a worried look on his face. I scooted in beside him and began to sift through our monthly statements. One from the electric company, one for water and trash, and one for gas which, over the summer, had been fairly insignificant since the fireplace had been sufficient for heating the cottage on a cool day. But winter was on its way, and the gas bill was rising more quickly than the temperature was dropping.

"I've only used the heater once," Alex sighed. "It will be a monster of a bill when we have to use it everyday." I looked at the bill and cringed.

"We could always just shut the heat off and snuggle. That's what people do when they're stranded after disasters like avalanches. They warm each other with their bodies."

Alex rolled his eyes, and I continued. "Really, they say that the body is an excellent source of heat."

"That's just great, Rae. Let me know when you figure something out that will actually work."

Alex was being a bit snippy with me, which was totally out of character for him. But he was right. I wasn't sure what we were thinking when we ran away. Living on love seemed like a good idea at the time, and I honestly thought the money from my savings would be sufficient considering we had a free place to stay and no car payment. Maybe it was because, in the past, I had never worried about money. My parents always handled it. I guess I forgot that, even though we had a car, we needed money for gas to keep it running, and even though we had a house, we would have to pay the bills so we could live inside. I took a deep breath and exhaled loudly, letting Alex know I fully agreed with him without having to actually admit it.

He looked at the bills again, then at a piece of paper where he had scribbled down the amount of money we had remaining between the two of us. Alex shook his head.

"We can pay our bills for another couple of months, but what about food? Your tuition?"

"You know how I feel about that. I can live on peanut butter and honey, you could cut back on the Mini-Wheats, and I don't need to go to school to be an artist."

Usually when I made a statement like this, Alex was quick to make a rebuttal. He would insist that school was nonnegotiable, but this morning, he said nothing of the sort: "We'll have to get jobs; that's all there is to it."

Getting jobs was something Alex and I had discussed at one point, but we had put the notion on the back burner because, unlike normal people, there were certain things we had to take into consideration. The law required employers to ask for proof of citizenship before hiring. If that was our only hurdle, I wouldn't be worried. Our concerns were colossal in comparison: Alex had no way to prove he was even alive. Keeping a low profile was something we both considered important, and living off the grid was something that, for the past couple of months, we had managed to do. All our bills were in the name of Ian Limbeaux, the ridiculous name Alex had come up with. We had gone to great lengths to maintain an anonymous lifestyle, and now we were going to have to get jobs. I would officially be in the system; I would be traceable.

"I saw a sign posted in the window of a shop downtown. They need a mechanic and I can fix cars. I can see if they would pay me cash."

"I can check the art store," I offered. Alex frowned. "I might even get a discount on paints if I work there."

"I'm sure Flynt would like to give you more than a discount."

"Don't start," I said, getting up from the table and making my way over to the fridge. I grabbed some lunchmeat, a pack of cheese from the deli tray, and bread from the brisker. "I'm making a sandwich. Do you want one?"

"No thanks," Alex scowled.

"Don't worry about it, Alex. Getting a job isn't all that bad."

"And this is coming from the same girl who doesn't even like to leave the cottage to run an errand?"

"No need to be snippy. Besides, what other choice do we have? If we don't get jobs, we'll have to leave." The truth of the matter was that I really didn't mind leaving the house to seek employment. After Chloe's visit, I no longer felt safe inside the cottage, and I was looking for any excuse to leave.

Alex scoffed and began to sift through the stack of bills.

"I don't see why you're so worried. We'll figure it out. We always do."

Alex's eyes were cast upon the table and a look of concern consumed him. He was holding an envelope in his hand, an envelope he had already opened.

"It's not just the bills, Rae. In several months, we won't even have a place to live."

I took a bite of my sandwich and sat down across from Alex. He pushed the envelope toward me.

"What's this?" I asked with a mouthful of bread and turkey. I cracked open a Diet Coke to wash it down.

"Just read it," he instructed.

I studied the front of the envelope. It was addressed to Circle B Enterprises and the sender was a law firm out of Seattle. I maneuvered a thick bundle of paper out of the envelope, unfolded it, and began to read. After several minutes, I set the document down on the table and looked into Alex's eyes.

"I have absolutely no idea what this means. Brief me, please."

"You know what a will is, right?"

"Yes."

"Before my parents died, they had a law firm draft their last will and testament. It included instructions for the management of their estate in the event of their passing… things like that. Nothing out of the ordinary. It's tedious reading, but I've learned a few things about my mom and dad that I didn't know before. They were rather wealthy and a huge chunk of their money has been in limbo for nearly twenty years. I was their only child, so they left everything to me. But since all legal documents show that I died nearly two decades ago, it's no longer mine."

"So what was to happen to all of the money… the property, if you weren't alive to accept it?"

"Under normal circumstances, the entire estate would have been turned over to the next of kin. But I have no relatives to speak of. Everything was left to a Joseph Gorem. He has power of attorney for my parents."

When he said the name Joseph, I flinched as though he had struck me. Joseph…. Joe?

"We have until March."

"March. What are we going to do after that?"

"I don't know, Rae."

"Your parents were wealthy, so what. I still don't understand why we have to leave the cottage."

"My parents owned their estate outright. That's the good news. Circle B Enterprises encompassed many things: their money, their stocks, their bonds, and their property. After their death, Circle B slipped between the cracks. No taxes were paid for nineteen years. Now it seems the government wants their money."

"Why now?"

"All of our accounts are in the name of the trust. Just by turning on the electricity, I put Circle B back in the system."

"But you used a fake name."

"It has more to do with the location than the name. I didn't think of that."

"How much do we owe?"

Alex shrugged his shoulders as if he had something more pressing on his mind. He began to ruffle his hair with his hand. This was followed by his newfound ritual of massaging his temples with the tips of his fingers.

"There's more. At the bottom of page seven, it says that this letter is part one of three. This is only a portion of the will. It looks like this document, part one, pertains only to my parents' dwellings."

"Dwellings? How many did they have?" I asked, shocked.

"It looks like five."

"Where?"

"Bartlesville, Alexandria, Bangkok, Florence, and Paris, France."

"Well, you might just get to Europe after all."

"That wouldn't be so bad. But right now, the last thing we can afford is a vacation."

"What about the other papers? You said the will was divided into three different parts."

A smile spread across Alex's face, the only smile I had seen all morning.

"On page three, a reference is made to a third document. Look," Alex said, pointing to a paragraph near the bottom of the page. I read it two times but gained no understanding.

On all matters concerning Alex Loving, son of Paul and Sara Loving, please refer to document two, section 4: The Godfather Clause.

Legal jargon was confusing, but after reading the page for a third time, I was beginning to get the drift.

"This is good news. I think this means I have a godfather, Rae! I think the second document pertains to how I was to be cared for in the event that my parents passed away and left me on my own. I need to get ahold of this law firm and see about having them overnight the remaining documents." Alex relaxed against the wall and sighed. "I can't believe it, Rae. I might have a godfather and there is nothing I want more than to meet him."

The odds had been stacked against Alex and me from the very beginning, and I knew it was going to be hard for us to be together. It now occurred to me that not only were the odds stacking up, but my lies were as well. My house of cards was about to fall, and I would be left to explain. The truth was going to have to come out, and I thought that it should be sooner rather than later. But first, I needed to know if Joseph Gorem, power of attorney, was also Pastor Joe, Alex's godfather. If so, I might just have the perfect solution to our problem.

I could smell the paints before I opened the door to the Artist's Edge. Flynt was standing behind the counter sketching something in a book. When the bell over the door jingled, he set down his pad of paper and laid his pencil on top.

"How's it going, Rae? Already out of paints?"

"Getting low. What I really need is a job to support my nasty habit. No money, no paints."

"Right. You could have much worse habits, I suppose."

"I guess. So, do you need any help? Because if I have to work, I can't really imagine working anywhere else."

"How many hours are you needing?"

"Enough to pay the bills with a little extra on the side to support my addiction."

"What are you working on?"

"Oil on canvas entitled My Evil Alter Ego."

"Sounds very.... very...."

"Freudian," I finished the sentence for him.

"Yes, very Freudian. You stole the words right out of my mouth. I'd love to see it when you're done." Flynt paused. He was looking down at the counter, his eyes focused on the drawing he had been working on when I walked in. "You still with the same guy? Boy Miro?"

"Huh?" I had a puzzled look on my face, but then smiled when I realized Flynt was talking about Alex. "Yes, I'm still with Boy Miro," I laughed.

"That's too bad," he said, looking up from the counter into my eyes.

"Your arm's better," I observed out loud, instantly relieved that I had changed the subject.

"Yeah," he nodded and patted his forearm. "I guess I'm back to my old self."

"So, do I have myself a job?"

"You can start as soon as you like. I can probably only give you twenty hours a week. I'm totally fine with you bringing projects to work on as long as we're not busy. I do inventory on Mondays, so if you're free then, I can always use the help."

I'd love to believe that it was one part charming personality and the other part my love for art that won me the job, but it was the nervousness in Flynt's voice when he spoke and the way his lips turned into a fragile smile when I walked into the store that revealed the reason for my recent employment. But still, I couldn't help feeling a bit of pride as I walked back to the Wagoneer with a new feather in my cap. I had come out victorious and this victory made me feel more confident about my next task, a task that would either make or break the both of us.

"You're all grins and giggles," Alex said when I slid into the car. "I take it you got the job."

"I got the job. He's paying cash. The hours are flexible. Plus," I added. "I can get some of my homework done if the traffic through the store is slow. Kill two birds with one stone."

"How convenient." Alex looked a bit annoyed when I thought that, on the contrary, he should be very pleased. "Sounds like Flynt might still be crushing a bit."

"Maybe," I agreed, hoping to get a rise out of Alex. If jealousy were the only way I could get Alex to visibly profess his love for me, then I would take it.

"Wouldn't surprise me. Should I worry?"

"You have about as much to worry about with Flynt as I have to worry about with Corrine."

It looked like things were going to take longer than I expected at the garage. I guess they wanted to see what Alex could do before they agreed to hire him. His ability was the least of my concerns. I'm sure Alex could wave his hand in front of the car and fix it, in much the same way as he had fixed my broken body on more than one occasion. Alex told me to run a few errands and pick him back up in a couple of hours. This was fine with me because I knew that I would need every bit of two hours to complete the second task on my agenda.

When I drove into the parking lot, the old black sedan was parked next to the back entrance of the church, just as it was before. I pulled into one of the visitor parking slots. I zipped up my coat, slid out of the Wagoneer, and walked the short distance to the back door. Now that I had made the acquaintance of Pastor Joe, I could say that I knew him, but I wasn't sure if I knew him well enough to enter the church on a regular basis and walk through the building unannounced. I decided that today, the answer would have to be "yes." Time was of the essence. If Pastor Joe's last name was Gorem, then not only was he Alex's godfather, but he also had power of attorney over the Loving estate. He might legally hold the key to Alex's financial future. Alex was going to figure out a way to get the remaining documents from the law firm in Seattle and when he did, he would know everything. It didn't bode well for me to let him find out about Pastor Joe on his own. I needed to be the one to bring him the news.

The glass door shut behind me, and I stood in the downstairs lobby for a moment before retracing my steps from several weeks before. I walked down the hallway with purpose, and when I reached the stairwell I climbed to the top floor. As I approached his office, I noticed that the door was ajar and a light was on, but I didn't hear any sound coming from inside. I pushed open the door and poked my head inside. The door creaked and startled Pastor Joe who was sitting on the sofa instead of behind his desk.

"Rae, you have a way of sneaking up on people. Come in."

"If now's not a good time I can come back," I said, hesitating a moment before stepping inside.

"Now's the perfect time. I was just getting ready to take a break from my reading." Pastor Joe set his cup down on the end table and began to shuffle through a stack of papers that were resting on his lap.

"Can I offer you something to drink? I'm having hot tea. There's a nip in the air today, and I find that something warm helps with the aches and pains."

"No. No thank you."

"And to what do I owe the honor of your visit?"

"The last time I was here, you made all of the confessions," I cut to the chase. "Shouldn't it be the other way around? Isn't that why people come to church? To confess."

"It has been my experience that everyone has something to get off their chest, even pastors."

"Well, now it's my turn. I have something I want to confess. I have something I need to tell you."

"Okay." Joe leaned back into the sofa, crossed his legs, and folded his arms across his chest.

"I've been lying." Pastor Joe raised his eyebrows in surprise. "I've been lying *badly*," I reiterated "and now everything is coming apart."

CHAPTER TWENTY-ONE

*P*astor Joe listened for nearly half an hour as I explained in detail the last year of my life. I told him about my longing to keep Alex here with me and about how I had been manipulating every situation in order to get my way. I told him about the lies I had been telling. I told him about Chloe and Ben and how they wanted me dead. I told him how we ran away to keep my parents safe. I told him about the walkie-talkie in the kitchen. I told him about the Loving's Last Will and Testament and how we desperately needed money for back taxes or else we would lose the family home. I told him about everything except the journal.

"I know that it's wrong to lie, but I've never told a lie without good reason." I paused. "Here's the thing. I do plan on telling Alex the truth and on several occasions, I have even come close. But just when I set my mind to do it, something gets in the way. Our situation changes... it twists... and my lie no longer seems harmful. But really, it's just the same old lie in the name of something new. I don't want Alex to leave me, and I'm willing to do whatever it takes to keep him here with me."

I was expecting Pastor Joe to look at me with scorn. I had been lying to his godson, after all. Instead, he began to laugh.

"It's the oldest trick in the book," he chuckled. Joe was looking at the ceiling with an easy smile on his face. "The cartoon character that has an angel on one shoulder and Satan on the other. The cartoon is meant to be funny, but the fact of the matter is… Satan is very real. Just as real as God. He is the great manipulator, the great tempter. He is the father of lies. He is the voice inside your head that tricks your heart. Just when you have made your mind up *not* to do something, he changes one tiny circumstance, making the temptation look all sparkly and new. And you are left to fight off the temptation once again."

For some reason, the last thing Pastor Joe said reminded me of my email. Ever since the Internet had been hooked up at the cottage, I had been getting more spam than mail. I would block emails from RiccoPBL who was trying to sell me Viagra, only to find that the next day, Ricco had been let back in as Ricco123, selling the same product but under a different name.

"Satan like spam," I said when I made this very loose connection.

"I have heard Satan called many things, but I have never heard him compared to potted meat." Pastor Joe laughed again, louder this time.

"Not like the Spam you eat," I said with a bit of impatience that, almost immediately, I wished I could take back. "Like the spam that fills up your email account."

Joe didn't say a word. He had a perplexed expression on his face and then he nodded in agreement.

"I suppose you're right."

"So how do I shut it off?"

"The computer?"

"My mind," I said with confidence.

"Let me think about this. You say that you're having trouble keeping out the junk mail." Pastor Joe scratched his head. "So how do you find the emails that you need? The ones you're searching for."

"If I'm looking for an email from Mom and Dad, I enter their name into the blank space at the top of the page and hit return. Gmail filters my account and then displays only those emails with my parents name attached."

Joe scratched his head again. "What I'm hearing you say is that you entered what you knew to be *true*. In the *blank space*, you entered the subject that you were searching for. In the *blank space,* you should enter the *truth."*

"Umhum." I gave Joe a blank stare, wondering where he was going with this.

"I think you're right, Rae. Satan is like spam. As long as you live in this world, temptation will exist and doing away with it, is a long and continual process. Turmoil within the body will linger as long as you let it. How long would it take for you to sit down and delete all the spam from your email account?"

"Hours."

"And it can take a lifetime to rid oneself of temptation; even after it's finally gone, you have to work daily to keep it out.... that is, if you do it on your own."

I felt a bit discouraged. I'm not sure if it was the sagging of my shoulders or the frown on my face that gave me away, but Pastor Joe quickly changed direction.

"I'm not trying to dishearten you. I'm trying to help you, really I am. You see, just like the blank space at the top of your Gmail account, there is a blank space in every person's life. Find the blank space in your life. When you find it, try entering the Truth." Pastor Joe laughed again. "'Then you will know the truth, and the truth will set you free.'"

"The truth, huh." I recalled how, last time I saw Pastor Joe, he had encouraged me to find the truth. "And *how* do I find the truth?"

"*How?*" Joe regarded me thoughtfully. "Everyone's journey is different, Rae. But I will be here for you while you search and I will do my best to guide you."

Much like my last visit to Joe's office, I was on my way out the door when something he said stopped me in my tracks. I had been so caught up in my confession that I had forgotten my purpose for coming.

"My full name is Joseph Aaron Gorem. I am not only Alex's godfather, I have power of attorney over the Loving estate, and I think I might have a way to help you."

I needed peace and quiet to sort through my feelings, and I could think of no better place than the church sanctuary. I checked my watch. I still had a good forty-five minutes before I needed to pick up Alex. I walked out of Joe's office and descended the stairs. When I reached the main lobby, I hesitated, looking through the two large wooden doors into the chapel. I admired the stained glass windows and wooden pews. A familiar feeling washed over me as I peered into the room. It was the same feeling that came over me when I walked into the sanctuary last month, and it was the same feeling that I experienced on the path last May when I knew for certain I was not going to die. I thought maybe that feeling was God. Regardless, I liked the feel of the hymnal in my hands, and I liked the words inside. I liked the feeling of peace that came from gazing upon the crucifix that hung behind the pulpit. In the middle of the small sanctuary with stone floors and a vaulted ceiling, I felt like I had God all to myself. I felt like he was really listening.

Slowly, I approached the sanctuary and, once inside, I shut the doors behind me. It was inevitable. I was going to have to tell Alex about Pastor Joe.

Alex was hired at the garage on an as needed basis. They couldn't guarantee him more than fifteen hours, but they did agree to pay him cash. This solved our immediate cash flow problem, but I knew we had bigger fish to fry. So, I spent the rest of the week contemplating the more pressing problem, losing our home, and I had decided it was time for me to come clean. I didn't see any way around it. Besides, Joe was right; I needed to get rid of the spam in my life and this was a definite start. When finally I gathered the courage to tell Alex about Pastor Joe, he reacted exactly how I expected he would. He was furious. He didn't talk to me for several hours. So, while Alex was fuming, I took the liberty of calling Joe and setting up a time for the two of them to meet. It wasn't until after I told Alex about his upcoming appointment with his godfather that he began to simmer down. I had also spent a lot of time thinking about the truth, and even though I didn't understand what Joe meant, I couldn't shake what he said. He told me I should find the truth if I wanted to be set free. He told me to enter the truth into the blank space of my life. The only blank space I could think of was the hole in my heart, and at the moment, Alex was doing a pretty good job of filling that. Maybe *Alex* was the truth. It was true that he was sent to earth to be with me. It was true that he loved me. It was true that he was here to keep me safe. It was also true that he would leave me one day, maybe very soon. So maybe the truth was bigger than Alex. Pastor Joe wanted me to begin my quest for the truth. But I didn't have the slightest idea where to begin the search.

My first day of work went as well as could be expected. Flynt spent several hours going over the ins and outs of inventory, but at eleven o'clock when three of Flynt's teammates walked into the store, he headed to hockey practice and left me to my work. I played around with Flynt's iPod for the first fifteen minutes, scrolling through an assortment of hockey fight songs that I had no interest in listening to. After finally settling on a playlist, I set to work. The stock room was in such disarray that I spent seven hours sorting and pricing products. I could see why he needed my help. When five o'clock rolled around, I finished tidying up the back room and had just begun to put a list together for supplies that needed to be ordered, when I heard the bell jingle over the door. Strange, I thought. I poked my head around the corner and was relieved to see Flynt. He was carrying a large white bag.

"Hey there!" Were you able to hold down the fort?"

"Making some progress. Your supply room is a wreck."

He shrugged and then laughed. "Right. I told you I needed your help."

"Seriously. I have absolutely no organizational skills whatsoever, but the seven hours I spent back there made a world of difference."

Flynt was still dressed in his practice clothes. He was wearing a pair of loose fitting navy blue sweats with a logo up the side and a long sleeved

Vikings tee shirt. Flynt placed something on the counter that was small, black, and rectangular with a BMW emblem on the front. It was the key to his car, but unlike my set of keys, there was no key at all. It was a keyless entry. I remembered reading about it when I was flipping through Alex's *Car and Driver* magazine. My eyes drifted to the bag Flynt was holding in his hand.

"Dinner?" he asked, holding the bag up so I could read the black writing on the side. The food was from Bugaboo Bay, a popular restaurant on Lake L'Homme Dieu.

"I thought that if you wouldn't meet me for dinner, I would just bring the food to you."

"I really better be going. I have homework... and a boyfriend."

"Come on. It's not like it's a date. Boy Miro can do without you for another hour or two."

"I don't know."

When I didn't respond, Flynt tried another approach. "It's a celebration. That's all. We're celebrating your first day at work."

"Fine. I can stay for thirty minutes, and then I have to go."

With a satisfied smile, Flynt began to pull the food out of the bag.

"I ordered a couple different entrees. I don't know what you like... not yet, anyway."

"I'm not picky."

"Good. I ordered you the penne primavera. I also ordered you a burger... just in case."

"The pasta's perfect. But you didn't have to do all this."

"I wanted to."

I took a bite of my focaccia bread while Flynt began to tell me about his life. He told me that his plans for trying out for the Minnesota Wild had been placed on hold due to his injuries, but after his arm was completely healed, he planned to fulfill this other life long dream. I asked who would run the store once he was a famous athlete. He told me there would be time for both. I envied Flynt. Unlike his stockroom, his life appeared to be in perfect order. He knew what he wanted, and he went for it. It was as simple as that. As for me, the biggest obstacle I had overcome was the fear of leaving my house. But I didn't tell him that. At six o'clock, I told him I absolutely had to leave. It took a bit of convincing, but finally he agreed to let me leave on the one condition that I take the extra burger home for Boy Miro because he might be hungry. I thought that it was a good idea. Alex loved burgers. I thought that it might just make him happy.... It did not.

"Where have you been? I was getting worried."

With the exception of making a spaghetti dinner on my birthday, Alex had never cooked a thing. He had grilled, and he had warmed up dishes courtesy of Corrine, but he had never prepared a single dish himself. But tonight, he had made me something special, and of course, I felt guilty when I walked into the cottage with a full belly and a bag from Bugaboo Bay in my hand.

"I don't think I like you working with Flynt," Alex said later that evening.

"What else can I do? We need the money and he's paying me cash."

"But he likes you and that doesn't work for me."

"Well, Corrine likes you," I said very matter of fact.

"But I don't work with her."

"But you don't turn her away when she brings you food."

"Brings *us* food."

"You're right. Besides, she's gone, and I really don't have to deal with her anymore."

Alex immediately looked uncomfortable. An awkward smile formed on his face just before he spoke.

"Corrine's parents brought her back home today. She wasn't making the grades."

I exhaled. "It hasn't even been a month, has it?"

"Not quite."

"I'd be willing to bet that she flunked out on purpose just so she could be near you. She missed you, Alex."

"You know that I can't change the way Cory feels about me, just like you can't change the way Flynt feels about you. But I'm sure there's something we *can* do."

"Because we're cosmic?"

"Yes, because we're cosmic."

That night as I lay in bed, I began to thinking about what Alex said. Maybe there was something we could do. I began to think of ways I could totally disgust Flynt so he would no longer have any interest. I had come up with a list of seven different ways to make him gag, when I had a revelation. Flynt and Cory created conflict between Alex and I, but up until this point, we had viewed them as two separate problems. I was elated when Cory left for college. When she left, I felt relieved... but then she came back. Maybe eliminating the problem was the wrong approach and maybe our two separate problems would make one perfect match.

CHAPTER TWENTY-TWO

I hadn't realized how dirty the cottage floors were until I was on my hands and knees cleaning them with an old rag and a bucket filled with water and bleach. It was very out of character for me to clean. In fact, since arriving at the cottage four months ago, I hadn't bothered to clean anything other than my room. Alex was the one who usually tidied up, and although he never said anything about it, I'm sure it bothered him. But today, I was the one who was cleaning, and it had everything to do with the solution I came up with on Monday night.

I had just found a thirty-year-old toothbrush under the sink and was working hard to remove the dirt that had taken up residence between the linoleum and the wall when Alex sauntered into the kitchen.

"What's gotten into you?" he asked, his voice on the brink of laughter. "This place is a mess."

"And you're just now noticing this?"

"I've had other things on my mind," I told him without looking up from the stubborn spot in the corner of the room that would not come clean no matter how many times I rubbed it with bleach.

"It doesn't strike you as odd that you're sitting under the kitchen table with a toothbrush in your hand?"

"Don't blame this mess on me. No one has lived here for twenty years. What do you expect?"

"I'm not blaming anything on you. All I'm saying is that you've never really cared before. Why now at three o'clock on a Friday afternoon?"

"Is it three already?" I stopped scrubbing and held very still. After having the revelation on Monday night, I woke up Tuesday morning eager to share with Alex my idea. He was not enthusiastic. He wasn't willing to foster any relationship that involved Flynt Redding, and he definitely did not like the idea of having him in our home. Because I knew that Alex did not support my matchmaking efforts, I had neglected to tell him I had set a firm date.

"Tonight's the big night. The double date," I told him, still holding my body still, preparing myself for his wrath, or at least one of his super-smart comments.

"Here?" he responded, aghast.

"I told them six. That should give us plenty of time. You know you could help. We still need to get cleaned up and cook dinner."

"I'm not cooking. You set this up, not me."

"I'm also reuniting you with your godfather. Remember that?"

"You lied."

"You owe me."

"Fine. Anything for you," he scowled. "I'm guessing you told Flynt why he was invited to our house."

I didn't respond; instead, I began scrubbing again, harder this time, putting all my weight into scouring the spot that was now turning from black to a yellowish-brown.

"Rae?"

"What?" I said still rubbing the spot with the toothbrush.

"Did you tell Flynt and Cory why you invited them?"

"Not exactly." I stopped scrubbing and crawled out from underneath the table.

"You do know that no one is going to be looking underneath the table for dirt."

"It has to be perfect. I have a lot riding on this… *we* have a lot riding on this. I must create ambiance so that Flynt and Cory will fall in love. What if things are going really well and then Flynt drops his napkin on the floor. What if he bends down to pick it up and he sees this huge brown stain. That, Alex, is not romance. Besides, once I got started I couldn't stop. I could scrub for hours and it still wouldn't be clean."

"I swear, it's either feast or famine with you."

"Speaking of feast or famine, we need to decide what to fix for dinner."

"Well, my little matchmaker, if I'm cooking then it will have to be something easy."

"How about spaghetti? You've made that before. All you have to do is cook the meat and add some sauce." Spaghetti had always been my favorite food. Maybe I loved it, not for the taste as I had previously thought, but rather, because it was a romantic cuisine.

"I think I can handle that. Besides, there's nothing like a plate of spaghetti to bring to two people together. It worked for Lady and the Tramp."

"You don't seem very excited about this. If I didn't know better, I would say that you don't want Corrine fixed up with Flynt. If I didn't know better, I would say that you like the attention she gives you. You can't live without the banana bread and her starry eyes."

"Well, you do know better. You *should* know better than that."

"I'm going to get in the shower," I said, flipping my hair over my shoulder smartly before making a dramatic exit.

I turned the hot water knob to the right and let the water flow, flushing out the rust that had settled in the pipes. While I waited for the water to warm, I sat on the toilet, with the lid down, and read a couple of pages from *Gone with the Wind.*

Several minutes later, I stuck my hand into the stream of water and found the temperature to be just right. I stripped down, threw my clothes in a pile beside the tub, and then turned in a full circle toward the sink. The hot water had made the bathroom steamy, fogging up the mirror, so I wiped my hand across the smooth, wet surface and stared at my reflection. My hair was a mess and a layer of dirt coated my face. I looked at my hand; it was splotched with paint and a variety of hues were caked underneath my fingernails. From now on, I would at least try to make myself presentable. I vowed to fix my hair and wear perfume on a regular basis, which was a definite start. I did not promise to paint my fingernails, but I would try my best to pick the paint out from underneath.

Forty-five minutes later, I emerged from my bedroom, dressed in something I had finally decided was appropriate. Picking the perfect thing to wear was a challenge. I wanted to look good for Alex, better than Corrine. But I couldn't look too good, because I didn't want Flynt's eyes to wander. I mean, he was supposed to fall in love with Corrine, not fall more deeply in love with me. I paired a top with some leggings that my mother bought for me last year. They accentuated my long legs, my only redeeming feature. The evenings had become downright chilly, and even though my toes were still in shock, still a light shade of blue from stepping out of the warm shower into the cool cabin, I put on a pair of Kelly green peep-toe heels and endured the numbing sensation because tonight, beauty trumped pain.

Alex was in the kitchen cooking spaghetti. I snuck up behind him and kissed him on the back of the neck. "Thanks for making dinner," I cooed. "It smells good."

"So do you." Alex let the spoon rest on the side of the pan and turned around, looking me up and down.

"And you think that Flynt is going to fall for Cory with you looking like that? I'm beginning to question *your* motives, Sunshine."

Flynt was the first to arrive. He had exchanged his sweat pants for a pair of jeans and his tee shirt for a lightweight v-neck sweater. He had put on cologne. It smelled good. It was a perfect mixture of patchouli and chocolate with a hint of vanilla and lavender. He was holding a bouquet of fall flowers, and when he stepped through the door, he handed them to me with a smile. His smile quickly vanished though when he saw Alex standing at the stove stirring the noodles. Alex didn't even bother to turn around and say hello. I eased the awkwardness by leading Flynt into the living room, so I could show him my painting, and I noticed how the smile returned to his face when he saw it. We had been discussing the symbolic nature of "My Evil Alter Ego" for nearly fifteen minutes when I heard a knock at the kitchen door. I cringed. Flynt's face went completely blank. I had never seen anyone look so confused. Alex was right. I probably should have told Flynt what I was up to. I could hear Corrine's voice carrying from the kitchen. I could hear Alex laughing, making me want to throw up. Wanting to get the show on the road, I ushered Flynt back into the kitchen to meet Corrine. As usual, she was wearing a low cut dress that accentuated her "features". I gritted my teeth. My eyes drifted from Corrine's assets to the chocolate cake on the counter; I began to grind my teeth a little harder.

The first thirty minutes were awkward to say the least. I should have realized that Flynt might know Cory. He was a couple of years older, but Alexandria was small. They had grown up in the same town... probably even went to the same school. I felt like a total idiot. Luckily, Corrine began to talk, and I no longer felt like the only idiot in the room.

"Alex's eyes were what I noticed first. I mean, I could just stare at them all day," Corrine giggled.

What Corrine said was both unexpected and ill-fitting. It didn't take a super genius to realize this evening was not going as planned. If Corrine continued to set her sights on Alex, my matchmaking was sure to fail. I checked the expression on Alex's face and was satisfied that he looked anything but flattered.

"I'm so glad you guys moved in," Cory continued, looking right into Alex's eyes as she spoke. I don't recall anyone ever living here, but my mom says that before I was born there was a family that used to come and stay."

It occurred to me that I had yet to tell Alex about the conversation I overheard in the Harvey's backyard. I needed to shut her up now before she spilled the beans.

"The cottage has been such an eye sore. At least someone is now cutting the grass." Corrine wasn't coming up for air and it didn't appear that she wanted to, either. Her mouth just kept running and running.

"Are you guys renting?"

"I guess you could say that," Alex responded without hesitation.

"So, do you guys sleep in the same room? I mean, your parents don't care, or what?"

I heard three gulps, one right after the other. I swallowed my food, almost choking on her words. Corrine was getting right to the heart of the matter. She asked exactly what was on her mind. Some sort of foreign energy was building up inside me, and I realized it was pride. Alex was the best-looking guy that I had ever seen, movie stars included. Suddenly, I felt the need to defend my territory. My claws were coming out. Up until this point, I wasn't even sure if I had any. I wanted with all of my heart to tell her that, yes, we slept in the same room. I sharpened my claws on the leg of the wooden table. I wanted to tell her that Alex was mine and would always *be* mine. But I couldn't tell her that our parents didn't care. It wasn't that they didn't care. His parents were dead and mine didn't know. It was getting confusing. I retracted my claws and tried to come up with something to say, and quickly.

"My parents are no longer living." Alex beat me to the punch.

I turned my attention to Corrine. It was the first time I had ever seen her at a loss for words.

"Rae's parents have been like my own. They trust us. They know that I would never do anything to break that trust," he finished, looking directly at me, reiterating the fact that I would never get the things from him that I was asking for.

"Wow, my parents could never be that cool." Corrine paused. "That's why I am here instead of living in the city." Corrine paused and then an ornery smile turned the corners of her lips. "My mom found out that I was living with some guy instead of at the dorms. My roommate ratted me out. I'm like, almost nineteen. Good thing she doesn't know everything about me or her feathers would really be ruffled."

"I thought you flunked out?" Alex covered his mouth and forced a cough. "That *is* what your mother told me."

"That's what she tells everyone," Corinne chuckled.

I couldn't be certain, but I thought Corrine was working pretty hard to construct an image for herself, an image she thought Alex might like. Evidently, she thought there might be more than one way to Alex's heart. I wanted to tell her that her efforts were futile. Maybe some guys would be impressed with her escapades, but not Alex. He was different. Or at least, he was different with me.

I looked silently at Flynt, who had not spoken a word since Corrine walked through the door, and I thought he couldn't have looked more uncomfortable. All at once, I remembered that he was my boss and that I actually needed my job. I was going to have to apologize. No, I was going to have to beg his forgiveness: first, for setting him up on a blind date without his knowledge, and second, for his date's terrible behavior. I tuned Cory out and began to put together my defense for the case I would be presenting to Flynt tomorrow at work. I could lie and tell him that Corrine was our friend, but that wouldn't really help my cause much either. It looked like a double date: I knew it, Alex knew it, and Flynt knew it, too. It seemed that everyone at the table knew except Cory. I was going to have to be brutally honest with Flynt.

As we ate our spaghetti, the conversation between Alex and Corrine continued to flow. I was beginning to realize that Flynt and I were invisible. Corrine was still rambling on about things that should have made me blush, talking directly to Alex as though they were the only ones in the room, but it didn't really matter. I wasn't listening. Instead, I was staring at her, thinking about how she was several months younger than I was and yet, she looked like a woman. I still looked like a little girl. I snuck a peek at Alex from the corner of my eye and saw that he was, once again, massaging his temples with his forefinger and his thumb. He had been doing this more and more frequently, and I made a mental note to ask him about it later.

"So how long *have* you two known each other?" Corrine looked shocked and dismayed. I wondered what Alex had said that caused the smile on her face to change into a look of disgust. I now wished that I had been listening.

"All of *her* life," Alex responded smoothly while looking at me through adoring eyes. "But it feels like I've known her for an eternity," he continued on and, as he did, I felt my cheeks begin to warm.

"I've always been with Rae. I have always loved her, even when she acted like she didn't know who I was."

"I'm sure you have a lot of stories, then." There was a vicious sparkle in Cory's eyes. My cheeks were now hot and the color scarlet, I was sure.

"Do I ever," Alex said bemused. "Would you like to hear one?"

"I don't think now is the time, Alex," I said, nudging him with my elbow. I looked around the table and realized that not a single soul was on my side. Even Flynt looked excited to hear the story. I leaned back against the wall and closed my eyes, preparing to accept my fate.

"When Rae was only ten-years-old, she had this doll she called, Roxanne."

"Oh great," I thought. "Here we go."

"Roxanne was not just any doll. She was *the* doll, Rae's favorite doll. She even had a nickname for her. She called her Roxie, and she talked to her doll as though her doll were a real person."

Talk about a plan royally backfiring. It seemed that everyone was against me tonight. I opened my eyes to a mere squint and peeked at Corrine. She looked pleased with the story and where it was heading. I glanced at Flynt. He looked sick. At least one part of my plan was working; if Flynt were in love with me before, he surely wouldn't be after this evening. Alex was talking about dolls, talking about how I talked to dolls. Once again, Alex was remembering me as a child. That was the problem. He was looking across the table at Corrine, who looked more like a woman than I ever would. But when he looked at me, he still saw a little girl.

I-AM-A-WOMAN, I wanted to shout so that only he could hear.

"So the Colberts had just moved to Paris…"

"Paris? Rae, I didn't know you lived in Paris. How exciting."

I nodded my head without saying a word. For once, my erratic life had redeemed me. For the first time I could see that the purpose behind my pain was to make Cory jealous.

"Alex. Can you speak French?"

"Only a little."

"Say something in French."

"Je m'appelle Alex Loving."

"Oh! Say something else," Corrine squealed.

Alex shook his head and continued with his story. "Like I was saying, Rae and her parents had just moved to Paris. They had only been there for a couple of days, and they were walking around Montmartre... near the Sacre Coeur."

When Alex said *Sacre Coeur*, he almost sounded French, and I nearly melted in my seat. I looked over at Corrine. By the way she was slumped in her chair with her elbows on the table and her chin resting in her hands, it was more than obvious that his voice had the same effect on her. In fact, everyone at the table, even Flynt, seemed to be mesmerized by the way Alex rolled his R's and stretched out his J soft and long when he said *je m'appelle.*

"I suppose that during the day, it's all art and mimes and cafés, but when the sun goes down, the streets tell a much different story. Just like in any big city, I suppose. The funny thing is, well, not really funny. I should rephrase. The sad thing is that if you look closely, the stories of the night can be found on the streets during the day. But those aren't the stories people like to hear. Rae knows what I'm talking about. The café on Rue Lepic. Rae, do you remember the little girl with her dirty face pressed against the glass?"

Alex repositioned himself and took a sip of his tea. When I didn't respond, he continued.

"Rae's parents were still sitting at the table inside the café. All of a sudden, Rae got up. Without telling her parents where she was going, she walked out of the café and gave her doll to the little girl." Alex paused for a moment. He was looking down at the table, a forced expression upon his face; it seemed as though he was trying his hardest to remember a portion of the story.

"What was it you said to her?"

"*Ça va.* I said *ça va* because it can mean several different things and because, besides *au revoir*, it was the only French I knew."

"*Ça va.* In case you're wondering, *ça va* means, 'Is this okay?' Rae was giving the little girl her favorite doll, and she was asking her if it was acceptable. She said the perfect thing and she didn't even know it. That is why I love Rae. Not only is she beautiful, she has a beautiful heart as well. It looks so nice when she chooses to wear it on her sleeve."

"So, you were there with her? I don't get it. You lived together? Is that it? Like brother and sister? Isn't that a little weird?" Cory's questions were becoming far too personal, but Alex seemed to be enjoying the conversation, so much in fact, that if he continued to divulge many more details about our life, he would surely slip. The cat would be out of the bag and our cover would be blown. In my opinion, the fewer people to know about us the better.

"Did we live together, Rae?" This whole time I thought the pleasant smile on Alex's face was because he was enjoying Cory's company, but when he looked at me to answer the question, I knew that wasn't it. He was taunting me. He was getting back at me for inviting Cory and Flynt over for dinner. He was going to make me pay.

"No, I would say that Alex lived very, very far away."

"Would you, now?"

"Yes, I would." I nodded my head in a very meaningful manner.

"Rae can be so forgetful at times. Sometimes she forgets how close I really was."

Flynt and Cory were obviously lost. Alex and I were in a world of our own, talking about topics they couldn't begin to comprehend. I rubbed my hands together in a nervous manner, and all at once, Cory gasped.

"Are you engaged?" she shrieked. For the first time, Corrine eyed the ring on my finger, and for the first time ever, I felt proud of what it meant.

"Not engaged, but promised to one another, none-the-less." Alex spoke up once again.

"So, in other words, you think the two of you are meant to be," Flynt said without expression. "I would like to know how Rae feels."

"Flynt," Alex said with a snarl. "The only way I can explain it to you is like this: Rae and I are cosmic." And with that, the smile permanently vanished from Flynt's face and the evening came to an end.

"Well, that was a complete flop," I confessed as Alex and I lay on the deck watching the stars and listening to the water lap onto the shore.

"What did you expect?"

"I took into account every possible scenario, with the exception of the scene that unfolded at our kitchen table."

"I think Cory kind of scared Flynt."

"Will you quit calling her that?"

"I think *Corrine* kind of scared Flynt."

"I think I might have lost my job."

"I doubt it. Flynt was staring at you all night."

"Really, I hadn't noticed. I was too busy listening to Corrine make inappropriate innuendos."

"Besides, if he fired you, he might never see you again. I think Flynt will do whatever he can to keep you at the store."

"I guess it doesn't really matter if Corrine is infatuated with you or if Flynt is in love with me; we love each other and that's what really counts. We're cosmic, right?"

"Haven't I been trying to tell you that all along?"

"I liked the story you told tonight, but it made me kind of sad. I had forgotten all about Roxie. I had forgotten what it felt like when I saw that little girl."

What I should have said was that I had forgotten what it felt like to feel sorry for someone other than myself. Did Alex see the part where I went home and cried myself to sleep? Did he know that, for a solid month, I thought about that little girl day and night? Where had that little girl gone? Not the girl with her face pressed to the window, but the one who cared about others?

"The stars are bigger in Minnesota, I think."

"So are the mosquitoes." I both heard and felt Alex swatting at his arm.

"It's October. The mosquitoes shouldn't still be out."

"They don't die off until we've had a couple of hard freezes."

"I think they like your blood. It's sweet," I said, rolling over and kissing his cheek. "So is your skin," I said, kissing him again.

"I'm welting. I can feel it."

"You're an angel. You're not supposed to welt."

"This angel needs some Off."

"Or a mosquito net." I envisioned the two of us lying under the stars beneath a mosquito net made for two.

"Somehow a mosquito net just takes a bit of the ambience away, don't you think?"

"You gotta do what you gotta do," I told him.

"Okay, that was a total Oklahoma accent. Flynt's right. You do have a twang."

"And you're beginning to sound like you're from Minnesota the longer you're here. Or France. Your accent tonight was amazing."

The year in which the world was proven round instead of flat is disputable, but what cannot be argued is that for thousands and thousands of years there were men like Pythagoras who believed with all of their heart in something they could not prove to be correct. I wonder what it was inside of Pythagoras that sparked this revolutionary idea. Did it just occur to him one evening as he was looking up at the sky that the world might be very different than people believed it to be? Was it something that someone had said, something he had heard a hundred different times in a hundred different ways, something common and ordinary perhaps, but something that struck him in a new way? Maybe it was something he saw. Or perhaps it was simply something he could just feel in his bones, a feeling that begged him to search for answers.

I never think about the earth being round or flat; in fact, I don't question the world at all. I rarely think about the ground I'm lying on when I'm looking at the stars. But on occasion, I do think about life, and sometimes, I wonder why I'm here. I wonder why life is filled with pain and sickness and loss. These are the things I think about. For eighteen years, I lived as though the earth was flat. I never questioned why my life was the way it was. I never stopped to think that there might possibly be a reason for every occurrence in my life. I never thought that tragedy could mix perfectly with joy to create a beautiful picture. I lived day by day. I thought about the pain and not the purpose behind it.

And then last April, something Alex said forever changed the way that I see life. It was an a-ha moment. I would have been less shocked if he had told me the sea was made of blue gelatin. What he said was something I couldn't shake, and after time that small seed of truth grew into a tree with many branches. Sometimes when I'm lying in bed missing my mom and dad, I think back to the day when life as I knew it began to change, the day at the park when Alex told me that my life was like the Monet I had seen at a museum in Paris.

I can hear Alex's voice as though he's right beside me; his words continue to evolve into an even greater truth that touches every portion of my life. He told me that life doesn't make sense until you step back and look at it from a distance. Only then can you see the whole picture. "I guess you could say each experience is one splotch of paint in the great masterpiece of life," he told me.

Although it was many years ago, I try to take myself back to the day when my family visited the Musee de L'Orangerie, the day I first saw the painting Alex was talking about: a massive canvas painted on by none other than Claude Monet. It encircled the entire room. With my eyes closed, I try to remember how I felt the first time I saw Monet's magnificent painting and the peace I felt as I let the colors envelop me. I imagine myself walking so close to the painting that I'm almost touching it. Irregular shaped colors that make no picture at all. That's what I remember seeing. Slowly, I move backward, noticing how I gain more clarity with each step. I continued to feed off the words that changed my world.

"When you try to look at it up close, in the present, it can look confusing.

But when you step back and look at your life in retrospect you gain clarity."

Sometimes I repeat these words aloud and sometimes silently, always hoping for enlightenment, and every once in a while another branch of understanding begins to grow. Tonight, as I was thinking about the distance between the canvas and myself, I began to think of my mom. She was a thousand miles away. Ample distance to see her in a different light and, like a Monet, when I saw her from this far away place, everything I saw was beautiful.

It was different when I lived at home. My life with her seemed such a mess, a canvas randomly splotched with paint. The scar on her arm was an ugly splotch of paint that reminded me of my dead sister every time I saw it. There was a splotch of paint that represented our gypsy-like lifestyle, another one that represented secrets, and still another one that represented lies. There was a blue splotch of paint in the center of the canvas that signified the sorrow in her voice and reminding me of her pain for which I knew I was the cause.

Tonight, I was thinking about my mother from a distance. The scar on her arm no longer reminded me of my sister's death but of my mother's strength. I envied her courage to live life to the fullest despite her pain. I envied that she never complained when life dealt her a difficult hand. Tonight, I could still hear the pain in her voice, but it was no longer *her* pain; for the first time ever, I realized it was *my* pain that she had sacrificially taken upon herself. And although my mother was a beautiful woman, for the first time in my life, I realized that her greatest beauty resided somewhere deep inside.

There are many things about my mother that I never considered until now. She was always just my mother, and she did the things that all mothers should do. She fed me, she clothed me, and she nursed me back to health when I was sick. I never stopped to look at all the separate pieces of my mother that made her who she was. The mosaic of experiences that made her character complete. There was a beautiful white splotch of paint at the top of the masterpiece that was her faith. It reminded me of how I felt when she prayed; my world stood still and I knew that God was listening. I wondered if God listened to me the way He listened to my mom. *If You are listening to me tonight, I would like to ask You one question: If everything does happen for a reason, and if each experience shapes us into the person we are supposed to be, what is it all for? Who am I supposed to be? I know You are God, and I know You exist, but why do You let me suffer? If You are God and You are love, then how could You let me feel such pain? How could You let my mother feel pain? How could You let my sister die?*

CHAPTER TWENTY-THREE

*B*ecause I stayed up so late last night, I promised myself I would sleep until noon. I didn't have to be at work until three o'clock, and I was extremely nervous about seeing Flynt. After what went down the night before, I was utterly embarrassed, and I feared I might even lose my job, which I desperately needed. But at eight o'clock, the phone rang and startled me out of my dream. When we first moved into the cottage, it had an ancient phone with a rotary dial. I had replaced it with a modern version that had caller id and a built in answering machine. Normally, I would fall back into a slumber, but since buying the phone, this was the first time it had rung, and I was scared of who was on the other end. So scared in fact that I didn't even get out of bed to answer. I let the machine on the phone take a message while I trembled under my sheets. For nearly five minutes, I lay in bed with an old quilt pulled high over my head. Not until my heart rate began to steady did I move from under the covers and make my way to the desk in the living room where the phone sat. The smell of breakfast was coming from the kitchen but the house was quiet. I assumed that Alex was awake and was taking his morning swim. I had told him the water was near freezing and he was crazy to go in. Not only did I fear he might catch a cold, but I worried he might draw unwanted attention.

"Swimming for miles in freezing water is not a normal human thing to do," I told him. When he tried to argue, I reminded him that even Cocoa, who so loved the water, wouldn't think of getting in. I looked out the large picture window and sure enough, I could see something bobbing in the distance. I looked back at the phone; the answering machine was blinking with a number one. I picked up the handset and pressed the arrow at the bottom to scroll through the list of callers. Only one name appeared: Manila Crow.

"If it's not one crow waking me up, it's another," I said aloud.

I was completely irritated because I was sure that it was a telemarketer calling us on a Saturday morning. And I knew how telemarketers worked: they worked together. It only took one telemarketer to find you and once they did, they all knew where you were. I would never have another peaceful Saturday morning again. Still annoyed over being woken up, I was tempted to delete the message, climb back into bed, and pull the covers back up over my head. But a small voice inside of me said, *push the button, Rae.* I couldn't deny my curiosity, so I pushed the button.

"Good morning, Rae. I'm sorry I missed you this morning. My name is Mary, and I know you don't know me. But I was calling very briefly this morning to share an encouraging thought with you out of the Bible. It's out of 2 Corinthians 1: 3-4. Please take the time to read it. Thank you."

How did this lady get my number? Pastor Joe. That had to be it. I looked out the window. Alex was still in the water but moving quickly to the shore. With haste, I pulled a scrap of paper out of the drawer and pushed play on the machine so I could listen to the message again. After pushing stop and start several times, I finished copying the message and hit delete, erasing the message for good.

Flynt was already at the store when I got there. I was very nervous walking in, but when I got close to the counter and saw his face light up, all my fears were put to rest. With a smile like the one on his face, there was no way I would lose my job. Still, I didn't say a word because I didn't know where to start. I wanted to apologize, but I had never been very good at that. I decided to wait and see if Flynt had anything to say. Thankfully, I didn't have to wait long.

"That Corrine is something else."

"What do you mean?" I tried my best to act naïve.

"I've known Corrine all my life. Let's just say that her behavior last night was very typical. I'm pretty sure she has her sights set on Alex. She was all over him."

"Oh that," I said as though I wasn't bothered.

"In any case, I think Alex handled it well." I didn't respond. "I mean, he would be crazy to want Cory over you."

I looked at Flynt and rolled my eyes.

"It's true. And by the way, thanks for inviting me over last night. Everything considered, I had fun."

I couldn't believe it. I had imagined that Flynt experienced many different things last night, but fun was not one of them. So far, I was sure of only one thing: My plan had *completely* backfired. Maybe it was Alex's fault, not mine. All the reminiscing last night, made me into something virtuous and compared to Corrine, I probably was. But while Alex had intended to push Corrine away, his stories only intensified Flynt's infatuation. How could I tell him nicely that I don't feel that way about him? But how *did* I feel about Flynt? It might make me a little uncomfortable, but I didn't *hate* it when he paid me compliments. The attention wasn't all that bad. Plus, our friendship was so easy. I didn't have to beg for his affection and that was nice for a change. I was completely fascinated with Alex and his superhuman abilities, but I couldn't deny that sometimes it got a bit old. His never failing strength made me feel weak. I didn't deserve him. Flynt was very human and right now, that felt very nice. I liked how he fumbled his words in my presence. I loved seeing his goofy smile form when I walked into the room.

"You're quiet this afternoon. I think I have something that might perk you up."

Flynt brought a smile to my face when he pulled a cup of hot coffee from behind the counter. When he handed it to me, I looked at the cup.

Mocha Latte
Milk: 2%
Sugar: Splenda X 2

If Alex had ordered the latte, he would have ordered it with organic sugar. And if he did order it with Splenda, he would have known that I liked four instead of two. My latte was proof of so many things: Flynt tried so very hard, but Alex would always know me better. I was reminded of all the things that I loved about Alex, and even though his super powers sometimes made me feel inferior, that was what I loved the most.

"Thank you," I smiled and took a sip of the yummy, hot liquid.

"Did I get it right?" Flynt asked hopefully.

"Perfect."

With the threat of getting fired out of the way, my mind became preoccupied with Manila Crow. I was completely confused. The caller ID read Manila Crow, but the caller said her name was Mary. I scratched my head and considered the discrepancy. I pulled the scrap of paper from my bag and read the phone number I had scratched down. Flynt was in the back room doing inventory, so I picked up the phone and dialed. I waited, but nothing happened. It didn't ring, and there wasn't an operator telling me I had dialed a number that was no longer in service. It was completely silent on the other end, so I hung up and twisted my mouth in confusion. But then I came up with another idea.

I swiveled in my chair and flipped open Flynt's laptop that was sitting on the counter. Quickly, I typed, 'phone number search' into Google. A list of websites bounced back, and I clicked on the first one. This particular service required a fee, so I closed it and clicked on another. Reverse phone number lookup. It sounded promising, so I entered the number into the blank space and clicked 'find'. What came back was not what I expected. I expected to see the name of a church or even the name Manila Crow. But much to my dismay, nothing came back, nothing at all. In fact, the area code I entered did not exist. I closed Firefox, shut down the computer, and folded Flynt's laptop shut. I was becoming more

and more annoyed. I was going to have to pay Pastor Joe a visit after work
to find out if he had given someone my name and, if he had, I needed him
to ask Manila Crow to quit calling.

"What a delight it is to see you, Rae."

I smiled, trying my hardest not to laugh. I wasn't usually addressed in
such a fashion, and I wasn't used to it. I was anything but a delight and it
seemed that everyone but Pastor Joe knew it.

"What brings you here today, my dear?"

"Nothing good, I'm afraid."

"Sit down. Sit down," he demanded in a sweet but serious voice.
"What seems to be the problem?"

"I got a phone call this morning." Joe didn't respond. He stayed
seated in the chair behind his desk and looked at me with anticipation.
This was going to be harder than I thought. I was about to accuse a pastor,
and I could no longer think of a good way to do it. The smile on his face
was so pleasant that I was almost willing to have Manila Crow call me
every Saturday morning for the rest of my life if it meant keeping Joe in
this happy state.

"Well, I'm concerned that someone might have gotten my number
from you." It felt good to say exactly what I was thinking.

"But my dear, I don't have your phone number. You never gave it to
me."

"Well, my name then. Maybe you gave someone named Mary my
name."

"I'm sure I don't know what you mean." The smile had vanished from
Joe's face and was replaced with a look of concern.

I couldn't say any more. I was so nervous that I was trembling. I did
the only thing I could think to do: I pulled the slip of paper from my bag
and pushed it across the deck in Joe's direction.

Joe studied the piece of paper for a moment, and then he spoke. "Ah,
2 Corinthians 1: 3-4."

Silence.

This wasn't fair. He couldn't sit in silence. He was a pastor and his job was to teach. I needed teaching. I need to know what he was thinking, and I need to know why Manila… or Mary had called.

"What is that verse?"

"You mean you haven't looked it up?"

"No. I didn't know how to find it," I lied. He was probably thinking it didn't take a super genius to figure it out and, truth be told, we had a Bible on the shelf at the cottage. If I had really wanted to, I could have figured it out.

"Why don't we look it up now," he suggested, pushing a thick, brown book across the desk toward me.

"You want *me* to look it up?"

Joe simply nodded his head. I didn't know where to start. Where would Corinthians be inside of a book with so many pages?

"Front or back?" I asked meekly.

"The New Testament."

"Front or Back?" I asked again.

"Back."

Much to my surprise, it didn't take me long to find it. Once I reached 2 Corinthians, I found the verse and read it aloud.

Praise be to the God and Father of our Lord Jesus Christ, the Father of compassion and the God of all comfort, who comforts us in all our troubles, so that we can comfort those in any trouble with the comfort we ourselves receive from God.

"What does this mean?" I asked, still staring at the verse.

"It means that during hard times we receive comfort and hope from God. Not so we can keep that comfort for ourselves, but so we can share that comfort with others who are in need. It is through God's comfort that we receive the strength to deal with our pain. It's not about hiding away the pain of the past. It's about opening our heart so that others may see the scars. Then they will ask us how it came to be that we were healed.

Our scars are proof that we survived and that will give others hope."

"*To open your heart to someone means exposing the scars of the past.*"

"I like that."

"It's something my grandmother... my nana used to say."

"Your grandmother is a very special woman."

"She was."

Pastor Joe sighed. "You have the name Manila Crow written at the top of the paper and also the name Mary?"

"Manila Crow came up on the caller ID, but the caller said her name was Mary."

Joe chuckled. "What a sense of humor."

He continued to chuckle and began to shake his head in disbelief. I had obviously missed the punch line.

"Throughout history, the crow has symbolized many things. In some parts of the world, the crow represents a prophecy or a bad omen. The Arabs call the crow the Abu Zajir or the 'Father of Omens.' Another story tells of how Satan disguised himself as a single black bird and flew into St. Benedict's face, causing him excruciating sexual temptation for a beautiful girl he had once seen. It is said that St. Benedict tore his clothes, which was an outward sign of grief or distress, and jumped into a bush of thorns. It was said that this painful act freed him from sexual temptation for a lifetime.

"The crow has been called the messenger of death, a devourer of flesh, a tattler, a spy, and a divulger of secrets. But in the Bible, the crow or raven represents Christian solitude, divine providence, affection, wisdom, hope, longevity, death, change, prophecy, and even an emblem of the Virgin *Mary*. In the book of First Kings, the crow or raven brought Elijah bread and meat in the morning and in the evening while Elijah was in hiding. So you see, in the Bible, the crow is a very important messenger indeed, delivering everything one needs to survive.

"But why me? Why did I get the phone call?"

"I don't know, but I will say this. Alex has come back from the dead to save you, and you are getting messages from Manila Crow in the name of Mary. I think someone is trying to get your attention, and I think it is time you listen. Examine your heart. Study the verse. What scars do you have that could help another heal? When you find this answer, you will understand why you are being called. I do know this: When the phone rings, you should pick up."

My heart had been through a myriad of changes. The shell that surrounded my heart last year was gone. I was now able to examine my heart, but I didn't like what I found. My heart was in dire straights. I was a mess. My heart was bleeding, and I couldn't stop the leak. Everything inside my body was mixed up. I was hiding away in Alexandria trying to survive in more ways than one. How could I help someone else when I couldn't even help myself? What did the crow mean to me? Was it a sign of good or a sign of evil? Or perhaps the crow was Satan and I was St. Benedict. Did I need to throw myself into a thorny bush to save myself from sin? I liked the other scenario much better. I liked to think this crow was good, that this crow was sending me a message, bringing me what I needed to survive. But what was the message? The message was 2 Corinthians 1: 3-4. I remembered it word for word.

Praise be to the God and Father of our Lord Jesus Christ, the Father of compassion and the God of all comfort, who comforts us in all our troubles, so that we can comfort those in any trouble with the comfort we ourselves receive from God.

All at once I remembered the question I had asked God the night before. I recited it aloud.

"If everything does happen for a reason, and if every experience shapes us into the person that we are supposed to be, what is it all for? Who am I supposed to be? I know You are God, and I know You exist, but why do You let me suffer? If You are God and You are love, then how could

You let me feel such pain? How could You let my mother feel pain? How could You let my sister die?"

All at once I realized that He had given me my answer!

CHAPTER TWENTY-FOUR

I should be grouchy, but I wasn't. It was Halloween. I was glowing... excited... and it had everything to do with the deluxe Wonder Woman costume Alex surprised me with yesterday morning. When I was a little girl, I wanted to be Wonder Woman for Halloween, but I had to be Mickey Mouse instead. One year, I was a hobo and another year, a clown. I often wondered why I hated Halloween so much. I attributed it to the fact that I wasn't really into dressing up, but when Alex walked into the cottage with the Wonder Woman costume, I realized that just wasn't the case.

"Oh goodie, goodie," I shouted when I saw it. The costume was perfect. It came with a star-patterned skirt, knee-high red boots with a white stripe up the front, silver wristbands, a bright red cape, and a gold headband. Even more surprising than the Wonder Woman costume was the next costume Alex pulled out of the bag.

"What are you going as?" I asked. He told me he was going as a beer garden guy and that the name of his costume was called Oktoberfest. I asked him why he wasn't going as a superhero. He laughed and told me it was because he was already a superhero, and he wanted to be normal for a change. I had to laugh with him. Sometimes I forgot that Alex was anything but normal. He looked real and felt real, but was he?

Halloween: the day when you get to be something out of the ordinary, something extraordinary and powerful, and Alex chooses to be a beer man. For the first time ever, it dawned on me that my boyfriend was what everyone aspired to be: incredible. He was supernatural. He could heal my body with the tips of his fingers. He could fight off demons and the darkest forms of evil. He had amazing strength and I was proud that he was mine. I pulled Alex's costume out of the plastic bag and held it up for a closer look. The ensemble included a tight, white short-sleeved button up shirt, a pair of green above the knee shorts with suspenders to match, white knee high socks with green stripes at the top, and a green hat with a yellow feather on the left hand side. I couldn't wait to see how he looked in it, but when I awoke this morning, the first thought that entered my mind was *my* costume and how *I* would look in it.

I crawled out of bed, tried on my costume, and stood in front of the mirror, staring at my reflection. I looked and felt invincible. I didn't even mind that we were going to a Halloween party at Corrine's house. Because Halloween fell on the weekend, all the local kids that had gone off to college were coming back just to attend the soiree. Plus, some of her new friends from the Community College would be there. It would be a full house, and for once in my life I would blend right in.

"Do you think we should just leave a bowl on the front porch for all of the kiddos?" Alex asked.

"Kiddos?"

"The trick-or-treaters."

"Oh, yeah, the trick-or-treaters. Sure, I guess. We live five minutes out of town. Do you think we'll even have trick-or-treaters?"

"I don't know, but I want to be prepared." Alex had bought eight bags of assorted candy, and he was dumping them into a metal tub he had washed out in the sink.

"Let me have a Twix," I said, grabbing two miniature sized candy bars out of the bucket and unwrapping them before shoving them into my mouth. "Now that's what I call breakfast."

"Do you need some coffee to go with that chocolate?"

"You know I do." The dark brown liquid had just begun to drip, and Alex had a mug sitting beside the coffeepot. Sitting next to the mug, he had purposefully placed a box of organic sugar and a spoon.

I rolled my eyes at Alex and grabbed my creamer out of the fridge.

"You don't even want me to get started on the creamer you use. There's nothing natural about it." Alex grabbed the bottle out of my hands and started to read the label. "I don't even think this is a milk product."

"You're right. I don't want you to get started. Now give me back my creamer," I said, grabbing the bottle and pouring a small measure into my cup until it turned a light and creamy brown. "You know what's going to happen if you put all of that candy on the front porch unattended. The first kid that comes by is going to take it all."

"That would be dishonest."

"Just saying. That's what I would do," I told him.

"What's wrong with humans?"

"Are you kidding? Absolutely everything."

"So, are you excited about the party tonight?"

"I guess so. Are you?" I asked, helping myself to another Twix.

"It will be good to get out. We can't hide away forever."

"What are you talking about? We get out of the house. We both have jobs. I even go to the grocery store all by myself."

"I just mean that since we've been here, we really haven't gone out of our way to meet anyone new."

"I object. We had a dinner party."

"And that went well. You nearly lost your job."

"Well, I don't mind going out so much anymore."

"And I'm proud of you. I don't mean to be the bearer of bad news, but nothing has changed. Chloe and Ben are still out there… somewhere. I can feel it."

I could feel it, too, but I wasn't going to tell him why. I was not going to tell him about Chloe's visit. Not tonight. I simply nodded in agreement. Alex interpreted the look on my face as one of concern and made an immediate attempt to correct his blunder.

"Don't worry, Rae. I am here to protect you, just like always. Like I said, nothing at all has changed."

"Can't we make it all just go away?"

"No."

"But we can pretend, can't we?"

"For one night, we can pretend."

"I guess Halloween isn't really all that bad. It's all about pretending, pretending you're something you're not."

Alex pulled his costume out of the bag and held it up to his body.

"What do you think?"

"I think I'll call you Franz."

"I think I'll stick with Alex."

Alex had admitted on more than one occasion that he was fairly fond of his name. So much so that he hadn't considered changing it to quiet my parents' suspicions.

"How about Englebert, then. I think Englebert is a German name."

"I'd take Franz over Englebert any day."

"Then Franz it is."

"Your costume is great, by the way. You look more like Wonder Woman than Wonder Woman."

"Thank you," I blushed, then turned full circle so he could see it in its entirety.

"No… thank *you*. Thank you for finding my godfather. I'm eternally grateful."

"You're going to meet with him again today?"

"Yeah. In an hour."

"You guys are becoming joined at the hip."

"I guess so. It's kind of nice. I feel like I'm really starting to know my mom and dad."

"I'm sorry that I kept him a secret. That wasn't fair."

"It's okay. I understand why you did. But no more secrets, okay."

I cleared my throat. "Okay."

"What are you going to do while I'm gone?"

"Finish *Gone with the Wind.* Maybe we can talk about it when you get home?"

"Can't wait."

Corrine's house was seven down from ours, and Alex and I chose to take the road instead of using the lane by the lake to get there. We stayed close to the forest on the other side of the street so we could see oncoming traffic. It was 8:30 when we started out and completely dark, not a star in the sky, and the moon was hiding somewhere behind the clouds. I could hear music coming from Corrine's before we even stepped out of our cottage door, but now that we were drawing closer to her house, which was at least five times larger than all three of our cottages put together, the music was so loud that my eardrums were pulsing. The fact that Mr. Finnegan had complained about my dog barking, yet had no complaints about the raging party at the Harvey house was further proof that he despised me. You could see the Harvey's house a mile away; it was lit up with strings of different colored lights. Corrine had gone a bit overboard with the decorations. I caught a glimpse of a devil (all bright red and shiny with little devil horns) running out the door and sloshing drink out of his cup as he chased Little Bo Peep down to the lake.

"Do you think her parents are home?" I asked, even though I already knew the answer. Mrs. Harvey was about as strict as they come. I couldn't envision her throwing a Halloween party for Corrine and all of her friends, especially when Corrine was still on probation for her behavior at school.

"The Harvey's are out of town for the weekend. Didn't you know?"

"No, I didn't. How did you?" I shivered.

"Word travels fast along the North Shore. Are you cold?"

"Freezing. But it's worth it."

"I wish I had a coat to give you. I guess my arm will have to do." Alex pulled me in close as we walked up the wide path to Corrine's house.

"It looks smoky in there."

"We'll survive."

"Are you sure this is a good idea?"

"No. I'm not sure it's a good idea at all."

With a houseful of guests, I thought it would take Corrine at least thirty minutes to find us. Unfortunately, I heard her calling Alex's name before we'd even made it through the kitchen. Her voice was loud and shrill over the music. I rolled my eyes when I saw her costume. She was dressed up as Swiss Miss. Standing next to Alex, she looked like *she* was his date. The skirt of her light blue dress was full, but stopped just above her knees. From the waist up, the tight, white material of the dress formed a bustier that she had stuffed herself into. I looked down at her feet. She was wearing black Mary Janes and white knee-highs. I glanced at Alex's knee-highs.

Well, aren't they just the perfect match, I thought.

It only took a second for Corrine to monopolize Alex. She was talking to him, but I couldn't hear what she was saying. I felt like the *Invisible* Woman, not *Wonder* Woman, and all at once, I hated Halloween all over again. All dressed up like Wonder Woman, ready to fight the world, and I didn't even have the strength to fight for my man. My eyes roamed around the room looking for someone, anyone I recognized. I slipped past Corrine and Alex, unnoticed, and made my way to the back of the house, observing the Harvey's gaudy décor along the way.

The living room was crowded with creatures of the night, but it wasn't hard to spot the oversized Spiderman conversing with Michael Meyers and a zombie. Spiderman was supposed to be fairly small, but this one was huge. As I walked through the smoke-filled room, my eyes began to burn, so I headed toward the back door. I snuck one last look at Spidey before slipping outside; he was waving at me from across the crowded room, obviously trying to get my attention.

The night was cool, and I accepted the fresh air with gratitude. I stood on the deck for a moment, taking in a deep breath and gazing into the distance toward the lake. A large group of Corrine's friends had built a fire by the shore, so I headed in the opposite direction, around the side of the house and back toward the front. A small building sat between Corrine's house and the road. I supposed it was the garage. I didn't hear any noise on the other side of the garage, so I advanced toward it quickly before Spiderman decided to follow. I wondered if Corrine still had Alex trapped in the corner of the kitchen. At the moment, I didn't feel the need to rescue him. In a way, I was tired of fighting. Keeping Corrine away from my man was futile.

Why did I even come here, I asked myself, sitting down on the hard gravel driveway, wishing I had a barrier thicker than Wonder Woman's skirt between my cheeks and the jagged stones. I stared at the darkness across the street that was the forest. I shuddered. Good things never happened in the forest, at least not to me. I ran alongside the forest everyday, but I had never entered. Maybe it had something to do with what happened to me the last time I went into the woods in Oklahoma by myself. Benard Bodin attacked me, and Alex had come to my rescue. I should be able to remember every last detail about that day, but I can't. When I looked into Ben's eyes I saw evil... that I do remember. I remember feeling his wrath more than I remember the feeling of his hands clenched around my throat. I remember the fear more than I remember the pain. I shivered just thinking about it. I wrapped my red, satin cape around my shoulders and hugged myself tightly. Wonder Woman defeated by the Swiss Miss. I picked myself up off the ground and without thinking, headed down the gravel driveway in the direction of the woods. If I disappeared into the night would anyone notice? Would anyone come searching for me? I had done it before. I had left my parents behind. I had vanished. My mother had sent me an email, but neither she nor my father had tried to find me. Not that I wanted the police involved, but shouldn't parents call the police when their children disappear? Was my presence in their lives that meaningless? It wasn't that I wanted them to come after me; if they did, it would defeat my whole reason for leaving. But it would be nice to know they had tried. And then there was Alex, who was so engrossed in his conversation with Corrine that he didn't even notice when I left. What would he do if I just disappeared into the night? Would he accept my departure, or would he come looking for me? What was it that was holding us together in the first place? Was it Ben and Chloe? What if Ben and Chloe ceased to exist and Alex was allowed to leave? If I were no longer in mortal danger, would he lose interest? If there were nothing left to fight for, would that make me boring? Was I what he found alluring, or was it the fight?

Fourth Way to Lose Alex Loving: Become so boring that he no longer cares

I decided to put the notion to the test. I glanced over my shoulder. I had an unobstructed view into the kitchen window, and I could see Alex. Corrine's hand was on his arm, her head thrown back in laughter. He seemed captivated by her. I checked my phone for the time. It was 9:15. I would see how long it took before he noticed I was gone. Night surrounded me on every side and dry leaves crunched beneath my feet as I entered the forest. I looked over my shoulder once again and saw the glow of the party fifty feet away. I stood still for a moment, listening, and then I shuddered. There was something about watching a party from a distance that was very, very lonely. In an instant, I knew how Alex must have felt in the halfway, watching me, a girl who didn't know he even existed. I couldn't think of anything lonelier than that.

Deep in thought, I moved through the darkness, crunching through the leaves and twigs until I felt my foot hit something hard. A searing pain shot up my leg, and tears leaped to my eyes. Hunched over with my right hand on my throbbing toe, I stretched my left hand blindly in front of me, and I ran my hand across the smooth surface of the object that was blocking my path. It was large and as hard as a rock. Actually, it *was* a rock. I released my toe and sat down upon the stone. Wrapping my cape around my shoulders, I watched from the woods as the party continued without me. In the quiet of the woods, I thought about Pastor Joe and what it meant to find the truth. I wondered what my truth was. Joe made it sound like the quest of finding it would be an adventure. I had just begun to consider Alex's meeting with Pastor Joe when I heard tree branches breaking in the distance. I sat stock-still and continued to listen.

"Rae," a voice called out of the darkness, a voice I recognized but could not place. All at once I was crippled with fear.

"Rae," the voice called again. It was a man's voice, but it was not Alex's. Someone else was in the forest with me, someone other than my boyfriend.

"What are you doing out here all alone?" The sound of crackling leaves grew louder as the man drew near. "Don't you know that the forest is no place for girls to go alone?"

His voice snuck up behind me. I took in a shallow breath. I swallowed hard and held perfectly still.

"Where are you, Rae?" The crunching stopped. "I know you're out here. Just tell me where you are."

I'm not sure if it was the closeness of his voice, or the familiar cologne that revealed his identity.

"I'm right here, Flynt."

"Where?"

"Sitting on a rock."

"Say something again so I can hear your voice."

"What do you want me to say?"

"Tell me that you like my costume."

"Um... I like your costume, Flynt."

"Ah, there you are, Wonder Woman."

"Where are you?" I whispered through the darkness.

"Right beside you," he said, touching my hair with the back of his hand. "Why are you out here all by yourself?"

"I don't know. I suppose Wonder Woman doesn't really fit in."

"Neither does Spider Man," he laughed.

"You're kidding, right. You're Spider Man?"

"Yep. I'm Spidey. Let me have your hand."

I reached my hand into the darkness until I felt the warmth of human skin on mine.

"I'm even wearing a mask," he said, moving my hand with his and not releasing it until it fell upon something silky.

I let my fingers linger on his face for a moment before returning my hand to my knee.

"So, what's the real reason you're out here all alone? It wouldn't have anything to do with Corrine talking to Alex, would it?"

"Maybe a little something to do with that."

"I wish I could say you have something to worry about, but you don't. I mean… you and Alex are cosmic, right?"

"Yeah, we're cosmic alright. And right now it feels like we're on opposite sides of the world."

"You mean the universe?"

"Even worse, but yes, that's what I meant to say."

"Don't be so hard on Alex. It's not him; it's Corrine."

"Maybe," I reluctantly agreed. "It's a little bit chilly out here. Do you want to walk?" I asked.

"Sure."

We started back in the direction of the house. At first, in silence, but then I changed the subject to something it didn't hurt to talk about.

"What made you choose Spider Man?"

"I'm fascinated by the webs that he shoots out of his hands. That's all there is to it." He laughed. "Why the Wonder Woman costume?"

"I've wanted to be Wonder Woman ever since I was a little girl," I told him.

"So then, this is a dream come true for you?"

"More like a dream that turned into a nightmare."

"This doesn't feel like a nightmare to me. And you make a beautiful Wonder Woman, by the way. I just want you to know that."

It was dark, and when Flynt slipped his arm around my shoulder, I didn't see it coming. If I hadn't been so cold I would have objected.

"I've been meaning to ask you a rather serious question."

"Oh no. I don't like serious questions. What is it?"

"Well, I was wondering. What is your favorite art supply?"

I began to laugh. "Of all of the questions that you could ask me, you want to know that?"

"I've just been wondering. You're a bit mysterious. You don't talk about yourself. I think your answer will tell me a lot about who you are."

"Wow. I didn't realize you were so deep."

"I'm not a complete idiot."

"Alex thinks you are."

"That's not surprising."

"Gesso."

"Huh?"

"Gesso's my favorite art supply."

"Gesso. Really? I wouldn't have guessed that. Do you mind me asking why?"

"Because it's thick and white and it covers up imperfections. I would like to believe that, no matter how bad I mess things up, I have the ability to start over... start from scratch."

"If you were a painting, I would never gesso over you. You're perfect just the way you are."

"That's a horrible pick up line, Flynt, but thanks."

By anyone's standards, Flynt was good looking. His thick, blond hair was always perfectly mussed, and there were many things about him that I liked. But when Flynt said that I was perfect, I didn't blush. I could relate to Flynt in ways I couldn't relate to Alex. Although Flynt had his life together, he was not perfect. I found comfort in his imperfections and warmth in his humanity. He was my friend... and maybe my best.

"So, how did you end up at Corrine's house, anyway? I thought you couldn't stand her."

Flynt knew I had just as many reasons not to be at Corrine's party as he did, and I was ready for him to say something smart in return like, *touché*, but he said nothing at all. When I felt his arm slip away from my shoulder, I wondered if I had said something wrong. I waited for him to respond, but he did not. In fact, I couldn't even hear him breathing. When I realized Flynt was no longer beside me, I stopped in my tracks and a chill that was completely unrelated to the cold night air swept over me.

"Flynt?" I whispered with uncertainty, but he didn't respond.

"Flynt?" I said again, louder this time, but there was only silence.

"Flynt, this isn't funny. Stop playing games and talk to me... right now."

If it hadn't been for the quiver in my voice, I would have sounded demanding. I looked toward the road and felt relieved when I saw the outline of Flynt's body; he was standing at the edge of the forest near the road, and the light from Corrine's house glowed behind him, allowing me to see his silhouette.

"Hey, Flynt, wait up."

"When will you ever learn that you shouldn't drag others into your mess?" His voice was deep and chilled me to the bone. This voice was not the voice of Flynt.

"Who's there?"

The stranger laughed. "Should you even have to ask? You really are just a silly little girl. You're all dressed up like a superhero, but you don't have the power to keep your only friend alive. Or is he more than a friend to you? He looked like more than a friend to me."

"What did you do to him? Did you hurt him? What do you want from me? Tell me right now why you hate me," I screamed.

"So that I can answer all of your questions with one simple sentence, let's just say that blood runs deep." His laugh was baritone, menacing, and his answer was anything but simple.

"Quit hurting everyone I love. If it's me you hate, then take me. I'm hardly worth all your trouble. I'm sure you'll only be disappointed in the end."

"Don't worry. I will take you, but I assure you that I will not be disappointed. While your boyfriend is busy flirting with… what's her name… *Cory*, I plan to finish you off. There's no one here to help, Rae. It's over."

I guess I should have been more fearful of his threats, but at the moment I was more focused on the way that he said Cory's name. I hated the sound of her name. It made me want to fight.

"Are you going to make this easy, or are you gong to make it fun? Just so you know, I prefer a fight. I'd really hate to see that Wonder Woman costume go to waste. Chloe is waiting at home for a story that is action packed. Besides, it will give me something to laugh about for years to come."

Action packed, I thought. Very quickly I tried to assess my strengths, which were practically nonexistent compared to Ben's. But there had to be something working to my advantage. Think. Think. And then all at once I knew. I thought about the wire-rimmed glasses he wore when I first met him at the American school in Amsterdam. He was as blind as a bat. So, what had changed? He no longer wore them. Why? Regardless, the night was as dark as I had ever seen. Ben was still standing with his back to Corrine's house, which was at least fifty yards away, and the light that poured out of the Harvey's home continued to form a soft ring of light around his body. I realized I had the optimal position. I was standing in front of Ben, surrounded by darkness. He couldn't see me, but I could see him. Without moving my feet, I reached out with my arms and felt first to my left and then to my right. I was relieved when the tips of my fingers brushed across the rough bark of the tree next to me. Without disturbing the leaves beneath my feet, I inched closer to the tree, leaning against it and silently pulling off my boots.

"I can't see you, Rae, but I can hear you creeping around. I'm getting closer. I'm going to get you." The tone of his voice filled me with fear, but I didn't speak; instead, I focused on my plan of action, which was to scale the side of the tree. It had crossed my mind that, once again, I was taking the flight instead of the fight option. I was taking the easy way out, trying to save my own life while Flynt, my good friend Flynt, was lying somewhere in these woods.

"You're not going to speak, is that it? You *are* making this rather fun, Rae. A real Halloween treat."

Trying my hardest not to make a noise, I stretched my hands above my head and held on tight to the highest branch I could reach. Silently, I swung myself back and forth, gaining both speed and height. After another full swing, my legs caught the next branch up, trapeze style. I was now hanging upside down with my knees wrapped around the branch of a tree, and Benard Bodin was standing directly below me. Using strength that I didn't know I had, I lifted myself up so that I was resting on the limb. I searched frantically for another limb of the tree I could use to pull myself up higher.

"Come out little birdie and sing me a pretty song. I have been trying to catch you for years, but you just keep flying away. But I *will* catch you tonight. There is no one here to save you now. Not your parents. Not Alex. There's no one here but the two of us… and Flynt. But he won't be here much longer, I'm afraid." Ben chortled.

I was now securely positioned in the tree, at least ten feet above Benard, which was high enough. I was safer now than I was before, but I felt horrible. I was a coward. I was hiding in a tree while Flynt was dying a horrible death below. To hear him breathing or moaning would be so much better than hearing nothing at all. But the only breathing I could hear was Ben's. He was still standing directly below me. I wondered if perhaps he was rethinking his strategy. I began to wonder if Flynt was already dead, and then I began to wonder how long I could sit in this scratchy tree.

The cold was creeping through my skin and into my bones. My teeth were beginning to chatter. I was going to have to do something and soon. I needed to save Flynt, and time was of the essence. I had just begun to contemplate my next move when I heard something in the distance. It was the fast crunching of leaves and limbs breaking underfoot. It was the swift sound of a creature leaping through the forest. I looked over my shoulder at Corrine's house. Light was shining from the kitchen window, and I could make out Corrine still standing there, but Alex was gone. It wasn't until the forest floor began to swirl with leaves and branches that I realized what was going on. With all my strength, I clung to the trunk of the tree with one hand while I shielded my face with the other. The rumbling freight train sound I heard on the path in Oklahoma months ago had returned, which could only mean one thing: Ben and Alex were at it again. Alex had come to my rescue. I retrieved my phone from my bustier. It was 9:30. It had only taken fifteen minutes for Alex to find me. He was fighting for me while I was sitting up high on the branch of a tree. I was disgusting. Flynt had followed me into the woods. I knew he cared about me. But he didn't know what I was. He was dead. I was sure of it, and I knew that it was my fault. As I watched my boyfriend fight for my life, I knew I would never forgive myself if something happened to him. If he died tonight, then I would die by his side.

My hand was no longer enough to block the debris that was swirling around me. Dirt was being pulled from the earth and dispersed into the air. I was gagging… choking. With my eyes closed, I hugged the tree and buried my face into its rough skin. Last May, when I witnessed Alex and Ben fighting for the first time, the wind blew so hard it stung; it was cutting, but at least it was warm. Tonight, as I curled myself into a ball, the wind was not only cutting, but also very cold. It felt like thousands of needles were piercing my skin, and I could feel my blood turn frigid as it dripped down my arms and legs. Only minutes had passed, but it felt like I had been listening to the freight train rumbling on for hours. And then all at once, it was silent and a bright light shown through the lids of my closed eyes.

"Are you going to come down, Wonder Woman?" His voice was smooth and beautiful. I looked below me and saw the angelic Alex. Alex, without his ruggedness. Angelic Alex, with chiseled cheekbones and ruby lips. Alex, with shiny, emerald eyes. Alex, without a single scratch on his body.

"Flynt." That's all I could say, and then I began to cry.

CHAPTER TWENTY-FIVE

*B*y the time the paramedics arrived on the scene, Flynt's heart rate was faint but steady, which was a good sign. Ben's attack had been quick but brutal, and the blood Flynt had lost from the attack was substantial. This news was hard for me to take. I could hear perfectly Ben's voice chanting, "Blood runs deep." How stained was the forest floor because of me? Flynt's blood might wash away, but this memory could never be washed from my mind. I would never forget. Flynt's life would be a constant reminder of the curse that surrounds me. I did the only thing that I could think to do: I prayed.

"God. Are you there for me like you are for my mom? I know you are there, but are you listening to me like you listen to her?" There was only silence. "If I were you, I wouldn't listen to me either. I am a mess. Everyone I care about gets hurt and some of them even die. I pray tonight that you will either give me strength or take my life. I cannot live like a coward any longer. Are you trying to get my attention, because you have it now? I am here, so what is it that you want? What is it that you want me to do? What kind of strength do I have that you could possibly use? Look at me. I am a skinny little girl in a Wonder Woman suit. I am pretending. Is there anything about my life that is real? Please give me some answers, and please, God, I beg you, please let Flynt be okay."

Luckily the hospital was less than ten minutes away, and once inside the ER, Flynt would get the transfusion he needed. The donated blood would bring his pressure back up to normal and slow his heart rate down a bit. I heard words like *hypovolemic* and *internal hemorrhaging*. Flynt was strapped to a stretcher and covered with a blanket. With great difficulty, the EMS started an IV. Apparently, Flynt had lost so much blood that his body had started to shut down, causing the vessels to constrict, making it next to impossible for the paramedics to find a vein. His natural sun kissed complexion that I found so uncharacteristic of Minnesotans was now snowy white, and his lips were a frosty shade of blue. He looked dead. He was unconscious, and I was scared. I was terrified of what could happen. I was terrified he would die. I hoped God had heard my prayers. If he could work a miracle for me, now would be a good time. I had done nothing to deserve an answer. I hadn't been good enough for God to listen to me. I had been lying for months, and I was pretty sure that *Thou shall not lie* was one of the Ten Commandments.

When the police finally arrived, I was sitting in the back of the ambulance while the paramedics treated my superficial scrapes and cuts. I told them not to worry about me and to take care of Flynt. I didn't matter. Besides, I knew that once we got home, Alex could simply touch me, and I would be healed. How long had Flynt been lying on the ground? An hour at least, I thought. He *should* be dead. Had Alex brought him back? Had he given him enough life to last until the paramedics arrived?

Of course, the police were asking questions, as they should in a situation like this. I don't remember what I told them or if I told them anything at all, but I do remember seeing Alex in a heated conversation with the cops. I made a mental note to ask him about it later. My appearance alone was all the evidence they needed to prove that I was not the cause of Flynt's near fatal accident. While waiting in the back of the ambulance, I thought back to the first time I saw Ben and Alex battle. They completely destroyed everything within a one mile radius, and I began to fear what the police might find when the sun shed light on the scene tomorrow morning.

I was a mess when I walked into the ER, but I was in such a state of shock I didn't care. My costume was ripped to shreds and bruises were already starting to form. I looked like I had been in a tornado. My hair was standing on end, and Alex had been plucking out bits of dead leaves for the past thirty minutes. The ER hadn't changed at all since my last visit. It was a different ER, but the smell was still the same. All of the furniture was hard and cheap, and there was a fish tank in the middle of the waiting room. Alex and I hadn't even made it to the front desk before a group from Corrine's party surrounded us, asking questions and begging for answers. Without their masks they looked familiar, but I didn't know any of them personally. I was in no state to answer questions, and Alex was certainly in no mood. He lifted his hand without saying a word, and the crowd of kids parted like the Red Sea parted for Moses. We walked up to the front desk, and Alex spoke for the both of us; however, we did not get the answer we wanted to hear. Only family was allowed back, and we were not kin. We would have to take a seat in the lobby with everyone else. I noticed Corrine was not present. I assumed she had her own set of issues to deal with. The police were very interested in the fact that she was having a party in her parents' house while they were away. I wondered how grounded she would be now. Mrs. Harvey would make her life miserable from here on out.

After emergency surgery, Flynt's condition was stable, but he would be staying a couple of nights. I closed my eyes and thanked God for answering me and for answering me so quickly. Maybe he was listening. "I owe you one," I whispered. "Anything you want I will do."

I picked the small, blue loveseat by the fish tank, and Alex sat down beside me. I rested my head on his shoulder and let out a sigh. The adrenaline was waning and reality was beginning to set in.

"Looks like you're going to need a new Wonder Woman costume. Yours is ripped to shreds." Alex laughed to ease the tension.

"It would be okay with me if I never saw this costume again. I'm not fit to wear it. I'm a coward. Ben is right. I'm a little bird that flies away. If I'm not running, I'm flying."

"I guess I still don't understand what you were doing in the woods with Flynt. Should I be worried?" The accusing tone of his voice was infuriating and all at once, I lifted my head from his shoulder and words came flying from my mouth.

"If you hadn't been ogling Corrine, I wouldn't be in this predicament."

"And if you would have been listening to what Corrine was saying, you wouldn't have gone into the woods."

"I don't want to fight with you," I said, staring at the fish tank. Alex's eyes joined mine, and we began to study the fish. We sat in silence, watching them glide through the water. The fish tank was elaborate, filled with a plethora of sea creatures and brightly colored coral that provided nooks and crannies and formed dark tunnels for the more adventurous fish to swim through.

"What did you tell the police?"

"I told them it was *Sasquatch*. The cop took one look at me in my lederhosen and laughed."

"Smart Alec. What happened to Ben?"

"He left."

"This earth?"

"No. He's still here. He just… ran away again."

"Again?"

"Yes."

"You're so strong."

"So are you."

"No, I'm not. I'm weak."

"Being a human is hard work," Alex stated.

I studied his beer boy costume. The thin white shirt was shredded and stained a dirty brown, but there wasn't a scratch on his body.

"It would be much easier being a fish," he said, still staring at the tank with interest.

"Not really," I told him. "Fish are a lot like humans… in a way."

"How so?" Alex laughed.

"Look at the yellow fish," I instructed. "He's the adventurous one. He has no fear. Do you see the tunnel over there?" I asked, pointing with my finger to the corner of the tank. "He is the only fish in the tank that dares to swim into the dark. Nothing scares him. Look, he's going in right now."

Alex and I watched the yellow tang. There was a crab stationed at the mouth of the tunnel. He stretched out his claw and nipped the tang, but the yellow fish showed no sign of retreat. After disappearing for a moment, the yellow tang swam out of the tunnel to mingle with the rest of the fish.

"Nothing bothers the tang. He's beautiful. He's a warrior. If you were a fish, you'd be the yellow tang."

"What about that slimy thing?" Alex pointed to a barnacle attached to the side of the tank. "Who would that be?"

"A lazy person, or maybe someone who is so comfortable in their life they have no desire to do anything greater. They have no desire to reach out into the world; instead, they wait for the world to come to them."

"Did you ever think that maybe they're not lazy at all. Maybe they're just scared. Maybe it's fear that holds them to the tank."

"Maybe."

"Well," I said, forcing a laugh. "The crab is easy." I pointed to the crab that was poking his head out of the dark tunnel and using his pincers to inflict pain on the passersby. Both Alex and I studied the crab at work. Every so often he would scurry out of his hole and swat at the yellow fish for no apparent reason.

"What a crab," Alex laughed.

I giggled. "The crab reminds me of Mr. Finnegan." Alex laughed again.

"Look at the sea anemone," Alex said, pointing. "I think that sea anemone is like a Mom. She is constantly moving in all directions to provide protection for those she loves, but she's not the first thing people notice. She never leaves her home, and she never stops protecting. I think she is the most beautiful creature in the tank."

"I agree."

"So which fish would you be?" Alex asked.

"Do you see that little gray fish at the bottom? Watch how it feeds. It swims in fast to get what it wants, and then it leaves before the other fish notice. It's sneaky. It's deceiving. I'm not proud of it, but I'm the gray fish."

Flynt was moved to hospital room 209, and when I got to the door I knocked softly, hoping he wouldn't hear, hoping for any excuse to turn around and walk away. Standing at the door to Flynt's hospital room took me back to the day about six months ago when I was about to enter my nana's room in the ICU. I had been terrified of what I might find. And now I felt terrified once again. I loved Flynt in a way that was different from the way I loved Nana. She was my strength, my rock; she was the glue that held all of my broken pieces together. Without her, I didn't know if I would ever be whole again. Standing outside Flynt's door wasn't quite the same. He was weak, and I preyed upon that weakness; my actions had almost cost him his life. If I had been brutally honest with Flynt, he wouldn't have followed me into the woods. Flynt was the kind of guy who would jump off a building if I told him to do it, and I was the kind of girl who would watch him fall.

"Come in."

I heard Flynt's voice, weak, above the beeping machines and the TV that was left on with the volume turned low.

I pushed open the door and felt a sudden shock. I guess I expected to see a hint of anger on his face, but I didn't. Flynt was sitting up in bed, a needle in one arm, a bag of blood hanging on a hook above his head, and a smile covering his face. He was still pale but not ghostly, and his lips were full and almost pink.

"I'm sorry," I told him hesitantly.

"For what?"

"For everything. But mostly, for being the reason you're here."

"I should be the one who's sorry." Flynt spoke just above a whisper. "It's embarrassing, really. I didn't do anything to help you." He paused and took in several shallow breaths. "You could have died, and it would have been my fault."

I wanted to tell Flynt he had it all wrong. That even if he had tried, he would have been no match for Ben. Instead, I said nothing.

"You shouldn't have followed me into the woods."

"I needed to talk to you."

"Why?"

"I needed to tell you something."

"What could you have told me that would have been worth all of this?"

"I think I love you." His voice was raspy, barely a whisper above the beeping machines. "You're not like other girls I know."

I swallowed hard. "You did lose a lot of blood. You're not making a bit of sense."

Flynt parted his lips to speak and quickly, but very gently, I put my finger to his mouth. "Shhh." My voice was so soft, I had to lean in closer for Flynt to hear. "Shhh," I told him again. "I need you to listen to me, Flynt. People I love don't last long. I need you to stay away from me... starting now. I'm not good for anyone."

"Except for Alex."

"Yes, except for Alex. But that's different."

"Because you're cosmic?"

"I wish that was the only reason why."

"You're not going to tell me why, are you?"

"No. I am not."

"There's something different about Alex. Am I right?"

I had grown fond of Flynt, and despite my increasingly impressive ability to lie, I couldn't bear to be dishonest with him, especially after everything that had happened. Not now. Not after he had come into the forest after me. Not after he nearly lost his life because of me. Not after he had professed his love.

"Yes," I whispered. "You're right. He's not like you."

"Is that why you don't love me back?"

"I love you. I just don't love you in that way. I promise it has nothing to do with you. You're perfect just the way you are. It has everything to do with Alex. There are things between us that you will never understand."

"I can't remember exactly what happened last night, but I do remember bits and pieces."

I nearly stopped breathing. That Flynt might have witnessed what took place between Alex and Ben while he was lying on the forest floor was something I had not considered. I so vividly remember how I felt the first time I saw Alex and Ben fighting. I was terrified beyond words. What had he seen? What if he remembered everything? Would Alex and I be forced to leave our cozy cottage, the cottage that I had grown to love?

"What did you see?" I tried to keep my composure.

"Bright lights mixed with darkness. It was hard to keep my eyes open. It felt like I was in the middle of a sand storm. Debris was flying everywhere."

"Like I said before, you lost quite a bit of blood."

"There are still gaps in my memory, but I will remember it all, I know I will."

"Please," I begged. "Don't try. Don't try to remember. Try to forget."

"Will I see you again?"

"I think it would be best if you didn't."

"You seem so sure of yourself."

"That's because I am. Everyone I care about gets hurt. I have a way of breaking everything I touch."

I knew that I couldn't spare Flynt's feelings if I was going to save his life, so I shook off the sentiment and the soft smile on my face turned into something hard and warning. I realized that in order to save Flynt's life, I would have to hurt him, just like I had hurt my mom and dad. I would have to be hateful. I would have to send him on his way. I would have to convince him that we never had a chance.

"I will take care of the shop until you're ready to come back. But then I'm done. Don't try to come by. If you see me on the street, don't look my way. I don't care about you. I love Alex. Goodbye."

I got up from the chair I was sitting in and turned toward the door without looking his way.

"Rae," he called in a voice that was weak, barely a whisper.

I walked out of the room and closed the door behind me. I was becoming quite good at hurting people who loved me.

I kept the store running while Flynt was away and, as promised, when he was strong enough to return, I left the key to the store beside the register and walked out of Flynt's life without looking back. Things for Alex and I changed drastically after Halloween. Ben and Chloe were no longer just a threat, they had made their move. If it had gone their way, I would be dead. I knew Alex was supposed to protect me, but I kept the paring knife in my bedside drawer for safe measure.

Alex thought it would be best to lay low for a while, not only for reasons that had to do with Chloe and Ben, but for other reasons too. There was talk along the North Shore about the happenings in forest on the night of the Halloween. Mostly they were just stories that came from overactive imaginations, but some of the stories that were circulating held a bit of truth. The dust that rose from the air, the blinding flashes of light, and the ear piercing sound of an out of control freight train had drawn attention away from Corrine's party and to the woods. As I had feared, the morning light shown down on an unexplainable, circle shaped clearing in the woods. The county road we lived on was now crowded with cars, and the clearing in the forest was becoming a tourist attraction for vacationers and townspeople alike.

Because Flynt had lost so much blood, and because Alex was at the scene when the police arrived, people began to speculate that he was a creature of the night. They began to say things like, "I just knew there was something strange about him." I even overheard someone at the grocery store discussing how Alex liked to sharpen his fangs in public. I wasn't concerned about the stories that were circulating, but I was concerned about the attention they directed toward us. If Flynt's memories matched the tales that were being told, then Alex and I were in trouble. We would most certainly have to leave.

It was the first of December, a month since Ben attacked me in the woods. I was thankful when each day came to an end and there was no new threat from him or Chloe, and I was thankful when the changing of seasons confirmed that ample time had passed for people to forget.

When the ice became thick enough to walk on, the game of ice hockey replaced the game of gossip. Some of the local boys cleared the snow from the lake and left a beautiful and perfect patch of ice for hockey. Alex and I would sit and watch with other neighbors, but I could tell by the way he clenched and unclenched his jaws that he was just itching to get out there with them. I tried to imagine what it might be like to watch him play: the boy with the power to move mountains playing ice hockey with a group of unsuspecting college boys. Normally, Alex could keep his strength in check. But in the heat of the game, with all of that testosterone flying around, I wondered what would happen if he slipped. Sometimes Alex would step onto the ice for a closer look, so I would talk about the weather and the coming spring with Mrs. Harvey. I hadn't seen or heard from Corrine since Halloween. After her soiree, I was pretty sure her parents had locked her up and thrown away the key.

Katie Ramsey was another bystander. Her boyfriend was Cole Hawthorn, a winger for the University of Minnesota Gophers. It didn't take much to tell that she was proud. Most of the time I didn't much care for Alex showing his strength in public. I feared his strength might draw attention. But when I saw Katie looking at Cole, it made me desperately want to buy Alex a pair of skates and a stick. Sometimes I would think about Flynt when I watched the boys play. He was still too weak to play. I thought about his dreams of going pro, the dreams he shared with me, the dreams I had shattered.

The lake wasn't the only surface that was slick. The road in front of our house was covered in snow and no longer fit for running. Three days was about the max I could go without running before I would go crazy, and it was now about a week and a half since I had been running, and I was ready to pull my hair out. Even Alex could sense I was cranky, and he knew exactly why. Under normal conditions, he would encourage me to stay inside where it was warm and safe, but today, he was shooing me out, practically lacing up my running shoes and pushing me out the door. The snowplow had come through and cleared the roads, and the temperature was an almost tropical thirty-four degrees. The forecast was calling for heavy snow later in the week, so I decided to double up on my mileage today. When I told Alex I was getting really tired of the snow, he reminded me that soon, we would legally own an apartment in Paris. He was more than willing to move.

I pulled on a hooded sweatshirt and threw a warm fleece over the top. I adjusted the cotton balls in my ears before putting on my hat, and donned a pair of warm, knit gloves.

"Come on, Cocoa," I said, watching her tail wag back and forth in delight. I wasn't the dog whisperer or anything, but I knew without a doubt that Cocoa had fallen into a state of doggie depression without her morning exercise.

"Be careful," Alex called after me as I walked out the cottage door.

I didn't realize how much I missed the miles until I heard the metronymic sound of my feet padding on the asphalt beneath me. I had just worked up to a jog when I approached Mr. Finnegan's house. The light in his kitchen was on, and he was sitting at his table by himself. I stopped for a moment and stared into his window. I felt many things for Mr. Finnegan, but sorrow had never been one of them. But I couldn't help noticing how lonely he looked. I wondered if he had always sat at the table alone, or if once upon a time he had had a partner. I couldn't imagine anyone loving old Mr. Finnegan, but my father always told me there was someone out there for everyone. I quickened my pace until I reached a speed fast enough to release me from my worries. Running was the form of venting that I loved. I could pound my problems out on the pavement. Sometimes I pounded out Chloe and Ben and other times it was Corrine; but today, I wasn't thinking about my problems as I ran.

The cold weather and the trees that were heavy with snow had me singing Christmas carols instead. Christmas was on my mind. I had a couple of hundred dollars left over from working at Flynt's, and I wanted to use it to buy Alex's Christmas present. More than anything, I wanted to buy Alex the hockey stick and skates that he wanted. If I had enough left over, then I would buy him a Minnesota Wild jersey as well. I had searched for the skates online, but I couldn't find anything cheaper than 400 bucks. I didn't have that kind of money, but I wasn't about to settle for anything less. We had spent last Christmas apart and for all I knew, he might be sucked up to heaven before next Christmas, so I wanted this one to be very, very special. And then I thought of it. The little thrift store might have just what I need. I hadn't been there in several months, and since the roads were good, today was the perfect day to visit.

CHAPTER TWENTY-SIX

*I*t was the middle of December and we hadn't heard a peep from Chloe and Ben. They knew exactly where to find us, but they had made no further attacks. I was beginning to wonder what they were waiting for. The longer they waited, the more sure I was that they were better prepared than Alex and I could ever be. We knew they were close, but we hadn't the faintest idea of where to find them. I was sure that Chloe and Ben must be scheming, coming up with a failsafe way to kill us both, and I was becoming edgy. Alex, on the other hand, remained cool and collected. In fact, he seemed to be ignoring the problem all together. A part of me just wanted to get it over with. If I had to die, I would rather it not be a drawn out process. I didn't really want to keep thinking about all the ways it might happen, all the pain I might go through before I breathed my final breath. I thought about these things at night, when I was alone and Alex wasn't there to ask me what I was thinking about. I was pretty sure my life would end with drowning, but I couldn't stop myself from imagining other equally vivid scenarios. Coming in second on the list of possibilities was death by strangulation, because that was exactly how Ben had tried to do me in before. Coming in at third place was death by a penetrating wound.

The weeks leading up to Christmas had been pretty close to perfect, but for some reason, my spirits were down and although I tried my best, I could not pinpoint the reason why. Alex had been busy planning festivities to distract me from self-pity, but on occasion, it made me feel even worse when I saw that he was truly enjoying himself, enjoying all of these things as though he were experiencing them for the first time... and then I realized he was. I was sure he did not remember Christmas on earth as a human. Sometimes I forgot that he was only two years old when he died. I had experienced eighteen Christmas mornings. Eighteen years of putting up a tree and decorating it. Eighteen years of hanging stockings and wishing for snow on Christmas morning without seeing a single flake. I had seen snow the week before and the week after Christmas, but never on Christmas day. It seemed as though my wishes had been compiled and delivered all at once. It had snowed eighteen inches since the beginning of December and each new inch only added to Alex's enthusiasm. We now had to shovel ourselves out of the cottage and clear the path between my place and his on a daily basis. The way the drifts had piled up around the outside of the house made it look as though we were living in an igloo rather than a small wooden cottage.

Alex and I picked out our first Christmas tree several days before Christmas and while I had tried to be practical suggesting that we get an artificial tree at the hardware store, Alex convinced me that we should go to a local tree farm instead.

"I like the idea of having a real tree inside our house. Plus, we'll have more fun picking it out," he finally convinced me.

When all was said and done, we spent a fortune on the tree, but it was the most perfect tree I had ever seen. The Tree Farm was filled with families. The fathers were equipped with saws and twine, and we watched as they struggled to free the trees from the ground. It was clear they enjoyed it as a family outing, but I think they would have been much happier if the trees were more cooperative. When Alex pulled out his pocketknife and sliced through the trunk of the tree like it was made of butter instead of wood, they had an altogether different look on their faces. I can say with certainty that Alex's pocketknife wasn't the reason he was able to cut through the tree with ease, and it wasn't hard to see that he was just showing off.

"At least try to make it look difficult," I told him. "People are starting to stare. Women are actually drooling."

These were the kinds of things I often thought but never said. I was accustomed to the attention that Alex drew. He had the kind of beauty that would cause a person to stop and take a second look, a face so kind it drew you in. Alex shrugged his shoulders and began to bind the tree with some twine. He was just about to sling it over his shoulder when I stopped him.

"Can't you just drag the tree like a normal person?" I begged.

Usually Alex would say something smart to retaliate, but it appeared he was so filled with the Christmas spirit that he was willing to do anything I asked.

Not until we pulled the tree inside the cottage did we realize we had definitely over done it. We hadn't taken into consideration the size of our living room when we picked out the largest tree on the farm. When Alex released the tree from the twine, branches burst out in every direction, exploding through the room in a very *Christmas Vacation* sort of way.

"I guess we could move out the furniture," Alex suggested as he pushed aside a branch so he could sit on the sofa and admire the fruits of his labor.

The next morning I strung lights on the tree while he hung them on the house.

"Once again, very Clark Griswold." I teased him, but really I couldn't have been happier. The tree. The lights. The snow. The love.

And then came Christmas morning and with it, eight extra inches of snow. This was the first Christmas for so many things: my first Christmas as an adult, my first Christmas with Alex, and unfortunately, my first Christmas without my parents.

Alex and I opened our gifts after breakfast. I made Alex open his gifts first, starting with the hockey stick and the pair of Easton Stealth skates he had seen on Cole Hawthorn's feet. They were the exact skates he wanted. I took a picture of him opening the package, so I could always remember the smile plastered on his face. I also bought him a vintage Beastie Boys tee shirt, which he loved, and a quilted black ski coat, which he did not. I saved the best gift for last: a copy of the Miro book he was so drawn to at Artist Edge. When it was my turn, Alex had for me a single box wrapped in silver paper. I peeled the paper back and took a deep breath before lifting the lid of the box.

"They were my mother's," he told me when I examined the princess cut diamond earrings nestled inside the silk-lined box. "I found them this summer while I was unpacking. They were in the top drawer of my dresser." The hint of sadness in Alex's voice seemed to surprise him. He offered a soft smile, trying to take the emphasis off his pain.

It was easy to see that Alex missed his parents with the same ferocity with which I missed mine. Holidays are supposed to be happy, but it's strange how they seem to remind you of all the things you no longer have. Alex and I spent the rest of the day on the sofa watching TV. We didn't have to express to each other what we were feeling. Instead, Alex held me tight, which eased me through the ups and downs of the day.

It was New Year's Eve, and Alex and I were sitting at the kitchen table, each with a blank sheet of paper and a pen, attempting to make a list of goals for the New Year. Two goals in particular came to mind, so I jotted them down on a piece of paper.

To be with Alex for the rest of my life.
Find the truth

I looked at Alex's sheet of paper; he had already written down nine resolutions and was working on number ten. His set looked more like a bucket list and it made me angry beyond belief. I craned my neck to read it:

Ride a snowmobile

Swim the length of the lake and back as soon as the ice begins to melt

Jump out of a plane

Travel across Europe: Paris in particular. See the Eiffel tower in person and visit the Picasso museum near La Place de la Bastille.

Break the record for the world's largest snowman

Read at least one good book

Write something new

Learn how to cook something other than spaghetti

Learn to be human

Take Rae someplace she has never been. Someplace absolutely beautiful and absolutely perfect. Someplace where she can be happy.

A tear snuck into my eye when I read numbers nine and ten. With a quick and discrete movement, I swept my hand across my face and cleared my throat.

"I think we can knock number five off your list before we ring in the New Year."

Alex looked up from his sheet of paper and gazed out the window. He held his eyes there for a moment as if there was actually something to contemplate.

"I don't know," he said, shaking his head.

"Why? I know it's not for the lack of snow."

"It's cold out there."

When Alex said this, I knew he was thinking only of me. To my knowledge, Alex had never been sick a day in his life... this time around, anyway. He bathed in the icy water of the lake and rarely wore a coat when he ventured out into the subfreezing weather.

"It's not the cold that makes you sick," he told me when I tried to persuade him into donning the coat I had given him for Christmas.

"No," I agreed. "But your immune system can't fight off infection when you don't treat your body right, either."

"Sometimes I forget that my girlfriend is not only an artist but an expert on the human body as well," he said sarcastically.

"Come on," I encouraged, sliding out of the kitchen bench and making my way over to where my furry boots were resting by the door.

"It's late and it's a blizzard. Are you sure you want to go out in this?"

"Yes, I'm sure. But if I help you with one of yours, then you have to help me with one of mine." Alex studied my list.

"What's the 'truth'?" he asked.

"Just something Pastor Joe told me about."

"If Pastor Joe's helping you with that one, then your list doesn't allow me much of a choice," he said.

Alex got up from the table and slid on his ratty work boots before walking out the kitchen door, clad in a thin short-sleeved tee shirt. I eyed the coat I bought him for Christmas. He left it hanging on the hook beside the door.

It was a hacking cough that woke me the next morning. I jumped out of bed to see who was making all the commotion. It didn't occur to me that it might be Alex. He was lying on the sofa in the living room with a wet rag over his forehead. The fire was blazing and the room was almost too warm for comfort.

"It's freezing in here," Alex coughed again.

"It's scorching," I corrected, removing the washcloth and pressing my cheek against his forehead. "You're burning up. Alex, I think you're sick." I took the washcloth into the kitchen and ran it under ice-cold tap water before returning it to his forehead.

"Brrr," he shivered.

"I hate to say I told you so, but you should have worn the coat I bought you."

"I thought the coat was for appearance's sake only."

"Not any more. We need to bring your fever down. It's not helping that you're lying so close to the fire."

"I'm fine," he argued.

"Go get in my bed, and I'll bring you some ibuprofen. You'll feel better when the fever breaks."

I helped Alex into bed, then went back into the kitchen and began to rummage through the cabinets until I found the bottle of ibuprofen. Still amused, I opened the lid and shook out two small, brown pills. I thought about what it meant for Alex to be sick. He wasn't supposed to get sick. The only explanation I could come up with was that Alex was becoming human, and I knew I was to blame. He warned me this could happen. But at the time, the idea of Alex being like me sent a very selfish excitement surging through my body. It gave me something to look forward to; however, I failed to take into consideration that, as Alex became more like me, he, too, might also feel physical pain much the same as I did. He was on this earth because of me. He was suffering because of me.

When I walked into my bedroom, Alex was asleep under the thin sheet with the washcloth still on his head. He started when I lay down beside him.

"I brought you some medicine."

"I've never taken anything in my life, and I don't plan on starting now, but thanks." He coughed again, louder this time.

I could hear rattling in his chest along with labored breathing, quick and shallow. I began to worry about all the things that could possibly go wrong with Alex being under the weather. I wondered what the outcome of a trip to the doctor might be. Would a physician discover there was nothing human about Alex Loving? And what would happen if they did? Would a single trip to the doctor blow our cover? And what if he needed an antibiotic but refused to take it? Would he die in a very human sort of way? These were normally questions I would ask aloud, but when I looked at Alex lying there so listlessly, I decided it best to keep them to myself. Instead, I folded my body around his, absorbing his heat, and kissing the back of his neck.

Fifth Way to Lose Alex Loving: Lose Alex to natural causes

"I was wrong about you, you know."

"What do you mean?" I returned, puzzled.

"You're still a Picasso, but you would have made a great Florence Nightingale, too."

"I think your fever's talking now."

"You take good care of me, you know."

"I know," I said and softly kissed the back of his neck again. But for the first time ever, I felt as though his skin beneath my lips might just be as fragile as mine.

In just one short day, Alex had made a complete recovery. It must have been his dangerously high fever that had rid his body of germs, because he held true to his word. Alex never took a single pill. His speedy recovery lifted my spirits but did little to free me of guilt. Speedy recovery or not, Alex was becoming human, and I was to blame. If he was susceptible to sickness, was he also susceptible to death? The time would come when we would once again face Chloe and Ben, and I wondered what would happen. I wondered who would win.

CHAPTER TWENTY-SEVEN

*I*n early January, I enrolled in both physiology and anatomy for non-majors to fulfill my degree requirements for science. I had no idea what I was getting myself into and because I enrolled online, I had no counselor to advise me against it. The subjects were so time consuming that I was barely finding time to paint. On a more positive note, I enrolled in music appreciation as well and quickly found that the laidback structure of the class would give me plenty of options for balancing the load. So far, I had been able to kill two birds with one stone by listening to the music online while studying for tests. Needless to say, I was not getting to spend much time with Alex, but he was having no trouble keeping himself busy. When he wasn't meeting with Pastor Joe, he was playing ice hockey in the backyard. He kept a large spot on the ice cleared away so he could practice. As a result, I had to move my easel away from the window so I could actually get some work done. I found it very hard to concentrate on my painting when he was on his skates. His strength never ceased to amaze me. The power with which he swung the stick would often cause the puck to explode on contact. After weeks of practice, he was learning to control his swing, and with a dead on but slightly gentler motion, the pucks were no longer bursting in midstroke; instead, they were flying through the air at unprecedented speeds and at distances of up to a quarter mile away. Needless to say, he was still losing a lot of pucks. The good news was that we could pick them up at the local sports store for about two dollars. The bad news was that, after losing nearly 100, the cost was beginning to add up.

On Sunday morning, I walked into the kitchen with my nose in Volume I of *Uncle Tom's Cabin*. Alex was sitting at the table, eating breakfast and reading the *Echo Press*. Alex had never been one to leave an article unread, but his primary focus had always been the sports section.

"How's the book?" he asked.

"I've only just started."

"Do you like it?"

"I'm only on chapter two and already I'm furious."

"What part's making you mad?"

"Well, there's this guy named George Harris. He's married to a woman named Eliza. They're slaves and, because they have different owners, they rarely see each other. That makes me mad. People who are in love should not spend their lives apart."

"It's all about romance with you," he teased.

"That's not all. So George Harris is both talented and smart, and his *owner* is horrible, more horrible than most. He hires George out to work in a bagging factory."

"I kind of remember that part. Doesn't he invent a machine or something?"

"Yes, a machine that cleans hemp."

"That's right."

"Everyone at the bagging factory respects George. He's treated like a man, not a slave; he's treated like a person, not a thing. He's finally allowed to use the gifts that God gave him. So his master, Mr. Harris, caught wind of George's genius invention and decided to pay the factory a visit. When he arrived, he found a slave that was happy, manly, handsome, and educated."

"So he took him back to the plantation and never let him return to the factory."

"Yep. He took him back to the plantation, assigned him to the worst possible job, then he beat him. He beat him worse than ever before."

"It's hard to read, huh?"

"Yeah."

"You should finish the book."

"I plan on it."

"But maybe you should take a short break from the book and read something else instead."

"I'm only on chapter two!" I looked up at Alex and he was smiling. "Did you have something in mind?"

Alex slid the *Echo Press* toward me.

"Your boy's in the paper this morning."

"My boy?"

"You know, Flynt. Alexandria's most eligible bachelor."

"Why do you have a smile on your face? Are you planning something devious?"

"Nothing devious, although, maybe I should. The stories in the paper have gotten a bit dull now that the town is no longer concerned with how long my fangs are. Perhaps I *should* give them something to write about."

"Don't get any bright ideas."

Alex set down his glass of orange juice and looked me in the eye. "I want to try out for the Redhawks. They're looking for another player."

There was an undertone to Alex's voice, and I knew right away he was seeking my approval.

I slid into the bench and held my head in my hands. "Why do you have to make everything so difficult?"

"I just want to play hockey, that's all. I'm wasting away in this cottage."

I looked up at the ceiling and sighed. "And what if they figure out who you are? Then what?"

"We'll leave."

"And go where?"

"I don't know, Rae. Everything has gotten so serious in the past couple of months. I just want to have a little fun."

"Serious, huh? Welcome to *my* life. Now you finally know what it feels like to be human."

"Sorry. I didn't mean any disrespect. But maybe you should have some fun, too."

I didn't respond; instead, I picked up the paper that Alex had discarded on the table and, when my eyes fell upon the picture of Flynt decked out in hockey gear, I began to read the article below.

My interview today is one that I've been looking forward to for months. Perhaps because it is the first interview in a series of seven that will feature one of the star players for the Alexandria Redhawks. Or, my excitement could be because this week I'm interviewing a legend, a real hometown hero. He is a college graduate, an accomplished artist, an entrepreneur, a star hockey player, captain of the Redhawks, and the newest addition to his repertoire, a survivor. This week's interview is with twenty-two-year-old, Flynt Redding.

Dan: Flynt, I would like to start with a question about the happenings on Halloween night. I hope you don't mind.

Redding: Well, I don't mind that you ask, but I'm afraid I can't give you an answer. I don't remember much about what happened. The Doc told me I hit my head pretty hard. Plus, I lost a lot of blood.

Dan: Police and witnesses have said that a newcomer to town, an Alex... I'm sorry... I'm searching my notes and can't find a last name. But that's neither here nor there. Witnesses say this Alex was at the scene when the police arrived. Rumor has it that he was involved. And after seeing the aftermath, some have even speculated that he is a supernatural creature of the night. I've heard him called a vampire, an alien, and everything in between. Do you have any comments that you would like to share?

Redding: The clearing in the woods would suggest an alien invasion, but I have to say this is not the most likely cause. I really hate to disappoint you, but Alex is just a regular guy. Had dinner at his house once, in fact.

Dan: So the rumors aren't true, then. There is absolutely no animosity between you and Alex over.... a certain girl perhaps? Is that what you're saying, Flynt?

Flynt: I think you're getting a little personal now, Dan. What do you say we talk about some hockey?

Dan: Sounds fair. Here I am bringing up accidents again, but you're no stranger to injury. Do you think after your most recent setback... the injuries you received on Halloween night... that you will be strong enough to play in the Regional Championships, should the Redhawks qualify?

Flynt: I'm on a strict physical therapy regime. Plus, I'm practicing with the team everyday. If we qualify for regionals, you can bet I'll be on the ice.

Dan: And you're not the only team member to receive a hard blow. Redhawks right winger, Joey Cochrin, is out for the season after a fight on the ice last week. Is it true his jaw is wired shut?

Flynt: That's the truth, I'm afraid. He's on a liquid diet. What can I say? Hockey's a rough sport.

Dan: Is it true that the Redhawks are looking for a replacement?"

Flynt: That is also true.

Dan: Any leads?

Flynt: There'll be an open try out next Wednesday. I am hopeful that we'll find the perfect guy for the team. Our team is tight knit. Always has been. We are looking to find not only a good player, but also someone to be a part of our family.

Dan: What's your take on the Duluth Rippers? They're owning every team they play this year. One more win, and they'll have secured themselves a spot at regionals.

Flynt: They're tough, that's for sure.

Dan: Well, you have heard it straight from the hero's mouth. Flynt Redding, team captain for the Alexandria Redhawks, is on the mend and ready for regionals. He denies the report that vampires are chasing him around and when asked about his feelings for a certain girl, he gives the answer that only a gentleman would give: no comment. Check back in next Friday's paper for a one-on-one interview with Redhawks left winger, Terrance Hawking.

I pushed the paper away and began to swirl my coffee with my spoon. I looked into the cup of liquid and for the first time ever, it didn't look so good. At the moment, nothing did. Nothing in my life was going right. Nothing was going as planned. We were almost broke, and if the legal issues didn't get straightened out soon, Alex would lose the cottage. Ben and Chloe were still out there somewhere and the anticipation of their next attack was worse than the fight itself. I missed my mom and dad like crazy. And to top it off, the whole town thought Alex was the villain and that Flynt Redding was some sort of local hero because he almost died in the woods. There was nothing I could do about it either. What was I supposed to say? *Alex is not a vampire! He's not an angel. He's not an alien. He's just a dead boy that has come back to life to keep me safe.*

No, I could not say that. For the past several months, we had been limiting our trips into town, waiting for the gossip to die down so we could resume our lives. And now this: Alex was planning to try out for the Alexandria Redhawks, and I couldn't think of a better way to draw attention to ourselves. Besides, I was suspicious of his motives. I knew that the article made him angry. It made me angry. But was he trying out for the team because he loved the sport or because he had something to prove? It wasn't for me to judge, and I couldn't exactly tell him no. The only thing I could do is sit back and watch our lives unfold. It was tearing me apart.

January was coming to a close and February was drawing near. I wasn't a bit surprised when Alex returned from open tryouts to tell me he had made the team. I was, however, surprised by the rigorous training schedule that was required of all team members and, because being a part of the team was so demanding, my time with Alex was dwindling even more. When Alex wasn't playing hockey, he was meeting with Pastor Joe. But there was a bit of good news: The lawyers were nearly finished tying up all of the loose ends concerning his parents' estate. It looked like there would be just enough money to pay the back taxes and save all five of his parents' dwellings. We were both thankful that at least one of our problems was about to be solved. Both Alex and I were comfortable using his parents' money that way. It wasn't that he needed five different places to live; instead, it had more to do with the fact that his parents had taken the time to pick these dwelling places. Alex thought that by visiting them, he might be able to reconnect with old feelings from his past. Plus, the Minnesota cottage had been in the family for years and it would break his heart to see it go. And for other equally sentimental reasons, I, too, had become attached.

"Except vicariously through me, have you ever been to Paris?" I asked Alex one night when he was discussing the option of moving from Alexandria to the capital city of France.

"I don't know. I mean, I don't remember. There's just something about that country that draws me."

"So, you want to move? Is that what you're saying?"

"I wouldn't mind. I have a few ideas about getting rid of Chloe and Ben once and for all. After that we can do as we please."

"I'm tired of talking about this. You know my feelings on this subject."

"I'm not so sure I do."

"How many different ways can I possibly tell you I am terrified you're going to leave me? When Chloe and Ben are out of the way, what reason do you have to stay? How can I make you understand that there will be no Paris if you leave?"

"I have to say, Sunshine, you're not being very romantic."

"And neither are you."

"I'm talking about taking you to Paris, the city of love. It can't get much more romantic than that."

"You don't have to take me all the way to Paris to woo me. Kisses are romantic, too. But I never get any of those."

"Oh, *please*. I kiss you plenty."

"Why can't we just stay here?" I whined.

I rested my forehead in my hands and groaned. There were certain things I wanted to tell him but couldn't. For instance, if I went anywhere I would like to go back home. I hadn't seen my parents in nearly a year, and I desperately missed them. I knew I could not be in their lives until I was certain of their safety, but I could not secure their safety without risking the life of the man I loved. I couldn't win. I would hurt no matter what.

"We could go to the Eiffel Tower and the Picasso museum."

"The Picasso Museum? That's not the museum that comes to mind when people think of Paris. I've never been there."

"It's near the Place de la Bastille. Remember. It's on a little side street… off the beaten path."

"See. How do you know that?"

"Are you sure? Because I'm picturing it right now."

"I'm positive."

"Hmm. Maybe I did live there for a time while I was human. Maybe we *should* entertain the idea of moving to Paris so that I can reconnect."

"You're not going to drop this are you?"

"No. I'm not."

"I've already told you that I do not want to go back to Europe! Nothing good happened to me while I was there."

Alex let out a sigh. "Look, I don't want to fight with you. That's the last thing I want."

"I don't want to fight with you either," I said as I scooted in close beside him.

Alex held my face in his hands and kissed me lightly on the lips.

"I'm sorry if I don't kiss you enough. I'm sorry if I don't always give you the attention that you want or need. But I do love you. I always have, and I always will."

"I love you, too."

"Everything is going to work out, you know that, right?"

"I hope so," I told him.

Alex brushed his lips across my cheek and moved his fingers through my hair.

"I love the way your hair smells."

"Thank you."

"And your ears. I have always liked your ears, too," he said, pulling a piece of hair away from my face and brushing his lips across the lobe.

I moved closer and put my head on his chest. I closed my eyes and listened to him breathing. I listened to his heart beating beneath my ear. These were my favorite things about Alex. These were the things that made his presence real. It was his beating heart that reminded me I wasn't crazy.

"You know what I like?" I asked. "I like the little freckle on your lip." I told him, still holding him tight. "And the scar on your eye," I said, turning his face toward me so I could see the scar as I traced it with my finger.

I felt Alex's hand on the small of my back and I shivered. "I like the curve of your back and the two little indentions at the base of you spine. I wonder if those have a name?"

"I don't think so," I laughed. "But I like your fingers. You have gentle hands despite your strength, you know."

Alex repositioned himself on the sofa cushion, moving his body away from mine and looking me in the eye. "Umm… and I like the spot between your eyes. The spot that dips between your forehead and your nose." He began to move his finger down the profile of my face.

"It's called the *radix nasi.*"

"That's not a very pretty name. I think I should give it a new one," he said, leaning in closer and pressing his lips softly between my eyes.

I took his hand in mine, studying the freckles that brushed across his fingers. My eyes drifted upward, examining the portion of his arm between his elbow and his wrist. "I like your forearm. It's the part of your arm you wrap around my waist. It's the part of your arm that makes me feel safe."

"And I like the hollow just above your lip. I love it when you pout. It makes it stand out even more. I wonder if there's a name for that spot."

"It's the *philtrum,* or the *infranasal depression,*" I said, pulling the names directly from my anatomy lesson the week before.

"These are horrible names." He kissed me lightly on the lips.

"In Greek, *philtrum* means 'love potion'."

"I'm not even going to ask how you know that."

I moved my hand up his arm and leaned closer so I could whisper in his ear. "I love the muscle of your arm just below your shoulder. It's called the bicep, in case you were wondering." When I slid my fingers under the sleeve of his tee shirt, I felt him flinch.

"Thanks for keeping me safe. Thanks for loving me," I whispered in his ear.

CHAPTER TWENTY-EIGHT

*I*t was Valentine's Day and I was studying. I hadn't even thought of a gift for Alex and because our funds were running low, I was pretty sure I would have to use every creative bone in my body to come up with something good. I could write a poem, I thought. But that was more *his* style. If I had been more thoughtful and started last month, I might have been able to complete some spectacular work of art with my paints. I doodled a heart on my notepad with my purple gel pen, hoping that seeing the symbolic shape of love would be enough to bring forth some inspiration. Nothing. I colored in the heart, making it a shiny and solid purple. Still nothing. I slid my notebook to the side and with a sigh, picked up my enormous Physiology textbook from the sofa cushion next to me.

I was good at science. I was bound to be with both of my parents being doctors. It was bred in me, I suppose. But there was nothing inviting about studying physiology when my easel and paints were less than ten feet away. I couldn't understand why I needed science credits for a fine arts degree, and I was beginning to wonder why I hadn't chosen a simpler class. The only good part about this class was that I could take it online.

I breezed through the first fifteen pages of chapter twenty-seven, which was a physiological overview of the heart and surprisingly, I was somewhat intrigued. It would have been pretty cool if it were just by chance that we were studying the heart on this particular day, but I was pretty sure the professor scheduled the lesson on the human heart to coincide with Valentine's Day. All of that aside, the human heart has always fascinated me. I honestly can't think of any other vital organ with such an emotional tie. The heart is more than an organ that pumps blood through the body; it can also represent love or even agony. You never hear about cupid, the god of love, piercing the spleen or a kidney.

Many times the heart is used in figures of speech. For instance, when my parents tried to psychoanalyze me, my mom would say, "Rae, I think we need to get to the heart of the matter." In other words, we need to get to the most important part. And I suppose the heart *is* the most important part. You can live without one of your kidneys, but I know for a fact that you cannot live without a heart for long. I've heard of artificial hearts. But they are only used to buy the patient time before a heart transplant. In other words, an artificial heart is a temporary fix. You can even live, comatose, with a non-functioning brain. But the heart, it just has to beat or else you die. I remember where it hurt when Alex left me: right in the center of my chest. It hurt with such ferocity that I found it hard to breathe. What a mysterious and powerful organ the heart is; it must work in such perfect harmony with the rest of the body at all times.

I was now in the middle of chapter twenty-seven and so far, I had not read anything that I didn't already know. But when I saw the title *Septal Defects* in bold print, my eyes were once again drawn to the page, and I began to read:

A septal defect is a hole in the heart between the left and right ventricles, or between the two atria. The hole allows blood to leak between the chambers. As a result, some oxygenated blood from the left side flows through the hole in the septum into the right side, where it mixes with oxygen-poor blood and increases the total amount of blood that flows toward the lungs, forcing the heart and lungs to work harder and less efficiently. If left untreated, septal defect may cause problems in adulthood, including pulmonary hypertension (high blood pressure in the lungs), congestive heart failure (weakening of the heart muscle), abnormal rhythms or beating of the heart, and an increased risk of stroke.

I was fascinated. Not fascinated like I wanted to change my major, I was simply fascinated that there was a physiological condition that described my emotional ailment. I was fascinated because I could relate. I, too, had a hole in my heart, and I noticed it shortly after arriving in Minnesota.

I skipped down to the bottom of the page where the heading read Treatments. Medication and surgery seemed to be the only treatment options. Surgery always seems like a last resort. I mean, who really wants to be cut open? Not me. I scanned over the section that reviewed the outcome of treatment with medications.

Medications will not repair the hole, but it may be used to decrease the signs and symptoms associated with a septal defect.

I skipped down to the subheading entitled *Surgery* and began to read.

Surgery to repair the septal defect is highly recommended and requires the hand of a skilled cardiologist. The surgery involves plugging or patching the hole between the chamber walls, by one of two highly effective methods: Cardio catheterization or open heart surgery.

I cringed, put down the book, and began to wonder what type of doctor might be able to help me. What kind of doctor could patch the hole in my heart? So far, Alex was all the medication I needed, but even so, over the past couple of months, the hole in the bottom of my heart had grown considerably larger. And while he was the only one who could stop the leak, what if there came a time when he was no longer enough? Besides, I knew that he was a prescription that had no refills, and I feared the expiration date was drawing near. I didn't need a cardiologist.

I also didn't think I needed a shrink. My parents were both head doctors and in the eighteen years I had lived inside their many houses, they had never gotten to the heart of the matter. I knew it was really my soul that needed a physician, and I was pretty sure I was out of luck, because a soul doctor just didn't exist. However, the paragraph I had just read gave me the perfect idea for Alex's Valentines present.

I shuddered when I pulled into the pharmacy. I hadn't been to a pharmacy since the night my mother was taken to the ER for heart palpitations. That was the night I found out Ben had tried to kill her... because of me. I opened the door and quickly walked inside. The boy at the counter ignored me, which I didn't mind at all. I walked to the back of the store and found the prescription counter. There was a huge line, so I grabbed a tabloid off a nearby shelf and began to look through the pictures. I looked down at my outfit after I found someone famous wearing something very similar on page ninety-nine. A smile emerged, and I was beginning to feel very self-confident. But then I glanced at the top of the page and saw that my outfit fell under the scrutiny of the fashion police. According to this magazine my choice in clothing was altogether hideous.

"Next please."

I glanced up and noticed that, while I was still standing in the same place, the long line in front of me had already been served. I scooted up fifteen feet until I was standing face to face with the pharmacist.

"I have a strange request," I started. The pharmacist looked at me as though he were annoyed or maybe tired, so I helped him out and continued to run my mouth. "I just need an empty prescription bottle."

The pharmacist continued to stare at me without saying a single word, which aggravated me beyond belief.

"It's for my boyfriend."

Still nothing.

"For Valentine's Day."

Finally, he spoke. He was actually human.

"We don't do that."

"Please." That was all I could think to say. What I wanted to tell him was that I didn't really have any money to buy my boyfriend a proper gift, so his lousy bottle was going to have to do.

"It's illegal to put anything other than the prescribed drug into a pharmacy bottle."

"That is… if it has a label on it. I don't need a label. Just the bottle will do."

The pharmacist's name was Doug. It was on the nameplate pinned to his stiff white coat. "Please, Doug."

Doug disappeared for a moment. When he returned, he had an orange colored bottle in his hand. He looked from left to right and then behind his back before giving it to me.

"Thanks, Doug."

"Next," Doug snorted.

I thought about giving Doug Mr. Finnegan's address before I left the store. I thought they might get along famously. Instead, I picked up a pack of heart shaped Red Hots and a pack of white sticky labels before heading to the front of the store to make my purchase.

Alex was in his cottage when I pulled into the drive. It was the first day in weeks that he had not had hockey practice. After qualifying for the Regional Championships, the coach thought they deserved a small break. I went straight to my room and locked the door behind me. I did wonder what he was up to back there. With the exception of coming out for breakfast, he had been barricaded in his cottage all day. I just knew he was writing me a poem.

I pulled the white labels out of the pharmacy bag, opened the package, and ripped one off. I needed a real prescription bottle to use as a pattern. I exhaled deeply because I hadn't thought of that. I got up and walked into the living room to fetch my computer. With it snuggly under my arm, I hurried back into my room and re-locked the door. I typed the word 'prescription bottle' and hit enter. I then clicked 'image' and there before me were about six dozen pictures of prescription bottles that I could choose from. I clicked on the first image. I could see the bottle, but the words were fuzzy. I clicked on another. This image was larger, and I could read it with perfection. On my homemade label, I would need to include the name of the prescription as well as its expiration date. Plus, I would need the number of refills, pharmacy name, and prescribing doctor. This would make my handmade label look legit.

I picked up my purple gel pen and began to scribble on the little white sticker. Unsatisfied with my penmanship, I crumpled it up and started another.

Rae Colbert
Address: ever-changing

Prescription: Alex Loving
Administer prescription as
frequently as possible
for the rest of your life

Expiration Date: Too soon, I'm afraid
Prescribing Doctor: God
Number of refills: None

I looked over the label I had been working on for the past five minutes and nodded with approval. I stuck it onto the empty prescription bottle, then filled the bottle with heart shaped Red Hots. It was the perfect gift from a girl with no money. I hoped he would get what I was trying to say. Alex Loving was the drug I could not live without. He was that patch that filled the hole in my heart. He made me happy in a way that I had never been before. He couldn't leave me. To leave would be the same as letting me die.

I was in the shower with the bathroom door unlocked, when I heard a knock on the flimsy bead board barrier.

"Wha r y ding."

"What," I shouted back. "I can't hear you when the water's on."

I heard the door open a crack, but he didn't him come inside.

"You can come in. I don't care."

"That's okay," he said, sounding embarrassed. I scowled and closed my eyes tightly as I worked the shampoo through my hair.

"Don't make plans for tonight."

"You know me, Ms. Social Butterfly."

"Just saying. I have a little something up my sleeve."

"I love it when you say that." I opened my eyes and smiled. "Should I... dress up?"

"You can if you want," he offered. "But you don't have to."

"Are we staying here or going out?"

"You'll have to wait and see."

I peeked my head around the shower curtain and made a pouty face that looked ridiculous, I'm sure, then looked at him sternly.

"You still have soap in your hair." He smiled and shut the bathroom door. I scowled again, and then I yanked the shower curtain shut and started to shave my legs, which I had neglected for the past week and a half because I had been so wrapped up in my newest painting.

I had been saving the white lace top I purchased at the thrift store for a very special occasion, and I thought tonight might just be the night to bring it out. I pulled it out of the closet and held the hanger in front of me. I admired the beauty of the blouse and its intricate, lace detail. A smile turned the corners of my mouth as I remembered how it looked much better on *me* than it did on the hanger. So I let my robe fall to the floor, slipped the blouse over my head, and zipped up the side. After pairing it with jeans and some high heel lace-up boots, I looked at my reflection in the mirror. The top. The hair. The make up. Everything was perfect. I just knew that tonight would be perfect as well.

It was just passed five o'clock, and we were on our way out of town. The car was silent. I decided to keep my mouth shut and enjoy the drive. Besides, the only thing I wanted to know was where we were going, and there wasn't a chance he was going to tell me. I looked out the window.

Everything was frozen. The road was clear but the shoulders were piled high with snow. I smiled when I saw the miniature sized stop signs. Only in Minnesota would they have stop signs for snowmobiles. I loved it. I thought riding a snowmobile might just be something I should add to my list of New Year's resolutions. Maybe it could be something Alex and I did together.

The world outside the passenger window was a winter wonderland. The sun was starting to set which made the trees along the roadside appear dark and cold, and the sky was beautifully illuminated in rays of pink and white and yellow. I could see the occasional sparkle of snow that glittered on the branch of a tree when the sun hit it just right. It would shine just for a second, and then it would disappear.

After forty-five minutes, I felt the car begin to slow and heard Alex say, "We're here." The sign at the entrance of the town said Glenwood. The sun had set and it was dark, save for the old fashioned lampposts that lined the streets of this quaint little town.

"Did I tell you, you look very pretty tonight?"

"No," I said. It's a strange thing to feel your cheeks burning when the temperature outside is below freezing. But I couldn't keep from blushing.

"You don't look so bad yourself." I blushed again.

Alex wrapped his arm around my waist and pulled me close to him, which warmed my body more than I expected.

"Are we eating?"

"You are terrible. Do you know that?"

"What?" I said with innocence.

"You've waited this long, and I know that it's been miserable for you... but I think you can wait one second longer," he said, half laughing as he pulled open the door to a restaurant called Café Bella.

"Oh. I'm so hungry. It smells like heaven in here."

"It was worth the wait, then?"

"You still could have told me, so I could have gotten my taste buds ready."

Alex sighed like he usually did when he was frustrated with me, so I gave him a hug and a kiss and told him that his surprise was perfect.

The hostess seated us at a table by the window. We had a picturesque view of the snowy street. The lampposts glowed halos onto the white sidewalks below. I breathed discretely onto the window, and I drew a heart with my index finger. Alex smiled when he looked up from his menu.

"What are you getting?" I asked.

"Chicken Parmesan. How about you?"

"The Marsala. It's my favorite. Everything on the menu looked like food fit for a king. I took in my surroundings. The restaurant looked expensive. I looked at the menu again, this time checking the prices. It was. I wondered if we could afford it. Alex and I were coming to the end of our stash of money, and the Loving's will had yet to be settled. Being able to afford Bella's was the least of my concerns. March was only two weeks away and if we didn't get the money soon, we would lose our home. Plus, Alex was totally spoiling me on Valentine's Day, and I felt bad that I had only a prescription bottle filled with Red Hots to give to him in return. I hoped he hadn't gotten me anything. That way I could weasel my way out of the whole gift exchange thing. I reached my hand inside my coat pocket and felt the bottle. It was still there. The feel of the warm plastic on my fingers made me nervous. Was I more worried about my gift being cheap, or the fact that I had stuck my heart onto that label? I had told Alex how I felt about him leaving me behind, but never so pointedly. Stuck onto this plastic bottle were my deepest feelings. What if he really didn't feel the same way? For the first time, I thought about how that might just be more painful.

"I have something for you," Alex said after the server had delivered our dinner and retreated to a table on the other side of the room. "It isn't much."

I swallowed hard. I was now going to have to give him the bottle of Red Hots. "I have something for you, too," I whispered.

"Ladies first."

"Really? Okay." I clinched my hand around the bottle in my coat pocket, and held it there for a moment before I pulled it out and slid it across the table in his direction.

Alex looked at it for a moment, perplexed, then picked it up and stared at the label.

It was only the second time I had seen tears in Alex's eyes. He set the bottle down on the table next to his plate, still staring at it.

"I love it," he said finally, his eyes now making contact with mine. He bit his lower lip, the side with the freckle, and all at once the small brown dot disappeared. Alex reached into his coat pocket and pulled out a crumpled but neatly folded piece of paper. It looked as though he had wadded it up into a ball, thrown it into the trash, and dug it back out. Still chewing on his bottom lip, Alex unfolded the paper slowly, staring at whatever was on the page. He cleared his throat and rustled the paper a bit before he began to speak.

"I wrote you a poem. It's called *White*."

Scarlet is the color of passion, love, and fire
So many different meanings: both danger and desire

Scarlet is for untamed heat you will soon learn
It feels good as you draw near, but too close and you'll get burned

Scarlet is for the blood that pumps through me and you
Yet beneath the flesh, blood looks very blue

But to me, your love is like the color white
Pure, beautiful, perfect, and always worth the fight

White. It is the color of my Rae
Just one drop of white will make the darkness run away

White. A girl who wears her heart upon her sleeve
White. The color that I never want to leave.

It felt like we were so very alone. Like it was just the two of us sitting at the table by the window in this restaurant. The room was quiet and the sound of laughter was gone. Warm tears were building up inside of my eyes, about to spill over. I felt so many things stirring around inside of me at once. In my life there were so many uncertainties, but I did know one thing for sure: Alex loved me in exactly the same way that I loved him. One could not live without the other.

CHAPTER TWENTY-NINE

*T*here couldn't have been a more perfect day for the Northern Minnesota Hockey Playoffs. The sun was shining for the first time in weeks, and the temperature was supposed to reach a high of forty-two degrees, which was higher than average for the end of February. While March brought the first signs of spring to many states, Minnesota still had a rough couple of months ahead of her. So when I woke up this morning to find the sun shining, I welcomed the warmth with open arms.

"Are you sure this is a good idea?" I asked, as Alex was getting ready for the hockey tournament on Lake Agnes near the city park.

"What do you mean?"

"I just mean that you're stronger than they are. What if something happens? What if you slip? Figuratively speaking, of course."

"I'll try to control myself, Rae."

"Just promise me you won't show off. I don't know much about boys, but I'm studying testosterone in physiology and...."

"I said I would try to control myself, Rae. Can't you just leave it at that?" he teased.

"Fine. But all the same, I'll be keeping my eye on you."

"Let's go if we're going to go. We're running late as is."

Alex began to make his way toward the kitchen when I stopped him. "Aren't you forgetting something?"

"No," he said with his back toward me.

"Umhm. What about this?" I asked, holding up his pads and helmet. Alex scowled and turned around.

"What?" he asked, staring at the protective gear I was holding in my hands.

"You need to put it on."

"Seriously?"

"*Seriously!*"

"I fought Ben in the woods and came out unscathed, not a single scratch, and you think I need pads to play hockey with a group of college boys?"

"Okay, now you're just being boastful. Besides, I wasn't really concerned that you might get injured. The pads and the helmet are for appearance's sake only. Plus, rules are rules. The referee won't let you play in a tournament without them."

"Fine," Alex reluctantly agreed, snatching the equipment from my hands. "Now I have to strip down and start all over. If I'm late it's your fault," he complained.

"It's not optional," I said, falling back onto the sofa and making myself comfortable. When Alex shed his first layer of clothing, a smile formed on my face and a giggle escaped me. When he noticed I was enjoying myself, the shedding of clothes came to a complete stop. Alex threw his long sleeved Vikings tee shirt on the ground and looked me in the eye.

"For appearances sake, my arse," Alex huffed. "You just want to see me in my boxer briefs." Alex began to rub at his five o'clock shadow, and as he did so, his mouth disappeared behind his hand. It didn't take a genius to realize he wasn't trying to smooth his whiskers at all, but rather hide a smile of his very own.

"Don't flatter yourself," I chuckled. "I have much better things to do with my time than sit around and gaze upon you in your unmentionables."

I picked up a magazine and began to flip through the pages while Alex stripped down to his long underwear and began to layer the pads on top.

When he was finished, he looked fifty pounds heavier.

"What about your jersey?"

"We're getting new ones for the tournament. I'll pick it up when I check in."

"Okay."

"So, are you happy now? I can barely walk in all of this junk."

"Almost. You're still forgetting one small thing."

Alex rolled his eyes when I dangled his mouthpiece in front of his face.

"We wouldn't want people to start talking now, would we?" I smirked.

We were running late, and Alex was relieved when he found a parking spot up close.

"We haven't been here since the art festival," Alex said as we walked down the snowy embankment to the park.

I nodded in agreement. "It looks a lot different all covered in snow, but just as festive."

We could see the frozen lake in the distance and the portable rink system on the ice that marked the boundaries for the game. The opposing team was already warming up. Their jerseys were white with their names across the back in royal blue. The players were holding their sticks at a horizontal slant and skating in circles. They looked like huge machines, smoothly gliding one behind the other in perfect alignment. The *Echo Press* described this team as tough. Only now did I realize that tough took on more than one meaning. Yes, the Rippers would be a tough team to beat, but these players were rough, strong... resilient. There wasn't a single player on the ice that stood less than 6 foot 5 inches, and it was hard to determine their weight with all the padding, but I was guessing that most of them were tipping the scale at over 200 pounds. I thought about Alex who was pushing six foot even and weighed in at just under 175. He was small in comparison to the other players, but he had more power in the tip of his finger than all of the opposing team combined. A smile brushed across my lips when I thought about the surprise they were in for. I had told Alex not to show off, but right now in the heat of the pre-game festivities, I was eager to see what he could do should he use all of his strength for the good of the game.

A commentator booth was set up behind the dasher board, just to the left of the penalty box; however, the two men who were supposed to be doing the pre-game announcements had yet to arrive. Music was booming from speakers that were positioned on either side of the stands. Shifting my gaze away from the rink and onto the grounds, I noticed vendors conveniently arranged on either side of the bleachers, selling various refreshments - everything from hot chocolate to bratwurst and beer.

"I need to go and check in." Alex had his helmet in one hand and his skates in the other. "You should try to get a seat up front," he said.

I watched him walk away. It didn't dawn on me that he would have to register in order to enter the tournament and get a jersey. I should be excited for Alex, but as I walked toward the refreshments, I began to wonder what name Alex had given the officials. What name would be on the back of *his* jersey?

The smell of buttery popcorn wafted through the air, and I crinkled my nose. Although I was hungry before leaving the cottage and had planned to eat lunch at the game, the smell of fake butter made me nauseous, and I decided on a small cup of hot chocolate instead. When I reached the front of the line, I recognized Gretchen's dad at the window. I pulled my hat down over my forehead and bowed my head, pretending I was looking at the menu on the side of the truck. I hadn't been overly excited about attending the event; I was worried about the possibility of running into North Shore natives. Over the past few months, our lack of community involvement and the absence of our presence in town had allowed the Halloween gossip to settle. The last thing I wanted was for our appearance at the event to stir everything up again. Alex and I were supposed to be lying low. Personally, I thought entering into a tournament like this was a bit risky, but I knew how much Alex loved the game and couldn't possibly tell him no.

By the time I reached the rink, my hot chocolate was nearly gone and the seats were scant. I hoped Alex wouldn't be disappointed when he didn't see me front and center. I climbed the stairs and took one of the last remaining seats on the top row. I placed my empty cup of hot chocolate by my feet and slipped my gloved hands inside my pockets for extra warmth. Although the morning started out sunny, I was downright cold. The sun was now hiding behind the clouds and fat flakes of snow had begun to fall. I checked out the rest of the crowd and was pleased to find that I didn't know a single soul. I thought this was partially because there were no separate stands for out of town guests; instead, the Ripper and Redhawk fans were mixed together and, unless team colors were donned, it was hard to determine who was rooting for whom.

I pulled out my phone and checked the time. It was 12:45. In exactly thirty minutes, the Alexandria Redhawks would be battling it out against the Duluth Rippers. It had been eight years since Alexandria had a team worthy to play in the Regional Championships and hosting the event only added to the excitement. The hockey tournament had been the talk of the town for the past two months. Alexandria was proud of their boys and *Echo Press*, the local newspaper, had done its part to boost team spirit and build the players confidence by promoting the event; a spot had been reserved on the front page of the sports section every Friday to interview a player from the team and discuss strategies for defeating one of the toughest opponents in the Northwest, the Duluth Rippers. I had made the acquaintance of a few of Flynt's teammates while I was working at the Artist's Edge, and Terrance Hawking was one of my favorites. He was quiet and eccentric and seemed to love the game more than the win. He had skin the color of milk chocolate and dreadlocks that were short and neat. There was also Zac Brophy. He, too, came to the store on occasion. He was the Redhawk's goalkeeper and liked to insinuate that it was his impeccable ability to block the puck that allowed the team to win. I didn't care for Zac. Danny Westbrook was the Redhawk's defender, and he was nearly as pompous as Brophy. I had never cared enough about the news to read the paper, but I had been keeping up with the pre-game hoopla, mostly because Alex was so pumped about the championships. Zac was the featured player in last Friday's spread, and when I read his response to the reporter's questions I wasn't shocked; each answer directly reflected his personality. If his ego were blown up any more, his head might burst.

The Redhawks skated onto the rink to begin their pre-game warm up. I searched the ice for Alex but couldn't find him. I glanced over to the registration table and saw that he was just finishing up. He had his Redhawks jersey pulled over his pads, and sure enough, "Loving" was spelled out in black letters across the back. He wasn't even trying to be discreet. I sincerely hoped that Mrs. Harvey, queen of gossip, wasn't here. I was certain that the back of his jersey would be all the refreshing her memory would need.

"Crazy Train" was blasting through the speakers, and the crowd was getting revved up. The bleachers were completely full. When people began to cluster around the dasher board, authorities quickly arranged a barrier and began to move the enthusiastic fans behind the line. A man with a cowbell was running back and forth in front of the stands. Despite the cold, he had his shirt off revealing a red "AR", for Alexandria Redhawks, painted on his chest.

Finally, Alex skated onto the rink. I expected him to join the others, so I was surprised when he came to a stop beside the goal. He was rapping his stick on the ice while searching the crowd. I supposed he was looking for me. When our eyes met, I gave him a thumbs up. He smiled and began skating backwards, showing off his fancy footwork. Alex wasn't the only one scanning the crowd for someone special.

A large boy in a Redhawks jersey was desperately searching for someone. I was too far away to tell who it was, but even if I were closer, it would be difficult with all their pads and helmets to tell who was who without seeing the back of their jerseys. I studied him as he searched the crowd and was surprised that when his eyes fell on me, his searching stopped. He immediately raised his hand and waved. I looked over my shoulder, forgetting that I was sitting on the top row of the bleachers and naturally no one was sitting behind me. I pointed to myself with my finger. He nodded his head and waved his hand again. Still not sure that he was waving to me, I returned the gesture. Perhaps he had mistaken me for someone else.

It seemed the hulk of a boy was reading my mind and, after coming to the understanding that I had absolutely no idea who he was, he reached for his helmet to pull it off. I smiled when I saw the mess of blond hair. It was Flynt and seeing him made me feel all warm and fuzzy despite the cold. I questioned whether or not he was strong enough to play. But he was here. He appeared well enough to play the game he so loved, and I was proud of him. I admired him for trying. I admired him for not giving up on his dreams. I admired him for being kind enough to wave when I had been so mean. I liked Flynt, couldn't help it; he was a good friend, the kind of friend that would stick by you through thick and thin.

Flynt was still waving when I stole a glance at Alex. He had seen the whole production. From where I was sitting, I couldn't see the expression on Alex's face, but I didn't need to. I knew he was angry by the way he was sharpening his skates on the ice and rapping his stick in a very defensive manner. It was no secret that animosity had been building up between the two boys over the past several months, and I was afraid the spirit of the game might bring out all their pent up aggression toward one another. Thank goodness the referee blew his whistle to signal the start of the game, because Flynt and Alex were staring each other down like two bulls about to charge. When all the players had cleared the ice, the commentator began to announce the players from the opposing team.

"Welcome to the Fifteenth Annual Hockey Playoff. Thanks for coming out. I am Jerry Harvey and with me is Jack Callawy. We will be the commentators for this afternoon."

The crowd began to make some noise and I began to panic. Jerry Harvey? Really? Corrine's dad was one of the commentators. There was no way Alex and I would get out of this one.

"ARE... YOU... READY... TO... MEET... THE... RIPPERRRRRS!"

The boos overpowered the cheers as the opposing team skated onto the ice and it wasn't hard to tell that the Redhawk fans outnumbered Duluth.

"Number 17, Defender, Blake Curtis." Blake held his stick horizontally above his head and pumped it up and down.

"Number 7, right winger, Troy Simpson." With his head down, Simpson skated quickly across the ice to show his speed.

"Number 40, Goalie for the Rippers, Drew O'Reilly." O'Reilly slid across the ice on his knees and put his hands out in front of him in puck blocking style.

Mr. Harvey went through the list and, when the last Ripper skated off the ice, the entire town of Alexandria began to chant for their team: "REDHAWKSREDHAWKSREDHAWKS...."

"ARE... YOU... READY... TO... MEET... THE... REDHAWKS!" The crowd went wild when Flynt skated onto the ice.

"Number 21, center for the Redhawks and captain of the team, Flynt Redding." Flynt modestly skated across the ice. He flashed a kindly smile and waved to the crowd.

"Number 19, left winger, Terrance Hawking." When Terrance got on the ice, he was a different person. He skated with fury, beating his stick in front of him as he moved across the rink. Flynt had told me once before that hockey was Terrance's life, and by the look on his face, you could tell he was determined.

"Number 34, goaltender for the Redhawks, Zac Brophy." I rolled my eyes. He looked more pompous on the ice than off.

"Number 2, defender, Danny Westbrook."

"Number 13, defender, Dustin Whitamaker."

"And last but not least, newcomer to the team, number 3, right winger, Alex Loving!" Alex was taking his time crossing the rink. His hands were raised above his head and the cheering from the crowd only egged him on. I wondered what had gotten into him. This was something that I expected from Zac Brophy, not Alex. He was completely disregarding the plans we had made to lay low.

When Alex was inside the box, the Zamboni came onto the ice and began to smooth the surface before the start of the game. The DJ turned on "Kernkraft 400" by Zombie Nation, and the crowd stood on their seats and began to cheer. The shirtless guy was running back and forth clanking his cow bell, but he was no longer the center of attention. The crowd was concentrating on the tall blond descending the stairs and, although a bit delayed, my attention, too, soon followed. I stood up to get a closer look. When my eyes fell on Corrine Harvey, I was only half surprised. Even at a hockey match, she had a way of drawing attention to herself. I was, however, caught off guard when someone on the ice opened a door in the dasher board, so she could walk onto the rink. The music died down, the Zamboni made its exit, and Corrine made her way to center ice wearing tight jeans paired with high heel wedge boots, and a plaid Tartan cape coat I would kill to have. It wasn't until the fans began to place their hands across their hearts that I realized what Corrine was doing.

"Ladies and Gentleman," Mr. Harvey began. "Will you all rise and join my beautiful daughter, Corrine Harvey, as she leads us in the national anthem."

The instrumental began, and Corrine's voice started out low but quickly jumped half an octave in the second verse. Her voice fluctuated up and down, hitting each note with precision.

"And the rockets' red glare, the bombs bursting in air..." Corrine flawlessly jumped an entire octave to hit the highest note in the song.

"O'er the land of the free and the home of the brave." Corrine ended the song with perfection. Not only could she bake chocolate cakes, she could sing, and sing well.

When Corrine was safely off the ice, the referee blew his whistle to begin the game. The players flooded the ice and the organ music began. Flynt put on his helmet and moved into position opposite the Ripper's center, Cory Cooper. Alex and Terrance were both wingers, Alex at right and Terrance at left, and as Alex skated past Flynt to assume his offensive position, I noticed the taunting way he nudged his shoulder into Flynt's back. Flynt returned the gesture, and I shivered. This game was going to be brutal... I just knew it.

Not wanting to support the rivalry between boys, I moved my attention from the ice to the crowd and without even having to search, I saw Mrs. Harvey and Corrine seated six rows down and to my left. Corrine had made it back to her seat and was sipping on a soda. I wanted to hide in a hole. It had been a while since I had seen Corrine. Partly because she had been confined to her house since her soiree. But also, I had heard through the grapevine, or perhaps more appropriately, the hedge, that Corrine blamed her party getting busted on me. Her reasoning being that, if I hadn't pulled such a dramatic stunt in the forest, the cops would not have come to her house. I swear, Corrine was absolutely self-absorbed. When the referee blew the whistle for the second time, my attention was back on the rink. The organ music faded when the ref dropped the puck at center ice, and the sound of sticks slapping together was the only noise I heard.

"And Redding has the puck, and he passes it back to number 19, Terrance Hawking. Hawkins hands it off to Loving."

Alex was moving up the center when the DJ turned on "Kickstart my Heart." Both Theroux and Browning, Rippers defensemen, were moving in fast. In an instant, Flynt checked Theroux to the right and Terrance checked Browning to the left. The sound of bodies crashing into the dasher board prompted the crowd to cheer.

"You would be expecting the intensity to be high between these two teams considering what is at stake and it looks as though it's starting off that way," Jack Callaway said to his fellow commentator, Jerry Harvey. "The winning team goes on to the championship game in Syracuse, New York."

"Look at that Jack," Mr. Harvey interrupted. "Up the center. Here comes Loving. Loving takes the shot. And he scores. The Rippers didn't have anyone there for that one."

"Bill Jacobs is our referee for this afternoon, and he makes the call."

"Kickstart My Heart" faded and Metallica's "Master of Puppets" resonated from the speakers as the players headed to center ice to face-off. The scraping of skates on the icy rink was fierce and cutting.

"Players at center ice. Redding taking the face-off against Cooper."

Once again, Flynt fought to get the puck away from the opposing center, Cory Cooper, but this time, Cooper took it in one quick sweep and passed it back to the Rippers' right winger, number 19, Troy Simpson.

The music faded out and Mr. Harvey's voice was loud and clear.

"Loving takes it from Simpson, and he is off. Both Hawkings and Redding are open, but it looks like Loving wants to play this game all by himself."

"AND... HE... IS... STOPPED... SHORT," Jack Calloway burst in. "By Rippers' offensive, Theroux. Thoeroux takes it from Loving.... and what is this. Loving's not going to let that one slide. He hooks Theroux, and Theroux is down! This game is starting out with a bang!"

"Penalty for the Redhawks. Powerplay for the Rippers."

As Alex skated off the ice, my heart began to sink. What was he trying to prove? He didn't need to play dirty to win the game. I absolutely could not understand his behavior. He was using his strength all right, but it wasn't for the good of the game. The match continued on, but my full attention was on Alex. He was in the penalty box massaging his whiskers. He was in the zone, completely focused on the game. The buzzer sounded, ending the first period. The players moved off the ice and the Zamboni moved on. Even with the powerplay, the score was one to nothing in our favor. Eyes still on the players, I could see Flynt leaning over the small wall that separated the penalty box from the bench. He was yelling at Alex, and Alex was yelling back. While the other team members were trying to restrain Flynt, Alex began to taunt. I couldn't see much from where I was, but I didn't miss the anger showing on Flynt's cheeks. I wondered what Alex was saying. Meanwhile, the crowd was chanting, egging the two of them on. After the incident on Halloween night, all sorts of speculations had been made. People had the audacity to say Flynt's massive blood loss was because Alex had sucked it out. I wanted to tell everyone that Alex was not cruel or mean. He had healed Flynt, not harmed him. He healed him just enough to save his life. The only thing Alex had sucked up and swallowed was his pride. He had rescued Flynt, the boy who was relentlessly competing against him for my affection. And this was the thanks he got. Only now did I understand why Alex was acting the way he was... he was giving the crowd exactly what they wanted. He figured that if the town was going to talk, then he might as well act the part. As tension heated up inside of the box, the town was divided in two. Half of the fans were yelling, "Bite him" while the other half was screaming, "Booooo."

When Alex turned toward the stands and began gliding his finger up and down his lateral incisor, the crowd went absolutely wild. While Alex was still focused on his performance, Flynt threw a cheap shot. Still facing the crowd, Alex unmindfully reached his hand into the air and blocked his punch. Holding Flynt's fist in midair, Alex turned toward him and shook his head. Flynt's cheeks were now red with embarrassment instead of anger.

Alex turned back toward the crowd and lifted his free hand into the air. "Bite him" could now be heard loud and clear above the "Boos."

The ref blew his whistle signaling the start of the second period. I kept my eyes on all of the players and the game as a whole; however, it was obvious a second game was taking place on the other side of the rink, a game between Alex and Flynt. They had their eyes on one another instead of the puck, and were circling each other, holding their sticks at the ready. I bit my lower lip and clinched my fists tight inside of my gloves. While the Redhawks were a bit preoccupied, the Rippers were controlling the puck, and Curtis, the Rippers defender, had an unobstructed path toward the goal.

"Taking full advantage of the breakaway, Curtis is coming at Brophy full speed." Even though Mr. Harvey was rooting for the Redhawks, you could hear the excitement in his voice as Curtis skated toward the goal.

"Looks like Brophy's a little out of his net. I'm guessing Curtis is going for a backhand deke."

"You might be right, Jack. He's coming in fast at an angle. He shoots. He scores!"

"You know Harvey, Loving and Redding are going to have to get over their differences if they want to win this one."

"I couldn't agree with you more, Jack."

Back at center ice, the buzzer sounded and the ref dropped the puck.

When the organ music started, I began to drift. I began to think about Alex shedding his clothes in the living room earlier today, and I began to wonder why he never took off his tee shirt. He didn't even bother to take it off when he went for his morning swim. Perhaps he was modest. I immediately recalled the fight that took place just moments ago between Alex and Flynt. I would forever be left with the image of Alex shining his incisor with the tip of his finger. No, Alex was definitely not modest.

Perhaps he was afraid he might get sunburned. His skin was fairer than mine. No, that wasn't it either. Alex never used sunscreen. Besides, he was superhuman, and he wasn't supposed to get burned. I knew he was hiding something under his shirt, but I couldn't imagine what it might be. I was pulled out of my daydream when the crowd began to scream. It took a moment to figure out why they were yelling. I stood on my seat, so I could see over their heads. All the commotion was taking place at the end of the rink. Two guys were hugging and skating in circles. It was Terrance and Curtis.

"I thought hockey was a rough sport," I said under my breath. "This is more like the Ice Capades." I stopped when Terrance thrust his fist into Curtis' head. The protective piece flew out of Curtis' mouth and blood and saliva sprayed onto the ice. The DJ switched on "Mama Said Knock You Out" by L.L Cool J., and the crowd began to cheer. Curtis responded by pushing Terrance away and slamming his fist into Terrance's face.

"Back and forth. Back and forth." Jack's voice rose above the music.

"Oh, this is getting nasty, folks," Mr. Harvey shouted. "Trying to get a hand free... Terrance falls... gets back up!"

"And there goes a helmet," Calloway shouted into the mic.

The lack of protective gear didn't stop the fight. They now had each other by the shoulders and were skating in circles again, building speed with each pass, and attempting to gain the leverage they needed to win the fight.

"Will you look at that," Mr. Harvey boomed. "Blake Curtis now has Terrance Hawking by the jersey. Oh look, will ya! He's trying to pull it over his head! This is exciting stuff, folks."

"He's got 'em! He's got 'em! He's got 'em DOWWWNN!!!"

Terrance was on the ice, but the fight wasn't finished. Curtis was ruthless, but Terrance was still fighting back. I wondered why the ref wasn't blowing the whistle.

"Simpson just went in after Hawking."

"Now Westbrook... now Whitamaker. O'Reilly has left his goal unattended and he has Theroux by the neck. Hey folks, the whole team has joined the fight."

All the players were now throwing blows at the opposing team. Stick and helmets were abandoned on the ice as each player found an adversary willing to battle it out. After only a moment, Theroux skated off the ice. With his gloved hand he wiped the blood from under his nose. His head was also bleeding, and his blond hair was wet with blood and sweat. My heart was thumping beneath my heavy coat, and my palms began to sweat when I realized that Flynt and Alex were at it again. It didn't surprise me, but I think it surprised the crowd.

"This might just be the first time in the leagues history that two members from the same team are going at it, Jack."

"With the tension between the two, it was bound to happen."

I agreed with Jack; however, I was a bit surprised that Alex was acting on his feelings. Up until this point, he had been able to keep his emotions in check. But if this was going to happen, then I supposed there was no better place. I was thankful that Flynt was fully padded, and I was hopeful that Alex would not use all his strength.

The fight between Flynt and Alex had not only gained the commentators' attention, but the attention of both teams as well. "Mama Said Knock You Out" was still playing while Alex and Flynt exchanged swings. Alex was agile, and he quickly redirected his body to avoid Flynt's incoming fist. Flynt wasn't so lucky. Alex looked at me. I shook my head with disapproval. He looked a bit torn, but did not let up a bit.

"This isn't going to be pretty, folks." Mr. Harvey continued. "And I'm not liking Redding's chances. After a nearly fatal accident several months ago, Redding has just made it back on the ice and HE… IS… STRONG. But it appears that he is no match for Alex Loving."

"Loving has flipped Redding onto the rink, and with surprising strength, he now has him pegged to the ice."

"It doesn't look like Redding's getting out of this one, Jack."

"I've never seen anything like this. Loving is holding him to the ground with a single hand and Redding isn't fighting back."

"You're right, Jack. Redding isn't moving."

The music shut off and the crowd was still. The commentators stared at one other, unsure of what to say. Just moments ago, three separate fights were competing for the crowd's attention, now the players from both teams stood united, staring at the situation taking place on center ice. The referee blew his whistle but Alex didn't budge. Flynt was still lying motionless. When the ref blew his whistle again, Alex looked into my eyes and held them there. A bit unsure of the protocol, the referee skated toward Alex and pried his hands away from Flynt's jersey. Eyes still on me, Alex skated off the ice.

"Looks like Loving is *loving* the penalty box this afternoon, folks. And it's a good thing, too, because that's where he'll be spending the next five minutes. One more move like that and he'll be out for the rest of the game." Mr. Harvey's voice wasn't the same. It was shaky and uncertain. The crowd was silent as they observed a motionless Redding still flat on his back. The referee was beside him along with a few medics. I was holding my breath. I couldn't believe this was happening. I couldn't believe Alex had used his strength in such a way when he promised me he wouldn't. It seemed like an eternity before Flynt stood up, and when he skated off the ice, he seemed more disoriented than injured. As he moved toward the penalty box, he looked me in the eye. There was something in his expression that let me know he knew. His expression told me he had just seen something similar to what I had seen on the running path last May. The look in his eyes told me he had seen something beyond this world, something out of the ordinary, and that something was Alex Loving.

"I don't understand you. Do you want everyone to know what you are?"

"What am I, Rae? What is it you think I am?" Alex was standing in front of the fire, and he was wearing the black vintage Beastie Boys concert tee that I had given him for Christmas.

"Up until this afternoon, I thought you were an angel."

"Now what am I, a monster?"

I rolled my eyes, let out a moan, and fell back onto the sofa. "You're impossible. That's what you are. It's like you don't even care. You skate onto the rink with your last name printed all over your jersey. Someone is bound to remember your parents. This town isn't that big. Someone's bound to remember that nineteen years ago, Alex Loving died in fatal car crash just outside of town."

"Don't worry. I have a feeling we won't be here much longer."

"Well, you've got that right. You should have seen the look in Flynt's eyes after the game. I think he knows about the fight between you and Ben. I think he remembers everything. Maybe the way you had him pegged to the ice was the same way Ben had him pinned to the forest floor. You were holding him down! He couldn't move! What were you trying to do, scare him to death?"

"I don't understand why you care."

"He'll never talk to me again."

"And that makes you sad, right?" Alex huffed.

"Why do you hate him so much?" I yelled.

"Because!" Alex screamed. "He can give you all the things I can't."

"You haven't tried to give me anything," I said, standing up and taking a more defensive position. "I can't even get a kiss without begging. And the way you wear that tee shirt around. You don't even take it off to swim. It's like you're hiding something under there."

Something inside of Alex changed. Still standing with his back toward the fire, he pulled off his shirt and threw it onto the floor. "Is this what you want, Rae? Is this what you've been waiting to see?"

I stood with my mouth agape, not because of his perfect torso, but because of what was spread across his chest.

"You'd better come and get a closer look. I'd hate for you to miss anything."

Slowly, I inched toward him, afraid that if I moved too fast he might suddenly disappear. Alex's eyes held no expression, and as we stood face to face, he looked as hard as stone. I brushed my lips across his but he didn't respond. I closed my eyes and placed my hand on his shoulder. Slowly, I moved my right hand down his chest and let it rest upon his heart; I could feel it pounding hard beneath my hand. His skin was smooth and warm beneath my fingers.

After a moment, I opened my eyes to examine his chest. At first, I tried to act as though I wasn't staring, but I had to lean back in order to get a good look and turn my head at such an angle that I could no longer be discrete. When I saw the tattoo on his chest, I was reminded of the game he asked me to play on my eighteenth birthday. He called it the 'OR' game. He would ask me a question, give me two optional answers, and then I had to pick one or the other.

"Tattoo or piercing?" he asked.

"Tattoo," I told him.

"Really?" He looked surprised. "Neither."

"You can't say neither, you have to pick one," I reminded him of the rules, and he ignored me.

I'm was not sure if I was more surprised about the fact that Alex had a tattoo or by the beautiful detail put into the eagle that spread its wings across Alex's chest. I had never seen anything like it. It was life like. Not inked, but etched into his skin by the hand of a skilled artisan.

"Is this the reason you never take off your shirt?"

Alex looked disturbed but did not answer. All the emotion I saw in his eyes was gone. Alex was at a loss for words. This wasn't the sort of thing that usually happened. He was always so in control.

I ran my fingers over his chest, out of interest rather than infatuation. I could see the etch marks in his skin, but smooth was all that I could feel with the tips of my fingers. I tried the palm of my hand and it was the same. Smooth and warm; not a hint of the eagle that was permanently carved into his pecs. There was only one flaw I could find. The eagle's left wing was nearly gone.

"It's beautiful. You shouldn't hide it."

Alex did not respond. His body was as stiff as a board.

"What does it mean that it's fading?" Once again, I ran my hand across the very visible eagle, but as soon as my fingers touched the skin of his chest I felt him push me gently away. Within a second, I found myself standing alone in front of the fireplace.

"I'm sorry," he said. "But this was a mistake." He cringed as though he were in pain.

"What part? The part when you actually showed an ounce of emotion?"

"I'm not sure that I can do this... any of this. I'm so tired of pretending to be something I'm not. Goodnight. I'm going to bed," he said, turning to leave.

"You're just going to walk out and leave me standing here?"

Alex paused in the doorway, his back toward me.

"You're so brave with everything except for me," I told him.

"Because you're the only thing that I can't bear to lose."

CHAPTER THIRTY

*F*or the past couple of days, I had been listening to a song on Alex's cassette player called "Looks Like Rain" by The Grateful Dead. I found the cassette in a basket of old tapes that Alex kept in the living room under the coffee table. It was the title of the tape that drew me to it: *Without a Net*. It reminded me of the net I was entangled in. What I wouldn't give to be without a net, and how nice it would be to not feel so entangled. When I slid the cassette into the machine and pushed play, "Looks like Rain" was the song that came out of the speakers. The lyrics told a story about a man who woke up one morning to find that the love of his life was gone. I realized immediately that I was meant to hear this song, and because of this, I played the song over and over again. I could relate to the lyrics. I knew how it felt to say goodnight when what I should have said was goodbye. I knew how it felt to let something you love slip through your fingers. I feared the emptiness that would come with Alex's absence should he leave this earth for good. I had tasted his absence before, and it was poison. The lyrics told the story of a man who wanted to hold onto his love without tying her down in the process. I hadn't considered it before, but perhaps I was tying Alex down. Maybe he would rather go on… to eternity… the place where he belonged. Maybe he wanted to complete his purpose so that he could finally leave. For the first time since he arrived on earth I realized I was nothing more than a hindrance. Yes, he loved me, but he wasn't happy, not here, not on this earth.

Several days ago, I got to thinking about the eagle on his chest and how it was fading. Was that a sign that he was becoming more human, or was it symbolic of the time he had left on earth? I thought about Alex's strength. He was still as strong as the day I met him. But things were different. In the past couple months, I had seen Alex go through numerous changes. The first red flag was when he got sick over Christmas. Alex was supposed to heal, not need healing. There was also the event on the hockey rink. Alex had never been fond of Flynt, but he had always been able to control his emotions. What happened on the ice seemed out of character. It seemed such a human thing to do. Was Alex allowing himself to become more human so that he could be with me? Was Alex giving up his strength so he could stay on earth? I was so incredibly selfish. I had been looking out for my own interest instead of his. Pastor Joe told me I needed to find the truth because the truth would set me free. For months, I had been thinking about what my truth might be, and I had come up with nothing. It was late in the evening on the night of February 27th when I had a revelation: maybe I was supposed to find Alex's truth, not mine. Maybe *I* wasn't the one who needed to be set free. For once in my life, I was going to do the right thing, the unselfish thing. I was going to read the journal so I could finally put an end to Chloe and Ben, and I was going to do this by myself.

Alex had already gone to bed, and when I was certain that the coast was clear, I pulled the journal out of the nightstand and held it to my chest. If this was the truth, then why did it feel so wrong? I had spent my entire life thinking only of myself. Now it was time to think about Alex and what Alex wanted… needed. I opened the cover of the book and read the title page: The Dark and Unfortunate Life of Eva Pierce

I knew that it was now or never, so I opened to the first journal entry and immersed myself in the life of Chloe's mother.

Dear whoever is listening:

The salutation was enticing. It made me wonder if Eva was hoping her journal would one day be discovered and, if so, by whom? Her husband or Chloe, perhaps? Surely she wouldn't have expected it to be a stranger like me.

Dear whoever is listening: April 15th, 1990

After several weeks of nausea and extreme fatigue my suspicions were confirmed. I am four weeks pregnant. Chloe is a little over a year, and I find it hard to keep up. What will I do with two babies? I thought the news would excite Carl. I thought he might be home a bit more now that I was expecting. Much to my dismay, he informed me that his new project would be keeping him abroad. I guess it's just Chloe and me. All alone in this big house.

Dear whoever is listening: April 30th, 1990

My thoughts on Prince Charming:
I would be willing to bet that little girls' dreams are all the same and it all begins when our parents read us stories of princesses who, despite all odds, find their prince charming. It seems that in most every fairytale, there is a source of evil that wishes to destroy the young girl's happiness. In Cinderella, it was the evil stepmother and her two daughters, Anastasia and Drusilla. And the wicked queen tried to kill Snow White by giving her a poisoned apple, all because she was jealous of her beauty. If I remember correctly, it seems that jealously was also a factor in the story of Sleeping Beauty. All these jealous and wicked women, and then you have King Triton, Ariel's father, who wanted to keep her under the sea and punished her for falling in love with a human. He was bound and determined to keep her under his thumb.
My sister and I have always been like night and day. Her good heart set her apart from others, while my stunning beauty was my only source of definition. If I sound vain, I don't mean to. I wish that people had noticed something other than my beauty. I wish that someone would have said, "Eva, you are so smart", or "Eva, you are so kind." Or even, "Eva, you are so talented. Your

paintings are beautiful." From a very young age, I knew it was my sister that my mother preferred. My sister was pretty, but almost ordinary compared to me. I figured that maybe my mother was jealous of my beauty. And my father, he was like King Triton: always trying to keep me under his thumb. I felt like Ariel. I felt like I was drowning in my very own home. I knew that one day, I would find my Prince Charming, and he would be nothing like my father. He would be strong and powerful. My new home would be nothing like my parents' house in the middle of Missouri. It would be a palace, a castle fit for a princess like me.

When I was twenty-four, I met Carl Pierce; he was everything I imagined my Prince Charming to be. He was thirty-seven. He was rich and beautiful and perfect. My parents' disapproval was a good as their consent. I married Carl and moved into his castle, the large family estate in the heart of Tulsa, Oklahoma. My new house is nothing like the home where I grew up. But the excitement of something new, something different has worn off. It is filled with riches but lacking in love. Chloe is only one and a half, and already I am pregnant again. Carl is rarely home and, when he is, he barricades himself in his basement workshop. It is hard for me to admit, and I can't bring myself to say it, so I will write it inside a journal that no one will ever see. I think maybe my parents were right about Carl. Maybe he is not the best for me. Maybe my life is not a fairytale. I am living in a castle, but my husband is no prince, and I am not happy.

Dear whoever is listening: June 18th, 1990

I found a shoe today. It was a size 8 with a small heel. It was tan and worn. I suppose I would have never found it if I hadn't ventured into the basement, which on more than one occasion I had been told, was off limits. But it was the earring I found last week that sparked my interest. I barley noticed it at first. It was a small silver angel shimmering near the basement door. I picked it up and put it in the drawer of my nightstand, and pulling it out of the drawer to study it became my nighttime ritual. A sick form of entertainment while Carl was away. Then I found the shoe in the basement, and subsequently it was Carl who found me. Lying flat on my back on the

basement floor with extreme abdominal pains. My detective work earned me
a lock on the basement door and a nanny named Linda to help care for Chloe.
She's an older lady and she is nice enough, but I feel like she is really here to
keep an eye on me.

Dear whoever is listening: June 23rd, 1990

The doctor told me that stress is the most likely cause of my contractions.
They are strong and close together. The doctor gave me an IV infusion of
Magnesium Sulfate. I think that was the name of the medicine. It seemed to
have worked. The contractions have stopped, and I am more comfortable. The
baby isn't due until the beginning of January, but Doctor Porter thinks I will
be lucky to make it through October. I have been put on bed rest. There is
something about being cooped up inside the bedroom of a 15,000 square foot
mansion that makes me feel so lonely.

Dear whoever is listening: August 1st, 1990

I can't sleep at night. The doctor prescribed me a sleeping aid. He says I
need my rest. He says my baby needs for me to rest, but I have been on bed
rest for a month now. I have read twelve books and have watched every movie
available on Pay Per View. I have asked Linda if she would bring up my easel
and paints. I told her I could paint while sitting on the side of my bed. She
said she would ask Doctor Porter. I'm bored, and I miss Chloe. Linda only
brings her up to me a few times a day. Not being able to take care of her makes
me feel so incompetent. On a more positive note, I just found out today that
our baby is going to be another girl. I'm so excited.

Dear whoever is listening: August 3rd, 1990

I got my paints today. Yay! The sleeping pill is working. It puts me out
like a light, but I feel a bit groggy when I first wake up. Carl called this
morning and said he might be home next week for a quick visit before he has
to leave again. Chloe and I watched All Dogs Go To Heaven in my bed, and

then we took a nap. Today was a good day. Things might just be turning around.

Dear whoever is listening: August 14ᵗʰ, 1990

The first thing I thought of when I woke up was the shoe and the earring that I had found in our home a couple months ago. My mind keeps wandering, and it never ends up anywhere good. Chloe came down with a fever last night and Linda said it would be best if Chloe didn't come to visit me today. I am left here in my bed all alone with nothing to do but worry.

Dear whoever is listening: August 15ᵗʰ, 1990

Sometimes I think I hear noises coming from the basement. Carl is gone and won't be home for several days, so I know it can't be him making the racket. The door to the basement has a padlock on it, so it couldn't be Linda. I told Doctor Porter about it. I told him I thought someone had broken into the basement through the cellar door at the back of the house. He told me he would check it out, which made me feel better. This morning I made the decision to stop taking my sleeping pill because I seem to be completely worthless the next day. I hope I can sleep tonight.

Dear whoever is listening: August 25ᵗʰ, 1990

Doctor Porter came today because my contractions resumed. They were strong and a minute apart. He hooked up an IV, and once again, flooded my veins with Magnesium Sulfate. I asked him if he had gotten a chance to check the cellar door. He told me that everything looked fine and that I shouldn't be concerning myself with nonsense. He reminded me that stress and worry are bad for the baby and for me. He also told me that the sleeping pill he had prescribed to me for rest had side effects. One possible side effect is auditory hallucinations. Perhaps he was right. But then I remembered I had quit taking the prescription days ago.

As I was reading over Eva's journal, something wasn't sitting right with me. I started at the beginning of the journal and reread each entry. Perhaps I was feeling disappointment because I had yet to find a single thing that might help me in my quest to find the truth. Eva didn't like her parents... so what? Eva married the wrong guy... so what? Eva liked to complain... so what? That she liked to paint was her only redeeming characteristic. Eva was annoying. Like mother, like daughter, I suppose. I thumbed through the pages, stopping when I came to the second entry in the book. My stomach sank when my eyes fell on a sentence near the middle of the page.

My new home would be nothing like my parents' house in the middle of Missouri.

Missouri?

Eva was from Missouri. My nana and papa were from Missouri... my mom was from Missouri, too. My mom's sister's name was Eva.
"No. No. Not possible."
I sucked in a breath and began to read a new entry from Eva's journal.

Dear whoever is listening: August 29th, 1990

I have been bound to this bed for a little over two months. Linda continues to care for Chloe. I sleep a lot because there's nothing else to do. When I'm not sleeping, Linda brings Chloe to me. Chloe is one and a half years old and Linda swears that she is already going through her terrible twos. Lately, Linda has refused to bring Chloe to me. She says that her tantrums have been more extreme, and she is afraid that Chloe might have temper tantrum around me. I just don't see it. My Chloe is a little angel. Carl is still gone. His plans changed, and he wasn't able to make it back as quickly as he promised. Most of the time, it's just Linda, Chloe and me all alone in this monstrous house. I feel lonely. The only person from the outside that Carl allows in is Doctor Porter. I've asked Linda to sneak me up a couple of friends, but she is scared to cross him. If I were totally honest with myself, so am I.

Dear whoever is listening: September 6th, 1990

I can't fall asleep. Despite my adherence to Doctor Porter's prescribed bed rest, the contractions are still coming… and so are the noises. I know that what I am hearing is real. I guess I could try praying. I think I'll pray for rest.

4 a.m.: Still awake, prescription free, and the noises are coming from beneath me. Pounding that seems to be getting louder and more desperate. It has been over a month since I have been out of this bed, but tonight I will take my chances. Curiosity has gotten the better of me and you know what they say about curiosity. Wish me luck, whoever is listening, for into the basement I must go.

4:30: Side effect of pregnancy: losing your noodle. My plan for sneaking into the basement seemed perfect until I got to the bottom of the stairs and remembered there was a padlock on the door and Carl has the key. I wonder if there is an extra key lying around somewhere. I think I will start my search in our bedroom. It took me nearly twenty minutes to get back up the stairs and the climb brought on painful contractions. I will keep my stair climbing to a minimum. The house is still quiet. Chloe and Linda are sound asleep, but I still hear the occasional noise coming from below.

6 a.m.: No luck finding a spare key in the bedroom. I think I heard Chloe crying, which means that if Linda is not up, she will be soon. My detective work has come to an end for now, and I am exhausted. Until tomorrow night. Au revoir.

I studied the dates at the start of each entry. 1990. That was the year Laney died. That was the year I was born. I set the journal in my lap and held my face in my hands. I rubbed my eyes and stretched my mind. Something wasn't right. Something wasn't adding up. There was a connection between the journal entries and the letter inside my scrapbook. What was the connection? I had been in this exact position before. I can remember sitting on the bed in my papa's house trying to make meaning out of the letters I found inside the scrapbook. It was the date at the top of each letter that linked everything together. Dates. I slid off my bed in a hurry and pulled the scrapbook out of my bag. I flipped open to the page with my mom and dad and Laney standing in the Loving's yard. I studied the picture. There was something about the picture that seemed unusual, something that I hadn't noticed before. I ran my finger across the glossy finish and sighed. If a picture was worth a thousand words, then what was this picture trying to tell me? The answer I was seeking was right in front of my face. What did a pregnant Eva's journal have to do with the letters, the pictures inside of my book? Pregnant. Pregnant. Pregnant. "Pregnant," I finally said aloud. I studied the picture again and read the inscription above.

Sue, Will, and Laney. September 13th, 1990---Alexandria Minnesota.

Pregnant. On September 13th, my mom would have been five months pregnant with me. I studied my mom. She was wearing a white fitted tee shirt. I studied her stomach. It was flat. A cold chill fell over me. I flipped through the pages until I found the picture of my mother and Eva leaving for the prom. Roth was my mother's maiden name. Sue Roth. Eva Roth... Eva Pierce. Both Eva's grew up in Missouri. My aunt Eva looked like me. My aunt Eva looked like Chloe. Goosebumps formed on my arms and legs, and I began to push away the thoughts that were swimming through my mind.

No... no, I cried. *I am my mother's daughter. I belong to Sue and Will.*

I focused on Eva's journal, allowing the words inside to delay my comprehension, and the acceptance of what I already knew to be true.

Dear whoever is listening: September 10th, 1990

Four days and still nothing has turned up. I have found nothing that resembles a key, and the noises are still strong during the night. I have limited my snooping to the bedroom and a few other rooms on the second floor. I have sifted through empty boxes in our master closet, but I have found nothing out of the ordinary.

Not a single contraction today. I am still hopeful that Doctor Porter will relieve me of bed rest. If it weren't for this bit of detective work I was doing on the side, I think I would be going crazy right about now. Or maybe the fact that I am hearing noises and snooping around is what makes me crazy. I'm exhausted. Maybe that's it. I'm going to try and get some shuteye. Goodnight whoever is listening.

3 a.m. I just woke up drenched in sweat, sitting upright in the middle of my bed. It was a dream that woke me. In my dream, I was running my hand across the top of Carl's antique wooden desk. I was moving my hand toward the bottom drawer when someone jerked my hand away, and I woke up. Carl's desk is a family heirloom. That's where he keeps all of our important documents such as passports and birth certificates. They stay inside a small safe he keeps in the bottom drawer of his desk. Oh, my gosh! The key. It just occurred to me that the key to the basement might be somewhere inside Carl's antique desk. I think I am going to venture downstairs and give it a try. Wish me luck, whoever is listening. Four days till Carl gets home. Four days to find the key.

5:30: I found the key. It was on a small ring with one other. I hoped the key I found would fit inside the lock. It did! Carefully, I descended into the basement. The noises were most definitely real. I had not been imagining them. There was a stench in the air so thick I had to cover my nose with a bit of my sweater. I followed the cries and found myself standing outside Carl's workshop door. I beamed my flashlight across the concrete wall, searching for a light switch, and was relieved when I finally found one. When I flicked it on, the room behind the door lit up and the voices stopped. Still standing in the dark, I shone my flashlight on the door and found the knob. I turned it. I wasn't surprised to find that this door, too, was locked.

I slipped my hand inside my sweater and felt for the keychain. I held my flashlight over the keys: the key I used to get into the basement was unmarked, but the second key on the chain was marked with a "W". I held the second key tightly in the palm of my hand and took in a deep breath. I put the flashlight in my pocket to free my hands. Still standing in the dark, I held the doorknob and blindly inserted the key. My hands were shaking and pain was now searing through my abdomen in sharp, relentless waves. A pain so strong it brought me to my knees. I felt heaviness in my groin, and I thought about how I didn't want to have my baby on the basement floor. A voice inside of me said, Get up; Open the door and you will be fine, so I did. But there was nothing about me that was fine. My gag reflex was immediate. I coughed and choked and held my arm over my nose to lessen the stench. It took a moment longer for my sense of sight to fully function, as my eyes had to adjust to the brightness of the room.

But it was comprehension that took the longest. I could not understand what I was seeing. There was a mattress on the floor and on top of the mattress, were three girls clustered together. The youngest couldn't have been more than seven years old. It wasn't their scantly clad bodies that I noticed first, but their eyes. Their eyes were filled with fear. They looked liked scared animals. Still covering my nostrils with the sleeve of my sweater, I surveyed the room. There was a video camera set up on a tripod in the corner by Carl's desk. There was a roll of paper towels on the floor beside the mattress. A dresser was pushed up against the back wall and on top sat a single roll of duct tape. There was a bucket in the corner by the closet. I gagged.

Very slowly, I backed out of the room and motioned for the three girls to follow. They didn't budge. I moved toward the cellar door and to my surprise, it wasn't locked. With vise-like pain still gripping me tightly, I pushed open the heavy doors and let the warm breeze into the basement, and the rancid smell out. The girls had ventured out of Carl's workshop, but they were keeping their distance. They were scared of me, and I was scared of them. I couldn't understand why they weren't leaving. They watched, but did not move. My contractions were increasing in intensity. I took short, quick breaths until I felt the pain subside, and then I began to search the pockets of my sweater. When my hand brushed across something crisp, I pulled it out. I held out a twenty-dollar bill and my cell phone. The oldest girl moved forward and snatched them from my hand. Quickly, she put them in her pocket and moved back into position, guarding the youngest with her entire body, much like a mother protecting her child.

"Go," I told them, but still they didn't move. "Go," I urged them once again. The youngest was the first to move. She pushed through the older girls legs and darted for the cellar stairs. When she ran, the others followed close behind. I watched the girls ascend the stairs and escape from our basement into the darkness.

I'm sitting on my bed writing this and my whole body is shaking because of this new reality. Three young girls locked away in the basement of my own home. I let them out. What had Carl done to them? What would Carl do to me when he discovers that I was the one who set them free? I am scared for them. I gave them my cell phone. I am scared for me. I have not called the police. I don't know why, but I can't bring myself to pick up the phone. Carl will be home in three days, and when he gets here I will be gone.

Dear God,

I have never acknowledged you. I have never come close to you. I have never wanted to… until now. I need you, and I need you to answer my prayer. I know I have done nothing to deserve a response. I pray for Chloe. In my condition, I cannot take her with me. Chloe is in Carl's hands. I know he would never do anything to harm her. He may be a monster, but he is a good dad. Please keep her safe. I pray that one day, we will be reunited. Please forgive me for leaving my daughter. It's not right. I am afraid of what Carl is doing, what he is involved in. I am afraid for my life. I don't want to die. I am not ready. I promise that I will do better, be better. But if I do not survive, if Carl finds me, please save my unborn child. I give my child to you. She is yours. I pray that my baby will have loving parents, and that they will give her a name that suits her well.

I traced the date at the top of the last entry. September 10th, 1990. My mind began to fire rapidly through thoughts and memories. I flipped through Eva's journal until I found an empty page near the back. I began to write down my thoughts in purple ink.

Eva was pregnant with a girl
Eva was from Missouri
Eva had a sister

My mom had a sister named Eva
My mom's sister is dead
My mom signed Sue at the bottom of her email
The package entrusted to Sue and Will was beyond repair,
but the contents of the package were saved
There was an odd lady staying at the Loving cottage
Maybe the package was a person
Was the odd lady that Mrs. Harvey referred to, Eva Pierce?
Was Eva the package that Sue and Will were supposed to protect?
Was the baby inside of Eva the gift?
Eva Pierce was my biological mother.
Chloe is my sister.
My father is a monster.
My name isn't Rae Colbert. My name is Rae Pierce!

The letter in Nana's scrapbook stated that ten passengers were involved in the accident. It also stated there were three survivors, but it never said how many lost their lives. I couldn't have been the tenth passenger. Eva was number ten. But because I was born after the accident, I *was* survivor number three.

CHAPTER THIRTY-ONE

*I*t was ten in the morning, and I was in the Wagoneer, a good forty miles away from home and in the middle of the most severe snowstorm I had ever witnessed. The flakes were coming down at a rate so heavy, I could barely see out the window. It had been a full twenty-four hours since I discovered my true identity: I was the daughter of Carl and Eva Pierce, and Sue and Will Colbert were my aunt and uncle, nothing more. They had raised me as their own and they had protected me, despite the fact that my mother, Eva, was the reason their only daughter, Laney, had died.

At eight o'clock, I was lying in bed, unsure of what to do. This new information was mind numbing; it left me listless. It was too much to process at once. When I opened Eva's diary, I had done so with the best of intentions. It wasn't my own curiosity I was trying to appease. I opened the journal for Alex. Now more than ever, I knew it was my fight, not his. And when the fight was over, he would return to heaven where he belonged. In the past year, Alex had saved my life on numerous occasions, and I had done nothing for him in return. It wasn't until I saw the fading eagle on his chest that I realized all he was doing for me, all that he was giving up. I began to consider all I had read. I was pretty sure Eva Pierce was the package. I was also pretty sure that Sue and Will were trying to help her escape from Carl's clutches. I knew that Sue and Will Colbert had been assigned to work with the Lovings. The Lovings were involved in the fight against human trafficking; Pastor Joe had told me so. Based on the last entry of Eva's journal, I had reason to believe that Carl Pierce was up to no good. I was even beginning to wonder if Carl had ties to trafficking as well. It was pure speculation of course, but maybe Paul Loving was about to blow the cover off Carl Pierce's operation. That would link the Lovings to the Pierces, and the blood ties between Sue and Eva linked the Colberts to the Pierces as well. Things were beginning to add up. But there was one portion of the story that didn't make sense, a piece of the puzzle that didn't fit. All the dots were connected… except for one. What did Ben have to do with any of this? Why were his parents on the road that night? Why Minnesota?

I had taken the journal from my nightstand and was thumbing through the journal for answers, thinking I must have missed something, and there at the back of the book among the blank pages, I found an address scribbled in black ink. It was a long shot, but I thought it might just be the piece of information that tied everything together. Below the address was a phone number. And below the phone number was the name M. Bodin. I had found the missing link.

I turned the wipers to the highest speed, but it hardly made a difference. Large flakes of snow were coming at me so fast, I could barely see fifty feet in front of my car. What was normally a very busy road, I'm sure, was completely vacant this morning. The blizzard that started late last night was strong enough to scare even the locals into staying at home. The only tire tracks were my own, and the snow was falling so hard that even the tracks Alex's Wagoneer left behind would be covered within minutes. I looked at the pad of paper resting beside my bag in the passenger seat and studied the address I had scribbled down with my purple gel pen.

16800 West Country Road 24
Fergus Falls, MN

I had been on County Road 24 for fifteen minutes. I had to be getting close, but finding the house was taking a little more work than I had expected. All of the mailboxes were covered in snow and getting out of the car to brush the drifts away so I could read the numbers was not the most warming task. The mailboxes were spaced about a half a mile apart, which meant each lot was rather large. I tapped gently on my brakes when the next mailbox came into view, eased to the shoulder and shifted into park. Quickly, I slammed the door behind me to conserve the heat inside the car. I raced to the box and with a gloved hand, brushed away the snow to find the number 17540. I was looking for 16800. The numbers were getting smaller. I was headed in the right direction.

I climbed back into the car, shifted into drive, pressed my foot onto the gas pedal, and continued down the road another half mile. The wind was whipping around outside the car and bursts of air were blowing through the small gap at the top of the driver's side window. I cranked up the heat and held my hand in front of the vent to warm it. When the next mailbox materialized in front me, I got a sinking feeling in the pit of my stomach. Unlike the other mailboxes, the numbers on the side of this one had been scraped free of snow. It was as if the owners were expecting company. I tapped the brake gently and pulled up right beside it. I read the numbers with ease. 16800. The address matched the one on my pad of paper. This was it. It was now or never. I could keep driving, or I could finish what I had set out to do. I had braved forty miles of treacherous highway in the middle of a blizzard and taken a full hour and a half to reach my destination. If I didn't see this through, I would never forgive myself.

With the car in park, I surveyed my surroundings. I was still the only car on the road. There was an absence of tire tracks in front of me and the snow on the drive leading up to the Bodin's home, too, was completely untouched. When I left the house this morning, I had done so with haste. I hadn't even bothered to come up with a plan of action. I hadn't considered what I might do if I actually found Ben's home. I began to contemplate my next move. My car. I was going to have to find a place to park it; pulling up the Bodin's drive was clearly not an option. It would give them time to think, to plan. I needed to surprise them, to catch them off guard. I needed to hide the Wagoneer and, being that it wasn't the smallest car ever made, camouflaging it could very well be a challenge.

I looked across the street and saw a large snow covered barn with a road leading up to it. It stood alone in front of a thick patch of trees. *Perfect*, I thought. I put the Wagoneer into drive and pulled off the highway and onto the private road leading up to the sturdy structure. The barn door was narrow. I rolled down my window and folded in the side mirror to allow for a little extra room. Carefully, I drove into the barn. Once inside, the world around me grew eerily quiet. The old wooden barn blocked the wind that had been pelting against my windows for the past hour and a half. I pulled in-between two rows of hay bales and turned off the ignition. I sat back in my seat and exhaled. I was about to confront my sister, and I had no idea what I was going to say. I was lying to Alex. If he knew where I was right now, he would be furious.

I looked at my phone and pushed a button. I had three bars out of five. Not great, but better than nothing. There was enough of a signal to make a phone call should I happen to get into a jam. I closed my eyes and kept them closed until I felt enough confidence to continue. Unplugging the phone from its charger, I slipped it into the pocket of my jeans and opened the door of the Wagoneer. I stood beside my car and took in my surroundings. Tools were hanging on the slatted boards. There was a shiny green tractor in the back corner. A bag of cat food was propped up against the wall just beside the door, but there wasn't a single cat to be found. I reached into my jacket and felt for my locket, making sure it was still there. Very quietly, I shut the door behind me and walked toward the solid wall of swirling white flakes.

From the opening of the barn door, I could see the Bodin's driveway. A dense forest of trees surrounded their house, and I would use the woods to my advantage. I decided quickly that I would hike northwest a couple hundred yards, circumventing their property, and then head southeast toward the house. This approach would take more time, but it would allow me to get fairly close without being seen. I wrapped my scarf around my neck and pulled my hat down over my ears. I reached into the pocket of my coat and pulled out two hand warmers. I shook them vigorously. When I felt them heating up, I stuffed them into my gloves.

Once inside the forest, the sound of the wind died down. The trees blocked the bitter cold wind, and I was grateful. It was so quiet I could hear my feet crunching through layers of snow and ice. It was so quiet I could hear the sound of snowflakes making contact with the ground. As I was sneaking through the woods toward the Bodin's, a thought occurred to me. What if the house is empty? The absence of tracks in the drive and the lack of light coming from inside led me to believe that no one was home. And then what would I do? All of this for nothing? I hadn't come this far to fail. But the mailbox. It had been wiped clean. Perhaps they were home and if so, were they expecting someone? Were they expecting me?

I moved deeper into the forest through drifts of snow that were knee deep. The trek was more exhausting than I expected. Even though I was trained to peak condition and even though I could out run most people on any given day, I wondered if I would have enough energy left to fight should it come to that. I wondered if I would have enough stamina to run away if that was the option I chose. I slipped my hand into my pocket and let it brush across the knife I had tucked inside. I reminded myself why I had come. I was here to talk to Chloe. I was here to talk to *my* sister. I was here to give her what she wanted, and I was hopeful that if I did, she would finally leave us alone. More likely than not, my presence would lead to a fight. More likely than not, someone would die. I wrapped my fingers around the knife. "Just a precaution," I whispered. "Just a precaution."

I didn't smell the smoke until I came upon the clearing. I knelt down behind a mound of snow. I could see light coming from inside Ben's house. Someone was definitely home, and I was beginning to have regrets. I was beginning to wish I had let Alex come along, but just as quickly as I let the notion creep into my mind, I pushed it out. This was *my* battle, not Alex's. This was *my* fight, not his. I was the one who needed to end this.

"I am strong. I am persistent. I am stubborn. I will not stop until this thing is done."

I thought about how much easier my life was when Laney was the only sister I knew. I would give anything to meet her. Sometimes I thought I might even give my life to meet Laney. Many nights, I wished for the sister I never had. My wish had been granted. I finally had a sister, but she was nothing like the one I had hoped for. I didn't think Chloe and I would ever be close enough to share secrets and makeup, and I was terrified to see her once again. It was not going to be a warm welcome, I was sure of that. Regardless the outcome, I needed answers. There were things I needed to know. I needed to know what our father was like. I wanted to know if there was anything that Chloe and I shared, besides our looks. Did she love to paint like I did? Like our mother did? And finally, I would ask her what our mother was like. I knew that Chloe was young when our mother died, but if there was anything she could remember about Eva, then I wanted to know.

On my stomach, I crawled through the snow at a snail's pace so I wouldn't be detected. From this angle, I gained a unique perspective. This modern home, constructed of cedar, glass, and corrugated metal, had a cellar door. "You have got to be kidding me," I said out loud. Déjà-vu. I laughed when I thought about the last time I entered a home through the cellar door. I wound up with broken ribs, but I had escaped with my life. A couple of broken ribs were the least of my concerns today. How was it that I always got myself into these sticky situations? I picked up the pace and moved across the snow toward the cellar, not stopping until I reached it. With my back against the house, I stretched out my hand and brushed the snow away from the handles. A plastic lock had been cinched around the handles, holding the doors together. I pulled out my knife and opened it up. I moved the blade back and forth across the plastic, using the serrated blade to saw. Back and forth. Back and forth. Back and forth. My hand was frozen, and I was having trouble getting my fingers to do what I wanted them to. I had to stop periodically and wiggle them so they wouldn't stiffen. Finally, I heard the sound of plastic popping and was surprised to find I had sawed the lock in half. I slipped into the cellar and shut the door behind me.

Once inside the basement, I took a moment to kick the snow off my boots, catch my breath, and look around. Unlike the Pierce's basement, this small, single room was bare... completely empty. There was a hot water tank in the corner of the room and in front of me, a set of stairs that led to the first floor. This situation was familiar... too familiar. I moved toward the stairs, taking notice of the thin gap around the edge of the door that was white with light. I ascended one step at a time, not stopping until I reached the top. I stood stock-still for a moment and listened. I pressed my ear against the door when I heard voices coming from the other side.

"You're just like her. And of course you would be. You're blood. I can't believe I thought you might be different," a man's voice huffed.

"Are you threatening me?" a feminine voice cried out.

"I am not in the practice of making threats, Chloe. You need to choose which side you're on. You can't have it both ways."

"I've already made that choice," the voice, now trembling, responded.

"Prove it," Ben chortled. "I'm going to hop in the shower. You'd better have an answer by the time I'm done."

"Can't you just give me...?"

"This has already gone on long enough," Ben interrupted. "I have allowed you to teeter back and forth, and I am done. You need to get her by herself. She's sharper than you think. But I promise, if you put out the bait she'll follow. Once we get rid of your sister, Alex will take care of himself."

What did he mean, I wondered, *that Alex would no longer be a worry if I was gone? Shouldn't it be the other way around?*

As Ben climbed to the second floor, I could hear his footsteps overhead. I held my ear against the door. It was now completely quiet. I waited.

"POP."

A deafening noise came from behind me. A gurgling, a snapping that nearly sent me toppling backwards down the stairs. I held onto the railing and closed my eyes in fear. The popping sound was followed by humming overhead. All at once, I realized the source of the sound. I opened my eyes and looked at the hot water tank in the corner. Ben had just turned on the water. I let out the breath I was holding. Ben was in the shower and Chloe was alone. I had ten minutes, tops, to confront my sister, human to human, without supernatural interference of any kind.

"I am persuasive. I am persistent. I am bound and determined to settle our differences once and for all."

With my ear still pressed against the door, I listened to the sound of footsteps growing distant. Without being able to use my sense of sight, I had to depend on my sense of hearing to determine how far Chloe had moved away from the door. It was now or never. I twisted the knob, cracked the door, and after peeking around it, found that my ears had served me right. The coast was clear. I pushed on the door, making an opening just large enough for me to slip through. I was now standing in Ben's kitchen. I felt for the knife I had slipped back into the pocket of my coat, and then glanced at the set of butcher knifes in a wooden block on the counter. All at once reality sunk in. Ben's weapons were bigger than mine. He was stronger. I was outnumbered. It was two against one, and I didn't stand a chance. Or did I? There was a hint of vulnerability in Chloe's voice. She was weak and that was the only thing I could use to my advantage. My legs were shaking beneath me as I walked out of the kitchen toward the living room. I could hear logs snapping in the fireplace and the sound of Chloe crying. A single wall was the only thing that stood between two sisters. I took a deep breath before rounding the corner. Chloe was sitting on the sofa beside the fire. She shot into to the air like an arrow when she saw me.

CHAPTER THIRTY-TWO

*I*t had been over a year since I had last seen Chloe, but when I looked into her icy blue eyes, it was like no time had passed at all. She hadn't changed a bit; however, because of newfound knowledge, I was able to see her in a different light. I now took notice of the features that we shared. Our high cheekbones, our olive complexion, our hair... our eyes. We stood facing each other, neither of us saying a word. I wondered when she would make her move. Only a coffee table stood between us now. I felt for the knife in my pocket. I didn't think I could bring myself to use it, but I did feel better knowing it was there. What was I going to do? Was I going to fight back, or was I going to make a run for it? And if I did run, where would I go? Back down the stairs and out the cellar door? No. I couldn't run. Not yet. There were things I needed to know. There was a very good chance that today would be the day I would die, and I hoped I wouldn't go to my grave not knowing the answers to all my questions. My lips were quivering with cold or nervousness or both, and Chloe stood still but startled on the other side of the room.

"Why do you hate me?" I quivered. My voice was shaking beyond my control. "I'm your sister. We're blood."

"You will never be my sister. You aren't good enough to be my sister," she hissed. "I'm embarrassed to say we have the same blood running through our veins."

"What do you want from me?"

"What's mine."

"What does Ben want from me?"

"Your life."

"Why?"

"You are evidence of something greater."

"You don't want me dead?"

"I haven't decided," Chloe returned. "You see, sometimes in life we get a choice. We get to choose between what we know to be right and what we know to be wrong. I wrestle with the wrong and today, I'm afraid the wrong is winning."

"Are you talking about me or the girls in your father's basement?"

Chloe's body snapped to attention. Confidence replaced bewilderment and she focused on me like a lion that was about to devour its prey, like a cat toying with a mouse right before it pounced.

"Here's the dilemma. Dad wants you back... alive. But Ben wants you dead. I love them both, but I can't please them both. It's like this, Rae. I hate you because Mom chose you. Is it right to do what you think is best if you leave the ones you love behind? Mom left me behind. She took you with her."

"It's not like she had a choice. I was kind of attached."

"It doesn't matter. Sue and Will took you in and gave you the kind of life I longed for. I hate you for that. But Carl's not so bad after all... and I do love him. He might be a horrible man by your standards, but he has always been decent to me. He gives me everything I need... everything I want. He is my only family."

"So Carl *does* know I'm alive."

What I said sparked a fire in Chloe's eyes.

"If you think for one minute that I will let you get close to him, that I will let him find you, then you'd better think again. You have taken everything from me, and I will not let you take my father as well."

"Is that why all those boxes were in your basement? He's been looking for me, hasn't he?"

Even from across the room, I could see the rage manifesting itself in Chloe's every movement. She was pacing back and forth in front of the fireplace. I had struck a nerve, and I knew that further provocation might be my only chance of finding out the things I needed to know. I needed to know how my mother came to be reunited with her sister. I wanted to know how the Bodin's were involved.

"Eva might be my mother, but she will never be my mom. Sue and Eva may have been sisters, but they were nothing alike. I asked Sue about Eva once. She told me that Eva was the black sheep of the family. My nana... *your* grandmother said that Eva redeemed herself in the end. Eva called on Sue and Will to help her. She might have wrestled with the wrong... but she didn't let it win. In the end, she chose the right path. You're just like Carl. You're evil, Chloe."

"Is that what you think? You think that my mom called Sue? No. She betrayed my dad by calling his best friend. She thought she was being smart when she called Marion. Little did she know that Marion was involved as well."

Marion? I immediately thought about the inscription at the back of Eva's journal. M. Bodin. Marion Bodin. Ben's father. Eva hadn't called my mother. Eva called on the Bodin's for help. How in the world did she wind up with Sue and Will? I was pulled from my thoughts when I heard the floor creak behind me.

"Chloe." I didn't need any time at all to identify the icy cold and razor sharp voice of Benard Bodin. I was standing between the two of them: Chloe in front of me and Ben to my back. I had answers to my questions. I had found the truth, but instead of setting me free, I was now trapped between my two greatest enemies. I was getting exactly what I had asked for, exactly what I deserved.

"Well, look what the cat dragged in," Ben chortled.

I glanced over my shoulder and saw that his black hair was shiny and slicked back on his head. He was wearing his glasses, and looked nothing like the boy I ran into on the path last May. Still, the mere image of his face sent anxiety pulsing through my body.

"I've given you ample time, Chloe. Have you made your decision? Are you going to finish her off, or are you going to make me do all the work?" Ben smiled as he thought about my situation.

"No, Ben. I will be the one. Her blood is mine. It always has been."

Chloe looked at me for a moment, and then she spoke again. "Did you bring what I asked you to bring? Did you bring back what is rightfully mine?"

"No. I didn't," I lied.

"Then that's that."

Ben leaned against the wall with his hands behind his head. "This is excellent," he laughed. "This is the kind of thing I *live* for. I've always been fond of a good cat fight."

Cat fight? I began to remember bits and pieces of the article Alex was reading in *National Geographic*. I had a vivid image of a lion pouncing on its prey, using its massive jaws to press the prey's trachea closed. Death by suffocation. What was I going to do? Would I fight back, or would I take flight?

My eyes drifted around the room, searching for anything that might free me from the mess I had gotten myself into. A door through which I could escape, an object I could throw, a distraction... anything. My eyes fell on Chloe. She was moving slowly toward me, taking a few steps at a time and then pausing to pace back and forth before continuing her approach. It was a form of intimidation, and it was working.

My fingers fumbled with the knife in my pocket. I was going to have to make a run for it, but Ben was blocking the path that led to the basement. I was going to have to find another route, and quick. I moved my eyes off Chloe and onto the living room window that served as an external wall to the house. I looked through the window at the endless blanket of snow. There was no door, just the window. Chloe took another couple of steps toward me. Ben was still leaning up against the wall, chuckling and taunting. I tried to ignore him as I came to the realization that I had only one option. I did want to win, but my chances were slim to none. Even if I fought Chloe and won, Ben had no intention of letting it end there. He would finish what Chloe couldn't. I needed to stall them.

Breaking the window would be my only chance of escape. With only seconds to think it through, I considered a white chair that was in front of the glass. It looked heavy, but if I could lift it, it might just do the trick.

As my eyes moved clockwise around the room, my chest grew tight. I couldn't catch my breath. My heart was pumping wildly. I used my gloved hand to wipe the sweat from my brow.

I am going to die, I thought. *I am going to die in the Bodin's home. I didn't tell anyone where I was going. No one is going to save me. I am going to lose.*

As Chloe inched toward me, I inched toward the chair. It looked heavier up close than it did from a distance. I would be lucky to pick it up, much less throw it through the window. But it was my only shot at escape, and I would have to give it a try. I grabbed hold of the chair with both hands, and I used all of my strength to lift it. I was surprised to find that my strength had exceeded my expectations: tiny shards of glass showered down on the living room floor and sprinkled across my face when I thrust it through the window. The vaulted ceilings amplified the sound of shattering glass. The chair broke through the window, leaving a hole large enough for me to crawl through. Startled, I stood staring at my escape route. Cold air funneled into the living room, but I couldn't feel it; my body was hot with adrenaline. Without stopping to look at the expression on Chloe or Ben's face, I dove headfirst through the razor sharp hole and landed in the powdery white snow just inches below.

I lay there for a moment, dumbfounded. I escaped Chloe and Ben, but I had not escaped the sharp edges of the broken glass. I was bleeding. I lifted my hand to my face and felt something warm and wet. The snow below me was now a pool of crimson. If adrenaline hadn't been pulsing through my body, I would have felt the icy cold air infiltrating my gaping wounds. I would have felt pain blazing through my body. But I didn't. Instead, I was focused on the flight.

I was running, but without direction. The storm had changed the landscape, and the tracks I had made in the snow less than hour ago were gone. The wind only aided the storm. It was blowing the snow about, further decreasing visibility. I had to shield my eyes to see. I began to turn in circles, searching for direction. In the distance, I saw a tree. It was marshmallow white and standing alone, strong and sturdy. It was my only hope for refuge. I turned toward it and glanced over my shoulder at the Bodin's house. A figure was moving toward me, a petite figure shrouded in a veil of snow; it must be Chloe. It was time to move.

I studied the tree carefully, trying to determine how I could use it to my advantage. There wasn't a chance I could climb it. The first limbs were far too high, and the snow coating the tree made the branches slippery and the task impossible. I examined the trunk. It was thick enough to provide a place for me to hide… to rest… to gather my thoughts… to come up with a plan. I began to run as fast as I could toward the tree. My muscles loosened and my body grew warmer, but making a path through the snow was exhausting, and as I began to breathe in the icy air more quickly, my lungs felt as though they were transforming into stone. With each breath came a sharp pain in the center of my chest, but I pushed forward.

When I finally reached the tree, I leaned against the trunk, trying to catch my breath. My chest still hurt. I peeked around the corner of the trunk and saw Chloe drawing closer. She wasn't wearing a coat. My sudden escape had caught her off guard and she reacted impulsively. She followed me into a blizzard without taking the necessary precautions. That I had caught her off guard, unprepared, was the only thing I had working to my advantage. The temperature was well below zero, and I knew that, being only human, Chloe could withstand mere minutes in the blizzard before she would begin to develop the first signs of hypothermia. If only I could keep Ben away. That would be my only shot at survival. The force with which he had thrown me onto the path last spring had not escaped my memory. I could remember the shattering pain like it was yesterday. So, where was Ben? It didn't seem his nature to miss a fight.

I looked toward the house, and through the snow, I could see the lights shining from inside. The living room was empty. I let my eyes fall back on Chloe. She was approaching me from the left. She was no more than a stone's throw away. Her progress was slow, but she was relentless.

It was when I heard the sound of a rumbling train that I knew Chloe was no longer my biggest concern. I turned my head toward the sound. As I looked to my right, I could not believe my eyes; a huge white wall of snow had spontaneously formed. A torrential blizzard was moving across the Bodin's property at lightning speed. It was a tornado in the middle of a snowstorm. It wasn't possible. No. It couldn't be. The huge white mass began to move quickly toward me, but an instant later the storm changed course and began to move in the opposite direction. It was a storm of unnatural strength, destroying everything in its path. I had witnessed something comparable twice before, and on both occasions Ben and Alex were present. But how had Alex found me? I thought I had covered my tracks pretty well. It couldn't be Alex, and I was about to discredit the notion when I saw a splash of color pushing through the wall of white. I was not mistaken. A head. An elbow. A foot. Different body parts were coming into view and then completely disappearing. Alex was here. I had not planned for this. He was not supposed to be here. His coming had defeated my purpose.

I stared for a moment longer, watching the wall of white move back and forth, back and forth. It had captured Chloe's attention as well. Perhaps she had never seen a fight of this magnitude. Perhaps she didn't know how destructive their battles could be. The fight had forced me to change my strategy; I needed to distance myself. I needed to move out of the path of destruction. I looked toward my only route of escape - a snowy wasteland that continued on and on without an end in site.

Time was of the essence. The distance between Chloe and me was growing shorter by the second. I moved toward the wasteland with uncertainty, but when I saw something in the distance, I began to run toward it. It was my only hope. What was it? Another house, perhaps? No, not a house. It was too small. What then? I ran as fast as my legs would carry me. If I could make it to the building without Chloe catching me first, I knew I would be safe. I could lock myself inside. She would freeze to death before she reached me. And as far as Ben was concerned, I would leave him for Alex.

As I ran I could hear the battle between Alex and Ben raging on. The deep humming and the rumbling was growing louder and louder. Snow covered debris was blowing past me, and I placed my hands around my head for protection. I was counting on a victory for Alex. I looked over my shoulder to check Chloe's position. She was so close I could see the white flakes of snow on her pastel green sweater. I needed to make it to the shack. I could do it. I was halfway there. Only another twenty-five feet to go. Blessed with another burst of adrenaline, I picked up the pace. Twenty feet. Fifteen feet. And then I stopped. A noise came from beneath me that left me startled. I stood stock-still and listened.

With the noise of the battle in the background, it was hard to decipher the source of the sound. It was the sound of a tree being uprooted from the ground. It was the sound of something ripping, tearing, breaking, and it was close. It was a bellow so deep that even Chloe stopped to listen. I took another step. All at once, I felt the ground go soft beneath my feet. I was sinking deeper into the snow. I studied the landscape between the shack and me. I looked over my shoulder. Chloe was now so close I could see her shaking. I took another step forward. I heard the deep sound of something cracking. I sucked in a chest full of air when I realized I was not standing on solid ground but frozen water. There in front of me was a five-foot by five-foot clearing in the snow, revealing a very thin layer of ice reforming on the surface of the water.

It took a moment for comprehension to set in: I was looking at the remnants of a recently vacated fishing hole. Someone had left this spot to refreeze without marking it properly, and the shack I had been moving toward was a house for ice fishing. My dream flashed through my mind, and so vividly I saw myself trapped beneath a layer of ice. I was going to die. I was going to drown. Today was the day. For months, I had avoided the water in an attempt to prevent this.

The snow was still so deep it was hitting the middle of my calf. Gingerly, I lifted my foot and took a few steps backward. I then began to sidestep around the hole. I swallowed the hard lump in my throat but kept moving. Chloe was still coming at me. She was shivering. Her pace had slowed, but there was a determined malice in her eyes that I couldn't ignore. I slid further to my right, but this time, I could feel the frigid water sinking into my boot. I was stuck. I couldn't go any further. Chloe had me trapped between the shore and the hole in the middle of the lake. I had to think fast. I had to distract her. I reached inside my jacket and felt for my silver locket.

At first, I thought it was the journal Chloe was after, but after reading it all the way through and discovering that Eva and Sue were sisters, another thought occurred to me. I thought about my locket and how it had been stolen. I thought about how, on my eighteenth birthday, Alex returned it to me. I asked him where he found it, and his answer was simple: at the Pierce Estate. Neither one of us could figure out why Chloe would want my locket, and it wasn't until I read Eva's journal that I finally understood: the locket was an heirloom and the only connection she had to her mother's side of the family. Perhaps she felt entitled to it. I wondered what Chloe wanted more: the locket or my life?

I held the chain tightly in the palm of my hand and with one quick movement, I pulled it from my pocket and let it dangle in the air. I was surprised to find that my plan was working, or at least it had stopped Chloe dead in her tracks. She stood rooted in astonishment, watching the wind blow the locket back and forth. I took a deep breath. I told myself that it was just a locket, just a thing, and in one unsuspecting movement, I threw the necklace into the air and watched it slide to safety on the other side of the icy hole. Like a magnet, Chloe seemed to be drawn to the charm. As Chloe honed in on the locket, I began to inch my way toward solid ground. When the surface of the lake felt completely solid, I began to run.

The battle between Alex and Ben was at its peak. I could no longer see the Bodin's home. When I was about fifty feet from the shore, I heard the familiar sound of ice cracking in the distance. Instinctively, I turned my attention toward the lake, searching for Chloe, but she was gone. Gone. There was only one place for her to go and that was down. I took one last look at the snowy shoreline, torn between saving my life and saving Chloe's. It would be easy to let her go. Letting her go would solve most of my problems. But I already felt responsible for losing one sister, I couldn't feel responsible for losing two. I had to save her. I had to try.

I ran across the lake toward the spot where I last saw Chloe and came to a screeching halt near the hole. I was standing on thin ice, looking down into a pool of freezing water. The ice that reformed on the surface of the water was now broken. Cautiously, I slid onto my stomach. I had a sinking feeling that I was too late. I pulled off my glove and stuck my arm into the hole. The icy liquid felt like needles pushing deep into my skin.

Reaching blindly through the water, I searched for something, anything I could grab. I cannot explain why I felt an overwhelming urge to save the life of someone who wanted me dead. Perhaps it was my conscience. Chloe was my sister, and if I gave it my best shot, I could save her life. I continued searching the water, amazed that I could still feel such excruciating pain in my fingers when they felt so apparently numb. I was beginning to lose hope when something brushed past my hand, and then tried to grab me. With every ounce of strength I had left, I clinched my hand around Chloe's rock hard fist and began to pull. I could feel the slight movement of her hand in mine, and much to my surprise, I felt resistance. I was trying my hardest to save her and she was trying to pull me into the water with her. But I wasn't going to give up. I pulled harder while Chloe continued to fight. And then all at once, I felt her hand relax. She pressed something hard into the palm of my hand and then I felt her slip away.

When her hand disappeared beneath the water, my world went quiet. I stared at the hole in the ice and the pool of water below. This wasn't how I imagined the scene to unfold. I thought about my dream. I had not dreamt that I was drowning. It was Chloe that I saw trapped beneath the frozen lake. Stillness came over me and at first, I misinterpreted it as sadness. But I realized almost immediately that it wasn't so. The stillness was not inside me, but all around me. Gone was the rumbling sound of a train. Slowly, I unclenched my fist and looked at the locket in my hand. She had risked her life to save it, and then she gave it back to me? What did this mean? Was she saying she was sorry for everything she had done? I began to question whether or not I had tried my hardest to save her. I didn't jump in after her. I would have jumped in after Laney; without any doubt, I would have risked my life for her. Overtaken with guilt, I crawled across the ice on my stomach, brushing the snow away from the top as I went, just as I had done in my dreams. I knew what I was going to find: the face of my sister staring back, lips blue and eyes cold.

I was sitting under the tree beside the frozen lake. My fingers were still numb, but I could no longer feel the pain. The only pain I felt was deep inside my chest. The hole in my heart was gaping, and my life was slowly leaking out. It was finally over. I stole a glance at the battlefield. This time more than just the ground was destroyed. In the middle of the havoc, Ben's home had been torn to pieces. The entire second floor was gone and half of the first. I gazed upon the crater the boys had left behind; it was at least a quarter mile in circumference. The fight had been fierce. I recalled how Ben always ran away from the fight when it got too intense, but there had been no running away from this one; this time they fought until the bitter end.

I leaned against the trunk of the tree, the only thing still rooted to the ground, and closed my eyes. I tried to let reality sink in. Chloe was dead and the battle between Alex and Ben was finished as well. The aftermath was all the proof I needed. I was assuming that, as usual, Alex had come out of the battle victorious. If Ben had won the fight, I'd be dead by now. With my archenemies out of the picture, Sue and Will were finally safe. I should feel relieved, but I didn't because I had nothing left. The eerie stillness was a tell-tale sign that Alex was gone for good. He had been sucked back up to heaven, and I was alone. Mission complete.

For the first time in my life, I had done the right thing. I should find comfort in that, but I didn't. There was a part of me that believed, hoped, that if Alex departed this earth, he might take me with him. I couldn't be angry with him for leaving, because he didn't have a choice. And if he had told me he wanted to leave, could I blame him? How could I have been so naïve to think he was becoming human? How could I have been so naïve to think he might stay? The signs were drawn across his chest. It couldn't have been more obvious. Like the wing of the eagle, Alex's time on earth was fading. How could I have misconstrued the marking? How could I have not seen it for what it was: a forewarning of his departure?

"Alex becoming human just like me," I scoffed. "That was wishful thinking."

Alex was dead. Period. He died nineteen years ago, and it was time for him to go home. I should be thankful that I got to meet him, to love him. It was a miracle that he had come into my life. But right now, as I reflected on Alex and the time we spent together, the memories seemed less of a blessing and more of a curse. His presence had filled my heart, and just as I had feared, his absence left me feeling emptier than I had ever felt before. I stared blankly into the distance at the empty landscape before me. What was my next move? I had no family; my mother and father weren't my mother and father. My *real* mother was dead, and my *real* father was a monster. Chloe and Ben were gone. Alex was gone. In all of my life, I had never felt so alone. I had nowhere to go and nobody to run to. I was alone. I was cold. I was numb. I was tired. I closed my eyes and had just begun to drift off, when out of the silence came the crunching of feet through the snow. I held my eyes shut and listened as the footsteps drew near.

CHAPTER THIRTY-THREE

"Your eyelashes are frozen. Did you know that?"

The closeness of his voice startled me, but to hear his gentle whisper was like music to my ears. I lifted my lids at once. It couldn't be. Impossible.

Emerald eyes. Ruby lips. Chiseled cheekbones. Transparent skin.

That was what I expected. So it was with a mixture of surprise and sympathy that I gazed upon my boyfriend.

"You're bleeding," I whispered. If I could have cried out, I would have, but instead the noise that came out of my mouth sounded fragile. "I've never seen you bleed before." Alex was a healer, I thought. That's what he did... he healed my wounds and he kept me safe. But now Alex was bleeding. Alex was hurting.

Alex simply nodded his head.

"I thought you were gone," I said, unable to conceal my wonder.

Alex shrugged his shoulders but didn't say a word. The expression on his face told me that he shared in my surprise.

"Chloe's dead."

"I know," he whispered.

"Is it over?"

"Yes."

"Is he gone?"

"Yes."

"Is he coming back?"

"No."

"How can you be sure?"

"Because this time, he didn't run away, he just… he just… disappeared." A wrinkle appeared between his brows and his mouth was slightly agape. "Ben's departure was a strange thing to see. Sublimation at its finest."

"You're saying he vaporized?"

"Yes. That's exactly what I'm saying."

"The storm that was blowing around… that was the two of you fighting… I know that. But when Chloe's hand slipped out of mine, the storm stopped. The timing couldn't have been more precise. Do you think her life fueled his? Do you think he took his final breath when she took hers?"

"Quite possibly."

"So, where did he go?"

"Where he belongs."

"It looks like things couldn't have worked out any better."

Alex's expression changed from stunned to stoic. "But what if it hadn't? You shouldn't have come here by yourself. You shouldn't have come here without telling me."

As I returned his gaze, he knelt down beside me and took my hand in his. I wrapped my free arm around his neck and held him tight. I buried my head in his chest and let out a whimper.

"Can't we just put this behind us?" I sniffled and gave a small cough, letting his coat muffle the sound. "Do you think you can ever trust me again?"

With my face still buried in Alex's coat, I waited for his response. Unfortunately, it did not come as quickly as I hoped it might. I felt like I was sitting in a courtroom waiting for the jury to bring in the verdict. I just knew Alex's answer was going to kill me.

"We made a promise to be honest with one another, Rae." Alex leaned backward, creating a small space between us so he could look me in the eye.

"But I couldn't tell you," I began to plead. I pressed my lips against his cheek and let them linger there. "I couldn't tell you this. You have to understand. This is very different."

"A twisting of the truth. A lie. The keeping of a secret. It's all the same."

"There's a big difference."

"No. There isn't. It's about trust. It's about being honest with one another."

"I wasn't trying to hurt you. I was trying to save you."

"From what? I'm supposed to be the one who's protecting you. But for some reason you seem to be bent on destroying yourself."

"You can protect me from Ben, but you can't protect me from myself. You can't protect me from my past. You can't change the person I am. This was my battle and for the past year and a half, you have been fighting it for me. It was time that I took a stand, that I did something right for a change. It was my turn to do something for you."

"I have no idea what you mean. What does that mean, Rae?"

"It means that you think you know everything about me, but you don't know the beginning."

"I'm all ears," Alex said with a trifle of anger still lingering in his voice.

As I told Alex everything from beginning to end, his expression began to soften. I told him about Chloe and the dreams I had been having, the dreams about drowning and how I thought I was going to be the one to die. I told him she was my sister, my flesh and blood sister who wanted me dead. I told him about Carl and Eva. In conclusion, I reiterated the fact that my entire life had been a lie. I hesitated a moment before I told him about the girls that were locked in my father's basement. Even though I loathed Carl, he was still my father, and the fact that we were directly related, made me feel shame for something I hadn't done, something that had been done before I was born. But I told him because I was tired of the lies, because if there was anyone I could trust, it would be Alex Loving. More than anything else, I needed him to trust me. Right now, he was all I had left in the world and the only thing I wanted.

"You feel ashamed and you shouldn't."

"What if I'm like Carl? What if I have some of his bad? To think that I might even have an ounce of his evil makes me sick. I'm not sure if I know who I am anymore. I'm not sure I ever did."

"You know yourself better than you think. You're an artist. We're both artists, Rae. Maybe you a bit more than me, but regardless, we both pour our hearts into doing what we love. You paint. I write. While I pour my heart out over a piece of paper, you're putting yours onto a canvas, and I have never seen a thing I didn't like." Alex hesitated before he spoke again. "You're strong. You're beautiful. You're smart. You're stubborn. You're talented. You're brave. You're impatient." Alex let a small laugh escape him. "And more than anything else, you're loved."

"I'm sorry. I'm so, so sorry."

"I guess that I can see why you did what you did… not that it makes it right… but I can see why you did it."

"Do you still love me?"

"I'll always love you. No matter where we are, I'll always love you."

And I knew that when he said always, he meant forever.

"I need to get you out of the cold. I need to get you home."

"I know. I can't feel my fingers… or my toes."

"I'd offer to take you inside the Bodin's home," Alex surveyed the aftermath. "but there isn't much left."

As I looked at the destruction, I felt him swoop me into his arms. Being carried in such a fashion made me feel helpless and normally, I would protest, but I was tired and cold and my muscles were too weak to fight his strength.

"I'm not trying to get out of the hot seat or anything but… how did you get here? How did you find me?" It felt like a question I had asked a dozen times before. Alex just had a way of popping into the picture. "Don't tell me you ran."

"George Finnegan's snowmobile."

350

"You're kidding, right? Mr. Finnegan?" I wasn't sure if I was more shocked or surprised. Surprised that he had already knocked yet another item off his list of New Year's resolutions, or shocked because my predicament could have been the perfect excuse for Mr. Finnegan to rid himself of me.

"You took it?"

"Borrowed it."

"He let you?"

"He doesn't hate you as much as you think."

"Please."

"He's lonely. That's all."

I recalled an evening not long ago when I was out for a run. I slowed to a jog as I passed Mr. Finnegan's house. From the street, I could see him sitting at his kitchen table eating dinner all alone. As Alex trudged through the snow I continued to think about Mr. Finnegan. Maybe Alex was right. Maybe Mr. Finnegan was lonely.

"And how did you find me?"

"You left Eva's journal lying open on your bed. I saw the address. I'm more clever than you give me credit for," Alex said as he lowered me to the ground.

When my feet touched solid ground, I felt Alex's arms slip away. I gathered my bearings. The storm had settled and I could see my surroundings. The forest was to my right and to my left, the remains of Benard's home; the damage done looked worse up close than it did from a distance. From where I was standing, I could see directly into the basement. The water heater had been torn loose and knocked into a corner, and a layer of ice had formed on the basement floor from the water that was spilling from the pipes.

Even though a majority of the house was gone, the front porch and the stairs leading up to it remained. And there, unscathed in the middle of the porch, was Mr. Finnegan's motorized sled.

"Typical," I laughed.

"What?"

"You just pull up to the front door like you own the place?"

"Of course. Why not? Where did *you* park?" Alex asked as he made his way toward the craft. "I didn't see the Wagoneer when I pulled in."

"Across the street in the old barn."

"Typical," he scoffed.

"What?"

"Secret Agent Sunshine. You always have been quite the sneak."

"You know how I hate it when you call me Sunshine. Sue and Will called me that, and I don't ever want to hear that name again."

"Do you know why they called you Sunshine, Sunshine?"

"No, and I don't care, either."

"You were their Sunshine after Laney died. You were the only Rae of light shining through their darkness."

His response felt like a slap in the face. I stood transfixed as Alex put the key in the ignition. He revved up the engine and back slowly down the snow-covered staircase. Tears were welling up in my eyes, but I blinked them away.

"Are you coming or not?" he shouted over the noise of the machine.

I hopped on behind him and held on tight. I never realized my name had so much meaning.

I was surprised that it fit. Once the seats were folded down, Alex was able to drive the small snowmobile up a bank of packed snow and ease it into the back of his SUV; however, the back end of the snowmobile was hanging out, so we had to take it slow.

"What does it mean that you're still here?" I asked Alex once we were both inside the Wagoneer and en route to the cottage.

"I hope it means I will stay. You still want me, right?"

"Are you crazy? Of course I want you here." I bit my lip and turned to Alex. Although the blizzard had let up a bit, the snow was still falling. Alex was squinting his eyes, leaning forward, and focusing on the road. He had come to my rescue, and now he was taking me home. I studied the frozen blood on his face. It was all the proof I needed that he was real. I ran my hand across his cheek. He *was* becoming human. He *was* becoming more and more like me.

"Do you think we can have a normal life?" I asked. "No wait. I said that wrong. What I meant to say was, do you think we might be able to do the things that normal couples do when they're in love?"

Alex turned to me and smiled. There was a hint of mischief in his eyes. "What did you have in mind?"

"Marriage... but not now, of course. I don't want to rush it. I'm just glad you're here. But maybe someday?"

"Someday. I promise."

I closed my eyes and listened to the wipers beat back and forth across the glass. The metronomic sound could have lulled me right to sleep, but the still small voice inside me wouldn't let me rest.

"Why don't I feel happy?" I opened my eyes, looked at Alex, and demanded an answer from him. "Chloe and Ben are gone, and you're here. I have exactly what I asked for, but something doesn't feel right."

"Do you think that it's Chloe? She *was* your sister after all."

"I don't know. I should feel satisfied. I should feel complete. My knight in shining armor has rescued me once again. But I feel sad. Empty. I feel like something's missing."

"Not the fairytale ending you imagined it to be, huh?"

"Not so much."

"I don't want to make you feel any worse, but what you did was stupid. Heroic and selfless perhaps, but stupid. And I know why you came here all alone."

"You do?"

"Yes. It's because of your desperate need to control everything. But you can't always manipulate the situation, Rae. Sometimes you just have to let go."

"I'll take that into consideration."

"And Chloe was a bit more than a pain, by the way." He turned to me and smiled.

"I know. But I found and lost my true sister in less than twenty-four hours. No matter how much of a pain she was, that's kind of hard to take."

"I can understand why you would feel that way… even if she did want you dead."

"I asked her that. I asked her if she wanted me dead."

"And what did she say?"

"She said that she hadn't decided. She told me she wrestled with the wrong. But don't we all wrestle with the wrong to some extent?"

"I suppose."

"Why do you think that is?"

"Because it can hurt to do the right thing. Chloe wanted you dead because your life was a reminder of the pain in hers. Your life was a reminder that her own mother left her behind. Sue and Will gave you more love in a day than Chloe experienced in a lifetime. They gave you all the things in life that money could not buy. I think she might have been able to open up to you if it hadn't hurt so badly."

"To open your heart to someone means exposing the scars of your past?"

"Precisely. It was easier for Chloe to hate you than accept you."

"I feel like I'm standing at a crossroads, and I don't know which way to go."

"That's not unusual. You've been through a lot."

"I can't keep from thinking about Carl's basement and what was going on down there. If I try my hardest, I might be able to push that image out of my mind. I might be able to ignore it. Or I could take the other path. I could fight it. I could fight Carl and whatever evil he was up to."

"What do you think you'll end up doing?"

"I don't know."

As Alex drove down the road I began to think about something my papa once said. He told me that Nana had decided to help young girls like her. He told me that she had wanted to make a difference in their lives, and that she wanted to change the world. I wondered what Papa meant when he said that Nana wanted to help girls like *her*. Like her? What happened to my nana? What happened to my nana that hurt her so? I remembered the story she told me about her father. He had been so awful that she had to run away. It wasn't the distance that healed her. It was the reaching out to others that healed her heart, and it was God.

I let my mind wander to the entry in Eva's journal. She had described with such detail the condition of the basement and the three young girls who were locked inside. My chest began to tighten at the thought. A video camera. A mattress. Duct tape. Stench. I wiped a tear from my eye and tried to catch my breath. The girls had been held there against their will. They did not receive their freedom until Eva let them go. Freedom. Emancipation. Slavery. Control. I thought about the book A-Omega sent me. *Uncle Tom's Cabin*. In my opinion, it wasn't just a book about slavery, it was a book about control. Why did a person need to control another person to feel important? I began to think about the Lovings. According to Pastor Joe, they were deep in the fight against human trafficking. They didn't turn their back on the evil, they confronted it, they moved toward it full steam ahead. Is that what this was all about? Trafficking? Had our families been fighting for the same cause? Still looking out the passenger window, I could see a sign in the distance. I watched until I could read the words:

Alexandria 14 miles

The snow was still falling in perfect, fat flakes, and despite the fact that the back end of the Wagoneer was wide open to accommodate the snowmobile, the heater was on high and I was warm. I looked at Alex. The blood frozen to the side of his cheek had thawed and was beginning to drip down his face. I used my finger to wipe it away, and he flinched at my touch.

"Alex?" I asked.

"Yes," he returned without taking his eyes off the road.

"What is it inside of a man that makes him want to own another? Is it power?"

"Maybe. But I think it has more to do with pride."

CHAPTER THIRTY-FOUR

*I*t was two in the morning, and I had been wide-awake for hours. I was lying on the sofa, spooning with Alex who had been sound asleep since ten. Alex never complained, but I knew he was exhausted from the fight with Ben and his deep, guttural breathing revealed the extent of his fatigue. But it wasn't his snoring that was keeping me up; rather, it was my own personal misery. In less than twenty-four hours, I had learned that my real father was a monster, that my entire life had been a lie, and to top it off, twelve hours ago, I lost my true, flesh and blood, sister. The extent to which she had hated me no longer mattered; I was truly sad that she was dead. And then there was Sue and Will. Even though I was angry with them for lying, I missed them now more than ever. But greater still was the miserable feeling that developed inside me each time I thought about the events that took place in Carl Pierce's, my father's basement. I had been trying to push from my mind the words in Eva's journal, but I couldn't seem to do it.

A year ago I made a single wish. I wished for Alex and I to be together forever. My wish had been granted. I prayed that God would keep him here, and God had heard my prayer. Against all odds, Chloe and Ben were gone, and Alex was still here on earth with me. I should be fulfilled. I should feel complete. But I was empty. Being careful not to wake him, I turned onto my right side so that Alex and I were face to face. The fire in the hearth was dying, but the glowing embers provided just enough light to make out his masculine features. The cut on his cheek was scabby and inflamed and showed no immediate signs of healing. The freckle on his lip was fading, as was the scar at the corner of his eye. In his chocolate colored locks were hints of red that I had never noticed. I continued to study him as he slept; the movement of his eyes behind his lids told me he was dreaming. Little by little, Alex was changing. He was becoming human, just as he promised me he would. It wasn't until I felt the warmness of his breathe on my cheek that I finally understood the source of my pain, and I shuddered as though his warmth had chilled me to the bone.

"You're supposed to fill me up. You're supposed to make me whole. You're supposed to stop my heart from leaking," I whispered. I traced the outline of Alex's lower lip with my finger and the deep, low sound he was making turned into a drawn out groan.

"How do you feel?" I asked him.

"Sore," Alex muttered. "How do you feel?" he asked, still half asleep.

"DARK."

It took a moment for Alex to respond, but when he did, his voice came out rough, a whisper that wrapped itself around my pain.

"It's always darkest before the dawn."

Pastor Joe's black sedan was parked in the usual spot behind the church, but the door to his office was locked and the light was off. I spent a good fifteen minutes wandering the third floor of Cherith Interdenominational, opening various office doors, searching for my friend, my mentor. When I reached the end of the corridor and found the last office empty, I came to the realization that I had exhausted all of my options. I was desperate to find Pastor Joe. I wasn't sure it could wait another day. Joe and I needed to have a heart to heart, and we needed to have it now. Instead of getting better, my lying had only gotten worse. I had opened Eva's journal. I had done the exact thing I had promised myself I wouldn't. I was taking responsibility for what I had done, and I was well aware that I needed to be accountable for my actions. But in a way, I felt as though I had been misled. Pastor Joe told me to find the truth. He told me the truth would set me free, but I felt more entangled now than ever. When I reached the stairs, I turned back and stared down the corridor into the darkness. I didn't want to wait until tomorrow for an answer. I sat down on a step between the second and the third floor. I let my head fall into my hands and exhaled in defeat.

"Why do I feel so sad?" I whispered. "Why isn't Alex enough?"

A chill stole over my body when I heard a noise that so closely followed my questions that it seemed like a response. It came from the main floor, echoing up the stairwell, beckoning me to get up and find my answer. I felt a twinge of wonder as I emerged from the shadow where I was sitting and descended from the third floor into the lobby. I saw a flicker of light out of the corner of my eye. The chapel doors stood open and several candles were glowing near the altar. Pastor Joe was seated in the first pew; his balding head bowed in prayer. I hesitated for a moment at the base of the stairs, wondering if it was appropriate to interrupt someone, especially a man of God, while in the middle of prayer. I stood in the doorway and cleared my throat.

"I have found the truth," I said, interrupting the silence.

Joe turned toward me. He looked both startled and pleased.

"So good to see you, Rae. But I must say, you have a knack for catching me off guard."

"I'm sorry to interrupt, but this couldn't wait."

"Now is as good a time as ever. Do come in and have a seat."

I made my way to the front of the chapel and joined Joe in the pew where he was sitting.

"I think I've finally found the truth," I said without hesitation. "You told me it would set me free, but I feel trapped. I feel lost. I feel scared. I feel confused. I feel sad. I feel empty. I feel everything but free."

"Then it is not the Truth that you have found."

"I know everything there is to know about my past. How can you tell me I haven't found the truth?" I responded flatly, overcompensating to hide the anger.

"You have found answers, but you have not found the Truth."

"You're right about that. I have plenty of answers."

"Would you like to talk about it?"

"NO!" I shouted. My voice echoed and filled the chapel with a noise that instantly made me feel ashamed. Pastor Joe raised his eyebrows in surprise but did not respond. I took in a deep breath, attempting to cool my jets before I spoke again.

"Sorry. What I meant to say is that I can't. This isn't something I feel comfortable sharing with you."

"You can tell me anything."

"Joe, do you think we all wrestle with the wrong?"

"Everyone does to some extent."

"I feel like I've been wrestling for so long that I can hardly tell the difference between good and bad... between right and wrong... between what is the truth and what is a lie. I have spent my whole life on the same path and now I'm at a crossroads. I have to make a choice, but I'm not sure I trust my own judgment. I'm not sure which way to go."

"And you don't want to talk about it?"

"No, I don't."

"Then how can I help you?"

"Just give me an answer. Tell me how to find the truth."

Pastor Joe stared at the crucifix and sighed.

"My grandfather once told me a story about the Truth. It was a story about a boy he grew up with named Roald. Roald was a few years older than my grandfather, but they were both born in the same small Norwegian town, a village so far north that they rarely saw the sun. It was a beautiful and mountainous land that most would never want to leave. But when Roald was fifteen, he developed a terrible disease of the flesh that left embarrassing scaly sores that, when healed, would leave tremendous scars. Doctors told his parents the only cure was sunlight and unfortunately, sunlight was something the small Norwegian village did not have much of, at least not in the quantity Roald needed. Moving was not an option because Roald's parents were poor. And although they loved him dearly, they couldn't imagine making such a treacherous journey in search of the sun. Without the cure, his future looked bleak. He promised himself that if he could make it to his eighteenth birthday, he would set out to find the cure that his parents could not provide.

"For Roald, his adolesence was filled with both emotional and physical pain. The only thing that pushed him through the pain was hope. When Roald's eighteenth birthday finally approached, he was covered in scars; his condition had only gotten worse. Everyone told him it was too late. He would have to accept a life of pain. The journey to find a cure was treacherous and the promise of a cure was not certain, but Roald remembered the promise he made to himself. So with his meager possessions in hand, he set off down the mountain, searching for the light, the kind of light he had heard about but had never seen.

"After months of traveling, Roald was growing weak and his supplies were running low. Instead of getting better as he had hoped, his problems were only getting worse. He wondered if he would ever make it to the bottom of the mountain. He wondered if he might ever see the sun. Just as he was beginning to think he should turn around, he came to a fork in the road and was forced to stop. This was not something he had anticipated. The journey was hard enough without having to make a choice. He sat down on a rock and stared at the road that veered to the left. It was wide and straight and looked well-traveled. It seemed the popular choice, so Roald read the sign that marked the path.

If relief is what you've come for
Then you have not come in vain
This path may not have the cure you seek
But it can ease the pain

"Roald continued to stare at the sign. It was inviting and, although he did want the suffering to be gone for good, something to ease the pain would be nice until he found a cure. Still sitting on the rock, Roald turned his eyes to the path on the right. The first thing he noticed was that it was narrow and winding. Plus, the lack of any traffic suggested that the narrow path might not be the most popular route. With reluctance, he began to read its sign.

Because this road is long and hard
Its travelers are very few
But while other roads might promise much
That they end in death is true

Although this winding path is steep
You will be given the strength you need to stay
It may also be very dark at times
But there will be a lamp to light your way

"Everything ends in death, he told himself and stepped onto the path that was wide and well-traveled. Not long after taking the path, he came across a small village where a woman was selling salve. 'Come near,' she said to him. 'I will heal you with this ointment.' Roald was desperate and, although he clearly remembered the doctors telling him that the sun was the only possible cure, he accepted the salve to coat his sores. Within seconds the pain was gone, and Roald felt better than he had ever felt before. He felt so good, he could hardly remember what it felt like to be in pain. Because he had no money to give her, he traded all the food in his knapsack for some of her salve and then continued on down the mountain in search of the next town.

"Not long after he left the town, Roald became very hungry. He sat down under a tree and began to search his bag for something to eat, but there was nothing. Inside his bag, he found a small jar of salve and that was all. After days without food, Roald came to another fork in the road. Once again he was forced to make a choice. Just like at the last crossroads, there was a sign at the start of each path. And like before, the path to the left was wide and well-traveled while the path to the right was very narrow. Starting with the sign to the left, Roald began to read.

362

Come this way if you are hungry
This road has everything you desire
Food for when you're hungry and a bed for when you're tired
More than you could ever dream
Treasure too great for you to hold
Don't listen to what others warn
What glitters is truly gold

"Roald could hear the pangs of hunger growing louder and calling him closer to the path that promised food and much, much more. As if out of obligation, he read the small sign to the left without heeding what it said.

Because this road is long and hard
Its travelers are very few
But while other roads might promise much
That they end in death is true

Although this winding path is steep
You will be given the strength you need to stay
It may also be very dark at times
But there will be a lamp to light your way

"Roald scoffed at this. His life had always been hard. That's what he was trying to escape. He was trying to escape from pain. So why would he take a road that promised to offer more? But what does it mean that all other roads lead to death? He paused for a moment longer, contemplating death and what it meant to die and what it meant to suffer. He decided he would rather die than suffer.

"So once again, he chose the wide path that was well-traveled. Roald continued on to the next town, and the smell of fresh baking bread was confirmation enough that he had made the right choice. His stomach grumbled when he walked into the café where he ordered a bowl of soup and some bread. Not having the money to pay for the meal, he offered the woman his coat. But the cost of the meal was steep, and Roald had to offer the woman his ointment as well. With a full stomach, he walked out of the café and continued his journey down the mountain.

"As the sun set and darkness took over, the air began to chill. Roald began to wish he still had his coat. The meal he had given everything for was no longer satisfying, and his stomach began to growl. He reached into his bag and found it empty. Roald had made it halfway down the mountain. The villagers hadn't expected him to make it this far, but he was hardly proud. He had less now than when he started and was no closer to finding a cure. He was discouraged, but more than anything, Roald was lonely. He missed his family. He missed his friends. Although his bag was empty, it was the emptiness inside himself that pained him most.

"That night, he fell asleep on the cold hard ground, and when dawn broke, he woke to a gentle whisper. He sat up quickly and began to search for the person behind the voice, but there was no person, only another fork in the road and two more signs. Tired and weak from the journey, Roald studied the signs with care. As usual, he read the sign to the left, first.

Don't pass by this path, I warn!
If you do you'll be alone
Because not a single soul has passed this trail
And despised what they've been shown

"There was something about this sign that angered Roald. He was finally able to see the sign for what it really was: a lie and a promise that only left him wanting more, a promise that left him empty and cost him everything in the end. Roald was tired, cold, and weak. After a day without his medication, his skin was beginning to fester. He looked at the sign to the right and began to read.

Because this road is long and hard
Its travelers are very few

But while other roads might promise much
That they end in death is true

Although this winding path is steep
You will be given the strength you need to stay
It may also be very dark at times
But there will be a lamp to light your way

Know this:
Before you step across the line you will feel your body fight
Still, take this path
Please, follow me
Step into a world of light

"It was only after seeing the sign for the third time that he realized something he had been blinded to before. The sign to his right had not changed. What it offered in the beginning was the same the thing it offered in the end. It did not promise to fulfill his immediate desires, but it promised to guide him on the path."

"Which path did he take?"
"The narrow path. The path to the right."
"And what happened?"
"It led him down the mountain. There were dark times just as the sign promised, but he was never alone. He was never left wanting."
"So this is just some parable, and Roald isn't really real?" I asked.
"He was as real as a girl name Rae."
I gulped. "I just don't see how any of this has to do with me." As I rose from the pew, I began to think my trip to see Joe had been a giant mistake. The empty spot inside of me was beginning to fill with anger. I wondered what Joe was trying to tell me. Was he trying to tell me that I was like Roald? My skin was fine. I didn't have boils. Without saying a word, I turned to leave the chapel, but something stopped me in my tracks.

"Joe," I said with my back to him. "What do you think about pride? Do you think it is generally good or generally bad?"

"It has been said that pride is the sin from which all others arise. It is the most serious of the seven deadly sins, my dear. Why do you ask?"

"No reason." I wanted to leave but my feet were rooted to the ground.

"Are you familiar with the story of Lucifer's descent to earth?" he continued.

As though on cue, I turned to face the pastor. He had a serious look upon his face, a more serious look than I had ever seen before.

"It was Lucifer's pride that caused him to fall from heaven. It was his pride that earned him the name Satan."

pride (prīd) *n.*: a feeling of pleasure from one's own achievements

This was the definition of pride I could most relate to. I could just hear Sue and Will saying, "I'm so proud of you, Rae." I had often heard people interchange the words proud and pleased. "I am proud to announce…" could so easily be substituted with "I am pleased to announce." To be pleased with something hardly seemed a sin. But like many words, pride, too, has many meanings.

A high opinion of one's own importance
Arrogance
Haughtiness
Vanity
Conceit: the desire to be more important or attractive than others. Failing to acknowledge the good work of others
A showy or impressive group
A company of lions
A disagreement with the truth

So, what is it inside a man that makes him want to own another? The more I thought about it, the more I believed that Alex and I were both right. While power had more to do with the action itself, pride has to do with picking the prey.

CHAPTER THIRTY-FIVE

*I*t was almost two o'clock on a Thursday afternoon when Alex and I pulled up to the cottage and found a black economy sized rental parked in the driveway. We had just returned from lunch at Bugaboo Bay, and it was the first time I had been out of the cottage since paying Pastor Joe a visit. Taking me out for lunch was Alex's last attempt at cheering me up. He had made various other attempts, such as reading me poetry from his journal and braving the Laundromat all by himself to clean my dirty clothes. But nothing had worked, and Alex was growing more and more concerned that I was sinking into a permanent state of depression. The hostess at Bugaboo Bay tried to seat us by the window so we could stare out onto the frozen lake, and she looked taken aback when I started crying and told her I wanted to sit in the back instead. Alex was right. I was depressed. I should be happy. Everything had fallen into place. Chloe and Ben were gone. Alex was here. And finally, after months of waiting, the legal matters had been settled, the back taxes had been paid, and Alex could keep his parents' properties. Not only that, there was quite a bit of cash left over. He wouldn't tell me the exact amount; he only told me that we would never again have to worry about money. That should make me happy. We could stay at the cottage. We had a home. But I wasn't happy. Not until I saw the black Toyota parked in our driveway did a little fire spark inside of me. I lit up at once.

"Expecting someone?" Alex asked as he grabbed our lunch leftovers. He slid out of the Wagoneer and walked over to the rental, pressing his face against the glass.

"No. I'm not. Come on." I pulled the sleeve of his puffy black coat and dragged him to the door. "If you think I'm going in there all by myself, you're crazy."

"No one's in the car. Do you think they went inside? What kind of person just walks inside of your house when you're not home?"

"That's what you get for leaving the doors unlocked," I scolded him.

Alex opened the door, and I walked into the kitchen. Cocoa raced into the room to greet us. Her tail was beating back and forth. She whimpered, then licked my hand. I gave Alex a suspicious look, took him by the hand, and pulled him into the living room. After everything that had happened in the past couple of weeks, I didn't think there was any room left for surprises, but nothing could have prepared me for what I saw when I rounded the corner.

"Mom!" I said out of habit. If she hadn't caught me so off guard, I would have called her Sue.

Mom was sitting in one of the floral chairs. When Alex and I walked into the room, she got up from where she was sitting and made her way toward me, wrapping me in her arms. I expected her embrace to feel different now that I knew the truth, but it didn't. And knowing the truth hadn't changed the way I felt about her either.

"You have no idea how worried we've been about you." Her hands moved to my shoulders and she leaned back to look into my eyes. Her face was stained with tears. For a split second, we were in a world of our own, and then she noticed Alex standing behind me in the doorway. A look of fear flashed across Mom's face. Her left hand fell limply to her side. Her right hand was still on my shoulder, and I felt it begin to shake. I knew exactly how she was feeling. It's not everyday that you come face to face with a supernatural being. With caution, my mom moved away from me and toward Alex. She studied him for a moment before she let her fingertips brush across his cheek, gently at first, but then with a bit more force. It was as if the harder she poked and prodded the more real he would become. I followed her fingers to the scar at the corner of his right eye, the scar that was beginning to fade. She cocked her head to the side and a puzzled expression appeared on her face.

"I can't wrap my mind around this, Rae." Her voice shook. "I'm not surprised you couldn't tell me more about him," she said, staring at Alex. She was talking about him like he was a statue. A nervous laugh escaped her. "But if you had, I wouldn't have believed you," she confessed, still cradling Alex's face in both of her hands.

All at once, an image flashed before me, an image of a woman holding Alex in the crook of her arm. It was the image of a lady who was confused and lost; the angel Alex remembered was my mom.

"Your eyes are the same," she told him with awe in her voice.

"That's not the first time I've heard that," he laughed and glanced over at me.

When finally he spoke, Mom looked taken aback. She cleared her throat and shook her head.

"Thank you for keeping her safe," she said, her uneasiness fading.

"I've done my best. Although I have to say, she's not the easiest person to protect."

Sue began to fish around in the pocket of her sweater and pulled out a tissue to wipe her nose. She sniffled and let out a sound that was a cross between a gasp and a laugh.

"I'm afraid I do know what you mean." She used the back of her hand to wipe a tear from her eye.

"She's quite the little sneak."

"She always has been." Mom blew her nose and gazed upon Alex with adoring eyes.

"Stubborn, too, that girl," Alex continued.

Even though tears were flowing down her face at a steady rate, my mother began to laugh. "Even as a child."

"Hello! I can hear you," I said, waving my hand in the air.

She looked at me and smiled.

"How did you know where to find us?" I asked, taking a seat on the sofa. Alex plopped down beside me while my mom walked over to the floral chair and grabbed her purse. Her hand disappeared inside of the bag, and when it came back into view, she was holding a small manila envelope. She held it in front of me without saying a word. I recognized the envelope and the handwriting as my own. Except for the return address, the penmanship at the top left hand corner looked more like Alex's than mine. I glanced in his direction and rolled my eyes.

"Sorry," Alex said without hesitation. "It had been lying on your dresser for months. I assumed you wanted it mailed."

"This place hasn't changed a bit," my mother said, changing the subject.

"You *have* been here, then?" Alex and I said in unison.

"Your father, Laney, and I stayed in this very cabin. We were here with Eva... your mother... for only a day before Carl tracked us down. We received word that he had sent someone after us... after Eva. We left immediately. That was the last time I saw this place, and I never thought I would see it again. I attached so many negative feelings to this cabin, but it's beautiful and quaint and perfect. Nothing like I remember it to be."

Sue was still standing in front of the fireplace clutching the envelope tight in her hand.

"Why don't you sit down, Mom?"

"No. I feel like I've been sitting for hours."

"Can I at least get you something to drink?"

"I already helped myself to the pot of coffee in the kitchen. I hope you don't mind. I want you to know that I haven't come here to intrude or to bring you back. I've come here to explain, and I'm sure you have a few questions."

"I pretty much know all the facts. I read Eva's journal."

"I didn't know she had one."

"She did. I found it in the Pierce's basement."

My mom's mouth fell open in surprise, but she didn't say a word.

"I know what Eva did. What I want to know is why."

"I'll try my hardest to answer. Eva was estranged from our family for years. There are things about her that I will never know."

"Eva didn't seem like an evil person. So, why did Eva marry a man like Carl?"

"The best answer I can give you is that she was young and she was confused. Eva and Papa never saw eye to eye. She was always a bit of a rebel. And stubborn. She was so stubborn."

"I can't imagine anyone not liking Papa."

"Nana and Papa didn't have a lot of money, but they always had enough. Don't get me wrong, we never went without, but extravagance never concerned them. Eva wasn't really fond of rules either, and she hated what our parents did for work. I have heard it said that a girl usually picks a husband that is like her father, but Eva chose a man that was nothing like her dad. He was rich. He was powerful. She didn't wait long before marrying him. Whether it was love or infatuation, I will never know. Regardless, she couldn't have known him well. I tell myself she couldn't have. I think that Eva made a bad decision and that decision was Carl Pierce. Unfortunately, it was a decision she couldn't easily recant. Plus, she was comfortable. She liked the money; there was no doubt about that. There was a time when I thought Eva was happy. I thought maybe she had finally found her niche. But I also felt something was very wrong. I guess you could say I had a sister's intuition. When Eva announced her engagement, Nana and Papa did not condone the marriage. Needless to say, we weren't invited to the wedding. I was hurt, but still I loved her with all my heart. I would have done anything for her. Anything. After that, we lost touch."

"Completely?"

"Yes and no. Because of the man she married, I was able to keep tabs on her. Not long after the wedding, Eva became pregnant with Chloe. Eva didn't even call to tell us that she was expecting. But because Carl *was* and *is* such a prominent figure, word of this high profile pregnancy made headlines. Shortly after Eva and Carl's pregnancy was announced, Will and I found out we were expecting a baby of our own. When Eva and I were little girls, we would talk about our wedding dresses. She promised me she would never leave my side. She promised that when we had children, we would raise them together. In return, I promised her I would treat her children as my own. Because we were so close in age and even closer in heart until we reached our teenage years, I had never considered that we wouldn't go through these life experiences together. But at that particular season of our lives, we couldn't have been further apart.

I watched her couture-covered belly grow on the pages of magazines instead of in person. I read about Eva's life in newspaper articles. Of course, on occasion, tabloids told dark tales that many refused to believe. I mean, how could it be possible for a man like Carl, a man with such high standing, a man who was on the board of numerous charities, to abuse his wife in private? Eva didn't help the situation. She fit the part to a T. She was so beautiful. Her clothes and shoes were perfect. She had the perfect house, and she wanted desperately for everyone to think she had the perfect husband, too. She had a beauty that I sometimes envied. She was beautiful on the inside as well; it was a beauty that rarely ever shone, but when it did, it was blinding. I think about how her life could have been. I try not to, but I can't help but wonder what she could have done with her life had she used the gifts that God had given her."

Mom cleared her throat a bit. I could see she was holding back tears. She sniffled and began to fish around in her pocket for another tissue. Alex got up and fetched the box of Kleenex from the fireplace mantel and handed it to her.

"I've gone off on a tangent, haven't I?" she said, sinking into the floral chair. "And I'm sorry for the tears. I haven't let myself think about Eva in a very long time."

"You don't have to talk about her if you don't want to," I said, trying to relieve her discomfort.

"I want to. I need to. You need to know about your mother." Sue ran her fingers through her short brown hair and took a deep breath before continuing. "Eva gave birth to Chloe, and Chloe was just as beautiful as her mom. But with motherhood came a few changes. Eva no longer graced the covers of magazines. In fact, it seemed she had dropped off the face of the earth. I never realized how much I enjoyed seeing and hearing about Eva, even if it was in a trashy tabloid, until the news was gone. The media had become the only link to my sister and after a while, I felt like I didn't have a sister at all."

"So how did you find her? How did she get to the cottage?"

"We received a letter from A-Omega. After that, everything got crazy. The letter changed everything. They wanted us to take a bit of a break so we could prepare for our next assignment. We were living in Kansas City, close to Nana and Papa, and that's where we stayed. Our sabbatical was supposed to last through January. That's all we were told. We were not given any details, and we didn't question the mission because that was how it usually worked; plans were always slow to unfold and information was always given in small measures along the way. But at the end of June, something unusual happened. Another letter from A-Omega arrived; the plans had changed. Our sabbatical had come to an end, and we had only months to sell our house and most of our belongings. Along with the letter came three airline tickets. We were to fly into the Minneapolis St. Paul airport and meet our liaisons, Paul and Sarah Loving.

We were also told to be on the lookout for a package. Our mission was to take care of the package. Fix it... I wasn't sure. The nature of the assignment seemed rather odd, and it was unlike any assignment we had ever been given. I was nervous, but still I trusted. We were supposed to arrive in Minneapolis on the twelfth of September. Will and I were to divulge the details of our assignment to no one, not even Nana and Papa. Nothing registered. Not even when I stepped off the plane in St. Paul and saw a very pregnant Eva standing in front of me with black rings under her eyes did I connect the dots. I could only think of two things: that I was so happy to see her, and what had happened to my perfect and beautiful sister? The worst of it was that Eva wouldn't speak. It was a classic case of Post Traumatic Stress Syndrome. But I had no idea what had happened to her."

"And the package?"

"It came. But I didn't recognize it at first. After getting off the plane, Will rented a car at the airport and Laney, Eva, and I followed the Lovings here, to this cottage. I kept waiting for some banged up package to be delivered to the house but nothing arrived. The next morning while I was fixing breakfast, I heard Eva's voice coming from the living room. It was the first time I had heard her voice in years. She was discussing with Will the events of the past couple of months. I hadn't realized what a mess she really was. Not until then did I realize that Eva was the package. Yes, she looked horrible, but the real damage had been done to her spirit. She was broken on the inside. She was an emotional mess. But as A-Omega told us in the letter, she was not beyond repair."

"And the contents of the package?"

"Inside the package was the baby, of course. Rae, the beautiful gift was you."

Deep inside, I knew this all along. Tears fell from my eyes without control. When Alex wrapped his arm around my shoulder and pulled me close, I barely noticed. Everything was jumbled up. Before Mom arrived, I was angry with her for lying to me. I was angry with her for letting me believe my cousin Laney was my sister. I was angry with her and my father for dragging me all over the world. But I was no longer angry. When I looked at my mom, I only felt respect. As she mourned the loss of her daughter and sister, she could have easily resented the fact that I was alive; instead, she took me in and loved me as her own. Sue and Will went above and beyond the call of duty. What was a mother anyway? A mother didn't need to be biological to be a mom. A mother, a *mom*, is a woman who cares for a child. I was her child and she was my mom, the only mom I ever knew. But still I had one question.

"Why didn't Eva take Chloe along?"

"I don't know what to tell you. If Eva had brought Chloe, it would have been so much easier for your father and me. Not a day goes by that I don't think about your sister."

"My sister is dead."

"Laney?"

"No, Chloe."

My mother let out a painful moan and rose from the chair at once. She walked over to the fireplace and stood with her back toward us.

"A mother should always try to save her child," I said. "If Eva had brought Chloe along, she wouldn't be lying at the bottom of the lake."

My mother's shoulders began to shake.

"If Eva hadn't abandoned Chloe, Chloe wouldn't have resented me. I would have had a sister."

My mother regained her composure. "You can't live your life saying 'what if.' You have to deal with what you're given. Eva wasn't herself when she arrived. She was in shock. She barely spoke, and when she did, it was only to Will. When I think about Eva's life, I try to remember the good. Eva made a few bad choices, but she died a hero. Think of the girls she saved by taking a stand. She knew letting the girls out of the basement was risky. She had discovered Carl's secret and because of that knowledge, she lost her life."

"So Eva ran away from Carl. But how did Carl find her?"

"He received a phone call from a friend."

"Marion Bodin?"

"Yes, the Bodin's. You know the Bodins?" My mother looked surprised.

"Let's just say I was acquainted with their son."

She raised her eyebrows in suspicion but didn't ask any further questions.

"Eva confided in Will that before she left Oklahoma, she called the Bodin's to inform them that she would be paying them a visit."

"And they didn't think that was odd?"

"No. From what I understand, the Bodin's were close family friends. Her visit did not seem out of the ordinary, and the Bodin's did not grow suspicious until Eva failed to show up at their house."

"She trusted them."

"She did."

"But you intercepted her?"

"Correct. The Lovings were there to greet her when she landed."

"She didn't want to go with you?"

"Not at first. But that is where the Lovings fit into the picture."

"They forced her?"

"They persuaded her."

"How?"

"Paul was finally able to convince Eva that the Bodins were not the friends she thought they were."

"What did he say? How did he know?"

"Paul and Sarah Loving worked for a government organization…"

"I know," I interrupted. "They were involved in the fight against human trafficking."

"You know quite a bit more than I thought."

"I know a little."

"This organization knew about Carl Pierce's involvement, and they were well aware of his connection to Marion Bodin."

"What connection?"

"Carl and Marion were more than friends, they were business partners. They ran their business under the name Pierce and Associates: International Relocation and Job Placement Services. On the surface, the company was legitimate. They had an office in Tulsa and another in Houston. Carl and Marion built the company from the ground up. They were headhunters."

"How did it work?" Alex asked.

"They were international headhunters. They received resumes from all over the world. Not every applicant was employable, but they held on to their resumes. After a while, they came to realize that these unemployable applicants could make them money, too. Carl and Marion put their heads together. And what did they come up with? Sex sells. They took their business underground. They carefully picked their victims based on social class, nationality, age, and gender. They never even had to leave their office. They promised each applicant money, job security, housing, etc. I'm sure it seemed like a pretty good offer to someone who was down and out. Plus, Pierce and Associates had built a name for themselves. They were trusted in the community and across the nation."

"But Marion lived in Minnesota, and Carl lived almost a thousand miles away. What they were doing was illegal. How did they make it work?"

"Traffickers typically work in rings. They transfer girls - children - from state to state. They keep them on the move. The longer they are in one spot, the greater their chances of getting caught."

"They were the kingpins?"

"Yes. I would say that Marion Bodin was a bit more involved than Carl."

"So Eva thought she was running into the arms of safety, but she was really running from bad to worse."

"Precisely. And it didn't take long for them to find us. Shortly after arriving at the cottage, we received word that the Bodin's were on their way. They had discovered our location. Eva was still weak and barely fit for another journey, but there was nothing we could do. We had to leave. It was raining that night. It was so dark. Will and I got Laney and Eva situated. Sarah, Paul, and Alex were in the car behind us. And then…" my mother's voice trailed.

"The wreck," I said, finishing her sentence for her.

"I lost a lot that day. I carried around a huge amount of guilt. But I finally realized I have a lot to be thankful for, too. Every morning, I pray a prayer of thanks that you were a part of Eva at the time. I am thankful that circumstances were set up in our favor so we could raise you as our daughter."

"What circumstances?"

"As I said before, after Chloe's birth, Eva dropped off the face of the earth. It was unforeseen how this might work to our advantage. With the exception of Carl, no one knew that Eva was pregnant with her second child. Not even her closest friends. After the wreck, after Eva's death, Carl assumed the child she was carrying died as well. There was a funeral and everything. It *was* a miracle that you survived."

"I have a gravestone?"

"Gosh. That sounds awful, but yes. It's next to your mother's."

Sue began to meander around the living room, eyeing objects and touching them as she passed.

"I see that you've added a few books to the shelf."

"Thrift store specials." My response was automatic. I was still thinking about my gravestone.

"You always did love to read." My mom's hand fell on the spine of a book, and she let it rest there for a moment. "Rae, I'm sorry we had to move around so much. I'm sorry you were never allowed to have things of your own. I'm sorry we could never give you a normal life."

"Normal isn't all it's cracked up to be."

Mom turned toward me and smiled.

"Why did we move around so much? Was it your work or was it because of me?"

"It was both. Purpose in life is a strange thing and something that can be very hard to understand. As far as Will and I were concerned, our main purpose in life was to protect you. I think you can understand the legal implications of running away with a child that isn't yours. Giving you back to Carl wasn't an option. After the accident, we moved in with Nana and Papa. We were safe for a while, and we were able to give you a relatively normal life. But when you were seven years old, Carl discovered that you had survived the crash, and he came very close to getting you back. We knew we would have to go someplace far away to keep you safe."

For a moment, Mom didn't say a word. What she wanted to say seemed to be on the tip of her tongue, but she couldn't seem to force it out. Her silence gave me a moment to catch up. She said that when I was seven, Carl almost got me back. I recalled the nightmare I had when I was seven years old on our first night in London. I recalled the stitches on her face and the swelling. I *had* been the cause.

"It's complicated," she continued, interrupting my thought. "Just because you have one mission in life doesn't mean you can't also have another. After your father and I graduated from college, we moved to Asia and devoted our lives to rescuing victims of human trafficking. Our goal was to free as many women as possible and then restore them, build them up, and provide a way for them to make an income. But freedom does not come easily, and when a woman is freed from trafficking she is in crisis... both physical and emotional. You can only imagine what they had been subjected to. Your father and I were devoted to rebuilding these girls from the inside out. We found that the physical wounds were easier to heal than their hearts. When we decided to start a family, Will and I moved back to the states. Trafficking seemed a million miles away... and then it fell into our laps. When Laney died, I was completely useless. I've told you all of this before. There were days when I couldn't pull myself out of bed. But when you were seven, we almost lost you to Carl. It opened my eyes to so many things. We moved abroad to keep you safe, picking up in Europe where we left off in Asia."

"And you decided this on your own, or did Nana and Papa have anything to do with your decision?"

"Not Nana and Papa. A-Omega. We consulted A-Omega after the *incident*. It was our first attempt at contacting A-Omega since the wreck. A-Omega gave us a new set of orders. We were instructed to move to London."

"And?"

"And that's it. That is how A-Omega works. They never brief us all at once, they never have. They give us information as they see fit. They give us information when the time is right."

"That's annoying."

"Depends on how you look at it. At that point in my life, I couldn't handle much. I found it a relief not to be entangled in the details. It's nice to know that A-Omega has everything under control."

"Did you trust A-Omega when you brought your family to Minnesota?"

"Yes."

"And did you trust them even after you lost Laney?"

"I cut all ties with A-Omega for seven years."

"But then you went back?"

"We went back. Life doesn't always happen how you want it to; regardless, I believe there is a plan. When you were seven, I realized that our life was like a puzzle and you were the final piece. That's all I needed. Your presence brought me back to my purpose."

"Why didn't you tell me?"

"As far as Will and I were concerned, you were never anyone else's daughter. You were ours. We couldn't bear it if you wanted to find your real father. We knew what he was, and we weren't ready to explain that to you. There are things that go on in this world that are so dark, Rae. Maybe we were wrong to shelter you for so long, but we thought you were too young to hear the truth. When you turned sixteen, we began to worry what would happen when you went off to college. We had protected you for so long, but what would happen when you left our home? We expressed our concerns to A-Omega, and they told us to come back to the States. We relocated to Oklahoma, which seemed crazy. We couldn't understand why A-Omega would move us so close to the man we had been trying to avoid. We feared for your safety more than ever. But we trusted that it would all work out. And by the looks of it, it did." Mom smiled, looking first to me and then to Alex.

"When you saw Alex for the first time, did you know it was him?"

"No, of course not. I'm a scientist, Rae. The supernatural existing on this earth was not a notion I had ever entertained. But when Alex introduced himself, it was like I knew it all along." My mom looked at Alex. "Your name. Your eyes. Your scar. It added up." Sue turned in my direction. "Your dad was able to calm me down, but I could tell that he, too, was shaken up a bit."

"Where is Dad?"

My mother inhaled deeply but didn't say a word.

"Mom? Is Dad okay?"

"Will is fine. He's upset with you, Rae. He's upset that you left the way you did."

"It's because of the letter, isn't it? It's because Ben and Chloe tried to poison you. It's because I knew, but kept it to myself. I should have told you, but I couldn't. I had to leave. You understand, right?"

"It is not because of the letter. And I do understand. So does your dad. Just give him time."

"The dad I love never wants to see me again, but the father I hate is hunting me down."

"Rae," my mother scowled.

"I just don't understand why Carl would keep girls locked in *his* basement. Isn't that a bit risky? Wasn't he afraid of getting caught."

"Money is a powerful thing. Rich people can hide things that others can't."

"So, is Carl Pierce still involved in trafficking? Did you make any progress in stopping him?"

"Of course, we did. We have made progress, but we're still not there. There was the issue of the cell phone. When Eva freed the girls from her basement, she gave them her cell phone. The DA thought that the girls' testimony and the cell phone would be enough evidence to lock Carl away for good. No such luck. Oh! Before I forget." My mother changed direction in an instant. "I received this just days before your letter came." My mom pulled a white envelope out of her purse and handed it to me. I studied my name, which had been written perfectly on the front of the envelope in black ink. I flipped it over and noticed it was still sealed.

"You didn't open it?"

"No. When I got this letter," she said, pointing to the envelope I was holding in my hands. "I knew I would be seeing you soon. It's yours to open."

I held the letter loosely between my fingers. It was with some hesitation that I finally broke the seal and pulled out the neatly folded piece of paper. Carefully, I unfolded it and began to read.

Dear Rae,

Today is the day that you have spent a lifetime preparing for. Every pain you have experienced has shaped you into the person you are today. The trials were a necessary part of the training, and we were with you through it all.

Regardless of what you might think, we know you are finally ready. But you should be warned: if you do accept this assignment, there are going to be bumps along the way. The path will be rough, but your assignment will be to make the road smooth for others. When you run into problems, please let us know so we can help. If you decide to accept our offer, it is essential that you keep the lines of communication open between us. We will be sending correspondence periodically. Often it will be through writing, but other times it will not.

So keep your eyes open, because it is the correspondence that will help you decide which path to take when you come to a fork in the road. I would like to go over the reasons why we have chosen you. You are strong and determined, stubborn and kind. Your lack of patience can be used to your advantage and will produce the quick and lasting results we desire. And last but not least, you have always worn your heart on your sleeve. Without the proper guidance, this is a very dangerous place for the heart to be. On the other hand, that you take the pain of the world upon yourself is your greatest attribute of all. Let us protect you, and you might just change the world.

Please give the offer consideration. If you do decide to accept this mission, please be at the Minneapolis-St. Paul International airport at five o'clock on the morning of March 17th. Proceed to the Southwest ticket counter in Terminal 2-Humphrey, Concourse H, to check in and receive your boarding passes. Make sure to have a photo i.d. ready. There will be three tickets: one for you, one for your mother, and one for Alex. Upon landing, you will receive further instructions. We at A-Omega are excited to extend this offer, and we have the highest hopes that you will accept. One last thing. We are aware that you have been searching for the Truth. We are also aware that you have yet to find it. Follow us and you will find It. Please consider our offer. We hope to hear from you soon.

Arm Yourself Well,
A-Omega
Ephesians 6: 10-18

That my weaknesses were also my greatest strengths was a concept I had never before considered. Maybe I did wear my heart on my sleeve when I was a little girl. Alex's stories confirmed that. But it hurt to have my heart out in the open. It had nearly killed me when I left it so exposed. At a young age, I put it in a shell because I didn't know what else to do. The shell protected me; it made me hard and indifferent. Now my heart was free, but I was still timid. They say old habits die hard. I've heard it said many times, and I always correlated it with change. But maybe I was wrong. Maybe the rest of the world was wrong. Maybe it wasn't about change. A-Omega wasn't really asking me to change. They liked me. They were simply asking me to redirect, asking me to use my gifts for something good. But how? That was the question. How could I use stubbornness and my impatience for the greater good? Right now, it seemed like it would be much easier to change than to redirect. I was familiar with change. If I was unhappy with a painting I would gesso over it and start again. If a situation made me unhappy, I would run, I would fly away. So how would I redirect? How could I use all my strengths without hurting others and myself in the process?

That night, before I fell asleep, I said a short prayer. I prayed that God would show me which path to take. I prayed that He would give me a sign. I prayed that He would give me the tools I needed to make the right decision. I prayed that He would keep the ones I loved safe, no matter what.

CHAPTER THIRTY-SIX

*A*fter Mom arrived, things did not slow down. The next afternoon, I awoke to find a box on the kitchen table addressed to me. Like the box I received on my birthday, there was only the name of the sender, no return address. This time, the sender was Jacobian House. The cottage was quiet. There was a note on the kitchen table beside the box saying that Alex and my mom had gone into town for breakfast. They probably needed that time; Alex needed to talk with someone who knew his parents. He needed to connect with the part of his life he could not remember, and who better to help him with that than my mom. Alex and my mother had a bond that could never be broken. She was his guardian angel. She was the woman holding his lifeless body in the crook of her arm. And I knew that in her other arm, she held my sister. Maybe my mom needed Alex just as much as he needed her. I took the box into my bedroom and shook it before collapsing onto my bed. Something inside thudded around. Setting it down beside me, I studied it. It was medium sized but heavier than I anticipated it to be. I ran my hand through my hair and sighed. I wasn't scared to open the box. Maybe I was a bit anxious, but I was not scared. I pressed my ear to the cardboard.

Nothing.

Finally, I grabbed a pair of scissors and sliced through the tape that was holding the box together. When I looked inside, I was a bit confused.

On top of several other items was a folded sheet of paper. A list of ten names:

Quinn Collins
Mason Armishaw
Katelyn Cross
Terry Dunbarr
Todd Catchitore
Steven Bellamy
Gracie Abbott
Baxtor Lavine
Shae Simmons
Peter Jovorskie

These names will form a belt. The Truth will be the buckle.

Arm Yourself Well,
A-Omega
Ephesians 6: 10-18

I set the paper down and looked inside the box. This time, something shiny caught my eye. I reached past the other items and fished it out.

"Now this is more like it," I said, staring at an antique golden brooch with jewels set into a *fleur de lis*. It was beautiful. My fingers were fumbling with the pin on the back when, instead of feeling something sharp, I felt something flat and crisp. I flipped the brooch over and set it in the palm of my hand. There was a handwritten note on a tiny slip of paper.

For where your treasure is, there your heart will be also
I walked over to my dresser and leaned in close to the mirror. The pin was made of solid gold and the clasp had been welded to the brooch itself. Definitely old. I placed my hand over my chest and felt for the beat of my heart. When I found it, I poked the pin through my sweatshirt

and fastened it shut. I studied myself in the mirror. The brooch was absolutely gorgeous.

I pulled a third item from the box: a pair of black combat boots. I held them by the laces and out in front of me. They were heavy. I peeked inside the boot and found a tag: 7 1/2.

"They got the wrong size," I scoffed.

I placed them on the ground and slipped my foot inside. No, they were right. It was a perfect fit. I laced up the boot and put on the other. I stood up and began to pace around the room. They were comfortable for boots. I gave the door a swift kick.

"Hmm. Steel toes and all."

There was no way I would be able to run in these boots. These were boots fit for a soldier, not a long distance runner. I fell back onto the bed, reached my hand blindly into the box, and came out with a notebook, a very pretty notebook, made of white leather and embossed with a decorative shield across the front. In the center of the shield was a single word: FAITH.

I had experienced a lot of crazy things in the past year-and-a-half, but this was insane. What was I supposed to do with all this stuff? I hated not knowing the answers. I sighed and reached in for the fifth item. This time I pulled out a small box. It looked like computer software. I read the cover. Antivirus. I knew what it was, kind of, but I had no idea how to install it. Besides, I had a PC and the software was for a Mac. It wouldn't work on my computer. I tossed it aside. Even though the items in the box were puzzling, and I had absolutely no idea what to do with them, I was still eager to see what else was inside. I pulled the last item from the box. It was a smartphone, the newest technology. Finally, something I understood. I pressed the button on top of the phone and held it down. Nothing happened. It was dead. "Figures," I huffed.

Boots fit for a soldier. If I was going to fight, the boots made sense. And I knew how to use a phone. But a list of names? A brooch, a blank journal, and computer software? I wasn't going to make it out of this alive.

I had just placed the phone back in the box when I heard the front door slam shut and laughter fill the cabin. Still wearing my gear, I walked out of my bedroom and into the kitchen.

"Good morning, sleepy head," Mom cooed, mussing up my hair with her hand and kissing me on the cheek. Alex handed me a coffee, which I graciously accepted. I held it up to my nose and inhaled deeply.

"I see nothing much has changed," Mom laughed. "If I would have let her, she would have been drinking coffee when she was two. I will never forget when she got into a bag of coffee beans in Nana's pantry. She opened the bag and ate the beans like they were candy. I think she liked the smell."

"I think it's too early for 'Rae' stories."

Alex looked at the clock on the mantle. "I beg to differ. It's nearly noon and you're still in your pajamas and... combat boots?" Alex had a peculiar look on his face. "That's quite an ensemble. You look like a soldier... or something."

"A soldier?" I laughed.

"You know you're not going to be able to run in those things," Alex said smartly.

"I know." I considered for a moment what he had said in joking. A soldier. A soldier. A soldier. Silently, I repeated for a fourth time the word that moments ago held no significance whatsoever, but now sounded very good. "Maybe it's time I stop running away."

"Where did you get them?" Alex asked and my mom smiled. She had a proud look on her face.

"The box that was on the kitchen table this morning, that's what was inside. That and a couple of other things."

"Who is it from? Did it say?"

"The package was sent by a company called Jacobian House, but there was a note inside from A-Omega. Actually, it was a list of names."

"I knew it wouldn't be long," Mom nodded her head with approval. "The box always comes right after the letter. It always works that way."

"This is all too weird. I can't make sense out of any of it."

"A-Omega wouldn't have sent it if they didn't think it was completely necessary."

"What else did you get?" Alex chimed in.

I pointed to the brooch pinned over my heart. Alex nodded with approval.

"Is that all?" my mom asked, surprised. "There should have been six items in the box."

"There are. They also sent a notebook, and some computer software. Oh, they also gave me a smartphone."

"That's not fair."

"Are you jealous?"

"I'd take the phone. And your boots are pretty cool. I'd wear them. But you can have the rest." Alex paused and began massaging his temple with his thumb. "What are you supposed to do with the list of names?"

"I have no idea. None of the names look familiar. Mom, did you get a package in the mail when you decided to work for A-Omega?"

"I did. But that was years ago."

"Did they give you the same stuff they gave me?"

"No. The contents of the box are as individual as the person."

"I was hoping you might be able to help me understand what I'm supposed to do with all this stuff," I huffed.

"I can't tell you that. That's for you to figure out. The answers will come with time. They always do."

"I'm pretty sure I know what to do with the combat boots. That's self-explanatory. And the phone, I'm pretty sure I know how to use that, too."

"You might be surprised."

"So are you going to do it?" Alex asked. "Are you going to work for A-Omega?"

"I'm leaning in that direction, but I haven't made up my mind."

I glanced at the clock on the mantle. Alex had gone to his cottage shortly after dinner, leaving my mom and me to catch up. We talked for hours about everything from A-Omega to boys. It was now three in the morning. Mom had long since fallen asleep, but I was still lying on the sofa, wide-awake. I couldn't rest; I had too much on my mind. For nineteen years, I had lived life not knowing then all at once, the answers I had been searching for hit me like a ton of bricks. Pastor Joe had said the truth would set me free, and I had told a plethora of lies in order to find it. The strange thing was that, when I found the truth, I felt more entangled than ever. The truth had definitely *not* set me free. But then, Pastor Joe told me I had not found the truth, only the answers. I didn't understand the difference. Suddenly, it occurred to me: if the answers I had found were not the truth, then maybe I was asking the wrong questions.

I thought about the contents of the box: one pair of combat boots, one brooch, one notebook, a list of ten different names, one smartphone, and some computer software. I wondered how I would be expected to use these items should I decide to take that path. I thought about the letter from A-Omega, the letter Mom hand delivered just a day ago. A-Omega wanted me to work for them. They wanted me to follow in my parents' footsteps. My parents were shrinks. Did that mean they wanted me to get a degree in psychology? My parents were involved in the fight against human trafficking and had been for years. They had done their best to end modern day slavery; did they expect me to pick up their torch? Not knowing my assignment was frightening, but it was reassuring that A-Omega accepted me for who I was. It was reassuring to know they trusted me with this assignment, whatever the job may be.

What was I going to do? Would I be able to accept the mission knowing there would be a degree of risk involved? A-Omega promised to reveal the truth. How could I say no to that? I wished someone could just make the decision for me. It felt like my entire life hinged on this offer. I closed my eyes and placed my hand on the brooch resting over my heart. My heart felt empty. There was still a hole. I had Alex. He was here with me, but my heart was not healed. I was reminded of the story Pastor Joe shared with me, the story of two paths. The story of a man at the crossroads. I was at the crossroads. I didn't want to make the same mistakes as Roald. The letter from A-Omega stated that I would be taking a specific path. My job was to smooth the path for others. A path. Yes, I was going to have to choose a path to follow. I tried my hardest to remember the words that were posted on the sign at the mouth of the narrow, winding path in Pastor Joe's story.

Because this road is long and hard
Its travelers are very few
But while other roads might promise much
That they end in death is true

Although this winding path is steep
You will be given the strength you need to stay
It may also be very dark at times
But there will be a lamp to light your way

My life had been full of bumps. Was I ready for more? But this was different. I wasn't expected to tackle life all alone. There would be someone there to help me. Was I ready for this? Yes. Yes, I was.

I would accept the mission. If A-Omega could trust me, then I would put my trust in them.

"Yes. I accept the mission. I am ready to discover the truth. I am ready to fight."

As soon as I said the words aloud, I heard a muffled noise coming from my bedroom. It sounded similar to a wind chime. Perplexed, I walked the short distance to my room and stood in the doorway, waiting for the chime to sound.

Silence.

Silence.

Silence.

And then it came. I followed the noise to the box that was still sitting on my bed. When my hands touched the box, I felt vibrations coming from within. Very slowly, I opened the lid and pulled out the phone. The chime sounded again. I pushed the round button at the bottom. It lit up. Strange, I thought. Just hours ago, my phone was as dead as a doornail. I held it in the palm of my hand. I felt queasy. I felt anxious. I read the words before me.

New Text Message

Not possible. With the tip of my finger, I slid the bar at the bottom to unlock the phone and a dozen icons appeared on the screen. There was an icon for the weather and one for the time. There was a camera and even an icon for voice memos. Finally, my eyes fell upon the green icon in the top left corner. It was an icon for text messages. I touched it and waited. The sender's name appeared in bold black letters: A-Omega. My hand was shaking as I touched the screen. In a split second, the text message appeared, and when it did, I couldn't believe my eyes. I thought I would have to wait for my first assignment, but I was wrong. I read the words below. The assignment, although vague in nature, was also very clear.

Your first mission: Carl Pierce